*Also by Michael Palmer
in Large Print:*

Silent Treatment

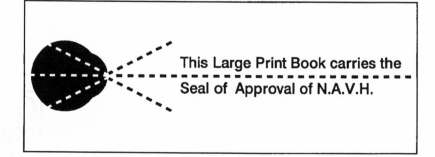

This Large Print Book carries the
Seal of Approval of N.A.V.H.

Critical Judgment

Michael Palmer

G.K. Hall & Co.
Thorndike Maine

Published in 1996 by arrangement with Bantam Books, a division of Bantam Doubleday Dell Publishing Group, Inc.

G.K. Hall Large Print Core Collection.

The text of this Large Print edition is unabridged. Other aspects of the book may vary from the original edition.

Set in 16 pt. Bookman Old Style by Minnie B. Raven.

Printed in the United States on permanent paper.

Library of Congress Catalog Card Number: 96-94639
ISBN 0-7838-1940-4 (lg. print : hc)

To My Sisters

Donna Palmer Prince
and
Susan Palmer Terry
For always being there for me

And in loving memory of our mother

Acknowledgments

In the process of getting a novel written, there is no substitute for long hours alone and in doubt. For helping me keep the isolation and uncertainty in perspective, my deepest thanks go to my agents, Jane Rotrosen Berkey, Stephanie Tade, and Don Cleary; my editor, Beverly Lewis; associate editor Katie Hall; my publisher, Irwyn Applebaum; my publicist, Stuart Applebaum; many friends of Bill W; and, of course, my family.

In addition, I have imposed on a number of friends to help me as critical readers or technical consultants. Steve Shapiro and Ellen Rosenthal, Dr. Steve Defossez, Dr. Donna Harkness, Kim Kelly, Dolly Fenton, Bunny Webb, Kelly Corbet, Ethan, Daniel, Matt, and Dad have each had an imprint on this book.

M.S.P.

It was just after noon when the flickering lights began again — countless slivers of rainbow bathing the inside of his eyes. Taken by themselves, the lights might have been fascinating, even beautiful. But as things were, they brought him only terror.

Noon. The last blast had been just six hours ago, waking him from a pleasant dream and dropping him into the midst of a nightmare. When the attacks first began, they came once every few weeks. . . . Then every few days. . . . And now. . . . The intensity, too, seemed to be increasing with each episode. It was living hell.

His palms began to sweat as he thought of what the next hour or so held in store. First the flickering lights, next the queasiness and a slight tic at the corners of his eyes. For fifteen minutes, twenty, even thirty, it would be like that. Then, with volcanic suddenness, his temples would seem to explode. He would writhe on the bed and fall to the floor, screaming. He would clutch pillows over his ears, futilely hoping to muffle the shellbursts inside his head. Then he would get violently ill, retching until it felt as if his stomach would tear apart. Sometimes he would even soil himself.

7

"Please, no," he whispered. "God, please, no more."

But he knew all the pleading, all the prayers in the world would not touch the pain. He was going mad. And nothing would stop the insanity. Nothing except the total and absolute destruction of the demons who had started it all — the vermin who had sent his life spinning out of control.

Bricker . . . Golden . . . Gentry . . . Forrester.

Only when justice was done, only when the four of them were dead, would he find peace again. Only when he had heeded God's mandate would the flickering lights and the violent headaches end.

But right now there was little he could do except take the pain pills and get ready. He shook three Demerol tablets from a plastic vial and washed them down with some bourbon. His best hope was that they would stay down long enough to do him some good.

The muscles beside his eyes began to tighten and twitch. The lights intensified. Within his skull the crescendo began.

Desperately, he snatched up the phone and dialed a long-distance number.

"Hello," said the voice he knew so well. "We are unable to take your call right now, but it is important to us. Please wait for the tone and leave a message. We'll get back to you as soon as possible."

"Please," he whimpered, his voice a small boy's. "Please help me. Make the pain go

8

away. Please make me stop what I'm going to do."

Then he realized that the words had only been in his head.

He set the receiver down and sank back onto the bed, resigned. No one was ever going to help him but himself.

Let this be the last time, he begged as the inevitable began. He tightened his hands on the headboard of the motel bed. *Let it end today.*

When consciousness returned, he was on the floor, his face pressed against the threadbare carpet, his cheek soaked with saliva. Pale sunlight brightened what was at best a dingy, pathetic little room. But the motel was close to *them,* and that was what mattered. He dried his face on the polyester bedspread and struggled to his knees.

He pulled the olive rucksack from beneath the bed and set it on the mattress. The two MAK-90 semiautomatic rifles were in mint condition, but he ritually began polishing them nonetheless.

Bricker . . . Golden . . . Gentry . . . Forrester . . .

One by one the faces flashed through his mind — faces of the people who had once been his friends. Faces he had once trusted. Now he knew they had been placed in his life to test him. He cradled one of the weapons in his lap and stared up, unblinking, at the ceiling light, testing his will and his strength. Two days before, he had bought the machine guns, gone to a landfill, and fired them for the first time. He hadn't held a gun since riflery class years ago in summer camp and was surprised at how comfortable he felt — all-powerful. But he had only been shooting rats in a dump. Next time would be for real. Next time the eyes glowing back at him would be eyes he knew well. Was he ready?

The last bit of pounding in his brain receded, then vanished. Some of the tension left his body. How long did he have before the next attack? He replaced the weapons and slid the canvas bag back under the bed. Then, totally drained, he allowed his eyes to close. He had never even struck a person in violence. Now, to regain his sanity, to send the demons back to hell, he was preparing to kill and kill again.

There had to be another way.

When he opened his eyes again, muted sunlight still filtered through the fake lace curtains. The clock radio on the bedside stand showed just two o'clock. The nap and the pills had blunted his rage some, but he knew that soon it would be as sharp as ever. He felt stifled, smothered. The room seemed postage-stamp small, the air stagnant and hard to breathe. He reached down for the rucksack, but before he touched it, he grabbed his key and bolted from the room. Even now, it seemed, he wasn't completely committed.

He left the motel and hurried down the street to a familiar bar — the Ghost Ranch Saloon. Once upon a time they had all gathered there after work. He almost laughed at the thought of Steve Bricker, drinking like a fish there and still beating all comers at darts. Then, almost immediately, the notion was preempted by another image of the man, grinning obscenely at him from behind his massive desk as he brought the hammer down on his life.

"I'm sorry. There's nothing I can do. . . ."

Bullshit!

He recalled the horrible, legless feeling of standing there before the man. The memory did much to dispel his uncertainty. He was going to go through with it . . . soon.

The Ghost Ranch was a windowless honky-tonk, lit almost exclusively with black light. It was decorated with Day-Glo cartoon ghosts of cowboys and Indians, horses and steer. From a dozen huge speakers some country warbler was begging someone for a second chance.

He smiled grimly. It was not the last time he would be hearing someone beg for one more chance. He ordered a bourbon, then another. The first one took care of his shakes. The second one he nursed. The place was nearly empty, but at the far end of the bowling-alley bar a cluster of hookers were plying their trade with three men in business suits. One of the women, the blond with Dolly Parton hair and cleavage, kept glancing over at him. Finally she decided he was worth a try. She took her time making it past the row of empty bar stools, giving him a good look. Then she introduced herself as Gloria. He nodded and made up a name on the spot. He wanted her company but had no intention of doing business with her. He had been monogamous for several years and had never done it with a pro even when he wasn't.

"Haven't I seen you in here before?" Gloria asked.

He shook his head, even though the whore was right. Bricker had done it with her on any number of occasions and once went so far as to bring her over and introduce her to the rest of them. Goddamn Bricker.

"So whaddaya doing in town?"

He wanted small talk, not the third degree. *Talk to me about the weather, for chrissakes. Or the Giants. . . .*

He realized that he was feeling irritable again and wondered if that was a sign. It had been only four hours or so since the last attack. He cursed himself for rushing out and leaving the pain pills in his room. *Pain pills, grimy motel rooms, hookers.* His life had once held such promise. How the hell had it been reduced to this? He felt his jaws begin to clench. The uncontrollable anger was back and building. Payback time was getting closer.

"So are you interested in a little fun?"

Gloria was saying. "I can give you a hell of a good deal."

He shook his head.

"Not today," he growled.

He wondered briefly what she'd look like without makeup. For all he could tell, underneath it all she might not even have a face.

Pouting, she stood. Then she began staring at him queerly.

"Hey, what's that in your eyes?" she asked. "Some weird kind of contact lenses or somethin'?"

"What are you talking about?"

"Those yellow rings around the colored part of your eyes. Oooee, is that weird."

"*You're* weird, do you know that? Now, get the hell away from —"

"Hey, Cindi, come on over here and get a load of this."

The woman was turned partly away from him when he leaped up, grabbed her breasts, and dug his fingers into them so tightly that she cried out in pain. Then he shoved her backward. Her spiked heel snapped off and she fell heavily to the sawdust-covered floor. Before anyone could make a move in her defense, he whirled and stormed out of the place.

Yellow rings. He had examined his face in the bathroom mirror a dozen times over the last day alone. Granted, he looked like hell. But if there was anything wrong with his eyes, he'd damn well have seen it.

13

His fury growing with every step, he stalked across the busy road without checking for cars. Horns blasted at him, but he didn't notice.

The sparkling lights had begun again.

He raced back to the motel. There was still time, he was thinking. Time to do what God had been telling him to do. Time to end the pain once and for all. The shimmering diamonds of multicolored light snapped against the inside of his eyes like hailstones. He fumbled with the lock, then threw the door open and snatched the rucksack out from beneath the bed.

"Not this time," he said out loud.

This time there would be no headaches. There would be no begging God to take him. This time there would be only vengeance. And then the headaches would be gone forever.

Chapter One

Three hundred joules, please. . . . Keep pumping. . . ."

Abby Dolan tightened her grip on the defibrillator paddles as she pressed them against the front and left side of the man's massive chest. He was in persistent cardiac arrest despite two electrical shocks and medication. His face and upper torso were mottled violet, reflecting inadequate circulation despite the ongoing CPR. Clearly, time was their enemy.

"Ready," said the nurse handling the defibrillator console.

"Okay everyone, clear!"

Abby pressed her thumb down on the square plastic button set in the handle of the right-hand paddle. Instantly, there was a muffled pop and an audible, visible spark from two spots where the paddles and skin did not make perfect contact. The man's body — 250 pounds at least — stiffened and arched. His arms snapped upward like whips. Then, just as rapidly, he was still.

"Pump, please," Abby said, checking the monitor screen.

The paramedic, up on a stool for leverage, wiped the contact gel off the man's chest with a towel, set the heel of his hand over the base of the sternum, and resumed his rhythmic compressions. For several seconds there was a slashing up-and-down movement of the tracing on the monitor. But Abby knew from ten years of ER work and countless code ninety-nines that the pattern was artifact, not related to any effective electrical activity of the heart.

She glanced up at the code clock started by the charge nurse at the moment of the man's arrival in room three. Nine minutes. So far, nothing. Abby had been working in the Patience Regional Hospital for over two weeks now, at once dreading and eagerly awaiting her first code. She had been busy, at times very busy, over those weeks. But no codes. Now it was happening. And "The Professor," as she knew some of the staff were facetiously calling her, was losing.

The patient, a married insurance salesman with a couple of kids and some grandchildren, was only fifty-two. He had collapsed while playing golf on one of the public courses in the town. When the paramedics arrived, he still had enough of a heartbeat to generate a pulse and measurable blood pressure. Then, as the ambulance was backing up to the hospital receiving platform, he arrested. All Abby had learned was that his name was Bill Tracy, that he took medicine for high blood pressure, and that his daughter, who worked in the hospital's record room, was on her way in with his wife.

Abby noted the low, irregular waves on the monitor. Persistent coarse ventricular fibrillation — the sort of electrical disarray that should have responded to a high voltage shock. But it hadn't. Something had to be off with the man's chemistry — something that had either contributed to the cardiac arrest or, more likely, was a result of it. But what? Abby fought a mounting sense of panic. At St. John's, where she had been an assistant professor of emergency medicine, there already would have been a cardiologist in the room to assist her. Maybe two. But that was a university-affiliated hospital in San Francisco. This was Patience, a landlocked mountain town with just two cardiologists, neither of whom was in the hospital today.

She looked back at the paramedic who was doing the cardiac compressions. Too mechanical. He was well trained, but he was using the technique he had learned on the CPR mannequin, Resusi-Annie. This was a 250-pound bull of a man. Abby pressed her fingertips into Tracy's groin, searching for the femoral-artery pulse that the paramedic should have been generating. Nothing.

"Harder, Tom," she said. "Much harder. You're not moving enough blood."

"But —"

"Please, I know you feel right with what you're doing, but you've got to do it harder.

17

A little faster, too. That's better. That's it. Good. That's it."

The man, like every paramedic Abby had ever known, took a great deal of pride in his work and his technique. Correcting him in front of the staff was hardly going to increase her popularity, but neither would losing this patient. The CPR, as he had been performing it, wasn't helping. She directed one of the nurses to keep her fingers on the femoral pulse and to call out if it began to disappear.

In addition to Abby, there were three nurses, a respiratory therapist, and the paramedic in the room. At St. John's there would often be that many *physicians* at a cardiac arrest. If the patient didn't make it, at least they all knew that everything that needed to be thought of had been. She wondered if anyone in the room knew how frightened she was about how this code was going — how concerned she was about missing something. Under the best of circumstances she was a worrier — meticulous in her approach to medicine and to life, always considering the potential downside of any move before making it. It was her best and worst quality, depending on whom you asked. But here, with no available backup, no one to bounce things off, and not much time left, she was very much on her own. In seconds she subconsciously but systematically flipped through dozens of possible sources of the trouble she was having.

"Are those labs back?"

"Three or four minutes, they say."

Abby knew that three or four minutes often meant five or ten. Bill Tracy didn't have that kind of time. She looked down at the dark, stretch-scar-like markings over his lower abdomen, and the fullness of his face. Then she reached under his shoulder and placed her hand palm up at the base of his neck. There was a prominence there, a definite fullness. Over her decade as a physician, she had seen only five or six cases of Cushing's syndrome, but this man certainly seemed like a candidate. The syndrome was caused by a small, benign brain tumor that chemically told the body to produce an excess amount of the hormone cortisol. The tumor itself wasn't usually fatal, but the high sodium, low potassium, and other derangements caused by the cortisol often were. Among the physical signs of the syndrome were obesity, a moon face, purple stretch scars along the abdomen, and a prominent so-called buffalo hump between the shoulders. Bill Tracy had all of those. Of course, many thousands of markedly overweight people without Cushing's had all those findings, too.

PRH had better-than-decent medical-specialist coverage, especially for a one-hundred-bed facility in a service area of twenty thousand. But there was no endocrinologist. And at the moment there was no cardiologist either.

She rapidly processed the possibilities. Without lab results, especially a potassium level, she was running blindfolded. If Tracy had low potassium from Cushing's, none of their resuscitative efforts would work until the abnormality was corrected. If he didn't have Cushing's, if his potassium was normal and she gave him more of the electrolyte intravenously, he would be as good as dead.

"Get ready for another shock," Abby said, struggling to keep panic out of her voice. "Three hundred joules again. Tom, keep pumping, please. As hard as you can."

She hesitated. Giving IV potassium without a serum-potassium level was about the most un–Abby Dolan thing she could imagine.

Just go ahead and shock him, the voice in her head insisted. *Do it!*

"Mary, I want him to get some potassium right now," she suddenly heard herself saying. "Ten milliequivalents IV."

"But I've never —"

"Please," Abby ordered sharply. "I don't have time to debate this."

The nurse's cheeks flushed. She quickly filled a syringe. For a moment Abby thought the woman was going to tell her to inject it herself. But no.

"Your potassium's in, Doctor," she said coolly.

"Thank you."

First the paramedic, now the nurse. How many more people would she offend before this code was over? She checked the clock. Almost twelve minutes, plus a few minutes to get Tracy in from the ambulance. Too long for him still to be in ventricular fibrillation. She took the defibrillator paddles, accepted some contact gel from the nurse, and rubbed the two circular steel heads together to spread it out. A negative outcome *and* controversy — the last results she would have wanted from her first code in Patience. But, then, she would never have been in Patience in the first place if Josh hadn't —

"Okay, stop pumping, please. Everyone clear!"

Forty-five seconds since the potassium. Now fifty. There was no more time. Abby hit the button. Again the muted pop, the single spasmodic contraction of every muscle in Bill Tracy's body, the faint odor of searing skin. And, again, the tracing showed only artifact.

"Resume pumping," Abby said, no longer trying to mask her dejection. "No. No, wait." The artifact had largely cleared. There was a rhythm on the monitor — slow, but regular. Abby felt her own heart skip some beats. "Check for a pulse, please."

"Go, baby," someone murmured. "Go . . ."

"I've got a pulse," the nurse called out as she pressed down over the femoral artery. Purposely looking away from the monitor screen to remain as objective as possible, she reported what she was feeling in her fingertips. "Now . . . . now . . . . now . . . now . . . now . . . now . . . now."

The pulse she was chanting correlated perfectly with the monitor pattern. The heartbeats were speeding up; the electrocardiogram complexes were becoming narrower, healthier.

"I've got a blood pressure at eighty, Abby," a second nurse announced. "Eighty-five. Hey, nice going."

A successful code was everyone's victory. But more often than not, Abby knew, the failures were left to the doc.

Bill Tracy's horrible, violet mottling rapidly and markedly improved. Tissue throughout his body was getting blood for the first time in fifteen minutes. No CPR, however well performed, could ever measure up to the real thing, Abby was thinking. Now all that mattered was getting him stabilized and praying that his brain had not been part of the tissue too deprived of circulation during that fifteen minutes.

A pretty woman in her early twenties rushed in. She was wearing faded jeans and a designer T-shirt. Her face was gray with concern.

"Dr. Dolan, I'm Donna Tracy," she said breathlessly. "I work part-time in the record room downstairs. That's my dad."

Abby checked the monitor. The encouraging pattern was holding, although Bill

Tracy was still unconscious. She lifted his eyelids. Midsize pupils, no wandering eye movements — both good signs.

"Can't tell," she said. "But things are going in the right direction."

At that moment the lab tech arrived, as breathless as Donna Tracy.

"His potassium's only one point eight," he announced. "Checked and rechecked. One point eight."

For the first time since the rescue-squad call had come in from the golf course, Abby Dolan smiled.

"Not anymore," she said.

Donna Tracy and her mother were at the bedside and Bill Tracy was beginning to regain consciousness when his private physician arrived. Tracy was still on a ventilator, but he was starting to buck against the tube. Before too long the decision would have to be made whether to sedate him or to take it out. Abby favored continued mechanical ventilation, but with the primary doc on hand, the decision was no longer hers.

The physician was a tall, angular, somewhat nervous-looking man in his fifties named Gordon Clarke. Abby had cared for a number of his patients. His manner was earnest enough, and he was certainly popular with his flock. But his diagnostic and therapeutic skills were badly in need of updating. If he had been on the staff at St.

John's, assuming he could have ever gotten admitting privileges there in the first place, he would have been assigned a monitor from the faculty to oversee his admissions and help him improve clinically. And, of course, he would have been exposed to weekly medical grand rounds and other academic presentations. But this was the boondocks, not academia. And although Patience Regional Hospital was incredibly modern and well equipped, modernizing a physician was often far more difficult than updating a building.

Abby could see the relief in Clarke's eyes as he looked down at his patient.

"The nurse who called my office made it sound as if he didn't have much of a chance."

"He's still in some trouble," Abby responded, "but certainly less than he was."

"I'm very grateful."

"So are we," Donna chimed in.

"What kind of coronary was it, anterior?"

Abby glanced down at the EKG she had just had taken and then passed it over. It showed some evidence of cardiac strain, but no actual heart attack. Clarke studied it. He looked confused.

"I don't see any damage," he said.

"His potassium was one point eight."

"Are you sure?"

"Checked and rechecked. His chloride was down as well, and his sodium was elevated. His serum pH was high — seven point six."

Abby hoped that when she recited the numbers, Clarke would come up with a list of diagnostic possibilities, including Cushing's and overmedication with diuretics. Now, she realized, she should have waited for a less public situation before bringing the whole business up. He was quite obviously clueless. The silence in the room was painful.

Clarke cleared his throat and stared down at the office record he had brought in. A slight tic had appeared at the corner of his mouth.

"I . . . um . . . I've gotten electrolytes on him twice in the last eight months," he said finally. "It appears his potassium was somewhat low on both occasions. I . . . guess I just didn't think much of it."

Abby was not surprised. Her inner voice was warning her to let the matter drop, to curb her redheaded-Irish temper and take this up at another time. But she had never been tolerant of incompetent physicians. Making mistakes was one thing. Every physician made them at one time or another. But ignoring abnormal laboratory results because they weren't *that* abnormal was quite another. Bill Tracy's death would have been her failure. And the two women standing beside him would have suffered a horrible loss. Horrible and quite probably unnecessary. Once again the small voice went unheeded.

"He has a moonish face, high blood pres-

25

sure, those purplish streaks on his belly, and a pretty prominent buffalo hump."

"I'm afraid I don't know what you're driving at," Clarke said, his cheeks as red as the nurse's had been.

"Dr. Clarke, I'm sorry. Maybe we should talk about this later. They should be here to take Mr. Tracy up to the unit any moment."

"No, that's okay. Go ahead. Tell me what I missed."

Abby saw the tiredness in the man's eyes. Never had she been out in a community caring for a busy, demanding general medical practice. And, in fact, until a few weeks ago, she had never even been detached from the university-hospital umbilical cord. She felt as if a sluice gate had opened, and all her feelings of irritation and impatience toward Gordon Clarke had instantly washed out.

"Dr. Clarke," she said, "I'm sorry."

"That's all right." Now it was Clarke who seemed irritated and impatient. "Just tell me what you think is going on."

"Okay. He looks like he might have Cushing's."

Clarke closed his eyes for a moment and then nodded and sighed. Abby was saddened by what she knew he was thinking.

"That's a heck of a pickup to have made under fire like that, Dr. Dolan," he said. "You certainly saved Bill Tracy's life." Wearily, he met the gazes of Tracy's wife and daughter. "Sorry Edith, Donna. I should have paid more attention to those potassium levels. I'll see you up in the coronary unit."

Quickly, he turned and left. As he passed through the door, Abby realized that George Oleander, the chief of medicine, had been standing there, taking in the whole scene. Oleander had been one of the staunchest supporters of her application to fill the ER vacancy at PRH.

He watched Gordon Clarke hurry away, then turned back to the room. His eyes met Abby's.

"That was a great save, Abby," he said, with much less emotion than the words warranted. "Perhaps when you have a few minutes, you could stop by my office."

Chapter Two

It was nearly three before a lull in the steady stream of patients allowed Abby to clear out the ER and call George Oleander. Besides Bill Tracy's resuscitation, the day had brought two more new cases of adult-onset asthma and one more of a skin condition that might have been hives, but really didn't look like any hives Abby had seen before. The asthma cases raised to five the number she had treated in just over two weeks. Most of them had responded reasonably well to standard therapy and had been referred back to their own physicians. One had required hospitalization in the ICU.

Asthma beginning in adulthood was fairly unusual. Five cases in six months would have been more like it. Abby's history taking had gotten more and more detailed, but so far no pattern had emerged. And no one on the medical staff seemed concerned or even interested. *Allergy Valley* was the way Oleander had referred to the area. *Pollen Central.*

The skin condition — raised, hard red welts that burned more than itched — was the second such case Abby had seen since starting at PRH. Dermatology was never her strongest suit, but at St. John's it didn't have to be. There was a derm clinic available during business hours, and derm coverage twenty-four hours a day for anything beyond the mundane. The welts looked to her more like vasculitis, an inflammation of the small blood vessels in the skin, than like hives. But, in truth, they really didn't look precisely like either. At their private doctors' request Abby put both patients on oral cortisone and antihistamines, probably the best initial treatment for any inflammatory or allergic condition.

After Bill Tracy had been taken to the coronary unit, Abby had some fences to mend. She began with an apology to Tom Webb, the young paramedic. The tension of the moment had caused her to be more brusque than she had intended, she explained. He was damn good at what he did, and his skill in the other emergencies they had shared matched the best she had known in the city. The young man claimed he understood, but his expression made it clear he was still smarting.

Soon after, Abby sought out the nurse she had snapped at, Mary Wilder, and made amends to her for not explaining the rationale for IV potassium before ordering her to administer it. Wilder, ten years or so older than Abby, had been at PRH since well before the place was rebuilt a decade ago. The nurse was genuinely embarrassed by her hesitation in following Abby's emergency orders and told Abby how much it meant to her and the other nurses to have a doctor of her caliber working in Patience. The two women shook hands warmly, and Abby returned to her patients with the sense that she had made her first genuine ally in the ER.

Gordon Clarke was the lone remaining ego casualty of the code ninety-nine. But righting things with him could wait until after her shift was over, and after her meeting with the chief of medicine.

George Oleander had an office in the Medical Arts Building, connected to the hospital by a covered passageway over the main driveway. The hospital itself, a three-story jewel of plate glass, brick, and cedar, was set in a meadow at the easternmost tip of the valley, right at the base of the foothills. Whether the mountains beyond those rugged hills were the southern Cascades or the northern Sierras seemed to depend on whom you asked. To the west of the hospital sprawled Patience, a boom town during the gold rush, a mining town for many years after that, and then, from what Abby had been told, nearly a ghost town. Hikers and other outdoors lovers had always used the place as a jumping-off point and might have kept Patience alive. But it was the arrival of Colstar International, twenty-five years before, that had really turned things around.

As she passed through the glass-enclosed

walkway to the Medical Arts Building, Abby gazed at the huge gray concrete factory, set atop a plateau a quarter of a mile from the hospital and several hundred feet up. The largest producer of portable power sources in the world, the Colstar brochures proclaimed; they made lithium batteries, lead acid batteries, alkaline batteries, solar batteries, rechargeables. Having been inside the factory once to see Josh's department and office, Abby saw no reason to dispute the claim.

The Medical Arts Building, clearly designed by the same architects responsible for the hospital, featured two dozen office suites with balconies facing the mountains or the town. George Oleander's second-floor office overlooked the flowering meadow, dotted with trees, that stretched out to the base of the Colstar cliff. It was a beautiful, pastoral view as long as one didn't look up. In addition to the usual array of diplomas, postgraduate certificates, and testimonials, there were pictures of Oleander with two governors of California, and another with longtime California Senator Mark Corman, a possible Republican nominee for President.

The medical chief greeted her warmly. He was fifty or so, with graying temples and the soft, broad-shouldered physique of an out-of-shape athlete. The redness in his cheeks and nose suggested to Abby that he might be a drinker. He motioned her to the

31

chair across his desk, where she had sat for two interviews before being hired.

"So," he said, "that was quite a performance."

"I hope you're talking about the code."

"Of course I am. Abby, there's absolutely no need to be defensive. You've been a wonderful addition to this hospital."

"Thank you."

No comment seemed necessary. Abby knew she hadn't been summoned to be told what a bang-up job she was doing.

"The nurses have been very pleased with the last three ER choices we've made — Lew Alvarez, you, and, of course, poor Dave Brooks."

This time Abby nodded her appreciation, not bothering to comment on the obvious — that if Dave Brooks hadn't died in a rock-climbing accident, her own appointment would not have been necessary. The other four ER docs were husband-and-wife Chris and Jill Anderson, Ted Bogarsky, who commuted in from someplace twenty or thirty miles to the west, and Len McCabe, an aging GP. During her orientation week Abby had been assigned to double-cover with each of them and with Alvarez. None of the five was a liability in the ER, although skittish, insecure Jill Anderson was close. But only Lew Alvarez showed a genuine flair for the work.

"The medical staff likes you, too," Oleander continued.

"I have my doubts about that."

"They do. I can tell. It's just that . . . Abby, we're small town here. Until we know someone, and know them well, the *way* they say things is as important as what they have to say. You're big city — and big city university hospital to boot. That makes you threatening to some people right from the get-go. One person told me that you seem tense and short with people. He said that a lot of the medical staff were . . . I don't know . . . intimidated by you. I didn't really understand why anyone would feel that way until this morning."

"Dr. Clarke."

"Gordon's an extremely nice man, and devoted to his patients. He's been here for over twenty years, almost as long as I have."

"And I made him feel like a jerk."

"I don't think there're many physicians who would have plucked Cushing's syndrome out of the air the way you did."

Abby stopped herself from pointing out that Clarke really should have paid attention to the two low potassium levels he'd gotten on Bill Tracy in his office. Oleander was right. She hadn't been relaxed about her job since the day she had accepted it. For the umpteenth time since then she wondered if she had made a mistake. As far as she knew, no one at St. John's, not even the good old boys who always had trouble accepting women docs in positions of authority, had ever felt anything but pleased at having her around. Now, just by being herself, she was a threat.

She tried reminding herself that being with Josh, planning their life together, was worth the decision she had made. But even that thought didn't fit as comfortably as it once had.

"The Cushing's was a lucky shot," she said. "Assuming it's even confirmed by the lab. A flat-out lucky guess. George, you're right. I have been too tense here."

"About what?"

"I don't know. Maybe just the newness of everything."

"I understand. Are things okay at home?"

"What do you mean?"

"You told me in our first interview that you wanted to move here because your fiancé had relocated to work for Colstar."

Actually, he's not technically my fiancé. We haven't really set a date. She could have said it but didn't. *And yes, the tension has everything to do with how things are at home.*

"Things are fine with Josh," she said. "Thanks for asking. It's me. You know, you may not believe this, but I've been scared stiff about coming here since the moment you called to tell me I had the job."

"I understand. Patience is a far cry from Union Street and Golden Gate Park."

"Believe it or not, it wasn't the town. It was the hospital. I went from med school to training to a staff ER position at St.

John's. Except for a little moonlighting I've always had the protective cocoon of knowing specialty help was never more than a few floors away. I have this overwhelming admiration for docs in remote ERs who have to do the whole thing themselves. Everything. The pediatric trauma and the adult codes. The stabilizing orthopedics and respiratory failure. Even the emergency neurosurgery."

"We're not *that* remote, Abby. We have a helipad. San Francisco's just an hour or so from here by chopper."

"Weather permitting. Don't misunderstand me, George. I love the feeling that no matter what happens, no matter what's thrown at me, I'll know what to do about it. It's just that for the last ten years I've always been able to call for help."

"We've got a hell of a staff for a hospital this size."

"I know. Hey, I don't mean to sound like a wimp. And I understand that the most any of us can ever do is our best. But I still don't like making errors."

"None of us does."

"For the four weeks between hearing from you that I got this job and actually starting it, I spent almost every free moment studying."

"Judging from your résumé and letters of recommendation, I would never have guessed that."

"Well, it's true. And I think if I've seemed

tense to people, that's the reason. A community hospital is uncharted waters for me. I don't want to make a mistake. Reputations in hospitals, especially negative ones, are created very quickly and recast very slowly."

"That's precisely why I called you in today. I want your reputation here to reflect the fine physician you are. Nothing else."

Abby's page summoned her to the ER at almost the instant Oleander's receptionist knocked and peered in around the door.

"That was the ER, Dr. Dolan," she said. "Just three patients waiting. Nothing critical."

"Thank you."

"I'm sorry I missed you when you arrived. I was over at the lab. I wanted to thank you for doing such a good job on my nephew Brendan's cut chin. He's only five. I'm sure you don't remember him, but —"

"As a matter of fact, I remember him very well. We redheads pay attention to one another."

"My sister said you kept whispering to him while you were getting ready to sew him up."

Abby smiled. "I was just reminding him that he was in charge, and that I would stop anytime he told me to. When I was a kid, I used to hate the feeling of losing control of any situation, especially one in the hospital or dentist's office. In fact, I still feel that way. I always try to make sure kids know they still have power."

"Well, my sister said you were just great with him. Do you have children?"

"No . . . no, my fiancé and I hope to have some before too much longer, though."

"Well, I hope you do."

The woman smiled, pulled her head back, and closed the door.

"I rest my case," Oleander said. "Everyone in Patience is connected in *some* way or other with everyone else. And no one is more important than the doctors. You've already made a great impression on the town. You just have to practice being a little gentler on the staff."

"Consider it done."

"Thank you."

Abby stood and shook Oleander's hand.

"I'm curious," she said. "Which doctor was it who said I seemed tense and short with people?"

Oleander debated responding.

"To tell you the truth," he said finally, "I think Dr. Alvarez said something to me in passing. Given that it was him, I probably shouldn't have even bothered mentioning it. Alvarez is an excellent physician, but if you'll excuse me for saying so, he's not much of a team player. He seems to have an opinion about pretty nearly everything and everybody. And he isn't the least bit shy about spreading it around. Sort of like fertilizer."

Oleander enjoyed a laugh at his own humor. Abby smiled politely.

Lew Alvarez. She supposed she should have known. Alvarez was clearly the top dog in the ER — at least until her arrival on the scene. But he was almost too self-assured. That and his irrefutable good looks had been something of a turnoff to her. It was hard to imagine his perceiving her as a threat, but she knew that was the sort of thing one never could tell about a person.

"Thank you for telling me," she said. "I'll see what I can do about changing his opinion of me."

"Suit yourself. Personally, though, I don't think Lew Alvarez's opinions matter all that much."

Abby wondered why the medical chief was so skeptical of Lew Alvarez despite the nurses' high regard for him. But this wasn't the time to get into it. She thanked him for his candor and left the office.

Heading back to the emergency room, she admitted to herself, perhaps for the first time, that of all those on the medical or ER staff, it was Alvarez she had most wanted to impress.

So far it appeared she hadn't done a very good job of it.

Chapter Three

Before returning to the ER Abby stopped by the ICU. Bill Tracy was extubated and propped up at a forty-five-degree angle, taking sips of water through a straw. His wife hovered over him from one side of the bed, his daughter, Donna, from the other. All things considered, Abby thought, he was looking damn good.

She stayed by the nurses' station long enough to take in the scene, then left without going into the room. Mindful of the situation with Gordon Clarke, she was purposely shying away from contact with Tracy and his family. Besides, she realized how easily things could have gone the other way. This was a time for reflection and gratitude, not celebration — and certainly not smugness.

It was almost five-thirty when she reentered the ER. Two and a half hours until her relief showed up. Ironically, it would be Lew Alvarez. She'd have a chance to practice her new, nonthreatening manner.

There were now four patients to be seen — one in the waiting room, one in X ray, and two on stretchers. None of them seemed too complicated at first glance, but she could recall dozens of examples, secondhand and personal, of the folly of relying on your first glance. She rubbed at the gritty fatigue in her eyes and wished she was home. She wanted to call and check in with Josh, but it was doubtful he would be back from work yet. The ER was just a patient or two from becoming backed up, and the nurses had already begun ordering tests on the two who had been there longest. Abby decided to make sure things were going in the right direction before she called home.

The evening charge nurse, Bud Perlow, met her at the chart rack. He was an imposing six foot four, but Abby had seen him use his puttylike face to put kids at ease. At five eight she had to step back several paces to make eye contact with him comfortably. She encouraged all the nurses to call her by her first name, but Perlow was one of the few who insisted on Doctor.

"Dr. Dolan, rescue is on its way in with Old Man Ives," he said. "He's been beaten up. Primarily facial lacerations."

"I don't know any Old Man Ives."

"Oh, sorry. I forgot you're new. Just about everyone in Patience knows him. He's a hermit. Very weird — retarded, I've heard. Lives in the woods. Someone told me he actually lives in a cave. He comes into town every few weeks to sell his carvings and pick up supplies. Usually people leave him alone, but apparently this time someone didn't."

Abby took two charts from the rack.

"I'd better get a move on, then."

"It may not be a problem," Perlow said. "Dr. Bartholomew's on backup for surgery, and he's in-house. I just saw him."

"Great."

The word came out more sarcastic than she had intended. Martin Bartholomew, one of four general surgeons on the staff, insisted on suturing every laceration that came in while he was on backup. Although Abby had yet to have a run-in with him, she had been warned by the other ER docs that it was only a matter of time. Bartholomew had an ego as bloated as his waistline, and unique requirements for even the most mundane procedures. It was sport for him to chastise a nurse in front of one of his carriage-trade patients for forgetting his special clamps or for opening a 6-0 instead of a 7-0 packet of suture.

"Shall I call him now?"

"Better let me at least check over Mr. Ives first."

Through the waiting room Abby could see another patient enter, this one a middle-aged woman, pale but ambulatory, supported by her husband. Probably a GI bug, she guessed. It was definitely time to get in gear.

The patient in X ray had a straightforward, nondisplaced wrist fracture. Plaster splint, a few Tylenol number threes, and an orthopedic referral. But the two patients on

41

stretchers were both enigmas. Neither was a true emergency, but their insurance probably didn't charge them a penalty for using the ER instead of contacting their primary doctor. One complained of fatigue and a low-grade cough, the other, a flamboyant fifty-year-old redhead, of chronic severe itching with no noticeable skin rash. Physical exams on both were negative, as was the chest X ray Perlow had obtained on the cougher. Abby ordered some additional laboratory studies but suspected that they, too, would be unrevealing. Two more in what was beginning to feel like a series of ill-defined or unusual conditions.

Was it her imagination, or had she been starting more and more of her discussions with patients by saying something like, "At this point I don't really know what's wrong with you, but . . ." ? The challenge with cases like these, maybe the most difficult in ER medicine, was to be certain that no one was discharged feeling that his symptoms were being taken lightly. Patients like that were lawsuits waiting to happen. Abby was constantly reminding herself that although a particular problem might not have been the worst thing she had seen that day, it was certainly the worst thing the *patient* had had.

While the two remaining patients from the waiting room were being evaluated by the nurses, Abby closed herself in the small doctor's office and called home, expecting to get the answering machine.

"Hello?"

Not only was Josh home, but it sounded as if she'd awakened him. Lately it had been more and more like that. For the two years they had dated, before he'd moved to Patience, sleep had been something of an enemy to Josh. Even during his months of unemployment he had stayed upbeat and energetic. Maybe those ten months had taken more of a toll than she'd realized, though. Or perhaps the expectations and pressures of his job at Colstar had been more than *he* had bargained for.

Over the five weeks they had been together in Patience, and even before she had moved up to join him, Josh had been irritable, distracted, easily fatigued, and bothered by headaches. A checkup with lab tests at the Colstar employees' clinic, done at Abby's insistence, had turned up nothing. But the disturbing changes in him had persisted. Recently, she had begun to wonder if she had wanted so badly for their relationship to work that she had never allowed herself to see Josh's darker side.

"Hi, honey," she said. "Are you okay?"

"What's that supposed to mean?"

"Nothing. You just sounded tired."

"I'm sorry. I was on the couch. I . . . I guess I must have fallen asleep."

On the couch . . . fallen asleep . . . The Josh Wyler she had fallen in love with

43

probably hadn't taken a nap since he was two months old.

"Well, you left for work at five-thirty this morning," she said. "Maybe you should start a little later."

"Do you want to do my job, too? Is that it?"

Abby refused to allow him to push any of her buttons, although lately he'd become something of a virtuoso at it. She wanted to ask him about the headaches he'd been having. But that might well have pushed one of *his* buttons, and she simply had no time or desire for a battle.

"I'll be home by eight-thirty," she said instead. "How about I bring home some Chinese food and rent a movie?"

"Sure. That'd be great."

There was no enthusiasm in his voice. The problem *had* to be his job. For the first few months after he'd started as director of new product development at Colstar, the job had been the best thing that had ever happened to him. Then, suddenly, there were constant deadlines — new products that always seemed to be at a make-or-break stage. He had never been particularly vulnerable to pressure at work. Now he seemed overwhelmed, disorganized.

Meanwhile Abby's decision to apply for the sudden opening in the ER at Patience Regional Hospital seemed only to have added to Josh's stress. Since her move up to Patience, there had been almost constant tension between them. Perhaps he had never expected her actually to give up the job she loved out of deference to their relationship. Maybe, over the months they'd been apart, he had simply discovered he liked being on his own. Or maybe, she sometimes allowed herself to think, he had met someone else.

The doors to the ambulance bay glided open, and the rescue squad wheeled in a stretcher. The man on it had his face swathed with blood-soaked gauze. Protruding from beneath the gauze, over the cervical collar, was a full, gnarled gray-black beard, matted with drying blood. Old Man Ives.

"Look, Josh, I gotta go," she said. "I'll tell you what. Count on me to provide dinner and X-rated entertainment. If you want to watch the movie afterward, we can do that, too."

"I'll be here."

Abby started to tell him that she loved him. Instead what came out was, "Great, see you later."

She set the receiver down and headed out to evaluate her new patient, thinking that she shouldn't have called home. The last thing an ER physician needed at work was to be distracted. The job was hard enough, the traps were everywhere. From now until her shift ended she would have to be especially vigilant.

The PRH emergency room had a row of five

treatment bays separated by curtains, and five individually numbered rooms, reserved for minor surgery and orthopedics, special procedures, major medical, pediatrics, and codes. Abby felt some relief at seeing Bud Perlow direct the rescue squad to wheel Mr. Ives into room one, where most of the routine suturing was done. She just wasn't up for anything major.

She paused to check on some of the lab results on the two enigmas. To no surprise, they were all normal.

"Ouch! Hey, easy. You just took half my hair off on that tape!"

Perlow met Abby beside the door to room one. From behind him she could hear their new patient jawing at the rescue squad.

"Some hikers found him facedown on a trail. Apparently two men followed him out of town, started yelling at him to stay away from Patience, and then beat him unconscious with their fists."

"I guess different isn't one of the best things to be around here."

"Pardon?"

"Oh, nothing. How does he look?"

"He's awake and alert, in case you couldn't tell. Deep lacs on both cheeks, through one brow, and across his chin."

"Alcohol?"

"I couldn't smell any. But, then, Ives is a few months short of a shower."

"I understand."

Abby liked that she heard nothing judg-

46

mental in the nurse's voice. It was human for any physician or nurse to be offended by a person's smell, or obesity, or age, or even illness. Everyone had an upbringing and a history to deal with. Everyone had sensibilities. But it was not acceptable to her when medical personnel withheld a full measure of care because of their prejudices.

She took the chart from Bud Perlow and was reading it as she entered the room. Old Man Ives was Samuel Ives. His address was given simply as North Hills, Patience. His age was fifty-one. She wondered if, in just sixteen years, the people of Patience would be calling her Old Lady Dolan.

She put on a paper gown and rubber gloves and began her assessment before even reaching the bedside. The man's face had taken a pounding, but it was not as fearsome as she had imagined.

"Mr. Ives, I'm Dr. Dolan. How're you doing?"

"They stole my money."

Abby glanced over at the paramedic, who shook his head.

"Mr. Ives," he said, with the overemphatic voice that most health-care workers seemed to use toward most patients, "I've got your wallet right here." He slipped a plastic bag under Ives's hand. "There's twenty-one dollars in it. Your book and what's left of your carvings are in the bag beneath your stretcher. They must have taken your groceries. We didn't see them anyplace." He turned to Abby. "The police came up to the trail with us. They think they know who did this, but Ives doesn't want to get involved. Whoever it was stomped on his carvings. There's not much left of them."

"Are you hurting anyplace except your face, sir?" Abby asked.

Ives shook his head.

Abby briefly checked his ribs, heart, and abdomen. There was no tenderness.

"Any problem with your vision?"

"Nope."

"Are you seeing double? Two of anything?"

"I know what double means. No."

"Mr. Ives, I think we should get some X rays of your face and neck."

"No. They're fine. I've had broken bones. I know what they feel like. I don't have any broken bones and I don't want any radiation."

Radiation. Not the word she would have expected from this man. She peered down at him, trying to look beyond the oil-stained clothes and the gashes and the beard, trying to see through her own prejudices. Samuel Ives's light-blue eyes were bright and piercing. *So what's your story?* she wondered.

She checked his eyes and cheekbones to be sure there were no gross signs of a fracture. Then she loosened his cervical collar and felt along his spine. No tenderness there, either.

"Okay," she said, "no X rays. I'll be back to examine you more thoroughly, then we'll get your face fixed."

Ives looked directly at her for the first time, as if surprised at the ease with which she had given in.

"Thanks, Doc," he said.

"Dr. Dolan," Bud Perlow called out from the doorway. "Could I see you please?"

"Hang in there, Mr. Ives," she said.

"Dr. Dolan, a woman just brought in her six-year-old girl with a nosebleed. It's a gusher. I put them in three rather than the pedi room because the table and the light are better."

"Perfect."

"What do you want to do about him?"

Abby glanced at the three other patients she had yet to finish. Samuel Ives's face was going to require several dozen carefully placed sutures. A good hour's work.

"Call Dr. Bartholomew and ask him to see Mr. Ives," she said. "Is the ENT tray in with the child?"

"On the counter."

The girl's nosebleed, like most such episodes, wasn't as bad as it looked. The few that *were* as bad as they looked were absolute nightmares, as often as not ending up in intensive care, or the operating room, or both. But though the bleeding point in this child was higher than Abby would have liked, it was reachable. She was in the process of cauterizing it with a touch of

49

silver nitrate when a shouting match began in room one.

"You know, you shouldn't be marching into town looking like you do," Martin Bartholomew was saying. "You scare the kids half to death."

"You probably scare quite a few of them, yourself," Ives countered.

"People like you feel society owes them," the surgeon ranted on. "Feed me, clothe me, educate my children, take care of me when I'm sick."

"I don't have any children to educate."

"And you don't have any insurance, either. Do you think I'm going to get paid for sewing up these cuts of yours? Twenty years of school and training, my family's home waiting dinner, and I'm here suturing this . . . this person who hasn't taken a bath in months."

"Years," Ives said. "Listen, why don't you just stop and go home? That's what I'm going to do."

"Hey, lie still! Dammit, lie still before I stick myself!"

"I'm getting out of here."

Abby apologized to the girl and her mother, set the silver nitrate stick aside, and hurried to the door.

"Bud, would you please get them to stop this right away? Call security if you have to."

She turned back to the child.

"These stitches need to come out in a

week," Bartholomew bellowed. "Come to the ER to have it done. I'm finished with you."

Abby heard him storm out of the room. He had been with Ives for only twenty minutes, yet he was done. She turned as he reached the doorway of room three. His puffed face was crimson, his eyes frog-like.

"I'll be home or on my beeper," he said icily. "Thank you for the referral."

He stalked off without waiting for a reply. Abby was reasonably sure, however, that *he* wouldn't be called on the carpet in George Oleander's office for his brusque-ness to a colleague.

She put the finishing touches on a Vase-line pack in the six-year-old's nose, went over the nosebleed instruction sheet with the mother, and discharged them to the waiting room for a precautionary half hour. Then she went into room one. Samuel Ives was off the litter, his back to her. He was gathering his things.

"Mr. Ives?" she said softly.

He turned, and instantly Abby felt her temper reach boiling point.

The sutures, probably 3-0 thickness rather than the much finer 6-0 or even 7-0 used for faces, were carelessly placed and tied in such a way that Ives's skin was bunched. Why hadn't the nurses let her know what was going on?

She took a deep, calming breath. Not only had Martin Bartholomew done a sophomoric job of suturing, but it appeared that no one had bothered undressing Ives to examine him for signs of less apparent injury.

Until we know someone, the way they say things is as important as what they have to say. . . . Practice being a little gentler on the staff. . . .

The world according to George Oleander. Abby forced herself to focus on the many kind, compassionate, intelligent, and professional things she had seen the nursing staff do over the weeks she had worked with them. It was really Bartholomew's fault. He had set the tone in room one. He had invited the staff to bring in their distaste for people like Samuel Ives. She closed the door behind her.

"Mr. Ives, could you please lie back down?" she said. "I want to examine you a little bit more, and then I want to suture your face over again."

For the second time Ives allowed his gaze to meet hers.

"No X rays," he said.

She peeked out at the treatment bays. Another patient was being brought in. She closed the door again, got Lew Alvarez's number from her clinic book, and called him. If he was free, could he possibly come in an hour early? She was already behind and was facing a complex suturing job. By their eight o'clock changeover, the place could be bedlam.

"Fifteen minutes," Alvarez said, no questions asked.

Abby next called Bud Perlow at the nurses' station. She would be in room one and did not need any help except for him to hold down the fort until Dr. Alvarez arrived. Oh, and one more thing. She would appreciate it if he told absolutely no one what she was doing.

Samuel Ives closed his eyes as she widened the narrow, shaved track Bartholomew had made in his beard. Then she cut away the sutures, numbed the edges of the lacerations once again, set a pair of magnifying glasses low on the bridge of her nose, and began a meticulous closure.

The repair took forty-five minutes. During that time not a word was exchanged between them. When the last knot had been tied and cut, Abby stepped back from the table, working the stiffness from her neck. She called it being "zoned." For forty-five minutes her brain had been free of all extraneous thoughts. She had probably not moved any muscle except in her hands and forearms through the entire procedure. *Zoned.* It was a joy to have been there.

She unbuttoned Ives's work shirt, which was heavy with drying blood. A more careful exam showed his chest and belly were free of discernible injury.

"Did they give you a tetanus shot?" she asked.

"They did."

"These stitches can come out in five days. Just come in and find me. No need to check in at the desk. I'm going to have the nurse give you a shot of antibiotic and five days' worth of pills. I'm also going to see if we can find you a shirt to wear home."

"I've been having a little trouble with my leg," Ives said. "Pick out some pills that will help that, too."

Abby gloved once again, and with Ives's help, lowered his fetid, bloodied jeans. The infection, covering five or six inches of his right shin, was long-standing and deep — undoubtedly deep enough to include the bone. Almost certainly chronic osteomyelitis, one of the most difficult, recalcitrant of all infections. She grimaced, not so much from the sight of the thick, raw inflammatory tissue, as from her knowledge of how difficult it was going to be to treat. Then she realized that he was watching her.

"How'd you do this?" she managed.

"A fall. I hit a rock."

"When?"

"Two, three years ago."

"And you can get around okay?"

"It hurts some."

She sighed.

"Mr. Ives —"

"Just Ives. That's what people I like call me. Ives."

"Ives, this is a pretty deep and serious infection. I don't know for sure if it's gotten into the bone, and I have no idea what germ is causing it. But if we don't treat it properly, sooner or later you're going to get very sick from it. You could even lose your leg."

"It really doesn't bother me that much. How about just giving me some medicine now and —"

"It's not that simple!" she snapped. She took another calming breath. Fatigue from the long, difficult day was catching up with her. She knew, especially after the debacle with Bartholomew, there wasn't a chance in the world that Ives would ever willingly be an inpatient. "Ives, listen. Let me at least take a small biopsy to send off for culture and some slides. Then I'll give you some intravenous antibiotics. Tomorrow I'll talk to the infectious-disease person and one of the bone specialists. Okay?"

"I don't —"

"Ives, please."

"Okay, okay."

"Thank you."

She opened the door and, for the first time in an hour, reconnected with the rest of the ER. Lew Alvarez was writing prescriptions for the last of the patients. She stood some distance away and watched him converse with the woman in fluent, animated Spanish. His English, she had noticed, was accent free. She wondered which was his native language. He was forty or so, and handsomer than any man needed to be. His eyes were dark and lively, and his thick brows and mustache were offset by rich copper skin. Of all the physicians in the ER, he was the one she found the most interesting.

George Oleander's description of him as excessively opinionated and not a team player did not easily fit the man she was watching — the man who had responded to her call for assistance without a single quibble.

He noticed her just as he was sending his patient away.

"Ta *da!*" he sang, motioning to the now-empty ER.

He moved toward her with a natural, easy grace. Regardless of what he had said about her to George Oleander, she could not imagine this man being intimidated by any-one.

"Thanks for coming in," she said.

"No problem. I understand you've had a day of it. Diagnosing Cushing's syndrome in the middle of a code. Hail to the chief."

"It hasn't been confirmed."

"It will be. And now, in comes Sam Ives."

"It's just Ives, he says. He doesn't like being called anything else."

"He was a college professor at one time. Or at least so I've been told."

Abby was instantly intrigued.

"Where? What'd he teach?"

Alvarez shrugged.

"No idea. A year or so ago he was looking for odd jobs, so I gave him some work on my farm. We never talked much. I don't think he gets many offers. People around here are scared of him."

"Has he ever hurt anyone?"

"Hardly. Just being out of the ordinary is all it takes around here, and he is certainly that."

"One of the nurses said he lives in a cave."

Alvarez laughed.

"His shack isn't much. No electricity, no plumbing. But it's not a cave."

"He's got chronic osteomyelitis on his anterior leg. He needs a surgical debridement and intensive antibiotic therapy. Maybe even a graft. Right now all he'll allow me to do is a biopsy and some IV antibiotics. Want to help?"

"Sure, if there's a chance something will rub off on me and I can diagnose Cushing's during a code."

Abby started to react to his sarcasm. But there was only warmth in his expression. He was teasing her, true, but not maliciously; he really was impressed. They got the biopsy kit and culture tubes ready, and set up an IV of powerful antibiotics. Then they brought them into room one.

Ives was gone. They checked the nearest bathrooms, but Abby knew he had skipped. She had come on too strong and frightened him away. Muttering curses at herself, she returned to the room.

Beneath the litter was the plastic possessions bag. Abby dumped the contents out on the mattress. All it contained were

57

sanded wood fragments — heads, torsos, and limbs of what might have been beautiful, delicately carved figures — and a well-worn copy of Conrad's *Lord Jim.*

Chapter Four

On the way home from Peking Pagoda, Abby ate an egg roll and half a carton of ribs. There was a time when she had smoked in response to stress — up to a pack a day of unfiltered Pall Malls. Soon after she'd given up cigarettes, she had found that, more and more, she was dealing with the people and events that upset her by drinking — only wine, and always top-shelf stuff. Eventually, she had felt obligated to limit her drinking to days when she wasn't worried about something or angry with someone, a move that effectively kept her on the wagon most of the time. With little time or inclination for regular exercise or meditation, food became and remained her pacifier. And the ten pounds between her clothes fitting well and feeling tight became a battlefield.

Tonight, with Bill Tracy, George Oleander, Martin Bartholomew, Lew Alvarez, and Ives competing for headspace with Josh, she felt fortunate to make it home with any dinner left at all.

The house Josh had rented was a six-room, cedar-shingled ranch on the north side of town. The charm of the place came from its setting at the end of a wooded cul-de-sac at the base of the hills. Over the weeks she had been living there, Abby had reconnected with her love of the outdoors.

The drive from the hospital to the house was about two miles, but she took a long way around, paralleling the north side of the valley, hoping she might catch up with Ives. By the time she pulled into their driveway, it was almost nine. The smell of cooking told her that Josh had decided not to wait for her to arrive home with their dinner.

"Honey, I'm home," she called out, knowing that their gravel driveway made the announcement redundant.

His not coming out to the kitchen to meet her probably signaled another evening of tension. She paused by the back door for one more rib.

"In here," he said.

As she passed through the kitchen, she noticed the bottle of pills on the counter. They were prescribed for Josh by the employees' clinic at Colstar. Fioricet — headache medication with generic Tylenol, some caffeine, and a moderately strong sedative. At least he had gone to see someone. If he mentioned having a headache, fine. But she had started enough skirmishes by bringing the subject up herself. Not tonight.

He was on the couch in the living room, his favorite spot, eating some vegetable stir fry, watching a baseball game, and doing a crossword puzzle. Taken as an isolated freeze-frame, the scene looked incredibly normal. She bent over and hugged him from behind. Then she took off his glasses and inserted herself between him and the puzzle.

"In case you can't tell," she said from breath-mint range, "I'm a little starved for affection."

He blinked as if he had just noticed she was there. Then he took her face in his hands and, for a moment, seemed to be peering at her through a fog. Even so, his blue-green eyes drew her in as they always had. Finally he responded to her closeness with a kiss, lips nearly closed, eyes open. It was hardly an invitation to anything more intense, but for the moment she would take it.

Josh was thirty-eight, an electrical engineer who had been married briefly in his early twenties and had been a gun-shy bachelor-about-town since. Two and a half years ago a mutual friend had fixed them up, accurately predicting that neither of them would be intimidated by the other's intellect and good looks. Abby adored him from night one. Josh wasn't as certain about her initially, but the time constraints of her job at St. John's required him to make something of a commitment if he wanted to see her at all. Within six months they were living together — an idyllic relationship, spiced with good friends and a wonderful merging of styles, humor, temperaments, and interests.

During medical school Abby had had a two-year relationship with a med student who decided in one tumultuous week that he was neither ready to be a physician, nor to be romantically involved with anyone. Over the years that followed she had dated as much as her demanding schedule allowed. But having a man in her life was never an overriding priority. She had good friends and a stimulating job in a city that she loved. If Mr. Right came along to share all that, so much the better. If not, she wouldn't be shattered. It was only after she met Josh that she was able to admit that, subconsciously, she had been kidding herself all along, purposely minimizing the importance of finding someone because she feared it simply wasn't going to happen for her.

From the very beginning the two of them were at ease with one another. Josh was more fun to be with than any man she had ever known, and it seemed as if there wasn't one aspect of her life that wasn't better, richer, because of him. Even her ER work became less stressful knowing that the end of the day meant sitting in a theater together or trading puns as they jogged through the park or squeezing into their small tub together before making love. She knew without doubt that this was the man she had held out for — the man she had somehow had in mind when she had worked so hard to find fault with the others.

And at almost thirty-five, she had no desire to begin the process again.

"Sorry I'm late," she said, setting what remained of the Chinese food on the table. "I finished up the day from hell with a really tough case."

"Tree resin, six letters, begins with *m.*"

"Mastic. Josh, listen to this. There's this hermit. He lives in the forest someplace north of town. A former professor, believe it or not. He got beat up and I sewed up his face. But he ran out of the ER before I could treat his infected leg. I think I scared him away."

"Hey, he wouldn't be the first guy you've scared away. How in the hell could any man not be frightened of a woman who looks like Nicole Kidman, knows about tree resins, and can put someone back together who's been run over by a bus?"

Abby smiled and felt some of her tension easing away. She brought him the last sparerib, and he ate it without comment. A truce had tacitly been declared over her getting home late with dinner, and his not waiting for it. Buttons had been pushed by each of them, but neither had reacted. The night might yet be saved. She sank down beside him on the couch and kicked off her shoes. Her feet sighed relief.

"His name's Ives. I brought some medicine and equipment home from work. Tomorrow I would love it if you could help me find him."

"Tomorrow we have plans," he said coolly.

It took several seconds before Abby remembered. Tomorrow was family day at Colstar — the first chance Josh would have to introduce her to his world. Forgetting his company outing was the sort of thing *she* had been doing that was adding to the stress between them. Thank God she hadn't innocently switched days at the hospital with anyone.

"Hey, the Colstar picnic," she said. "Just a momentary lapse. I've got my outfit all laid out and I'm ready to go."

"You don't have to come. In fact, I have things I need to get done at the office."

Another button.

Easy, she thought. *Tread easy.* If she simply didn't react, they still might make it through the night without a blowup.

"Josh, seriously, I've been looking forward to it. That's the truth. I just lost track of the days. I'm sorry."

"Look, I don't want you to come. Just forget it."

Damn. It was happening again.

"Honey, please, I —"

"You know, you don't see it, but you've been so damn wrapped up in that hospital, I might as well be on the moon. What is it? Are you upset that I went and got myself a good job again? Are you trying to make sure everyone in Patience knows you're still number one?"

"Josh, that's not fair."

"What's not fair? When I got laid off, tell me you didn't lord it over me for all those months. Tell me you weren't smiling every time you came home from your big-shot job with all those strokes from all those patients and students and fellow professors, and all I could say was that someone had promised they'd keep my résumé on file. Tell me it didn't feel great to be the only one in the house bringing in the bucks."

Abby felt her neck get hot. *She* was the one who had encouraged him to take the Colstar job, even though it meant trying to make it as a long-distance couple. *She* was the one who had begun a dialogue with the people at Patience Regional. And, ultimately, *she* was the one who had made the sacrifice of her job and teaching career in order for them to be together.

And now, once again, she was being treated like the enemy. He was so fragile, so volatile, she always ended up on the defensive. It had to be that he was disappointed with his job — that he was overwhelmed or unstimulated or having trouble with his boss — and just couldn't admit it. No other explanation made sense.

"Josh, honey, I'm sorry. Work has been tough for me, and today was a real bear." She took his hand and was relieved when he didn't pull away. "Believe me, I'm really looking forward to meeting the people you work with. I just hope they don't think I'm a jerk."

She saw some of the tightness leave his face. His fist unclenched. She touched his lips, then set her hand on his lap and stroked him in a way she knew he loved. He moaned softly, closed his eyes, and leaned back onto the cushion.

"I told them we'd be there at ten to help set up," he said without opening his eyes. "Maybe we can get up early and I can help you find your guy."

"That would be great. You may even like him — he's sort of a grown-up version of those kids you used to bring home from the basketball court for dinner."

She unsnapped his jeans and undid his zipper. It was no longer automatic that she could arouse him, but this time there was no problem.

"Doc," he said, "for what you're doing, I not only help you find this guy, I carry your medical bag."

Chapter Five

Abby lay facedown, trying to convince herself that she was still asleep, but knowing that she wasn't. She reached across the bed, but Josh wasn't there. Then she realized why she was awake — the repeating sound of an ax slamming into wood, and the crunch of logs splitting. She squinted at the pale sunlight filtering through the blinds. *Before six,* she guessed. She fumbled for the clock radio and groaned. Twenty after five. From the backyard the wood splitting continued at a furious, nonstop pace. A new chapter.

Josh, what in the hell is going on with you?

She rolled onto her back and blinked until the ceiling came into focus — more specifically, it was the poster of Albert Einstein that Josh had tacked there the day she'd arrived six weeks ago, telling her it was the sort of thing that happened when engineers finally felt comfortable with a mate. Six weeks. It seemed more like a year.

She pulled on a T-shirt and scrub pants and squinted at herself in the dresser mirror. She was certainly no Nicole Kidman, even with her contacts in, and five in the morning hardly brought out the best in her. But she still had decent looks and a better-than-decent body. And it was an almost sure bet that Nicole Kidman wouldn't know thing one about reducing a dislocated radial head in a screaming three-year-old. She ran her brush twenty-five times through her shoulder-length hair and, in spite of herself, wondered if Lew Alvarez was living with anyone. She knew he was a widower — one of the nurses had told her that much.

She went to the kitchen and loaded up Josh's fancy European coffeemaker. The bottle of Fioricet had been moved from the counter to the table. Sometime between the end of their lovemaking and now he had taken some. The label, dated two weeks ago, read fifty tablets. There were ten left. Forty in fourteen days was at the high end of the prescribed dosage, and the pills did have addictive potential. Was that what was behind his volatile, erratic behavior — drug dependence? It was hard for her to believe. He had always been a health nut, obsessive about conditioning and diet. Until now she had never seen him take a pill other than a vitamin.

She peeked out the window. Josh, his back to her, stood barefoot on the dew-covered lawn, stripped to the waist. His sinewy body glistened with sweat. Vapor rose from his shoulders and in his breath. The ax blows he was delivering — vicious, roundhouse, over-the-head swings — made her shudder.

She opened the door and stepped out onto the back stoop. The air was cool and utterly clear, with a sweet mountainy smell that blended wonderfully with the chips of oak and ash. From just beyond the yard the dense fir forest extended a hundred yards or so to the base of the rocky foothills. There were many things she missed living away from the city, but there were compensations.

"Hey, Bunyan," she said, "how about stopping for some coffee?"

One more swing, two more pieces of log. Wiping his brow with the back of his hand, he turned to her. His expression was peaceful, his broad smile genuine — pure Josh.

"Sorry if I woke you. Coffee would be great."

Abby packed her medical bag into Josh's large backpack, along with the surgical equipment, culture tubes, and IV antibiotics she had appropriated from the hospital. Then she added some of Josh's old clothes, some canned food and pasta, and an eclectic bunch of paperbacks, ranging from Daphne du Maurier to Stephen Crane to John Grisham, and loaded the carton into the back of Josh's Jeep. The khaki Wrangler Safari, more specifically the down payment on it, had been a gift from her when he'd landed and accepted the Colstar position.

"We've got about two hours before I have

to be at the park," Josh said, hopping behind the wheel. "Think we can find your hermit in that time?"

"I think so. Lew Alvarez, the doctor who knows him, told me where to park and what to do once we found the trail. He hadn't been there in over a year, so his directions were a bit shaky."

"Alvarez. Dark hair, mustache, looks like Omar Sharif in *Doctor Zhivago*?"

Abby was startled.

"A little, I suppose," she managed to say, "now that you mention it. You know him?" She sensed the heightening color in her cheeks and quickly looked out the window to her right.

"He's the one who sewed up my thigh when I tore it on that nail, remember?"

"I remember your telling me about the accident, but I don't think I ever knew who did the suturing. At that time I didn't have much interest in PRH. He did a fine job, though."

"Damn fine. Seemed like a nice guy, too."

Abby continued staring off to her right. What had been going on in her head since the end of her ER shift was nothing more than a perfectly innocent little fantasy — and a G-rated fantasy at that. But somehow she felt caught out.

Josh was animated and relaxed as they drove east toward the hospital and the Colstar cliff, then cut north across the valley. Morning was in full force now, cloudless and already warm. Perfect picnic weather. Abby wondered if nature had ever dared to frown on a Colstar function.

They easily found the street Lew had directed them to. It was paved and built up for half its length, then reverted to dirt for a quarter of a mile or so before ending.

"This is it," Abby said. "The trail should be right over there."

They were about two miles from the hospital. The hills on the north side of the valley were steeper than on the south. She felt sadness at the notion of Ives, battered and exhausted, making his way down this road and up into the woods at night with no light. Then she reminded herself that, for whatever reason, he had chosen his life of solitude.

Josh swung the backpack on and buckled it with practiced ease. Abby followed as he set off.

The trail was rocky and fairly steep, but quite well defined. It wound eastward through awesome, dense forest, made all the more imposing by the muted sunlight filtering through the branches.

Lew had guessed it would be a mile before they had to leave the trail and cut straight up. The markers for the turn would be a large boulder overseeing the valley, and a narrow brook, spanned by a fallen tree. Josh climbed with the vigor and confidence of an athlete and outdoorsman. Abby worked a bit harder at it, though she was pleased to realize that she was still in reasonably good shape. During the first few weeks after her move to Patience, before she had started at the hospital, they had hiked the hills and even done some quasi–rock climbing almost every day or evening. Lately, not at all.

The cutoff was exactly where Lew had depicted — a scuffed area at the base of a rise of boulders. The next hundred feet, almost straight up, had Abby breathing heavily. Then, through the trees, they saw it — a small clearing hewn into the forest. At the rear of the clearing, pressed against the hillside, was a crude hut of scrap lumber, corrugated aluminum, and roofing shingle.

Beside the hut was a workbench with carving tools and partially completed projects. To one side of the clearing, hanging from a tree, was a thick straw dummy, roughly human in shape, with half a dozen long hunting arrows protruding from it. Pinned to the base of the dummy in a most persuasive spot was a No Trespassing sign.

"I confess I didn't really think we'd find anyone living up here," Josh said. "It's still hard to believe someone does. But I suppose if you're a hermit, this is the Ritz."

"Ives," Abby called, without approaching the hut. "Ives, it's Dr. Dolan from the hospital. Hello . . . Ives?"

For several seconds there was only silence. Then, from somewhere up and to their left, came the snap of a bowstring. Almost simultaneously, with a crack like a bullwhip, an arrow slammed into the dummy chest high. Reflexively, they stumbled back behind a tree.

"Be right down, Doc," Ives hollered, his voice sounding fairly distant.

Josh walked cautiously to the dummy and inspected the arrows.

"Just one of these could bring down a jet," he said.

Ives emerged from the woods carrying a long, richly polished bow. The tissue around his eyes was badly swollen, and, in fact, his entire face was puffed and bruised. He had changed his bloody clothes for worn chinos and a frayed work shirt with the name Norm stitched above the breast pocket. There were still some flecks of dried blood in his beard, but Abby felt certain he had tended to that as well. She also noted that her suture lines were holding nicely.

"Sorry I took off on you last night," he said. "I have this thing about hospitals and doctors."

Abby said she understood and introduced him to Josh.

"Nice shot," Josh said, gesturing to the dummy. "Especially with your eyes nearly swelled shut."

"Only fifty yards or so. I could do that blindfolded."

"You hunt deer?"

"Don't hunt anything. Don't eat meat.

73

There're a few dummies like that one I've got scattered around in various places. I shoot at *them*. A long time ago I spent some time in Japan and ended up studying archery. I still like shooting — especially since I finished making this new bow."

Abby could tell that Josh was intrigued.

"Ives, I want to help you with your leg," she said, "but I'd also like your promise that if I get in over my head, you'll see a specialist and at least consider doing whatever he recommends."

Ives didn't respond. He was studying Josh's face.

"Olive-drab Jeep Wrangler, California license eight-two-eight, C-J-W," he said.

They stared at him, puzzled. There was no way he could have been at the bottom of the trail to see them arrive, and then deep in the woods with a bow and arrow when they reached his camp. His expression suggested he was enjoying the game.

"Okay, Ives," Abby said. "We give up."

Ives entered the hut and emerged with a weighty burlap gunnysack. Without a word he led them onto an ill-defined trail beyond the hanging tree. After a hundred yards or so the woods gave way to a rocky plateau, about thirty feet wide. Beyond the plateau was a sharp drop-off revealing a magnificent vista of the valley and the mountains. To the west was the town, perfect in miniature, stretching along the floor of the two-mile-wide valley as far as they could

74

see. And almost directly behind them, slightly to the east, was Colstar, looking from above like an airfield with smoke-stacks set on a broad mesa. Ives gingerly lowered himself onto his belly and motioned for Josh and Abby to do the same. Then he reached into his sack and withdrew an impressive pair of field glasses.

"One of my hobbies," he said, adjusting the focus, then passing the binoculars over to Abby. "For night viewing I fixed up an old pair of infrareds that work pretty well, too."

"Josh, these are incredible," Abby said. "See that car coming up the drive?"

"Barely. Black, Matchbox sedan."

"Volvo. And it's dark blue, not black."

She passed the glasses over. Josh scanned his workplace and whistled softly.

"Amazing. Big brother Ives is watching you," he said.

"I recognized your face because that Jeep is sort of distinctive and you have the top down a lot. By the way, you drive too fast."

"Do the people at Colstar know you do this?" Josh asked.

"Nope. And I hope you won't tell them. It's just a harmless hobby. Something to pass the time when there's no wildlife around to watch."

"I won't say anything," Josh said. "I prom-ise."

"Tell me something, Ives," Abby said. "If you have to resort to a hobby like this to pass the time, why not come down the hill and live with the rest of us?"

"I already did that," Ives said. "Too many cannibals. Too many rules. Too much hypocrisy. Too many bills. Too much hatred. Shall I go on?"

"No," Abby said, though she still wanted to know more of what, specifically, had pushed him up into the hills. "Now it's my turn. Do we have a deal about your leg?"

"No promises, but I will listen to what you recommend, and I'll do it if it seems right to me. Believe me, there's too much I enjoy about life to want to get sick or crippled. But you also have to understand that self-satisfied fops like that surgeon you referred me to do not make me want to have much to do with your sacred profession."

"I'm sorry about that."

"Don't feel sorry for me," Ives said, leading them back to his clearing. "Feel sorry for him." He motioned at Josh.

Abby was taken aback.

"What are you talking about?"

"I'm talking about white Mercedes number MD three-oh-three. Dr. Pomposity, himself."

"Dr. Bartholomew?"

"Precisely. Drives up to Colstar every Tuesday and Friday at nine A.M. and leaves at three."

Abby turned to Josh.

"He's talking about Martin Bartholomew. You know him?"

"He runs the employee health clinic."

"He's a surgeon. Is he the one who checked you over for those headaches?"

"He didn't really check me over. Just ordered some tests and then had the nurse call in a prescription."

"Lord. Josh, I think you should have a neurol—" She stopped herself in midword. The morning was simply going too well for her to spoil it. "Listen," she said, "we'll talk about it another time if you want."

Josh wandered back toward Ives's observation post while Abby took some shallow and deeper biopsies of the chronic infection on the hermit's leg. Then, with the cultures secure, she administered the IV antibiotic. Routine lacerations, and facial lacerations in particular, were usually no cause for IV antibiotics. With cut faces and scalps, tissue circulation was so good that severe infection was rarely a problem. But Ives's leg was another story. Treating him this way wasn't perfect, but it was better than the alternative of doing nothing. As she worked, cleaning away the superficial damaged tissue with forceps, scissors, and scalpel, she glanced around the clearing and smiled at the notion of what her high-powered university colleagues would say if they could see her at this moment.

When she was finished, she dressed the leg lightly and promised to return in a few days to remove the stitches from Ives's face and to continue work on his leg. Then she left the books, food, and clothing she had brought, called Josh back to the clearing, and hiked with him down the hill.

Once in the Jeep again, they headed for the park where the Colstar picnic was being held.

"Josh," she said, "have you ever read a remarkable little book called *Zen and the Art of Archery*?"

"No."

"I read it for a philosophy course at Cal, and I can't recall the author's name. But remember when Ives joked about being able to hit the dummy blindfolded from fifty yards?"

"Yes, what of it?"

"Well, I think that was more than a figure of speech. I think he does make that shot blindfolded."

Chapter Six

By the time Josh had reached Colstar Park, four miles west of the plant, Abby had already noticed a change in him. It began with some gestures that outwardly appeared benign — squinting as if the glare of the morning sun was uncomfortable, rubbing at his eyes and temples, wetting his lips, putting his sunglasses on, taking them off. His conversation, so animated on the drive across town earlier, had all but died.

"You okay?" she ventured.

He glared at her for a moment as if she had intruded on some cosmic thought.

"Of course I am. I'm fine." He didn't snap at her, but almost. "I was up at four-thirty, remember?"

If recent experience was an indicator, over the next hour or so he would become more withdrawn and irritable. Sometimes he would admit to having a "little headache," sometimes he wouldn't. Eventually he would take to bed, or fall asleep on the couch, or pick a fight with her. Occasionally he might have a drink of Scotch, often at an inappropriate hour, and in a way — no ice, no sipping — that was hardly typical of him. And that was only what she observed at home. She wondered what might be happening at work.

Colstar Park was a showplace — lush, perfectly maintained, and grand enough to encompass several duck ponds, a mile-long jogging track, playgrounds, large picnic groves, three ball fields, a grandstand, and a small lake. If there was another town the size of Patience that had such an oasis, Abby had yet to see it.

An outstanding park, a phenomenally equipped hospital, an unemployment rate close to zero, schools reportedly as good as any in the state — Colstar International and the town of Patience seemed to have formed a remarkable partnership, a symbiotic relationship as perfect as any in nature. As they parked the Jeep, Abby watched the early-bird families heading for the outing. Scrubbed kids with their bats and gloves, fishing poles and Frisbees. Relaxed parents, a few of whom she recognized as ER patients, shouting orders to their offspring as they tried to keep up. She had little trouble imagining what it would be like to raise children in this community.

But with Josh?

"Hey, *muchacho*," she called out with less enthusiasm than she had intended. "How about waiting for me?"

Josh glanced back and slowed his pace.

"Sorry," he muttered.

"I'm looking forward to meeting some of

the Colstar people I've heard about," she said.

"Well, they'll all be here."

His voice was hollow.

The truth was, Josh had not told her much about his work or his colleagues. And she had visited the plant only once, shortly after her arrival in town. All she really knew was that he was involved in the development of sophisticated, state-of-the-art plastic batteries, his department's research sponsored in part by the company and in part by grants from the federal government.

Colstar was the only large employer in the valley. In fact, anyone who didn't work directly for the company probably had a job or business that depended upon it. The picnic would fill several of the park's groves, Josh had told her. Maybe all of them.

"Wanna play a little catch?" she asked.

"Maybe later. I've got to go help organize the food."

He motioned to where several men were unloading a large Ryder truck. Near the truck were a dozen or so oil-drum halves on stands — the portable barbecue pit.

"Want help?" Abby asked.

But he had already walked away. She stayed where she was, following him with her eyes. When he reached the truck, he leaned, almost slumped, against it for several seconds. She was moving toward him when he seemed to gather himself and joined the others unloading the truck. She sighed and looked away. It was going to be a long day.

Abby was casting about for something to do when a man approached her.

"Dr. Dolan?"

"Yes."

He was broad-shouldered, fit, and military straight. His thick hair was swan-white, prematurely, she was sure, and his outfit — black turtleneck, black sports coat, black slacks, and spit-polished wing tips — seemed absurdly inappropriate for an outing in the park.

A Johnny Cash impersonator? she thought.

He reached out his hand and she took it tentatively. His grip was firm; his smile revealed pearl-perfect teeth.

"Lyle Quinn," he said. "It's a pleasure to meet you. I've heard a great deal about you."

"From Josh?"

She hated to acknowledge how unlikely that was.

"Yes, from Josh. From others, too. Would you like me to show you around?"

The strange man-in-black had piqued her curiosity. She glanced over at where Josh was hoisting large sacks of potatoes and corn on the cob with the same frantic vigor he had exhibited chopping wood.

"Sure," she said.

He guided her away from the barbecue pits and toward the lake.

"I heard about your saving Bill Tracy's life," he said.

Abby looked at him uncomfortably.

"Are you connected with the hospital?"

Quinn favored her with another practiced smile.

"In a manner of speaking. I'm on the board of trustees. Have been for, I don't know, six . . . no, seven years now."

There was a smugness to the man that had already impressed Abby negatively.

"Exactly what is it you do?" she asked.

"For Colstar?"

"If that's who you work for."

She was finding Lyle Quinn more annoying by the moment. Even worse, she had the strange sense that he wanted her to.

"It is," he said. "I guess you could call me chief security officer, head of security, something like that."

Abby recalled asking Josh why the entire plant was surrounded by an eight-foot-high chain-link fence, topped by three rows of tightly strung barbed wire, slanted outward. His only response was that they were working on a number of classified government projects.

"Classified batteries?" she had asked.

Batteries of the future, was the way he had phrased it.

"So," she asked now, "is this walk we're on security business?"

Looking at the strange fellow striding purposefully beside her, all she could think of was G. Gordon Liddy.

Quinn laughed, but his pale-blue eyes did not.

"Hardly. I just wanted to meet the woman who has become such a sensation at the hospital in such a short time."

Obviously you haven't been speaking with the same people I have, Abby thought.

"Please thank whoever said that about me," she said.

"You *did* save Bill Tracy's life. I have that on the best authority."

"How do you know Bill Tracy?" Abby said, reluctant as always to acknowledge that she had saved anyone's life. "Is Colstar involved with insurance?"

For a moment she thought Quinn was going to say that Colstar was involved with everything.

"Bill's a friend," he said. "He writes the health insurance for a lot of our folks."

"Well, I'm glad I was there when he came in."

"So are a lot of people."

They reached the tree-lined lake. Several brightly colored pedal boats were already out on the water. The laughter of children echoed through the sparkling morning. For a time neither of them spoke. Abby sensed that Quinn had more of an agenda than he had presented so far, but she could wait to find out what it was. She just hoped it had nothing to do with Josh.

"Nice place to live," Quinn said finally.

He motioned that he had seen enough and turned back toward the path.

"Very nice," Abby replied. "Do you have children?"

"Two. Grown and gone."

"But you like it here?"

"I do. And I like working for a company that takes its responsibility to the community seriously."

The agenda, Abby thought.

"It certainly seems like Patience wouldn't be much without Colstar," she said.

"Correction, Doctor. Without Colstar, Patience wouldn't *be.* That's why we're all very concerned when people with an antibusiness mentality try to impugn our company in any way."

"And are there such people?"

"A few. Very few. They're harmless because no one takes them very seriously. But anyone new to Patience is fair game to them, especially physicians, who often tend to be swayed by so-called liberal causes. I don't know your politics, or anything about you that wasn't in your application for staff privileges. But I'm sure that sooner or later they'll be approaching you to join them."

Abby had to control a knee-jerk flare-up of outrage. An application for staff privileges was, in most hospitals, personal and confidential — even from members of the board of trustees. She was quite sure Quinn knew that and had brought the matter up on purpose. He was displaying his resourcefulness and issuing a tacit warning at the same time. No doubt her under-graduate degree from Cal Berkeley and M.D. from Stanford had labeled her a leftist in his mind.

"Who are these people?" she asked.

"I'd rather not say. What I will say is that they are misguided and selfish individuals who are willing to put their own interests ahead of the community's."

They had arrived back at the field, where Josh was still helping to set up the barbe-cue. The crowd had grown considerably, and several organized games and sports had begun. Abby felt an urge to grab her glove and play some softball, and an even stronger one to get away from Lyle Quinn.

"Well, Mr. Quinn," she said, leading him to the backpack where she had stored her medical bag and makeshift first-aid kit, and Josh had packed their other gear, "thanks for the walk and the information."

Another unsettling smile. His eyes were locked on hers.

"A great many people are very pleased you're here, Dr. Dolan. Good doctors are a critical part of this community."

"Just like Colstar."

Her retort brought a flicker of reaction. No more.

"Exactly," he said. "Just like Colstar. Well, it's been very pleasant getting to know you. My wife and I look forward to entertaining you and Josh sometime in the near future.

Perhaps you will allow us to propose you for membership in the Patience Country Club. I'm on the board there, too."

He shook her hand and turned to go.

At that moment, from across the field, a woman began shrieking hysterically, again and again.

The commotion was coming from the west end of the field, just in front of a dense pine grove. At the first shriek Quinn whirled catlike and sprinted across toward the gathering crowd. Abby, still clutching her baseball glove, trotted behind him. By the time she arrived at the grove, a hundred or more people were there. Others, especially those with children, were trying to move away quickly.

"It's just Angela," Abby heard someone say.

The terrible wailing continued.

"Get back," the woman screamed. "Get back or I'll cut you, too! I swear I will!"

"One side, please," Quinn ordered. "Step aside."

Abby caught sight of Josh to one edge of the crowd and headed toward him.

"Somebody do something!" a woman exclaimed. "Help her."

Chapter Seven

It wasn't until Abby was almost at Josh's side that she saw the problem. A markedly overweight young woman was backed up against a tree, brandishing a ten-inch hunting knife and bleeding from a dozen or more shallow cuts that she had inflicted on her arms and thighs. Abby's first impression was that none of the wounds was dangerous. But the woman's beige shorts and white blouse were rapidly becoming soaked in crimson.

Quinn, at the front of the crowd, was about thirty feet from her.

"Angela, put the knife down," he said with the firmness of a parent confronting a recalcitrant child.

"Stay away from me!" she screamed. "Come any closer and I'll kill myself! You know I will."

She pulled up her blouse and ran the blade across flesh that she had already sliced several times. People gasped.

Abby could not see through the blood, but she strongly suspected that the woman's body would be covered with scars from previous episodes such as this. A self-mutilator — the ultimate form of self-loathing and masochism. Angela was hardly the first case Abby had seen. Such patients tended to be well-known to emergency wards and ER docs. The psychopathology was complicated and not always consistent from one patient to another. And all too often, despite intensive therapy, the end result was self-inflicted death.

"Oh, God," Abby said, moving past Josh.

"Stay back here," Josh ordered in a harsh whisper. "That woman worked on one of the production lines at the company. She still comes up to Colstar and does stuff like this all the time. Quinn and the police will know how to handle her."

Abby glared at him.

"I can't believe you just said that to me."

"Angela," Quinn ordered, taking another slight step forward, "you've got to stop this right now and put the knife down. We'll take care of you."

"Stay back!" she screamed. "Do you all see now what can happen when you make fun of people just because they're fat? Always snickering. Always pointing. I can't stand it anymore!"

Moaning piteously, she made a series of puncture wounds along the underside of her arm. From one of them Abby saw the scarlet spray from a small artery.

"Josh, please get the backpack," Abby said over her shoulder. "My medical bag is in there."

"No! You stay out of this. Quinn can handle it. There's no need for you to rush all over the valley playing hero wherever you go."

"Jesus." Abby turned to a husky man with tattooed deltoids, standing to her right. "Excuse me," she said. "I'm Dr. Dolan from the emergency ward. There's a big gray backpack over there near the picnic table. My medical supplies and bandages are in it. Could you bring it here for me, please?"

"Sure thing, Doc," the man said, sprinting off.

Abby half expected her lover to chase the man down and tackle him. Josh was entering the irrational, nasty phase of whatever was eating away at him. The pressure cooker was boiling and the safety valve was stuck. Sometime between now and late afternoon he would blow. Well, she was near boiling point herself.

"All right, everyone," Quinn was saying. "You all know that Angela has this problem. It doesn't help to stand around gawking at her. Go on. Get your kids out of here and get back to the picnic."

Immediately, the crowd dispersed. It was as if the onlookers had wanted to go but had needed someone to break the stranglehold of lurid fascination. In seconds there were only fifteen or so remaining, mostly men, who seemed ready for action.

Pointedly ignoring Josh, Abby moved next to Quinn.

"I have first-aid supplies in my backpack," she said softly. "A man's bringing it over."

"Oh, Angela's okay," Quinn replied, clearly annoyed with the woman and frustrated that he could not simply end the matter with a frontal assault. "Just nuts. She's been doing things like this for months — smashing her head against the wall until she's a bloody mess, cutting herself. We're all getting a little sick of it. I just want to make sure no one but her gets hurt."

"She's cut an artery in her arm. I think we should be trying to stop the bleeding soon."

"Someone went to call the police and rescue." Quinn risked another step forward. "She'll be all right. People get arms and legs cut off and survive."

"Not always," Abby said sharply. Could anyone really be that callous?

She moved up next to him. They were now about ten feet away.

"Stop it!" Angela screamed, slashing the air in their direction, cutlass style. "Stop it! Let me die! I deserve to die!"

Her eyes were wild. Tears washed through the blood smeared across her cheeks. The ground at her feet was becoming sodden.

"Damn her," Quinn muttered.

A woman hurried up to Quinn on the side opposite from where Abby stood. She had short graying hair, tortoiseshell glasses, and a Save the Planet T-shirt.

"Lyle, I've called rescue and the police," she said breathlessly. "They're at an accident at Five Corners. It'll be another ten or fifteen minutes."

"Jesus."

"Poor Angela. This is worse than I've ever seen her. After I spoke to Sergeant Brewster, I called her mother. She'll be right over, but she lives in Green Gables."

"Oh, great, Kelly," Quinn snapped. "The last thing we need is another hysterical member of the Cristoforo clan."

"Sorry."

"Look, call Brewster back. Tell him I want a cruiser and two men here in five minutes or less."

The woman nodded quickly and left.

Panting, the large man arrived with the backpack and set it beside Abby. Without taking her eyes off Angela Cristoforo, Abby withdrew her medical case and the plastic bag with the bandages and dressings she had leftover from treating Ives. There were at least two sets of rubber gloves inside. She was relieved that she didn't have to deal with the healer's dilemma of whether to treat someone in the field if it meant touching her blood without protection.

"Angela, I'm Dr. Dolan from the hospital," she said. "I want to help you. I want to stop the bleeding and fix those cuts."

At that moment Abby caught a flicker of movement — a man — through the trees behind Angela. She could tell that Quinn saw him, too.

"The doctors at the hospital hate me,"

Angela sobbed. "They hate the sight of me. The nurses laugh at me."

Abby was careful not to dispute what the woman believed, and what might very well be true.

"I'll make sure nobody ever does that again, Angela. I can do that. I promise."

Angela began singing a children's song, jabbing the point of the huge knife in rhythm against her chest. From somewhere out in the valley, Abby could hear sirens. She hoped that the commotion that was about to descend didn't push Angela Cristoforo the final inch. Nobody wanted to believe that a woman could bleed to death in plain sight of dozens of people. Abby knew better.

The man in the trees was now no more than five feet from Angela. Abby tried not to give his presence away with her eyes. He was tall and dark, wearing light jeans and a tan work shirt.

"Who is that?" she whispered, struggling to keep her eyes focused on the woman.

"A maintenance man from the plant. Willie Cardoza. He's kind of a flake, big practical joker. I don't know what in the hell he thinks he's doing."

"Too late to stop him now," Abby whispered.

She took a pair of rubber gloves and pulled them on. Then she held up a roll of gauze bandage.

"What are you trying to pull?" Angela

shrieked. "Stop right there! I mean it! I mean it!"

She raised the hunting knife to her throat.

"Angela, *please* — don't!"

Willie Cardoza took one step out from the cover of the trees. If Angela whirled now, there was no way he could escape being slashed. To Abby the seconds that followed were slow motion. Willie made his move at the instant Angela began to turn. He was taller than she was by six inches or more, but she was considerably bulkier.

"Angela!" Quinn shouted.

The distraction was just enough. Willie grabbed her right wrist from behind and brought his left arm around her neck. She struggled ineffectually as he braced his legs behind hers and pulled her down backward on top of him.

"Angie, it's me, Willie," he said, holding fast to her wrist, his lips next to her ear. "It's Willie. Angie, you've got to stop. It's over."

For one frozen moment, Angela Cristoforo's body went rigid. Then, with a final, pathetic wail, she released the knife. Lyle Quinn quickly moved forward and kicked it aside.

Willie Cardoza gently rolled her off him and onto her side.

"Angie, you let them take care of you now," he said. "You just rest and let them take care of you."

The sirens approached, then were cut off

as the first police cruiser pulled onto the ball field.

As Abby knelt beside the wounded woman, her gaze met Cardoza's. His long, narrow face, weathered and creased, had the look of having seen hard times. But his eyes were kind.

"That was a very good thing you just did," she said.

Cardoza's smile was self-effacing.

"She would have done the same for me," he replied. "We company grunts have to stick together."

He pushed himself to his feet, turned, and left without a word to Quinn.

Abby assured herself that Angela's pulses were intact and strong, and that none of her wounds was immediately life threatening. Then she began to tend to the individual cuts. She had two of them bandaged when the rescue squad arrived. After a brief report she turned matters over to them. When it came to first aid, nobody did it better than an EMT.

"How long has this been going on?" she asked Quinn.

"I don't know. Six months, maybe. She's spent a lot of time in mental hospitals over that period."

"And before?"

Quinn shrugged.

"She was — what was the word Cardoza used? — a grunt."

Abby packed up the knapsack and

watched as the EMTs finished inserting an IV and prepared Angie for transfer to the hospital.

She put the pack on and buckled the support straps, realizing with dismay that she had blood on her arms, legs, and clothes. She would wash it off as quickly as possible. With a terse good-bye to Lyle Quinn, she walked away.

The barbecue was now in full swing, with a dozen aproned chefs — according to Josh, the officers in the company — serving steak and chicken to their employees. But Josh was not among them, though he had told her he would be. She checked the picnic area and the path to the lake. Not there. Then she walked to the parking lot. The Jeep was gone.

She waited for five minutes but knew he was not coming back. The debate about approaching Lyle Quinn for a ride home lasted only moments. Abby found a pay phone and called a cab. She was feeling as frustrated, worried, and angry as she had at any time since moving to Patience.

Josh would get help or she was moving out.

She glanced back just as the ambulance began its trip to the hospital. There was something surreal about the scene — the magnificent mountains, the perfect ball diamonds, the shimmering emerald grass, the smoke rising from the barbecue pits, the laughter. And at one edge of the perfect scene, an ambulance carrying a woman slashed by her own hand — a woman consumed by the most virulent hatred imaginable. Hatred directed inwardly . . . at herself.

Chapter Eight

Abby parked her three-year-old Mazda in the doctors' lot and entered the hospital through the ambulance bay. For seven-thirty in the evening the ER was busier than she liked it, but still a notch or two from utter chaos. It was just as well, she thought. A few hectic hours would help keep her mind focused on work.

Five days had passed since the Colstar family outing. For Abby they had been days of tension and turmoil at home, sandwiched around relatively uneventful shifts at the hospital. Shortly after returning by cab from Colstar Park, she had moved her things into the small guest bedroom. And there she had stayed despite Josh's daily assurances that he would never behave so irrationally again.

Getting away from the stress at home wasn't the only reason she was pleased to be at the hospital tonight. The day-shift doctor she would be replacing was Lew Alvarez. Their paths hadn't crossed since the evening of Bill Tracy's resuscitation. But on her shifts Abby had managed to draw a nurse here or a doctor there into conversation about him. She could not, in all honesty, deny that she found Alvarez intriguing and attractive. But she refused to admit to herself that she had anything like a crush on him. The deteriorating situation with Josh was simply opening her eyes to other people. That was all.

What she did learn about the man only intrigued her more. He had been at PRH for just over three years and was now a partner in the ER group. Despite George Oleander's curious irritation with him, not one nurse had anything negative to say, except for the backhanded compliment that because he spent so much time with each patient, the ER tended to get jammed up during his shifts.

He was most definitely single. And although one nurse was certain he was involved with a woman, another felt equally certain he was gay. Abby knew enough of hospitals to be sure there was almost no way an attractive single physician — male or female — could be involved with anybody for long without some colleague getting wind of it. So she labeled him, unofficially and in pencil, heterosexual and unattached. In addition to his ER job he had a small working farm in the hills west of town, frequently moonlighted as the attending physician at the state mental hospital in Caledonia, and coached Little League soccer. His teams hardly ever lost.

Abby skirted the patient area and went directly to the on-call suite — a good-sized office, sleeping room, and bathroom. She changed into a pair of blue scrubs and her clinic coat, and then, as she routinely did when starting a shift, stopped to get centered. She rinsed her face with cold water, headed to the door, then stopped again and returned to the sink. Almost in spite of herself she adjusted the band holding back her hair and put on a dash of lipstick.

Alvarez caught sight of her as soon as she entered the ER, made a theatrical display of looking at his watch, and gave her two thumbs up.

"It's been like this since we had a code at three this afternoon," he explained. "Seventy-five-year-old guy with a massive anterior MI."

"Make it?" Abby sensed the answer to her question even before Lew shook his head. "Sorry. . . . Well, listen. Why don't I get started on that chart rack? Maybe together we can outflank them."

"I'll stay until the place is cleaned out," he said.

"You don't have to do that."

"You didn't have to come in early."

The first patient Abby dealt with was another of the *I don't know what's wrong with you* group. He was a thirty-eight-year-old father of three with profound fatigue. In Abby's experience fatigue and headaches were two of the most difficult complaints to evaluate and diagnose. And she had seen a significant number of both since starting at PRH. There was an almost limitless number of causes for each symptom, with perhaps the most common of those being stress — psychosomatic illness. Abby had never doubted the power of the human mind to cause *or* cure disease. The problem was that psychosomatic illness was a diagnosis of exclusion, to be made only when all other reasonable possibilities had been systematically ruled out. To assume an emotional etiology for a symptom like fatigue was asking for trouble.

Abby sent off what she considered to be a reasonable battery of tests and was launching into her "I don't know . . ." speech, when the nurse, Bud Perlow, motioned her over to the minor trauma room and handed her a chart. The patient's name was Hazel Cookman. She was eighty-four years old and a widow. Her presenting problem read simply, "Fell."

"I know you've got about ten things going on at once," Perlow said, "but I just needed you to take a quick look at her arm and tell me if you want films. I don't think they're necessary. You'll love her. If she wasn't a schoolmarm, she should have been."

The woman, propped up on the stretcher, wore a navy-blue short-sleeved cotton dress with a lace collar. She had on pearls and an extravagant amount of rouge, and overall looked as if she were dressed for a church social. The glint in her eyes and the set of her jaw were defiant.

Abby introduced herself.

"I assume you are well qualified to fix my arm, young lady," Hazel said, her voice strong.

"I am. Could you tell me what happened?"

"Why, I fell. Doesn't it say that there?"

"It does. But *how* did you fall?"

"I just fell. Nothing complicated about it. I was cooking some chicken and I fell. I think I must have hit the edge of my kitchen table. I checked my arm in the mirror and knew that I would need some stitches." She eyed Abby sternly. "Now, Doctor, I would like you to tend to my injury and let me get home. I left my house in such a lather that I forgot the chicken simmering on the stove."

"How did you get here?"

"Why . . . why, I drove, of course."

"Of course," Abby said, smiling toward the nurse.

Hazel Cookman's injury was one common to older people with "tissue paper" skin. Just below her elbow a flap of delicate skin had peeled back. It would need to be stretched out again and tacked in place with some fine stitches and Steri-strips.

"Well?" Hazel asked. "Can you fix it?"

"I can."

"And?"

Abby was checking the left and right ca-rotid-artery pulses in the woman's neck as she kept two fingers on the radial artery pulse at her wrist.

"I'd like to examine your heart and check

102

over your nervous system," she said. "And I think you should have an electrocardiogram and a blood count."

"My lord, it's just a cut arm. I simply have no time for all this rigmarole, young lady."

"Mrs. Cookman, I may be a young lady to you, which is fine. I'm pleased you think me one. But I am also a doctor. And I worry a lot about missing things in my patients. Right now I'm very worried that you don't know precisely why you fell. Now, these tests won't take long. And I promise as soon as they're done, we'll fix your cut."

"But —"

"Thank you." She turned to the nurse. "We'll need postural blood-pressure checks, lying, sitting, and standing, but not until I've seen the EKG." She waited until they were out of earshot, then added, "I don't know why, Bud, but something doesn't feel right. I don't think she just tripped. I think she lost consciousness and fell. In fact, before you do anything else, hook her up to the monitor."

"She'll bite my head off."

Abby patted him on the arm.

"Charm her with one of those great faces you use to win over the kids."

Abby saw one more patient, a straightforward splinter removal, then met Lew by the chart rack. There was no question that together they were getting ahead of the backlog.

"Anything interesting?" he asked.

103

"Not really. A cute LOL with a flap of skin pushed back off her forearm. Listen, Lew, why don't you go on home?"

He glanced about at the beds, which were still almost all filled.

"Another half hour, forty-five minutes. All I had planned for tonight was paying bills. The more tired I am, the easier that job is to take."

Not a team player? Abby wondered what could possibly have gone on between Lew and George Oleander to put off the medical chief so.

"Dr. Dolan!" Bud Perlow shouted from Hazel's room.

Abby charged to the doorway with Lew close behind. Hazel Cookman was drifting into unconsciousness. Her monitor showed a heart rate of ten.

"She's in complete heart block," Abby said instantly, her own pulse pounding. "Lew, call a code. Bud, get a line in her. I'll pump. As soon as we have another pair of hands, I want five-tenths of atropine IV."

She kicked a low metal stool in place next to the litter and stepped up on it to give herself enough leverage for effective CPR. At that moment Hazel's complete heart block reverted to a normal rhythm and rate. Abby checked both carotid-artery pulses and felt them easily. In seconds Hazel moaned. A few seconds more and she was wide-awake.

"Bud, get cardiology in here stat," Abby

said. "She needs a pacemaker. Do we have an external pacer?"

"Sure thing."

"Set it up just in case."

Abby's suspicions about the woman's fall were confirmed. Hardening of the arteries into Hazel's heart was causing a blockage to the spread of electricity from her body's natural, inborn pacemaker — the spot in the right atrium chamber where heartbeats are normally initiated. The result of the blockage was a pulse rate too slow to generate an effective blood pressure, and the pressure drop had caused her brief faint. For the moment the blockage kept reverting to normal. But that situation could change, quite literally, in a heartbeat.

The cardiologist would insert a guiding needle into the vein located beneath Hazel's collarbone and then thread a wire through it until the tip made contact with the inner lining of her right ventricle chamber. The other end of the wire would be connected to a temporary pacemaker box, which would kick in any time the inborn pacemaker rate dropped below seventy per minute. Once she was stable, a permanent pacemaker could be implanted beneath her skin. But until the temporary wire was in, she was in the gravest danger.

Hazel blinked twice, still clearly unaware of the commotion beginning to swirl around her.

"Well, Doctor," she said, "are you or are

you not going to fix my arm?"

"Not just yet," Abby said. "Mrs. Cookman, you and I need to talk."

Bud Perlow finished inserting an IV. Then he wheeled over the external pacemaker. Strictly an emergency apparatus, the pacer had paddles that were placed beneath the spine and beside the breastbone. The electrical pulse would shoot through the patient's chest, contracting all the muscles in her body, including her heart. Not at all pleasant, but lifesaving. Abby noted that, unlike almost all the equipment in the hospital, the rarely, if ever, used machine was quite an outdated model.

Her gaze never leaving the overhead cardiac monitor, she did her best to explain the situation to Hazel.

The octogenarian listened with surprising interest and patience. She even asked about what the permanent pacemaker would feel like beneath her skin.

Abby had just started her explanation when the large, regular waves indicating heartbeats vanished. Heart block again. Hazel's eyelids drifted down.

"Give the atropine!" Abby ordered, again kicking the footstool into place. "Lew, do you know how to use that external pacer?"

"Not really."

"I do," Bud said as he injected the cardiac stimulant. "We had an in-service on it a year or so ago."

"Start it up. Clear, everyone!" Abby called

out. "The external pacemaker is being turned on."

Abby positioned the heel of her hand just above Hazel's sternum, ready to set it down and pump, just in case the pacemaker failed to produce an effective heartbeat.

"I can't get this machine working, Dr. Dolan," Bud said. "I think it's shorted."

Her mind racing, Abby set her hands down to begin pumping. Then, as it had before, Hazel's heartbeat reverted to normal. And as before, in seconds, the woman was wide-awake and completely unaware she had passed out.

"Have we reached the cardiologist?"

"It's Dr. Price," the head nurse said. "He's not in-house. We've paged him, but no answer yet."

"Doctor, I'm still waiting for you to fix my arm," Hazel said.

"Soon," Abby replied. "You had another one of those spells."

"I didn't feel anything."

"I know."

Abby told the nurse to keep a steady eye on the monitor and have more atropine and another drug, Isuprel, ready. Then she motioned Lew to one corner of the room.

"I don't think we should be relying solely on the atropine or Isuprel."

"Agreed."

"How many pacemakers have you inserted?"

"One, a few years ago. You?"

"Same. I've always had cardiologists around. Well, that's two between us, and I don't feel like standing around waiting for disaster to strike."

Lew glanced up at the monitor.

"I like your style, Doctor," he said. "Let's do it. But let's not let anyone know we're both scared stiff."

With Hazel Cookman grousing at them almost continuously, Abby and Lew completed the temporary-pacemaker insertion without a hitch. Abby numbed up the area beneath Hazel's collarbone and disinfected it. Then, guided by landmarks she could only feel, she smoothly inserted the large-bore needle through the skin beside the bone, and into the subclavian vein. Lew handled the electrocardiograph machine, calling out directions and encouragement as Abby slid the fine wire through the needle, along the subclavian vein and the superior vena cava into the heart, then across the right atrium and tricuspid valve, and finally into place, wedged in the right ventricle.

"Hold it," he said. "You're there. You're there."

He hooked the wire to the small pacer box. The capture of Hazel's heartbeat was instant.

Abby angled her body to shield her hands until they stopped shaking. If Lew hadn't been there, she doubted she would even have attempted the insertion, much less completed it.

"Fine job," he said as she sutured the wire to Hazel's skin to keep it from dislodging. "The capture threshold is excellent. You can put one of these in me any time."

"Dr. Price just called," the head nurse announced. "He was seeing a consultation at the state hospital in Caledonia. He'll be here in half an hour."

"Okay, Mrs. Cookman," Abby said, "I'm ready to fix your arm now. After that Dr. Price, the heart doctor, will admit you to the hospital. Even though the pacemaker Dr. Alvarez and I just put in is working fine, I'm sure he'll want you in the coronary-care unit until he can put in one of those permanent pacers I told you about. Do you understand all that?"

"Oh, yes. I certainly do, dear. You've done a wonderful job explaining everything to me. And I really would be happy to come into your coronary unit."

"Great."

"But, unfortunately, I can't."

"But —"

"At least not until I turn off that chicken I left simmering. It would be a terrible waste of chicken and an even worse waste of my house when it burns down."

Abby glanced at Lew but managed not to react to his amusement.

"Aren't there relatives who could do it?" she asked.

"None."

"How about a neighbor or the police?"

"I don't think Holly and Alex would like that very much at all."

"Well, couldn't one of them do it?"

The woman patted Abby's hand.

"My dear, Holly is a one-hundred-pound German shepherd. I don't know exactly what Alex is, but he's bigger and meaner than Holly. Since my husband died, I've always had big dogs. These two are wonderful friends, and I certainly don't have to worry about locking up at night. But unless I'm there, no one could get inside the house without being attacked or having to harm my babies. I would never allow either thing to happen."

"I see. . . . Mrs. Cookman, I'll be right back."

"Just don't be long, young lady. I really do have to get home."

Once again Abby motioned Lew to the far corner of the room.

"This is crazy," she said. "Can she do this?"

"Sign out against medical advice to turn off her chicken? I believe so."

"But —"

"Listen, her pacemaker's working fine, and her heart's totally protected," he said. "She lives just a mile or so from here. I think you should have her sign out AMA,

110

then just load up on a few cardiac meds, call the ambulance, and go home with her."

"Actually, since I'm on and you're done, I was thinking —"

"No, no. Please. I'll do my part by staying here. She's your patient. I'll call my vet, Hank Tarver. He tends to my animals. He'll meet you at Hazel's house and take the dogs to his kennel."

"I can't believe I'm going home with an eighty-four-year-old in complete heart block to turn off the gas under a chicken."

"Welcome to Boondocks General, Professor. Wait until you start getting *paid* in chickens."

Ω Ω Ω

Abby returned via ambulance from Hazel Cookman's bungalow prepared to tell someone — anyone — that her mission to turn off Hazel's chicken had gone like cluckwork. Actually, she couldn't remember ever feeling more energized about being a doctor.

Hazel, her stove turned off and her dogs on their way to the kennel, took Abby's hand as they were hooking her back up to the monitor.

"Thank you," she said. "Thank you for being so kind."

"Nonsense," Abby replied. "You've fought the good fight for eighty-four years. You deserve the best any of us can give you."

Abby wrote admission orders that would hold until the cardiologist took over in the critical-care unit. Then she sought out Lew. He was in the office, finishing up a dinner that dietary had sent up. Even after a tough fourteen hours in the ER, he looked fresh.

"You're all caught up," he said. "And I am ready to pour a glass of Chianti, turn my stereo on, put my feet up, and fall asleep to Villa-Lobos. I've decided paying my bills can wait for another day. I don't know if you've looked at the schedule or not, but tomorrow morning I'm your relief."

"I hadn't looked," she said. "Come on. I'll walk you out."

As they passed by the waiting room, a woman was just registering at the intake desk. Abby recognized her as one of the diagnostic problems she had seen — the redhead who, someone had told Abby, had once danced with the Rockettes. The woman caught Abby's eye, waved sheepishly, embarrassed at being back, and immediately began scratching her arm.

Abby motioned that she would see her shortly, then walked with Lew across the ambulance bay and into the parking lot. The night was the sort never seen in the city — a glimmering full moon low in the northeast, a velvet star-laden sky to the west. The Milky Way was easily visible.

"Just beautiful," Lew said.

A car stopped at the patient drop-off space, and a man pulled himself up on crutches and hobbled in through the front ER entrance. Abby waited until the car had driven off and it was quiet once again.

"Lew, I really appreciate your helping things go so smoothly tonight," she said.

"No problem. I really enjoyed our pace-maker adventure. Besides, I actually feel as if I owe you more than just a little help in the ER. I owe you an apology. When you first got here, I found you a bit intimidating and standoffish. You're neither, and I'm sorry for thinking so."

"You know, that's really funny, because I found you standoffish and intimidating, too."

"I heard from the nurses that you've been going up to Sam Ives's hut to tend to his leg. That's a very kind thing to do."

"He's got a deep fungal infection, maybe osteomyelitis. The cultures grew out asper-gillus. I've been going up there because there's not much chance he'd come back here."

"Not after the way he was treated the other night by Martin Bartholomew, there isn't."

"Bartholomew's got big problems. But in general I've been really impressed with most of the staff. The town is growing on me, too. When I first moved here, I had serious doubts. I only left my job at St. John's and came to Patience to be with my . . ."

Her voice trailed off. *My what?* "Fiancé" seemed a more remote possibility than ever.

"Yes, I know. The man in charge of new-product design at Colstar."

"My, this *is* a small town."

She found herself a bit peeved that personal information about her would be making the rounds. But the truth was, even in the big city everyone was curious about everyone else — especially new docs.

"So how about you?" she asked. "Do you like it here?"

"I do. Most things, anyhow."

"Most things? What do you have problems with?"

She could tell immediately that he was having difficulty answering the question. He turned and looked away toward the east. When he spoke, it was in a harsh whisper.

"I have problems with *them*," he said with unexpected force.

Abby followed his line of sight. There, silhouetted against the full moon, was the Colstar cliff. Perched atop it, illuminated by dozens of floodlights, looking somewhat like a penitentiary, was the company. The letters of its name, filling much of the west-facing wall, were done in red neon.

"But why?" she asked.

At that moment another car drove up to the entrance. An older woman hauled out a wheelchair from the trunk and spread it open. Lew and Abby helped her move her husband from the passenger seat.

"It's his chest pain," the woman explained. "It's all right now, but Dr. Robbins is on the way in to check him over."

114

She hurried through the sliding doors and into the ER.

"I'd better get in there just to keep an eye on things," Abby said to Lew. "If it's not too late when I finally get caught up, could I call you to finish our conversation?"

"No calls about this," he said, too quickly. He realized she was taken aback and added, "Tell you what. I'll come in an hour early if you'd like, and we can talk."

"If you don't mind getting up that early."

"I work a farm, Abby. I'm *always* up that early. Meet me right out here at seven. If you're busy, I'll wait. And, please, don't say a word to anyone about all this until we've talked."

"O-okay," she said, bewildered by the precautions and by his tone.

"Abby, I'm sorry if I seem paranoid," he said in his near whisper. "But I have every right to be."

Ω Ω Ω

The woman's name was Claire Buchanan. She had been born and raised in the Midwest and had gone to New York City at eighteen to make it in show business. Her hair was colored flame-red.

"I was a damn good dancer," she said, talking almost nonstop as Abby carefully examined her skin, eyes, and ears. "At least for Sioux City I was. But New York is a different story. Thankfully, though, I got lucky. I met Dennis Buchanan, and he took me the hell out of there. A few years later we were living outside of LA and Dennis was selling carpeting. He has a gift. Like they say, he could sell refrigerators to Eskimos. Anyhow, one day we were just driving around up here and we found this town on a map. Dennis liked the name. We decided to spend the night, and we weren't here fifteen minutes when he saw the For Sale sign on the John Deere tractor place. 'Claire,' he told me, 'this is it. This is as far as we need to go.' That was almost ten years ago. Now I'm beginning to wonder if maybe I've developed an allergy to the damn place or something. Or maybe I'm allergic to Dennis. I'll tell you this, I can't stand this itching anymore."

"Mrs. Buchanan —"

"It's okay to call me Claire. Everyone does."

"Claire, tell me. Did your itching get at all better with the cortisone pills I gave you?"

"Maybe for a little while. The Benadryl might have helped a little, too. Then it just got bad again. Especially at night. I went to see Dr. Oleander, but he said he couldn't find much. He was very complimentary about you, though. He said that you had done a very thorough workup on me."

"Except I can't figure out what's wrong."

"He thinks it's nerves."

"Are you the nervous type?"

"I don't think so, except that I'm very claustrophobic. My mother and sister are, too. Dr. Oleander did one of those MRI tests on me for some stomach trouble I was having. If he hadn't given me a tranquilizer and a blindfold, I would have never made it into that tube."

"What stomach trouble? When?"

"I don't know. Six, eight months ago. The tests were all negative and my indigestion went away. But, Dr. Dolan, I can't sit around waiting for this itching to go away. You've got to do something to help me before I just throw myself into one of Dennis's combines."

"I don't know what's going on with you, Claire, but I don't think it's in your head. I can sort of feel a fullness in places beneath your skin, a thickening, but I just can't see anything. And I can't tell if the thickness is from your scratching so much. I think the next step is a dermatology consult and maybe a biopsy."

"Whatever you say."

"Actually, it's whatever Dr. Oleander says. He's your primary-care physician, and we try to defer making any referrals to him. But I'm sure he'll be happy to send you to the dermatologist."

"I don't think so," Claire said. "The last time you saw me here, you suggested I see a dermatologist. But Dr. O said this itching was either nerves or hives, and that all I would be doing was traveling thirty miles each way to have a so-called specialist tell me the same thing."

"Well, now that you're no better after a course of oral cortisone, I think Dr. Oleander might be ready to change his mind," Abby said, certain that would be the case.

For an area its size Patience had excellent specialty coverage. Cardiology, pulmonology, neurology, even rheumatology, as well as most of the surgical specialties like urology, ENT, and orthopedics. But no dermatologist. Actually, Abby did not disagree with Oleander. Treating many of the common skin problems was a matter of applying common sense. The old and useful maxim regarding the specialty was: *If it's dry, wet it, if it's wet, dry it, and when in doubt, use steroids.* But from what Abby could tell, Claire Buchanan's skin problem went beyond the bounds of common.

"I'll tell you what," she said. "It's only a quarter of ten, and Dr. Oleander is my medical backup for tonight anyway. Would you feel better if I gave him a call?"

"Oh, I would. Thank you, Doctor. Thank you very much."

Abby never liked encountering patients who were overawed by their physicians, although she did acknowledge that some patients seemed to be genetically bred to be so. It seemed to her to be the doctor's responsibility to break down such barriers to communication. From all she could tell, George Oleander was a damn fine primary-care doctor. As chief of medicine, he unquestionably ran a tight ship. But he did have an air of confidence that might inhibit some patients from questioning his decisions or from asking for a second opinion.

She sent off another series of routine blood studies on Claire, just in case, and went back to the doctors' office. Oleander answered before the second ring.

"George, hi, it's Abby Dolan. Sorry to call you at this hour, especially since this isn't about an emergency."

"No problem, Abby. I was just reading and wondering why the hospital seemed so quiet."

"Actually, it hasn't been. But our one admission was a unit case, and Brian Price is in with her."

At Oleander's request she reviewed her odyssey with Hazel Cookman.

When she finished, the medical chief laughed roundly.

"I know those dogs of hers," he said. "And they are tough. But I think I'd prefer a run-in with them to one with Hazel. It sounds like you did a great job, Abby. And you can bet that within a day or two everyone in Patience will have heard about it — or at least some *version* of it. It's exactly what this community needs."

"Thank you."

Community. Abby tried to remember how many times Lyle Quinn had invoked the word.

"I'm glad to hear this story, too," Oleander

continued, "because I'd been meaning to speak with you."

"Again?"

"I'm afraid Dr. Bartholomew and just about everyone else has heard about what you did the other night, replacing the sutures he put in old Sam Ives."

"Ives isn't that old," Abby said, feeling her temper begin to build. "And Dr. Bartholomew's suture job was unacceptable."

"He didn't think so. Abby, Marty Bartholomew's been a part of this community for years. At times he can be a bit of a horse's behind, I'll give you that. But he's been available to folks in snowstorms at three in the morning. He delivered babies before our obstetricians came on board. He's very much loved here."

Abby knew that there was nothing to be gained by arguing her case in this court. Still, she had to choose her words and maintain her composure carefully.

"I did what I thought was best for the patient."

"I understand, Abby. But as I said last week in my office, sometimes things in a community hospital work a little differently than in the big city. Now, what do you have for me tonight?"

His tone left no room for retort. The discussion was over. The point Abby had scored for her treatment of Hazel Cookman had offset the one she had lost for her abuse of the ego of Martin Bartholomew. It was time to move on.

Picking her way through her presentation so as not to say anything Oleander might interpret as inflammatory or confrontational, Abby reviewed Claire Buchanan's case. Her hope was that Oleander would come to the conclusion himself that a dermatology referral was in order.

"Sounds like classic neurodermatitis to me," he said when she had finished, employing the diagnosis given to any and all skin symptoms believed to have an underlying emotional cause.

"I was wondering about some unusual kind of vasculitis. She's quite uncomfortable."

"I can tell you want me to send her to Dr. O'Brien in Caledonia, Abby. And I might. But I like to be certain we've done all we can for our people here in Patience before shipping them off to doctors elsewhere."

"I understand," Abby said, though, in truth, she didn't.

"Well, then, why don't you go ahead and put Claire on some mild tranquilizer like Valium or Xanax and tell her to give me a call in the office tomorrow? I'll see her. If she needs a little punch biopsy, we can do that here. If we're absolutely stumped, I'll call O'Brien. We're trying to get him to open an office here in Patience. Our case is weakened if he believes our people can just pull up and drive thirty miles each way to see him."

"I'll be anxious to know what you think."

"I'll send you a copy of my office note, Abby. That Bartholomew business not-withstanding, you're doing an excellent job. Keep up the good work."

"Thank you."

"Oh, and Abby, tell Claire she really ought to be calling me before she runs to the emergency ward. You folks have enough to worry about. I'll be here all night if you need me."

He hung up without waiting for a reply. Somehow he had read and deflected Abby's agenda before she had even presented it. As a result, Claire Buchanan would be treated according to the wishes of her regu-lar doctor, not Abby's. It was the downside of the medical specialty she had chosen. Abby returned to her patient feeling vaguely uneasy that she hadn't battled harder on her behalf.

Chapter Nine

The flow of patients through the ER remained steady throughout the night, though never close to overwhelming. With a little over an hour to go before the end of her shift, Abby showered in the on-call room and took the chance of putting on her street clothes and clinic coat, rather than scrubs. She had been awake since treating a three-year-old with an earache at five-thirty and had spent most of that time thinking about Lew and the concerns he had offered to share with her about Colstar.

She made one quick pass around the deserted ER, then told the night nurse where she'd be and headed out into an overcast morning. To the east the Colstar cliff was still in shadow, but sprawled above it, the massive plant glowed in the pale morning haze. Lew was right where he had said he would be, standing beside an isolated low bench on the far side of the tarmac. Even at a distance she sensed his tension.

"Hi," she said.

"Morning. How was your night?"

"Manageable. Two NIWWs. But otherwise not much."

"NIWWs?"

"The abbreviation for 'no idea what's wrong.' My chief resident taught it to me. Lately, it seems, I've been seeing more of them than I'm used to."

"NIWWs. I like that. I really do."

Lew's expression and ironic laugh suggested he knew something she didn't.

"So," she said, "what's this all about?"

Lew stopped her with a finger raised to his lips and glanced about warily.

Thirty yards away two nurses crossed the parking lot, clearly — to Abby at least — out of earshot. He shook his head, warning her not to continue the conversation until they had entered the hospital.

"I'd like your promise not to share this discussion with anyone," he whispered finally. The intensity in his eyes was startling.

"Lew," she replied, just as softly, "nobody can hear us."

"Don't be so sure. I think my home phone may be tapped. I don't know what else they might have done."

"Who?"

Lew turned his gaze toward Colstar.

"The same people who built this place — them."

"Lew, I'm sorry, but I don't understand."

"Those patients you've been seeing — the NIWWs?"

"What about them?"

"What sorts of symptoms do they have? Headache? Rash? Fatigue? Chronic cough? Insomnia? Mood swings? Low-grade fevers?"

She looked at him queerly. He wasn't asking her, he was telling.

"Those kinds of things," she said. "Yes."

"Well, I've got news for you. Patients with those kinds of unexplained symptoms are all over the place here. Far more than one would expect."

"Maybe I'm just dense, Lew. But I still don't get it."

He glanced around again.

"Look, this isn't a good time or place to talk. I don't trust anyone in this hospital. In fact, I don't even trust the building. That's why I want you to be very careful what you say in the doctors' room. It might be bugged, or worse."

"Cameras?"

Abby was sickened by the thought. She was also wondering about Lew. "Believe it or not, it's possible," he said, seeing the doubt in her face. "I've looked all over for microphones or cameras with no luck, but I'm no secret agent."

"Maybe you'd better get to the point."

"Abby, listen. We really shouldn't stay out here like this too much longer. They already know I'm the enemy. Pretty soon, if they see us together too much, it will be guilt by association for you. I may sound paranoid about Colstar, but believe me, I have every right to be. You'll understand if you give me the chance to explain."

"Go on."

"Okay. There's a group of committed people who are trying to do something about all this. Trying to do something about your NIWWs. I'd like you to come to our next meeting."

Abby looked toward the cliff and then back at Lew. Were the "committed people" in his group the ones Lyle Quinn had warned her about? It certainly seemed that way. Being asked to choose sides between Quinn and Lew Alvarez would pose no problem for her. But she was still very new in town, and she had enough problems of her own at home.

"Oh, Lew, I don't know," she said. "I'm not much of a crusader, and I've never been a joiner."

"At least come and hear what we have to say," he said. "We call ourselves the Alliance. We meet every three or four weeks at one member's house or another. Tomorrow night it will be at mine." Lew handed her an envelope with directions. "Whether you come or not, please don't tell anyone about this, especially your friend."

"Well, the truth is, Josh has been very tense lately. Pressures at work, I think. So I don't know that there's much to be gained by telling him I've been approached by people who want to cause problems for his company."

"No more problems than they're causing for all of us," Lew interjected.

"Lew, I just can't tell you yes or no right now. What I said about not being a crusader is really true. I'm not proud of it, but I was on duty in the ER during the last election, and I never even made the effort to vote."

Lew's expression was deadly serious.

"Believe me, Abby," he said, "your involvement with the Alliance and what we're determined to do would more than balance that."

"I understand that's how you feel. I'll just have to see."

"Fine. Meanwhile, you might start keeping a log of those NIWW patients. I do."

Before leaving the hospital Abby called Claire Buchanan. The tranquilizer had given her a few hours of sleep, but the profound itching persisted. She would be calling Dr. Oleander in an hour or so, she said. Abby encouraged her to give herself a break for at least one day by taking the sedation as often as was safe. She set the receiver down, still feeling as if she hadn't done all she could have on the woman's behalf.

With Josh already at work there was no need to rush home. And as usual following a night shift, even those when she got *no* sleep, Abby was reluctant to go right to bed. If she did, she would be asleep in minutes and would have trouble waking up no matter what the time. Further, she had found that ten or eleven hours of sleep often left her feeling logier than her usual seven. It was better to try to put at least part of the morning to some use before surrendering to Morpheus.

She drove through the park for a time, then stopped for a brief walk down to the lake. It was all so peaceful, so picture perfect. On the way back to her car she stopped and gazed across the ball field at the spot where Angela Cristoforo had stood, her blood cascading onto the sparkling, manicured grass. Abby had followed up on Angela and learned that soon after her lacerations were repaired, she was transferred to a locked ward at the state hospital in Caledonia. A long-term, competent, dependable Colstar employee one minute, then suddenly a pathetic self-mutilator. It did not make a great deal of sense, but mental illness in its many guises often didn't.

It was after nine when she started up the Mazda and headed home. There were some letters she wanted to write. And if, by some miracle, she was still awake, there was the book on making the most of the passage into midlife that she had been reading so slowly, her midlife might be over by the time she finished it. She had always loved the eeriness, the unpredictability, and the strange characters she encountered working the night shift in the ER. But she invariably had trouble reconnecting with life outside the hospital when she did.

The moment she turned into the drive and

saw Josh's Jeep, she knew there was trouble. He should have been at work hours ago. She pulled up behind the Wrangler and became even more convinced something was wrong. Josh was in love with his car and was obsessive about caring for it. Now it was an absolute mess. There were thick streaks of dried and still-drying mud all over it, as if he had been off-roading in and out of quagmires. The tires were caked. The windshield was splattered as well. There were three empty beer bottles and crumpled-up food wrappers on the floor. Even the driver's seat was smeared with dry mud, as if he had fallen someplace and then, sodden, had crawled back behind the wheel.

The back door to the house was open. The kitchen had been treated as rudely as the Jeep. It smelled of alcohol and stale food. A wrapper from a sub shop was crumpled on the table along with two half-eaten Hostess cupcakes. Josh was enough of a health-food nut to patronize a sub shop only as a last resort. The cupcakes simply didn't compute at all. Next to the sink were bottles of Tylenol, Fioricet, and ibuprofen. Their caps were off, but none of the bottles was close to empty. Beside the pills, on its side, was an empty pint bottle of tequila.

Fearing the worst, she called out his name once, then again. The second time, from the living room, he moaned. He was on the couch, passed out, but in no obvious danger. He had on jeans, a sleeveless T, and his high-cut hiking boots. All were filthy. There were muddy tracks on the carpet.

Abby checked his pulses, which were strong, and his pupils, which were somewhat dilated. Two and a half years together, and she had never seen him drunk. In fact, she always teased him about being something of an alcohol snob, preferring to savor his microbrewed beer from a tall glass or stein while she drank Bud from a can. Now he reeked of alcohol. Looking down at him, she felt no anger — only the concern of a physician and the sadness of a woman watching the love relationship that had meant so much to her slip away.

Without trying to rouse him she checked the answering machine. The only message was from someone at work, calling a half hour ago, wondering where he was.

Numbly, Abby went to the kitchen and began to clean up, playing the nightmare scenario over in her mind.

Could it possibly have turned out worse?

When the moaning from the living room became louder and more purposeful, Abby wet a dish towel and brought it in. She wiped his face. His reddened, rheumy eyes fluttered open. He struggled to focus on her.

"They've called from work looking for you," she said, surprised by her first words and the coolness in her voice.

He pawed at his eyes and tried to moisten his lips with his sandpaper tongue. It took several seconds for his condition to begin to register. As it did, there was no mistaking his confusion.

"What time is it, Abby?"

"Nine-thirty . . . A.M."

"I never oversleep."

"You do when you're smashed on tequila and pills and out driving all night in your Jeep."

He struggled to a sitting position and surveyed himself again.

"I never went driving off-road."

"I think the Jeep would beg to differ. Go look at it."

"Jesus." He rubbed at his eyes. "All I remember is this headache. Right here." He pointed to the middle of his forehead.

"Sounds like you were in a blackout. The Jeep is filthy. Mud all over it."

"I . . . I don't remember going out at all." He brushed at the filth on his boots. "But I guess, if you say so."

He stumbled to his feet, nearly falling over the coffee table.

"Josh, you need help. I've been telling you that for weeks. I want to call Dr. Owen right now and have him see you and order an MRI or CT scan."

"No! . . . I mean, I've already scheduled an appointment with him. I'm okay now. I just had a little too much to drink. I'm no big drinker, and it just got the better of me. Now, I just need to get cleaned up and get into the office. I have a report to do and —"

"Josh, I will not stand by and watch you destroy yourself — destroy us — like this."

"Dammit, Abby, why in the hell can't you see what your part is in all this?"

"*My* part?"

"Yes, your part."

He was pacing now, as agitated as she had ever seen him. His voice was getting louder, shriller. For the first time in their life together Abby felt a spark of fear.

"You work all night," he ranted on. "You study when you're not working. You sleep when you're not studying. You have no idea the stress you're causing around here. And then, just because I'm having some headaches and get a little drunk, you come home and demand that I go and see a goddamn neurologist on top of the shrink you've already told me to see! Why can't you understand the stress *I'm* under? Why can't you see that I have needs, too?"

For the briefest moment the attack worked. Abby felt herself weaken.

"Josh, I meant what I said." She forced the words out.

"Well, I meant what I said, too, dammit." He was screaming now. "And no one's going to tell me what to do. No one! Especially not you!"

She glared at him and then turned away. He grabbed her shoulders and spun her around to face him. His eyes were glazed with anger. Remote. Almost unseeing. Reflexively, Abby braced herself to be hit.

Instead, Josh whirled suddenly and slammed his fist through the living-room wall. Then he stumbled out to the backyard and threw up on the lawn.

Shaking from the assault, Abby started out to comfort him. Then she stopped by the doorway, held in place by a powerful feeling of distance and detachment. Shutting out his retching as best she could, she raced to the small guest room and threw herself onto her bed. She had played her last card in their relationship. Now it was up to him.

Chapter Ten

Psychiatrist Graham DeShield cherished his reputation as the therapist to the stars. Whether it was a football superhero, a movie star from Carmel, or any number of San Francisco's elite and powerful, DeShield would see them at whatever hour and place their notoriety required. He was not at all bothered that some in his field disparaged him as a social climber with minimal academic credentials, while others made light of his "cheerleader" approach to psychotherapy and even of his intellect.

His professional plate was full and fascinating, and his successes, especially in dealing with phobias and narcissism, were well publicized and substantiated. The key, he knew, was prescreening. If a case was too mundane, too complicated, or held little chance for recovery, he would simply be too busy to take it. If the prospective patient was of sufficient stature or resources, he might agree to institute therapy, provided the grimness of the prognosis was clear.

Today DeShield had just finished a Bay Club luncheon at which he was the featured speaker. Later in the afternoon he would be having an initial evaluation appointment with Bebe Washington, the actress. He had seen several of her films and had to agree with those who put her among the most beautiful women in the world. Her agent, also a patient, had referred her.

Unfortunately, sandwiched between his luncheon talk and Bebe Washington was twenty-seven-year-old Ethan Black. As the son of Ezra Black, one of the wealthiest men in the country, Ethan was automatically accepted as a patient. That he had failed, so far, to respond to treatment was a source of frustration and even angst for DeShield. Black Ezra, as his father was known, had a legendary, hair-trigger temper and a reputation for utterly destroying people who crossed him in business or disappointed him in any other way. Of course, there were others who were set for life because they had, for whatever reason, ingratiated themselves with the man.

DeShield heard the door to his waiting room open and close, and knew it was Ethan. He took a few final seconds to gaze out at the panorama from his twenty-third-story office — views of Alcatraz, the bay, and the Golden Gate — and then reviewed his notes.

Ethan Black was working as comptroller for some sort of family-owned company up in Patience. His psychiatric history dated back only a year or so. Following an automobile accident in which he sustained some head trauma and multiple minor lacerations, his passive, introspective personality underwent a radical change. After a number of fights, including one in which he'd bludgeoned a man with a baseball bat, he was referred to DeShield and placed in the Hempstead Institute just outside the city.

All neurologic tests and scans had been negative, and postconcussion syndrome seemed the obvious diagnosis. The prognosis for that condition was excellent. Just the way DeShield liked it.

In each of their previous sessions, DeShield had outlined what seemed to him to be a reasonable therapeutic program for Ethan to use in dealing with his aggression, hostility, and acting out — a program calling for the summoning forth of Ethan's inner child. Each time, it seemed, there was complete understanding between them. Each time Ethan left with the promise that he would employ his mental exercises and avoidance maneuvers before lashing out at anyone. Each time, when Black Ezra phoned to check on his son's progress, DeShield had given him a hopeful response. And each time Black's scion had gone right out and hurt someone. Money had been able to smooth over the damage so far. But Ezra Black clearly hated paying off anyone. And more and more DeShield sensed the man was blaming him for the failures.

Referring Ethan to another therapist

was, of course, out of the question. Black Ezra had hired him because of his reputation as the best. How could there be anyone better?

With a sigh DeShield pushed himself back from his desk and opened the door to the waiting room. Ethan was there with his driver/bodyguard, smiling the same bland smile that the therapist had learned not to trust at all.

"Ethan, please, come in. Come in."

Black was five nine, but built like a wrestler. He had thick, curly dark hair, and a perpetual five o'clock shadow. In truth there was nothing about the man DeShield liked. His appearance and demeanor annoyed the doctor to distraction. His high-pitched voice sounded like a perpetual whine.

"I had more headaches," Black said.

"Tell me about it."

DeShield glanced at his desk clock and tried to will a faster sweep to the second hand.

"Well, you know those dreams? The ones where I lose an arm, then a leg, then the other arm and leg, and then my penis and my balls, and finally my head?"

"Yes, Ethan, I remember."

How could I not when you tell it to me every session?

"Well, I've been having them every night. Bloodier and more painful than ever. They're horrible. Really terrifying. I think

137

what you've been telling me is true."

"What's that?"

"That the villain in the dreams — the one chopping my parts off — is me."

"Of course it is. But you can overcome that sense of low self-esteem by simply employing the positive-mental-attitude exercises I have taught you."

"PMA. I know. I've tried. Really, I have. Well, I think the dreams set me up again, because yesterday and again this morning the headaches hit."

"Tell me about them."

Tell me about them. Tell me about them. DeShield wondered how many more times he would have to say the words before the hour was over. He began thinking about Bebe Washington.

"The same as all the other times, only maybe worse. First there's the smell I told you about, sort of like rotten eggs. Sulfury. As soon as that hits, I know I'm in trouble. The smell gets worse and worse; then, after twenty or thirty minutes, my head explodes."

"Ethan, did you hurt anyone this time?"

"I . . . um . . . I got sick."

"But did you *hurt* anyone?"

"I think I hit a guard."

DeShield felt his stomach knot. Another ten or fifteen thousand in hush money from Black Ezra. Another black mark on Graham DeShield's scorecard.

"Ethan, Ethan," he said, summoning his

138

strength for one more all-out attack. "Let's try some relaxation exercises."

"Sure."

"Okay. Now, close your eyes and concentrate on my voice. You must believe in me, Ethan. You must believe that I love you, that I believe in you."

"You believe in me," Ethan murmured.

"That's it. Okay, now picture yourself on a mountaintop. A beam of shimmering golden light is shining down on you from beyond the clouds, bathing you in its warm glow. Can you feel it?"

"I can feel it. I can feel it."

Ethan stood up. Arms spread, eyes still closed, he turned slowly, basking in the golden light.

From behind his desk, feeling vaguely nauseous, DeShield watched him, thinking about how absolutely ridiculous he looked — the pirouetting hippo in *Fantasia.*

"That's it, Ethan. Feel the warmth. Feel your inner child take over."

Ethan continued his slow spin.

"The inner child, Ethan. Listen to your inner child and do as he says."

"Okay," Ethan said.

He stopped, hands on hips.

"Okay what?"

"I hear my inner child. I know what he's telling me to do."

"Wonderful. That's wonderful."

Ethan's expression seemed more animated. His body posture more confident.

Hang in there with me, Black Ezra, DeShield thought. Maybe this really was a breakthrough.

"Dr. DeShield?"

"Yes, Ethan."

"Tell my father you tried."

With two strong steps Ethan hurled his stocky body upward against the huge picture window. The glass shattered almost noiselessly as he hurtled through it. He fell without uttering a sound. In an instant, there was only silence — silence and the rush of warm summer air into the air-conditioned office.

Numbly, Graham DeShield moved to the window. He had always suffered from vertigo when looking down from any height, and he had to hang on to the wall to peer at what remained of his patient. His phone had rung several times before he noticed it.

"H-hello?" he heard himself say.

"Dr. DeShield, Ezra Black here. I'm sorry to disturb your session, but I need to speak with my son."

Ω Ω Ω

Abby's alarm went off at seven P.M. Her next shift at work wasn't for two days, but after an all-nighter, her body needed to be eased back into normal-world time. Sleeping some during the day, then getting up and staying awake until midnight, usually did the trick. Her shades were up — another trick of the trade — so that the early-evening light could help her get oriented. She rolled out of bed, aware that the house was very quiet. Josh was either passed out in his room, or he had pulled himself together and gone into work.

For a few minutes she sat on the small chair by her window, gazing at the mountains as she sorted out her emotions. She was uncomfortable with the coldness that had worked its way into her heart. But, in truth, there was nothing she could do about it. The look in Josh's eyes as he grabbed her shoulders would never be erased from her memory, regardless of what became of their relationship.

Stretching, she walked to the living room. Even before she saw the note on the dining-room table, she knew that he was gone. The computer and printer that were his lifeline were missing as well.

Abby —
I've made a terrible mess of things. I never wanted to leave San Francisco. I never wanted to come here. But what could I do? They offered me so much money and so much respect. You were paying for everything and trying to act like it didn't matter to you. Well, it did to me. Now, I just don't know what's going on except that I put my hands

on you in anger and came close to striking you. Maybe I'm going crazy. Maybe there's something wrong with my brain. Maybe it's just the pressure at work, and the adjustment I haven't made to living here. It isn't my feelings for you, which are as strong as ever.

I've taken some time off from work to do some hiking and some thinking. When I return, it won't be to the house. Until I straighten myself out, I just don't want to be around you. I've spoken to a realtor and rented a place west of the valley. I'll call soon and arrange to pick up some more of my stuff. I'll go to those doctors. I promise I will. Meanwhile, at least I won't be doing any more damage.

Take care, and forgive me for wrecking everything. I'll be in touch.

I love you,
Josh

Abby sank down onto the sofa and reread the note. After so many recent arguments and so much verbal abuse, she knew that her overriding feeling at that moment was relief — relief that there would be some space between them; relief that Josh had agreed to get help; and, finally, relief that her conflict about attending the Alliance meeting had been resolved.

Chapter Eleven

It was seven-thirty in the evening when Abby smoothed out Lew's map on the passenger seat of the Mazda and headed across the valley. Dense clouds made head-lights helpful, and a drop in the tempera-ture suggested rain might be on the way. Just over twenty-four hours had passed since she had read Josh's note. There had been no word from him since. Nor had she tried to find out where he had gone. As isolated as she was feeling, as apprehensive as she was about the future, she knew that separating was the best thing they could have done. There might not be healing yet, but at least the bleeding had stopped. She *had* called Garrett Owen, the neurologist, and learned that Josh had scheduled an appointment several weeks away for an evaluation of headaches.

"If he had told my nurse that it was an emergency," Owen told her, "she would have spoken to me, and I would have found a spot to squeeze him in."

Abby was about to ask Owen to do just that but stopped herself. It was Josh's game now, and he could call the shots.

The route on Lew's map took her past the cutoff to Ives's trail, then along the base of the northern hills. Finally, about a mile west of town, she found the dirt road labeled on the map "my driveway." At the base of the road was a crudely cut and painted arrow that read, The Meadows — Alvarez.

The stony dirt drive sloped steeply upward for half a mile. It was hard to imagine Lew getting home at all when it snowed. At the crest of the hill was his farm, an unpretentious patchwork of wooden-fenced meadows, stretching out around a rambling whitewashed two-story house, a large old barn, and two garage-sized outbuildings. The spectacular vista, south and east, spanned the entire town and included a long-distance view of the Colstar cliff and the mountains beyond. There were several cows grazing nearby. Farther out, in a field of wildflowers, a pair of horses moved slowly toward one another.

She had no idea how many members of the Alliance would be there and was somewhat dismayed to see just two cars, one of which she assumed to be Lew's. Alvarez greeted her warmly at the door. He was wearing worn jeans, a plaid denim work shirt, and scuffed cowboy boots. The outfit looked as natural on him as did blue scrubs and a clinic coat.

"This place is lovely," she said as he led her through a fireplaced kitchen that looked as if it had been designed by someone who had a passion for cooking.

"I knew you'd like it."

They passed through a short paneled hallway to a spacious den. The walls of both were covered with framed photographs. Most of them seemed to be taken in a foreign country, and a number of them featured a woman — a slender, dark-haired beauty with a luminous smile. Abby asked where the pictures had been taken.

"Paraguay. That's where I was born, and where I chose to practice after I finished my training here. The woman in the pictures is . . . was . . . my wife. She's dead."

"I'm sorry."

His sadness was palpable.

"Thank you. So am I," he said.

The den was set up with a wet bar, some dishes of pretzels and chips, and a slide projector and screen. The only other person there was a stout, middle-aged woman named Barbara Torres, the associate director of the Patience Valley Region Visiting Nurse Association.

"I'm very pleased you've come," she said. "We've been hearing so many good things about you."

Abby thanked the woman and accepted a Perrier and lime from Lew.

"Are you expecting many people tonight?" she asked.

Lew and Torres exchanged brief glances.

"Gil Brant, who owns the pharmacy in town, should be here shortly," Lew said. He paused, searching for the right words. "The

Alliance used to number several dozen, but for now, at least, I'm afraid we're it."

. . . *Very few. They're harmless because no one takes them very seriously.*

Lyle Quinn certainly seemed to have his facts in order.

Lew motioned her to an easy chair positioned to get a good view of the screen.

"Perhaps while we're waiting for Gil," Lew went on, "Barbara and I could fill you in on our group's history and goals."

"Please."

"I was the last ER physician to come here before you. By the time I arrived, David Brooks, who'd been here for a couple of years, had been noticing a disturbing number of the sort of cases you refer to as NIWWs."

"NIWWs?" Torres asked.

"Abby's abbreviation for 'no idea what's wrong,'" Lew said. Barbara's smile suggested that, like him, she appreciated the irony in the label. "Well," Lew continued, "over the months after I started here, David and I began talking about these cases — the strange rashes, chronic fatigue, adult asthma, headaches, and the like. We became convinced that some sort of environmental exposure had to be at the root of them all. And, of course, the most likely source was up there on the cliff."

The doorbell rang. Lew left and returned with Gil Brant, a tall man with a cheerful, ruddy face.

"Let me congratulate you on your hand-writing and the accuracy of your pre-scriptions," Brant said after their introduction. "And let me also thank you for your commitment to see this cause of ours through."

Abby felt her cheeks redden. Lew spoke up quickly.

"Gil, Abby has made it clear that she's not committed to any cause. She's come to hear what we have to say and to see if there's a unifying explanation for the strange cases she's been seeing in the ER. That's all."

"Yes, yes, I see. Well, then, why don't we have at it?"

"Barbara, why don't you show Abby what we have?" Lew said.

Torres took a computer printout from her briefcase and handed it over.

"This is a list of one hundred seventy-five patients who have been seen in the emer-gency ward by Dr. Alvarez, Dr. Brooks, bless his soul, and by some of us at the VNA. The ages and diagnoses are beside each name. Some of them may have had definite diagnoses made by their private doctors by now, but we have no way of knowing."

Abby scanned the printout. The patients she had seen during her own brief experi-ence at PRH were a microcosm of this group.

"I could probably add an additional

twenty or so patients myself," she said. "What about enlisting some of the other doctors in town?"

"When David first confirmed my sense that there was a pattern," Lew said, "just as I did when you told me about your strange cases, we decided to do just that. Without even suggesting that Colstar was at fault, we sent out flyers announcing an organizational meeting of a group we named Alliance for a Healthy Patience and describing the symptoms we'd seen. About fifty people attended that meeting, including at least fifteen doctors from the hospital staff."

"Well, what happened?"

Lew turned to the pharmacist.

"Gil?"

"Well, the people at Colstar got wind of what we were doing and started a campaign to discredit us almost immediately. Attendance at our meetings dropped each time. Then, when we tried and failed to prove our theory about what was going on, we began to be looked on as . . . as —"

"Go ahead, Gil, say it. As quacks."

"Well, what *was* your theory?" Abby asked.

Brant looked to Lew, who nodded that it was fine for him to go on.

"Cadmium," he said. "This Colstar plant, in addition to being the company headquarters and research center, manufactures all of their rechargeable batteries. Cadmium is one of the main components. Colstar has it shipped in by the ton. Our theory right from the beginning has been that all of the varied symptoms we've been seeing have been caused by cadmium poisoning either through the air or the water."

Abby strained to remember what little she knew of the adverse effects of the heavy metal.

"Toxicity somewhat like mercury, yes?"

"Exactly," Brant said. "It's in the same column as mercury in the periodic table of elements. You know your chemistry."

Lew lowered the lights with a dimmer and flicked on the slide projector. The first slide, expertly prepared, was headed, "Symptoms and Signs of Cadmium Toxicity." The list was extensive.

"These slides were put together for presentations to both OSHA and EPA," he explained. "Obviously, they didn't make much of an impression, or we wouldn't be here tonight."

The list included all of the symptoms and findings Abby and the others had been seeing, plus a number of additional ones. Kidney failure, which Abby had not encountered in the ER, was the most serious common manifestation, along with severe respiratory disease. But everything from headaches to skin eruptions to gingivitis and even sterility was listed as well.

"So," Abby said, "don't keep me in suspense. What were the blood levels?"

Again, the three Alliance members exchanged glances.

"We managed to get fourteen or fifteen samples sent off on various patients," Lew responded. "They were all negative."

"Done at the hospital or sent out?"

"Mostly here. The hospital lab has a contract with employee health at Colstar to monitor nickel, cadmium, lithium, and the other potential toxins used at the plant. So they have all the equipment and expertise."

"We think the hospital lab is under instructions to keep any positive test under the tightest wraps," Torres added.

"Another possibility is that someone in the lab replaces all blood sent in for cadmium levels with blood they know will be negative," Brant chimed in.

"But why?"

"The usual reason," Lew said. "Money. It would cost millions for Colstar to close for any length of time, locate the source of contamination, and do whatever is necessary to correct it. In addition, Colstar competes with a number of other companies for very lucrative government contracts. Anything that forces them to retool would also make them ineligible or unable to stay in the game. Did you know that Senator Corman is from Patience?"

"Most definitely. It was always the first thing I was told whenever I asked anyone about the town."

"Corman's tight with Ezra Black. Colstar's

one of the companies in Black's empire," Lew went on. "Plus, Corman has as much support around here as he does clout in Washington. He's responsible for ensuring that huge government contracts keep coming this way. But if there's an environmental disaster involving the company, it's doubtful even he could protect it. Let's show you some more of these."

The first ten shots were different views of the plant itself, perched atop its massive butte.

"These were taken by Dave Brooks about eight years ago. Note the smoke coming from those stacks. The company — and their story's backed up by the EPA — tells us that's just steam. We have doubts. Now they only emit whatever it is at night. You hardly ever see smoke during the day."

"And what are those?"

Abby pointed to three identical dark, ill-defined areas in one of the shots, each one tall and narrow. They were situated one directly above the other and spaced vertically down the sheer cliff face beneath the plant. The angle of the other shots was such that the rectangles were not apparent in any of them.

"I've never even noticed those before," Lew said. "Have you two?"

"I would have thought they were just shadows," Barbara said, "or else some sort of optical illusion. But now that you call my attention to them, I can see them clearly."

152

"They look like slits in the rock," Brant added. "Windows of some sort? I don't know if they're even there now."

"Curious," Lew said. "Well, we'll have to check. Thanks for noticing them. I knew we brought you up here for a reason. Next, take a look right here in the corner."

"That stream?"

"Almost a river in the melting season. Only it's not visible anymore. Colstar built a huge addition right over it. I have no idea where the water goes, except it eventually must end up in the quarry where the town gets its water."

"Has the quarry water been tested?"

"All tests negative."

"What do the people from EPA and OSHA say?"

"Mostly they don't bother paying attention to us anymore. They came on-site two years ago at our request but reported finding nothing significant. But, remember, we're talking about the potential economic death of an entire town here. That's powerful stuff, especially when it involves an influential senator. We think EPA is closing its eyes to whatever is going on.

"The story I'm going to tell you may be hard to believe, but it's absolutely true. There's a tire company down south that has about the same relationship to the town it's in as Colstar does to us. A few years ago the workmen's-comp cases reported by the company to OSHA began piling up. Many of them involved limbs lost or mangled in substandard, obviously dangerous machines. The secretary of labor, who is the ultimate head of OSHA, rode into town personally and closed the plant down for innumerable violations. He expected a bushel of public-opinion points for the administration. But surprise! The outcry from the town was immediate and the political pressure intense. The plant was reopened within a day or two pending more in-depth investigation. It has never closed since. And as far as I know, the manglings just continue."

"Do you think Patience would become a ghost town without Colstar?"

Gil Brant answered.

"I believe we'd go through some hard times, but I think we'd rebound — especially if some other manufacturer took over, or Colstar retooled."

"I think we could manage off tourism," Barbara said. "And with time I'm certain something else would come along."

"But you haven't been able to get the community behind you?"

That word again. Only this time it was Abby herself who was using it.

"In the beginning," Lew responded, "we had a pretty staunch core group, even after our posters got torn down, the *Chronicle* stopped covering our meetings, and we started getting intimidating phone calls. But then David died."

"What do you mean?"

"David told me he had proof — a tape of a conversation and some papers — that Colstar was tampering with the blood samples sent to the hospital lab. A few days later he was found dead at the base of a rock called the Spike. It was ruled an accidental fall by the police and the coroner, but we all have our doubts. David was an experienced free-hand climber, and the Spike wasn't that hard. He'd climbed it alone many times. After he died, we decided to make our meetings less conspicuous. In fact, we've virtually gone underground."

Not far enough to escape Lyle Quinn's notice. Abby felt a chill at the thought of her predecessor's death not being accidental.

"If he was murdered, who do you think is responsible?"

"I'll show you in a minute," Lew said.

"So now there are just the three of you?"

"We would certainly like to have more," Barbara said. "But the truth is, it makes no difference to the commitment we feel. We believe the company is making a lot of people ill, and we can't just stand by and allow it to happen."

"What if it means forcing Colstar to close down?"

Barbara shrugged helplessly.

"Then Patience has to hitch itself up and move in another direction. In the twenties, after the Patience mine failed, it looked like

155

the end. But some enterprising people attracted Colstar here in its place, and Patience became a winner. We can do it again."

"We want to get the government to close Colstar down until it locates the source of the environmental contamination," Brant added. "I think there are people who care as much as we do and would support us."

"But that support depends on finding proof," Abby said.

"Exactly."

Lew flicked to the next slide, a newspaper head shot of Lyle Quinn.

"We believe that this man and the woman I'll show you next are the two main villains of the piece," he said. "Lyle Quinn is ex-CIA. He's the head of security at Colstar and is politically well connected, especially with Corman. He's also tight with just about everyone who matters in Patience — the mayor, the police chief, our esteemed hospital president, Joe Henderson, you name it. You asked who I thought was responsible for David's death if it wasn't an accident. This man's your answer."

Abby considered recounting her run-in with Quinn but decided not to. She was there to listen and learn, and, right or not, these people had a definite bias.

"Who's the woman you spoke about?" she asked. "The other villain?"

Lew advanced the carousel to the slide of an austere-looking woman with tortoiseshell glasses and short, conservatively styled hair. She looked familiar, but it took most of a minute before Abby placed her — the woman at the picnic in the Save the Planet T-shirt; the woman whose sensitivity toward Angela Cristoforo was such a contrast to Quinn's displeasure and disgust.

"Kelly Franklin," Lew said. "Director of environmental health and safety — EHS. Franklin has been at Colstar for about five years. She acts as if she would do anything to uncover dangerous practices at the company, but we're convinced she's a fraud — a puppet of Quinn and the company officers."

"Why do you say that?" Abby asked.

"Franklin told us on any number of occasions that she'd conduct an exhaustive investigation of the plant and even send blood off, in our presence, to an independent lab. But she never followed up."

"Maybe she's just waiting for some objective proof," Abby said. "Or perhaps we — I mean *you* — should be more aggressive about forcing her to give your concerns more than lip service."

"We intend to be," Lew said. He flipped on the lights and gave her some time to process what she had seen. "So, then," he said finally, "what do you think?"

Abby stared into her glass, her thoughts a swirling montage of Lyle Quinn, Josh, Colstar medical director Martin Bartholomew, Kelly Franklin, George Oleander, Lew, Claire Buchanan, and any number of other NIWWs. She could feel the silent expectation in the room. Should she even bother telling them that there was a very good chance things wouldn't be working out with her boyfriend, and that she would soon be looking for a job back in the city?

"I think there's something environmental linking many, if not all, of these patients," she said, carefully choosing her words. "And if that's true, it's hard to believe Colstar isn't responsible."

"Then you'll join us?" Brant asked.

"Not in any formal way, not yet anyway. I just don't feel as strongly about these issues yet as you do. Besides, the man I moved up here to be with works for the company. I'd have to see a pretty solid case against them before taking a stand."

"Is there any way your friend would listen to what we have to say?" Torres asked. "If we could get just one person we trust inside the company —"

"Barbara, please!" Lew snapped. "That's not fair."

The woman deflated visibly.

"Sorry," she said. "We've been at this for a long time, and I'm just getting a bit frustrated."

"I understand," Abby said. "Show me more conclusive proof, and I'll certainly consider sharing *that* with Josh. Meanwhile, I'll tell you what I *can* do. I'll begin keeping a log of the patients I see whose conditions are suspicious. And if I have time, I'll bone up on cadmium toxicity. If it seems appropriate, I'll send blood on any suspicious patient off to a toxicologist friend of mine at St. John's in San Francisco. If Sandra Stuart says the blood is clean, believe me, it's clean."

"As long as you go at least as far away as Caledonia to mail it to her," Brant said.

The four of them walked together to where the cars were parked. Torres and Brant expressed their appreciation to Abby for coming and left.

"I'm grateful, too," Lew said as the others pulled away. "I honestly didn't think you'd come. Will you promise to think over what you've seen tonight?"

"I will."

Abby sensed that he didn't want her to go home. If he asked, she had already decided she would stay — for a while. The craziness with Josh had worn her down, and she craved Lew's saneness, the warmth of his company. But, instead, Lew extended his hand and shook hers in a most businesslike way.

"I'll see you in a couple of days," he said. "Abby, if you think it's appropriate, I'd like to meet your friend Josh sometime."

"Actually, Josh isn't in much shape to be meeting anyone. He's been having a bad time lately. Some pretty striking mood swings. Plus headaches. I've been very worried about him."

"Has he been evaluated?"

"Only by the physician's assistant at the Colstar clinic. Today he made an appointment with Garrett Owen. It's anyone's guess whether or not he keeps it."

"Tell him he really should."

"I would if I could. The truth is, we had another blowup and he left. I don't even know where he is."

"I'm sorry. Are you two engaged?"

"Unofficially, I guess. But all bets are off until the current situation gets straightened out."

There, she thought. *Now you can ask me to stay.*

"Then we must help you do just that," he said instead, opening the car door for her. "Based on what you've told me, and what we've observed in a number of others, I would suggest part of Garrett Owen's evaluation of your friend should be a measurement of his serum-cadmium level."

Chapter Twelve

Abby drove home in no particular hurry, stopping at a convenience store for a quart of skim milk and a can of Maxwell House. On the way out she yielded to a wave of self-pity and snatched up a package of Oreos. The last place she felt like going was back to an empty house at the end of a dead-end street on the south side of Patience, California.

She flipped on the Mazda's interior light and checked herself in the rearview mirror. There was strain around her eyes, all right. But she still looked pretty much like the woman who had been pursued by interesting, attractive men throughout medical school and residency and, in fact, right up until the time she'd met Josh. The hints she had dropped on Lew Alvarez could have broken his toe. But here she was, heading home alone. The man was either a modern Sir Galahad, or he was simply not interested in her as anything other than a 33 percent increase in the membership of the Alliance.

As she drove, she mulled over Lew's suggestion that cadmium poisoning might be at the root of Josh's symptoms. Emotional lability, lassitude, and brain atrophy were among the signs and symptoms listed on Lew's cadmium-toxicity slide. Still, it was hard to believe. Josh was so meticulous about his health. How could he allow himself to be exposed at work to a known toxin? And if it had happened outside of Colstar, why hadn't *she* been affected as well?

One thing was certain. When she and Josh finally did see one another again, it would not be wise to bring up the subject of Colstar and cadmium pollution — not as long as he felt she was trying to outdo him or undermine his success. She *would* give the neurologist a call and suggest that he might squeeze in Josh's evaluation sooner if possible, and also that he might send off some blood for a cadmium level. If he seemed approachable on the subject, she might even offer to make a trip down to her toxicologist friend, Sandy Stuart, with a few tubes of Josh's blood. Heavy-metal poisoning was serious, but if diagnosed in time, it was treatable and curable.

As she pulled into the driveway, Abby was thinking that cadmium poisoning, as awful as it sounded, might be a better thing for Josh to have wrong with him than migraine variant or temporal lobe epilepsy, two of the diagnoses that ranked at the top of her list of possibilities. Both conditions had fairly effective treatments, but no cure.

The house was completely dark. *The first lesson in living alone,* she thought. *Leave a light on.* She locked her car — an unnecessary precaution in Patience, but a vestige of her days in the city — and was halfway to the back door when she suddenly sensed someone was watching her. She whirled, her pulse hammering.

"Josh? . . . Josh, is that you?"

A man *was* there, by the garage. She could see his silhouette now. Desperately, she tried to think of what move to make. The back door was locked. Even though her keys were in her hand, she would never make it inside before he got to her. There was a fist-sized rock not far from her foot. She could use it as a weapon while she screamed, hoping that one of her neighbors, none of whom was very near, might hear. But before she could act, the man emerged from the shadows.

For a moment she felt her heart stop. Then she recognized him. Quinn.

"Sorry if I startled you, Dr. Dolan."

He was dressed in black, exactly as he had been at the picnic. But the effect as he emerged from the shadows at eleven-thirty at night was much more menacing. Abby had no doubt that was exactly what he intended. His silver hair glowed in the dim light.

"What do you want?" she asked.

"To talk."

"Josh is inside. Let me go tell him you're here."

"*Josh* moved into the Sawicki place last night, out beyond Five Corners. They're off in San Diego tending to Sally Sawicki's mother, who has cancer. Today he called to say he wouldn't be at work. Wherever he is tonight, it isn't here."

"I don't think I like you, Mr. Quinn. Besides, I'm tired. And I know I don't like being dealt with by men who skulk around on my property."

"Ten minutes," Quinn said. "If you want me to leave then, I will."

"Maybe some other time."

"I want to talk with you about that little meeting you just attended at Dr. Alvarez's place, and also about your friend Wyler's place at Colstar. . . . Ten minutes."

Abby was too stunned by Quinn's revelation of Josh's movements to be surprised that he also knew where she had been. She felt wary of the man, even a bit frightened of his power and confidence. But she was also intrigued. She reminded herself that if what Lew and others believed about David Brooks's death was true, she would be strolling off with a murderer. But if Quinn was going to harm her, this didn't feel like the time or place. Still, she had no intention of being alone in her house with him.

"Ten minutes," she said, motioning him down the street where they would at least be closer to her neighbors.

"I assume that Wyler's moving into the Sawicki place means things aren't going well here. I'm sorry."

"Is that what you wanted to speak with me about?"

"Josh Wyler works in a very sensitive, crucial position for us. Problems at home could definitely have a negative effect on his job performance."

"We're working out our differences."

"Great. Keep at it. And let me know if Colstar can help in any way."

"We have plenty of help, thank you."

"Just offering."

Quinn walked along beside her in silence.

"I told you they'd be making a move to enlist you," he said suddenly.

"Yes, you did."

There didn't seem to be any sense in asking him whether he had followed her to Lew's, or whether one of the three Alliance members was a spy. His answer was not to be trusted, whatever it was.

"Did they come at you with all that cadmium hogwash?" he asked.

"You tell me."

"I'm sure they did. That's been their approach with all the others they've tried to recruit. They're wrong, Dr. Dolan. Way, way off base. We control every one of our toxic metals as closely as any plant in the country does."

"Then what are you worried about?"

"I told you at the company picnic that I'm paid to worry about anything that might be a threat to the welfare or viability of Colstar. As I'm sure Wyler has told you, we're cur-

165

rently the principal agency for a number of important government research projects involving portable power sources. Much of our work is highly classified, including several projects in his department. Any situation that closes the company or limits its production for long could result in the loss of those contracts. I'm certain the few people left in the Alliance for a Healthy Patience made you aware of that."

"They did."

"Dr. Dolan — would you mind if I called you Abby?"

"Dr. Dolan will do fine."

"Suit yourself. Dr. Dolan, I believe that the Alliance means well. But they're misguided."

"What about the symptoms we've been seeing?"

"An example of what can happen when overzealous physicians use their knowledge and status to influence lay opinion about health matters. It's pure Chicken Little, instituted by Drs. Brooks and Alvarez. And believe me, Dr. Dolan, the sky is not falling. The unconnected threads they pulled together impressed people only because two charismatic physicians said they should. Stare at even the most perfect complexion long enough and close enough, and you will think you see blemishes. There is no ecological epidemic, and certainly no ecological epidemic caused by cadmium. Not one other physician in Patience has supported their position."

Until me.

They had reached the intersection of Abby's road with the two-lane state highway, a paved wagon trail that wound its way through the mountains, connecting southern Idaho and northern Nevada with the ocean. They stopped by a streetlight. For a minute, maybe more, the only sounds were crickets, some peepers, and the rumble of an approaching semi. Finally the truck roared past them, headed west, toward the center of town.

"So, Mr. Quinn," Abby said as the sound died away, "you don't seem any more or less devoted to *your* position than the Alliance is to *theirs*. Exactly what is it you want me to do?"

"I want you to put any commitment you've made to them on hold until you know all the facts. The Alliance has almost ceased to be. Nearly everyone who started with the group has seen the truth and dropped out. New blood — especially new physician blood — is essential if they're to remain in existence at all. They don't pose a serious problem to us. But believe me, Dr. Dolan, I know enough about you not to want to have you on their side."

I know enough about you. . . . The implied threat again. He had used the same technique at the picnic. This time, though, he had lost the element of surprise.

"Mr. Quinn," she responded deliberately,

"what you do or do not know about me doesn't matter to me a bit. What's best for my patients does. And if you know so much about the Alliance and the meeting tonight, you should also know that I have made no commitment whatsoever to them at this point."

"Excellent."

"But the moment I see an elevated cadmium level in one of my patients, or any other evidence of illness caused by Colstar, I promise I will become an enthusiastic recruit in their attack on you."

"That's certainly fair. Meanwhile, I'd like you to consider assisting us."

"What?"

"I'd like to hire you as a consultant to Colstar — occupational medicine and the like. The stipend would depend on how much you're called upon to do. But I promise you that along with what we — I mean what *the hospital,* of course — is paying for your ER work, you'll be doing quite nicely, indeed."

"And, of course, part of the deal would be my staying away from the Alliance."

Quinn glanced at her.

"On the contrary," he said. "There's nothing I'd like more than to have you on a retainer *while* you're attending the Alliance sessions. Forewarned is forearmed."

"You want me to spy for you?"

Quinn didn't react to her question immediately. Instead, he walked along beside her quietly until they were nearing her home.

"What I really want is for you to come and tour Colstar. I'll introduce you to Kelly Franklin, our environmental health and safety officer. She has detailed maps of every inch of the company. Pick an area, any area, and she'll take you there and let you inspect it as long as you like. If you see any possible way we could be contaminating any part of the environment, we'll help you call in the regulatory agency involved, and comply with any mandates. You have my word on that."

"When do you want me to do that?"

"Why, right now. Kelly is waiting for us in her office. It's the perfect time, because the third shift is sort of a skeleton crew, and you'll be able to move about easily."

"Mr. Quinn, I'm not up for this tonight. And at this hour I can't believe Kelly Franklin is either."

"Dr. Dolan, I happen to know that you had today off, and you're not on the schedule again at the hospital until the day after tomorrow. This business is very important to us. That's why Kelly is quite anxious to meet with you. And I assure you, as a trustee of the hospital and a vice president of the company Josh Wyler works for, it's very important to the two of you as well."

Abby felt almost relieved. At last Quinn had taken off the gloves. His warning was oblique enough, but Abby had no doubt he was at least holding Josh's job hostage,

169

if not hers as well. She would most likely be able to find ER work without much difficulty, although probably not at a place like St. John's. But Josh was another story. If she was responsible for his losing his position at Colstar, what remained of their shaky relationship would surely crumble.

The nugget of fear inside her grew. She was hardly a threat to Quinn or Colstar, but he was setting about methodically to control her. And, yet, if Lew was right about Josh's symptoms being due to cadmium, she was far better off inside Colstar than off somewhere looking for work.

"No promises," she said at last. "Whether I notice anything on this tour or not. No promises."

"Of course. I knew you'd understand."

"And if I decide I don't want this . . . this consultant's position, I want Josh and me to be left alone."

"You have my word."

"You'll have to excuse me for not knowing how much that's worth."

Quinn's car, a black Range Rover, was parked in front of a neighbor's house. Abby followed him up the serpentine drive to Colstar. She wondered if Ives was up on his hillside, watching them through his infra-red glasses. She also wondered how long he would last up there if Lyle Quinn knew that one of his hobbies was observing the comings and goings at the plant. The uniformed guard waved them through into the massive, sparsely filled parking lot. Quinn pulled into a spot reserved for him and motioned Abby to the next one, which belonged to someone named Mr. Wang. A second uniformed guard smartly opened the front door at their approach.

"Tight ship," Abby said.

"I'm pleased you appreciate that."

The plush reception area was deserted. Quinn paused long enough for Abby to take in the many community-service citations and performance-award plaques lining the walls.

Salt of the Earth, Incorporated, she thought. Except, of course, for a security chief who lurks in the shadows to frighten women, an occasional ex-employee who stabs herself in public, and maybe, just maybe, a carelessly handled, toxic heavy metal.

"Kelly Franklin's office is in the A Concourse, the same as your friend, Josh's. Someone told me the two of you were planning on getting engaged. I surely do hope things work out between you."

"You seem like a very sentimental person," Abby said.

The smooth concrete concourses, three of them, were boulevard wide and brightly lit. There was a pod of numbered white golf carts parked at the head of each one.

"During our day and evening shifts, almost all of those carts are in action," Quinn said proudly.

"What's your handicap?"

"Excuse me?"

"Nothing. Nothing."

Quinn led her down A Concourse, deserted except for an occasional worker in a knee-length lab coat. One of the golf carts rolled silently away from them for what seemed like a mile. There was another cart parked against the wall next to an opaque glass door labeled "K. Franklin, Environmental Health & Safety." Quinn knocked briskly, the sounds echoing down the vast corridor like pistol shots.

Kelly Franklin greeted Abby professionally, but with apparent warmth. She was neither as informal as she had been at the picnic, nor as severe as in Lew's slide. Quinn completed the introductions and then left after reminding Abby that she should take as much time as she wished to explore the facility, and Kelly that Abby was to have free rein to inspect anything she wished.

"Dr. Dolan," he concluded, "we appreciate that you're an emergency physician and not an expert on occupational health and safety. But we also know that *you* will be able to appreciate the precautions we at Colstar take to ensure the safety of our workers and the town."

Abby thanked him icily.

"So," Franklin said once they were alone,

172

"can I offer you something? Some tea? A soft drink?"

"Nothing, thank you."

Abby scanned the office, which evidenced a woman who had two teenage daughters, a couple of environment-related graduate degrees from Cal and Washington State, a love of the outdoors, and an extensive academic interest in her field.

"You don't seem too thrilled to be here, Dr. Dolan," she said. "I'm sorry. Lyle has a single-mindedness about his job and his own way of doing things. And he doesn't care too much about who's inconvenienced, or who thinks he's a horse's behind, as long as he accomplishes what he sets out to."

"Well, obviously, Quinn's goal tonight was to get me here," Abby said.

Kelly Franklin looked genuinely embarrassed.

"I don't think I want to know how he did it," she said. "But at least I have the chance to make this part interesting for you. I promise you, giving someone — *any*one — free rein to look around Colstar is not Lyle's way. Your opinion of us must mean a great deal to him."

"I'm not sure why."

"Perhaps it has something to do with Josh," Kelly said. "Lyle told me you two live together. Josh is a great guy. Highly intelligent, nice, and extremely funny. He's been a very positive addition here."

"I'm glad."

173

So much for her concerns about whether Josh's erratic behavior had carried over to work. Clearly, to this point at least, she was the primary casualty.

Kelly seemed to expect Abby to say more.

"Well, then," she said finally, "why don't we get started?" She took a large sheath of cardboard-bound computer-typed pages from the floor beside her desk. "Lyle told me that your chief concern regarding Colstar is cadmium. This is an extensive annotated bibliography on the toxicity of cadmium. I got it from the NIH library in Bethesda. At some point I'd like it back, but there's absolutely no rush."

"Thank you."

"And here's a list of the hospital patients who have had cadmium levels performed at their physician's request. Their inpatient-discharge or emergency-room diagnoses are included. As you can see, every single one was negative. This next list is of the almost five hundred tests for cadmium, nickel, and other metals that we've done randomly on our employees. That program is ongoing and I oversee it."

"Are the tests run at Patience Regional?"

"Yes, as a matter of fact, they are. Why do you ask?"

"Just wondered."

"Any other questions so far? . . . Fine. I have a floor plan of the entire plant on my cart. If we try to see everything, we'll be here until tomorrow afternoon. But if that's what you'd like, I'm perfectly willing to do it."

With Kelly Franklin driving they rolled off down A Concourse as Abby studied the floor plan. The plant was built on two massive stories, one at ground level and one below. In the manufacturing wing, located on C Concourse, the basement level extended upward in part for two stories, and there was no ground floor. Most of the remainder of the basement was devoted to production. Abby chose to start with the research wing off A Concourse. Then they would tour rechargeable-battery manufacturing, the heart of cadmium use in the plant.

Bit by bit, as she learned about Colstar, Abby also learned about her guide. Kelly Franklin was divorced, and had been when she had taken the Colstar job five years before. Her two daughters, at their father's insistence, went to private school just outside of San Francisco. Although there wasn't much of a social life in Patience for an educated single woman, Kelly managed to meet people through the Sierra Club and shipboard-based scuba trips, which she took twice a year. She was sustained in Patience by the natural beauty of the area, the excellent money she made, and the fact that she loved her job.

As she listened to Kelly describe her life, Abby thought about herself and her own situation. If the separation with Josh became permanent, it was doubtful she'd last long in Patience alone.

The research wing was deserted save for a security guard and one scientist. It was a huge rectangle with a central glass-enclosed atrium, which Kelly explained was for work with any toxic or potentially toxic substance. It was superventilated into a complex series of filters. The air emerging from those filters was perfectly safe to breathe.

"We're very much aware of the toxicity of some of the substances we work with," Kelly said. "With cadmium, for instance, which is one of the more toxic, we exceed OSHA and EPA standards for air quality by a good margin."

"That's reassuring," Abby responded with no enthusiasm.

"Perhaps it would be *really* reassuring if I told you what those standards are. Essentially, the maximal acceptable ambient-air content for cadmium would be equivalent to pulverizing two aspirin tablets and blowing the dust into the air in the Astrodome."

"That *is* impressive."

Surrounding the atrium were a dozen or more individual laboratories, each featuring the sort of organized clutter Abby had come to expect in any busy research space.

"This is Josh's unit," Kelly said. "It's the most demanding area of the business, because the competition from other manufacturers is so fierce. From what I've seen, he's standing up to the pressure pretty well."

Look again, Abby thought as she inspected the equipment and quarters. Every inch of the vast space looked spotless and carefully maintained.

C Concourse featured a fifteen-foot billboard that proclaimed:

COLSTAR INT'L, PATIENCE, CA. PLANT.
EMPLOYEE SAFETY
IS OUR HIGHEST PRIORITY
101 DAYS WITHOUT AN
ON-THE-JOB ACCIDENT.

The manufacturing wing was as carefully maintained as research and development. All cadmium, nickel, and other toxic metals were handled by robot arms controlled by workers in mask, gloves, and jumpsuit. The huge vats in which the metals were mixed and prepared for injection into the battery casings were covered and sealed. Ventilation and air filtration were high priority.

In spite of herself, Abby was impressed. Colstar seemed to have safety precautions built upon safety precautions.

"I do have a couple of questions," Abby said as they glided back up the concourse. "First, do you know anything about a stream that once ran beside the plant?"

"Of course."

"What happened to it?"

Kelly smiled.

"I don't know if anyone outside the company has ever even seen this," she said. "But Lyle has given you the run of the place, so here we go."

She drove Abby to the very rear of B Concourse and then used a key to open a large metal door. Inside was a spacious natural-rock swimming pool, complete with a corkscrew water slide and waterfall. An extravagantly created jungle paradise. The vaulted ceiling was a massive opaque skylight. One wall was clear glass, behind which was a glittering health club.

"This space is reserved for Mr. Ezra Black and the rest of the officers. I'm part of the club, though I don't use it. They tolerate women in management here as long as we don't get in the way or try to act like men. The truth is, I'm a little embarrassed that we have such a thing at Colstar. If Josh isn't a key holder yet, he will be."

"The pool is fed by the stream?"

"Yes, but the water's heated to eighty-three. The excess from the stream and outflow from the pool drop down nearly fifty feet into a filtration plant located outside on the south wall of the mesa. From there it flows into the Oxbow River, which runs along the north side of the valley and empties into the quarry. The outflow water is monitored frequently for coliform bacteria and other toxins, and I test it personally every two weeks."

An executive swimming pool! Lew and the others were going to be sharply disappointed by the solution to the case of the vanishing stream.

"I've seen enough," Abby said, glancing at her watch. It was two-thirty. "And you must be exhausted. I appreciate the tour."

Kelly drove them back to her office.

"It was a pleasure to meet you," she said. "Perhaps we could go out for dinner sometime."

"Perhaps," Abby said. Then she realized that her response was unreasonably cool. Not once during the hours they had just spent together had she felt Kelly Franklin was hiding something from her. "Listen," she added suddenly. "I'd like very much to get together. I'll call you here in the next day or so and we'll set something up."

"Terrific."

Kelly paged Quinn, then stacked all the computer printouts together and passed them over.

"Thanks," Abby said. "I'll cadmium myself to sleep the next few nights."

"Have fun. Is there anything else?"

Abby tried to think of what Lew might want her to ask. Then she remembered the shadows on the cliff face below the plant.

"One last question," she said. "Are there any other floors beneath the basement?"

"None at all. The basement level rests on solid rock. The filter house is the only thing below it, and as I said, that's built outside."

"There are no openings cut into the face of the cliff on the northeast side?"

179

"No. Why? Do you have reason to think there are?"

For a few moments Abby studied the woman's expression, searching unsuccessfully for any hint of evasion.

"No. I was just wondering," she said.

Chapter Thirteen

Abby set aside the reading she had been doing on cadmium toxicity and packed her things for another trip up to Samuel Ives's hillside home. She recognized her anticipation at seeing the eccentric again and realized that he was one of the bright lights in the loneliness and isolation that had been engulfing her since moving up from the city.

The early morning was cool and already bright. In an hour and a half she would be starting the day shift in the ER. With any luck the twelve hours there would be interesting and hectic enough to be totally engrossing. Her mind certainly needed a break from the outside world. It had been a week since Josh had moved out. He had come back three days ago for some things, but she'd been working at the time. All she found on the dining-room table when she returned home was a ragged bouquet of wildflowers, and a letter.

I believe I know who is responsible for my problems, the rambling note read, in part. *Once I am CERTAIN, I will act. Then, and only then, will I be FREE. I PRAY that you are not one of them.*

The bizarre note brought a heavy dose

of reality. Over the days she and Josh had been apart, memories of the way things had been between them over their first eighteen months together had begun bidding for space in her head. Now, she realized, Josh Wyler was no longer someone she could count on for anything. Worse, he might actually have become someone to fear.

With time to fill, Abby had started taking an aerobics class and had even begun jogging. As a result, the hike up to Ives's place was getting easier. She made it this morning without even breathing hard.

As she suspected, the germ causing Ives's chronic leg infection had been identified as a slow-growing fungus called aspergillus. The treatment was amphotericin B, a potent intravenous antibiotic. To accommodate the hermit's adamant refusal to return to Patience Regional Hospital for any reason, Abby had reluctantly inserted a short, indwelling catheter in a vein in his forearm. On the days when she could not get up to see him, he administered the medication himself. And she had to admit that in spite of her doubts about the treatment approach, day by day the deep-seated infection was improving.

"Ives, don't shoot, it's me!" she shouted as she reached the clearing.

He looked up at her from his workbench.

"No shooting today, Doc. Just polishing my bow."

"It's so beautiful."

The hermit admired his handiwork.

"It's getting there," he said. "Another year, maybe."

"Then what?"

"Then I'll make another one, I guess."

Abby motioned toward the straw-dummy target.

"So, tell me — blindfolded or not?"

She had asked the question before several times and still had not gotten a straight answer.

"If I can see," Ives said this time, "what does a rag tied across my eyes mean?"

The lacerations on his face were healing nicely, and the bruising was all but gone.

"You've got great healing powers," Abby said.

Ives reached down beside his bench and held up a can of Chef Boyardee spaghetti.

"It's all in the diet."

"Ives, tell me something," she said as she re-dressed his leg. "How long have you been up here?"

"I don't really know. Nine, maybe ten years."

"I have a question about Colstar."

"Try me."

"I saw a slide of the plant taken about eight years ago. It was shot from a distance, and the quality really isn't that good, but on the face of the cliff it looks as if there are three long slits in the rock."

"But they're not there now." Ives finished

183

the thought for her.

"Exactly."

"They were windows of some sort, eighteen inches, maybe two feet across, and five or six feet high. Almost looked like the ports in medieval castles that were used to shoot arrows through without getting shot yourself."

"What happened to them?"

Ives shrugged.

"One day they were just gone — filled in, I guess."

"Can we see where they were from here?"

"We can try, but I think they did a pretty thorough job of sealing them up."

Ives retrieved his burlap sack and an army blanket and led her to his observation point. She hadn't been out there since the first day she had climbed up to the camp with Josh. Looking out across the valley now, she wondered where he was, what he was doing, and whether or not he had kept the appointment with Garrett Owen. She *had* called the neurologist and gotten him to move it up two weeks.

The sun was beginning its ascent, and the Colstar cliff glowed amber in the light. Ives spread out the blanket and lay prone next to Abby.

"I can never get over how huge the place is," she said.

"It's a fortress all right."

Ives focused his field glasses and passed them over. Having been inside the plant,

184

Abby found it easy to get oriented. First she scanned down to the roof of the hospital, and then the adjacent professional building. Next came the narrow field of wildflowers, and then the high barbed-wire-topped fence that essentially separated the valley from the plant. Beyond the fence was a broad, undulating rocky meadow, and then the almost-sheer cliff. Abby located the filter house Kelly Franklin had told her about. Next she panned across the face of the cliff. Nothing.

"Exactly where were those slits?" she asked.

Ives checked through the glasses and then handed them back.

"Look at the name Colstar on the side of the building. Believe it or not, those letters are each eight feet high. Now go to the S and head straight down the rock. I think that should be about it."

The resolution of the binoculars was magnificent. Abby studied the cliff carefully from top to bottom. Then again.

"Hey, Ives," she said excitedly, "I think I can see where they were. If you stare hard enough, you can tell that the shapes are still there, only it looks like they were sealed with cement or painted wood."

Ives examined the wall himself.

"Some sort of plywood with small stones glued on, I'd guess," he said.

"What's behind them? That's the question."

185

And why doesn't the health and safety officer know the answer? That was an even bigger question.

Ives set the binoculars aside.

"Well, doesn't that just beat all," he said. "Here I've been lookin' at the place all these years, top to bottom, side to side, and you come along and show me something I've never noticed." He grinned over at her. "So am I blindfolded, or not?"

Chapter Fourteen

The headache began, as all the others had, with the strange chemical taste at the back of his tongue. His anger had been building, even between the attacks, but now he felt as if a fuse had been lit somewhere deep inside him, and he was powerless to stop the explosion. He didn't deserve this. All his life he had tried to do what was right. He didn't deserve to be going insane. Three years in the Corps. Two rows of ribbons. He should have stayed in a few more years. Hell, he should have stayed in forever. If he had known what lay in store for him, he would have. First the failure with the diner, the goddamn bankers who wouldn't wait, then job after job. Then two jobs at once just to stay even, three when he could find the work. And now he had been let go at the plant. And for what? For taking too many sick days. But who in the hell could work thirty feet up on a ladder with cannons exploding in his head?

He felt the throbbing begin behind his eyes — the horrible, pulsating pain. The taste in his mouth grew sharper, more unpleasant. This one was going to be a bitch. He took a drink of water, then spit it out. There was no sense swallowing it. Before long he would be throwing up anyway.

He raced into his bedroom and tore the dry cleaner's plastic off his dress uniform. The Marines might not approve of his wearing it for this, but what the hell. They had spent all those years teaching him to kill. Now he would find out how much he'd learned.

His hands were shaking so badly, he could barely fasten the buttons on his jacket. But even after nearly fifteen years, it still fit damn well. It had been wrong to blow up at his boss for suggesting that he was faking the headaches, and wronger still to have sucker punched him. But he was only underlining what everybody already knew — the man was an asshole. Mr. Country Club Snob.

The throbbing became an electric drill, boring holes into his brain. He sank to the floor, squeezing his temples, then stumbled to his feet and out of the house. Straightening his dress uniform hat, he lurched to the car.

The country club, he thought. That was it. That was the fucking problem. All the country clubs set up all over the country to remind folks like him they were poor, worthless failures, not good enough now, not good enough ever. But, hey, don't forget that the good folks at the country club had let him in the elegant clubhouse once for three whole weeks . . . until he had finished painting it!

He gunned the engine of his Chrysler, a beast with 170,000 miles on the odometer and its second rebuilt engine under the hood. His vision was blurred, his brain on fire. What a rotten existence — what had he ever done to deserve this? Nothing. Absolutely nothing. He sped off in a shower of gravel, then screeched to a stop, opened the door, and heaved up the contents of his stomach. That was the end, he vowed, coughing and sputtering. He had thrown up for the last time. They could step all over him, they could take away his job for no good reason, but they couldn't break him. He was a goddamn Marine, for chrissake, and if Marines knew nothing else, they knew how to fight back.

The beautiful people had the money and the power and the Jags and the houses and the diamonds and the country clubs. He had a twelve-year-old tank of a car and the spirit of a Marine. No contest!

Fifty-five . . . sixty . . . sixty-five . . .

The Chrysler began to shudder. He gripped the wheel tightly and pressed his foot to the floor. The headache was as horrible as ever, but this time, at least, he didn't care. The country-club people had done this to him. Now it was his turn.

Seventy . . . seventy-five . . .

The cross streets flew by. The trees and telephone poles were blurs. The car was shaking mercilessly. An acrid smoke began billowing in around him. He was off the seat now, his right leg rigid, his foot jammed on the accelerator. Mission: enemy destruction. *Target in sight, sir.*

"From the halls of Montezuma, to the shores of Tripoli . . ."

He barreled off the road, across a stretch of grass, and up a small hill. The fence, shielded in green vinyl windbreaker, was just ahead. *No problem, sir.*

Eighty . . . eighty-five . . .

"We will fight our country's battles in the air, on land, and sea. . . ."

At last the pain in his head was gone. At last the hideous taste had left his mouth. At last he had stopped taking the punishment lying down.

The screeching of the engine . . . the crunch of metal on metal . . . the screams . . . more screams . . . the crash . . . the pain . . . the blackness . . .

Mission accomplished, sir. . . .

Chapter Fifteen

STANDON, CARL,
 — TOXIC METAL SCREEN INCL.
CADMIUM, NICKEL — NONE DE-
TECTED.

ANDERSON, JAYE,
 — TOXIC METAL SCREEN INCL.
CADMIUM, NICKEL — NONE DE-
TECTED.

MCELROY, THOS.,
 — TOXIC METAL SCREEN INCL.
CADMIUM, NICKEL — NONE DE-
TECTED.
 — ORGANOPHOSPHATES — TRACE
FOUND; LEVELS PENDING.

Seated at her desk in the on-call room, Abby studied the results from the first three NIWWs on whom she had ordered cadmium levels. All were negative. One of the three, a farmer named Thomas McElroy, had come to see her. His complaints were a lack of energy and a chronic cough that had not responded to two courses of antibiotics. His physician was George Oleander. Abby had ordered the cadmium level, then, on a hunch, she ordered a test for organophosphates as well. Organophosphate was a neurotoxin, commonly used in gaseous form as a chemical weapon during World War II. But it was also a component in many fertilizers. Apparently, Thomas McElroy had somehow gotten exposed to it.

Trace positive. She had no clear idea what, if anything, that meant. The tongue-in-cheek law taught to medical students was never to order a test unless you were ready to have it come back abnormal. The corollary to that law was that the best response to any abnormal blood test was to repeat it.

Abby decided that a better approach would be to set the whole matter in George Oleander's lap. If, in fact, Thomas McElroy's symptoms *were* due to organophosphate poisoning, the first definitive diagnosis for one of her NIWWs had been found. And it would *not* be cadmium. She peeked out to be sure that the ER was still quiet. Sundays often started peacefully, with families in church or beginning their days slowly. But with none of the medical offices open, and minimal coverage for each practice, the afternoons and evenings were predictably busy. At the moment things were very quiet. She was heading back to the phone when the wall-mounted intercom sounded.

"Dr. Dolan," the receptionist said, "Dr. Oleander's on line two."

"This is one efficient hospital," Abby muttered, punching the line open. "George, hi. I was just about to call you."

"To explain yourself, I hope."

"What?"

"I just got copies of some laboratory tests you sent off on two of my patients, Carl Standon and Tom McElroy."

"Yes."

"Abby, what on earth are you doing ordering cadmium levels on these people? And how many more patients have you ordered them on?"

"Just one other. I don't understand what the problem is."

"Well, it's time you did. Just what were your indications for ordering these studies?"

"The symptoms were different for each patient. I've been reading a lot about cadmium toxicity and —"

"I am telling you here and now that I don't want extraneous tests ordered on my patients without consulting me. And I can tell you also that most of the other doctors on the staff here feel exactly the way I do."

Abby felt her self-control begin to unravel. She glanced about the small office and wondered if what Lew had told her about bugs and cameras could possibly be true.

"I don't feel they were extraneous," she said stonily. "I also ordered an organophosphate level on Mr. McElroy, and that was positive."

"McElroy's a farmer. Every summer he

uses that damn stuff, and every summer he gets exposed, and every summer I treat him if his levels are high enough to warrant it. It's not *that* test I'm upset about, and you know it. If you've set about trying to cause trouble for Colstar and this town, you may find yourself looking for a job."

"Don't threaten me, George. And please don't speak to me in that tone of voice. I did what I felt was best for those patients."

"You did what you did because a certain other emergency-room doctor has been putting pressure on you."

"That's not true."

"Now, just listen to me. I thought when we spoke in my office last week that we had an understanding about what it means to work in this town."

You *had an understanding,* Abby thought.

"We're here to do what's best for this community," Oleander went on. "And trying to undermine the company that keeps us all afloat is not being a team player. Besides, I promise you, Colstar is not responsible for any illnesses. I would have thought you were convinced of that by now."

So, she thought, the Lyle Quinn dot was connected to the George Oleander dot. But, of course, Quinn had already gone out of his way to tell her he was on the board of trustees at the hospital.

"George," she said, "I'm doing the best I can to be a good doctor to the people of this

194

town. If that's not being a team player, I'm sorry."

"Abby, the bottom line is this: I don't want any more cadmium levels being sent off on my patients without speaking to me first. What happens when these people get their bills or insurance statements, and they learn that a doctor on the hospital staff thinks they've been poisoned by Colstar?"

"*Might* have been. I —"

"Please, Abby. I mean it. Back off."

"Whatever you say, George. They're your patients."

"Good. Now, I'm on backup for medicine today."

"I know."

"Well, I'm calling from the car on my way to my wife's cousin's. I'll be twenty minutes away from the hospital. Twenty-five at the most. My service has the number. Treat anything that's not life-and-death. Write holding orders on anyone you want to admit. This is an anniversary party. I'm going to try to stick it out here until five or six. Thank you."

He hung up without waiting for a reply.

"Mr. Team Player," Abby muttered.

She washed her face to cool down. Josh or no Josh, if life at PRH was going to be like this, she would take her chances somewhere else. It was hard to believe that two months ago she had been sitting with friends at a café by the water in Sausalito, talking about what sort of wedding she and Josh might have.

She was drying off when the charge nurse, Mary Wilder, pounded on her door and opened it a crack.

"Abby, come quickly," she called out. "We've got big trouble."

Abby grabbed her clinic coat from the chair and raced out.

"There's been a bad accident at Patience Country Club," Mary said, clearly anxious, but doing a decent job of remaining composed. "Some guy crashed his car through a fence onto a tennis court. He hit three women and then hit a pole or something. Apparently the injuries are bad. One ambulance is already on the way in, two more are on the scene. That's it for the town's ambulances. Tom Webb, the paramedic, will be calling back in just a moment."

Abby felt her heart respond to a jet of adrenaline. Instinctively, she checked her clinic coat pockets for her instruments and the two thick loose-leaf handbooks she had put together over the years crammed with treatment protocols, medication interactions, and other pearls of experience. Multiple trauma on a Sunday morning with a reduced crew and limited backup. Her fears about leaving the shelter of St. John's for a remote ER were about to become reality.

They hurried across to the communications area where the radio and telephones were clustered, along with a telemetry ECG unit.

"Do you want me to start the disaster drill?" Mary asked.

The drill, which each shift practiced once a year, was a telephone pyramid that would mobilize almost the entire hospital staff — medical, nursing, technical, and administration — within ten or fifteen minutes. Over a hundred people. Disruption, confusion, expense. The protocol was an on-off switch. Go or no go. There was no such thing as partial disaster drill. Abby knew the choice was the first of dozens, maybe hundreds, of critical decisions she would have to make over the minutes ahead.

"Not until we have a little more information," she said. "Find out who's in-house and get them down here, please. Also, get whatever nursing help you need for — how many did you say?"

"I think four."

"For four patients. Notify X ray and lab and have them call in their backups now."

Mary used the phone on the counter to begin making calls. At that moment the radio crackled on.

"This is Fire Rescue Three, paramedic Tom Webb reporting."

Behind the man's voice Abby could hear the wail of the siren.

"Go ahead, Rescue Three," she said. "This is Dr. Dolan."

"Dr. Dolan, we are on route to your facility, four minutes out, with two — repeat, *two* — priority-two patients, both female in their thirties. Both were struck by an automobile while playing tennis. One has an obvious compound fracture of the lower leg. The other has multiple lacerations and abrasions. Both are conscious and alert. Vital signs in both are stable at present."

"Received, Rescue Three. How many other victims?"

"Two. Another woman and the man who was driving the car. They're in bad shape. Both are going to be priority one. Two squads are on the scene."

"Received. We'll be waiting for you."

She turned to Mary Wilder, who had just finished a call. The nurse's expression was grim.

"There are only two doctors in the house. Dr. Levin is doing a C-section, Dr. Mehta is doing the anesthesia."

Abby threw the switch.

"Start the disaster drill," she said. "Set up the two patients coming in now out here in the bays. Save the trauma room and major medical for the other two."

Almost instantly the ER began to fill with nurses and technicians. But no physicians. Two crash carts were already in place. A third was brought down from one of the floors. Mary Wilder and the nursing supervisor for the hospital quickly formed teams to work on each of the victims. Admitting clerks readied their clipboards. The blood-bank technician checked her stock and notified regional blood-supply centers to stand by. The X-ray tech moved the portable unit into position. The phlebotomist prepared his blood-drawing equipment and moved to a spot out of the way. Suddenly, eerily, for one frozen moment, the ER was completely silent, waiting. Then, from some distance, wailing sirens could be heard.

"Okay, everyone," Abby said, sipping water to dampen the desert in her mouth, "let's all keep cool and do what we know how to do."

She gloved and hurried out to the ambulance bay just as a police cruiser and the ambulance sped in. The first victim, moaning piteously, had her right leg bundled in a bulky splint. Blood had already begun soaking through the gauze. Abby scanned her quickly — IV in and running wide, cervical collar on. Her face and tennis dress were blood-smeared and dirty with the red clay from the court. There was a nasty abrasion on her left shoulder. Abby glanced at the second woman and decided to follow this one in. One of the nurses was already cutting away her clothes.

"Rebecca Mason," the EMT said. "Thirty-four. The only things we found are what you can see." He lowered his voice and added, "Her leg's pretty bad."

Abby stopped the litter, checked to ensure that the *dorsalis pedis* arterial pulse on the top of the woman's foot and the posterior tibial pulse behind her ankle were palpable. Then she marked the location of each with a pen and motioned the team into bay three.

Her first job was a primary assessment — airway, breathing, circulation. The ABCs of trauma. Speaking softly to the woman, Abby reassured her as best she could while she systematically checked vital functions, critical pulses, then skull, chest, and abdomen. She heard her own voice, calm and firm, but felt oddly detached, as if it were someone else issuing the orders.

"Keep the saline running at five hundred. Routine labs and clotting studies. Type and cross-match for five units. Have X ray do a shoot-through and lateral of her neck. Clear those films with me before you do anything else. Then we'll do portables of her chest and leg before we send her over for real films. Catheterize her bladder. Be sure ortho is on the way in, and be sure to check those foot pulses every minute."

"Yes, Doctor."

"Anything else anyone can think of? Good. Keep me posted."

One down. Abby changed gloves and hurried over to the second woman, Katherine McNamara, who had already had her clothes cut away, and was covered with a sheet. Her head was swathed in gauze, which was becoming bloody over her right eye. Like Rebecca Mason, her neck was in a hard cervical collar, and her head was secured to the body-length fracture board. The nurse, whom Abby recognized from the floor, gave a quick report. Lacerations on her back that no one had gotten a good look at because of the need to protect her neck, and a deep gash on her forehead. Otherwise nothing obvious.

Abby knew that from here on she had to prioritize the treatment of each case relative to the others. This was triage, the ongoing process of evaluating multiple patients with illness or injuries to ensure that sicker patients would be seen first. The idea was to get the maximum benefit from the personnel and facilities available. But in disasters such as this one, another wrinkle was added. Treatment had to be given first to those who needed it to survive, and not to those who had no chance regardless of the efforts of the caregivers. If that situation did arise, the call would be hers.

Abby's assessment of Katherine McNamara put her on a lower priority level than the first. No triage problems so far. Of the two Rebecca Mason would go to X ray first and would be cross-matched for blood first. Mary Wilder hurried over just as Abby was finishing issuing orders.

"They're four minutes out with the next one, a forty-one-year-old male. Priority one. Barely conscious, hypotensive, multiple trauma."

"Another tennis player?"

Mary shook her head.

"No, this one's the driver. The one responsible for all this."

"Put him in the trauma room," Abby said. "And, Mary?"

"Yes."

"Let's all do our best to stay as objective and professional as possible."

The older woman's glare quickly softened.

"I'll try," she said. "But I know both of these women, and I know the one who's still out there, too."

"What have they reported about her?"

"Her name's Peggy Wheaton. Multiple trauma. She's unconscious. Her husband, Gary, is the president of the Patience Savings Bank. They have three kids."

Despite Abby's plea the nurse failed to mask the judgment in her voice.

"Get together the team assigned to this man. Then have another one ready when Peggy Wheaton arrives."

She stood on her tiptoes and scanned the ER, which was in barely controlled chaos. Several police officers were there now, along with the paramedics, technicians, nurses, and even two people from housekeeping — one of the downsides of calling a disaster drill. Abby motioned one of the policemen over and asked him to be sure that anyone not essential to the care of the patients be sent to the waiting room. Then, across the ER, she spotted the first doctor to arrive, a competent young pediatrician named Susan Torrance.

"Tell me what to do," Torrance said.

"Become an orthopedist."

"I wish."

"Any problem suturing?"

"None."

Sirens again. The first priority one. Abby directed Susan Torrance to do a detailed examination of Katherine McNamara but to be sure neck films had been cleared by Abby or a radiologist before moving the woman.

Abby gloved again and headed out to the ambulance bay.

"Where are all the doctors?" she asked Mary Wilder.

Everyone, whether on call or not, was part of the telephone pyramid and was expected to drop whatever he or she was doing and get into the hospital.

"I think a lot of them are away on vacation or at meetings. The telephone system breaks down some when too many people aren't home. They'll be in, though. I promise. Meanwhile, you're doing just fine."

Abby managed a tense smile.

"Thanks," she said.

"Here they come."

With another police cruiser whooping along ahead of it, the ambulance swung onto the long drive up to the ER. Abby moistened her lips and rhythmically tightened, then loosened, her fists. Priority-one trauma. At St. John's, since her residency, she had always been a relatively small part of the team evaluating and treating such

203

patients. During her residency she had trained in all aspects of trauma technique, usually working on anesthetized sheep. And at one time or another she had performed many of the techniques on patients. But after she had joined the faculty, there had always been residents about, anxious to hone their skills, and staff surgeons available to oversee and teach them. Now it was just Abby.

The police officers, two of them, hurried in first.

"He's under arrest for attempted murder, Doc," one of them said. "Just keep us posted with what's going on."

"Exactly what happened?"

"He hauled himself off the road at a high rate of speed, drove up a little hill, and crashed through a fence onto the tennis court. Slammed through these poor girls like a bowling ball, then slammed into the steel light stanchion. Crazy idiot was wearing a Marine uniform. He's no more a Marine than I am."

"Was he conscious? I mean, did he pass out at the wheel with his foot jammed on the accelerator?"

"Hell, no. Two people heard him yellin' and singin' before he hit the fence."

"Okay. Thank you. Mary, here we go."

The litter was raced out of the ambulance, right past Abby and into the ER. She hurried in behind it. All she had seen was a man, covered with blood and glass fragments. He was moaning and struggling against the restraints that held him to the fracture board. His neck was in a soft cervical collar, not the sort of rigid collar that had been secured on the first two victims. Had the rescue squad run out of rigid collars? Or had someone already placed a value on the man's survival?

The fracture board was lifted onto the hospital gurney. Abby stood back for a few seconds as the nurses cut away what clothes they could. Then she took a towel to brush away glass and moved to the bedside.

"Pressure's seventy," a nurse said.

"Wet a towel and hand it to me, please," Abby said. She swept aside some of the glass stuck to the blood on the man's face and caught in the corners of his eyelids. When time permitted, they would use inverted loops of tape to remove the fragments. Right now there was more important business at hand. "Open that IV wide and get me set up to put in an internal jugular line."

"Right away."

"My eye," the man moaned. "There's something in my eye."

"We'll get to it, sir. Just try to hold still."

Abby began her primary assessment. His respirations were shallow and grunting. There was a gauze pad taped to his chest, beneath his right nipple. Abby removed it, revealing a jagged gash. There was no air movement in his right lung.

"Get me a chest tube setup, please," Abby said, pressing the gauze back over the wound.

The lung had been punctured and had collapsed. Each time the man breathed, air was going straight through the bronchial tubes and into the right chest cavity. The increasing pressure from that side was making it impossible for the left lung to get enough air. That mounting pressure had to be released, and the right lung had to be reexpanded.

Abby wiped off the blood from the man's face to assess his color. There were a number of scrapes and shallow cuts, but nothing that would compromise his upper airway.

"Help me," he moaned. "Please help me."

Abby stared down at him.

"Mary, I know this man," she said suddenly. "I saw him at the Colstar picnic. His name is Willie Cardoza."

Chapter Sixteen

They're two minutes out with Peggy," Mary Wilder said as she wheeled in a cart with the equipment to insert a chest tube into Willie Cardoza. "Still no change. Vital signs are stable. She's breathing on her own, but she's not conscious."

"Okay. Get everyone ready. Right now I've got to get this line in, then the chest tube. I'm very concerned about this man."

Mary's expression left no doubt which patient *she* was concerned about.

Cardoza's condition was deteriorating. In addition to the collapsed lung, he almost certainly was bleeding internally. His blood pressure was barely discernible, and his consciousness was fading. Abby found no fracture in a lateral X ray of his neck, and removed the soft collar. Several other views in addition to the lateral would have been more reassuring, but there simply wasn't time. She numbed up a spot just to one side of his larynx. In trauma victims large-bore IV lines were critical for the rapid infusion of fluid and blood. Like most ER physicians, Abby was highly skilled at getting them in, either by way of the "blind" subclavian stick she had used to insert the pacemaker in Hazel Cookman, or by a "blind" stick into the internal jugular vein, which she was preparing to do now.

"Any more doctors?" she asked.

"Dr. Cohen just got here," Mary said. "The two in the OR will be done in ten minutes."

Les Cohen, an older GP, would be better than nothing, but just barely.

Abby felt for landmarks in Cardoza's neck and found the spots she wanted. She then inserted the large needle, keeping suction on the attached syringe so she would know the instant she was in the vein and could avoid pushing through it. The path was inward and slightly downward, toward the hollow just above his breastbone. After three quarters of an inch, blood shot up into the syringe. *Bull's-eye!* She detached the syringe, threaded a polystyrene catheter through the needle, and quickly sutured it in place. Central line in. One less thing to worry about.

"What about the other ER docs?" she asked.

"Dr. Bogarsky's your ER backup. He's on the way in, but he lives in Millerton. I don't think they've been able to reach the Andersons or Dr. McCabe. Dr. Alvarez is working until eight tonight at the state hospital in Caledonia."

"How about a surgeon?"

"Dr. Bartholomew's on. He'll be here in ten minutes."

"Tell Dr. Cohen to take over on the lady with the fracture. Have him give her some

IV antibiotic. Make it a gram of Unisyn. She'll be pre-op as soon as orthopedics gets here, but this guy's almost certainly going to have to go to the OR first."

"And we don't know about Peggy yet," the nurse reminded her.

"Dr. Dolan," another nurse called from the doorway, "they're here. They're wheeling Mrs. Wheaton into the trauma room now."

"Damn," Abby muttered. "Pressure, please?"

"Still seventy."

Cardoza was no longer conscious. His color was poor and his respirations labored. In addition to the chest tube, he needed to have a line placed in the artery at his wrist to monitor his blood pressure continuously, and an irrigation tube inserted into his abdomen to check for internal bleeding. A blood return from that abdominal lavage tube, and he would need to be taken quickly to the OR for exploration.

For Cardoza alone she desperately needed at least one other pair of surgically skilled hands. What she had instead was another priority-one patient to evaluate.

"I've got to get this chest tube in before I can leave him," she said.

"Dr. Dolan," Mary Wilder said, "it's Peggy Wheaton. Go ahead in there. We'll keep an eye on things here."

Abby felt a spark of irritation.

This is hard enough! she wanted to

scream. *For God's sake, don't make it worse!*

Quickly, she composed herself.

"Mary," Abby said evenly, "I'll be in there as soon as this tube is in. Meanwhile, please send Dr. Torrance in to evaluate her."

"But she's a pediatrician."

"She's also a doctor," Abby said, no longer able to cull the impatience from her voice. "Now, I've got to get this tube in."

The nurse glared at her and then stormed off. Abby was aware of an immediate coolness from the staff remaining in the room. But there was nothing she could do. Without the emergency procedure Willie Cardoza would be dead within a few minutes. She was his doctor, not his judge.

Working now in total, icy silence, she made a slit with a scalpel in a spot between two of Cardoza's ribs. Then she snapped the flexible rubber chest tube tightly into the tip of a heavy hemostat. With all her strength she jammed the tube and hemostat tip through the slit, worked it beneath a rib, and then popped it through the chest-wall muscle into the empty space where the lung had been. There was a hiss of escaping air as the dangerous pressure was released.

"Hook this up to the suction/drainage system, please," she said to the two nurses as she sutured the tube in place. "Pressure, please."

"Eighty, Doctor." Almost reluctantly, the

nurse added, "It's a little easier to hear."

Cardoza's color improved instantly, although it was far from satisfactory. The circulation to his head improved as well. He began moaning once again and making purposeful movements.

"I'll be needing a setup for an arterial line, and also one for an abdominal lavage. I'm going to check on things in the next room. Then I'll be back."

"How's it going in there, Doc?" asked the policeman standing guard outside the door.

"I don't think he's going to escape," she replied, rushing past him.

The moment she entered the trauma room, she did not like what she saw. Peggy Wheaton lay motionless on the gurney, her eyes closed, her breathing somewhat labored. A solid cervical collar was in place. Her tennis dress had been cut away, revealing an athlete's body with no hint of having carried and delivered three babies. There was a gauze bandage around her head, with blood soaking through the back left side. Her feet and hands were turned slightly inward. Their variation from normal position was minimal and might have no significance. But Abby sensed it meant serious head injury.

"What have you done so far?" she asked Susan Torrance, the pediatrician.

"I just checked her airway, heart, and lungs. They all seem okay."

"Blood pressure?"

"A hundred ten."

"Pupils?"

"I haven't looked yet. I did order a lateral neck film."

"Thanks, you did great. Is your other lady stable?"

"Perfectly."

"Excellent. Could you stay here, then, please? I may need another pair of hands."

The pediatrician stepped back from the bedside. Abby moved into the spot, took her ophthalmoscope in one hand, and gently lifted Peggy Wheaton's eyelids with the other. But even before she checked the woman's pupils, she noticed something more disturbing than anything she had seen so far. Above the collar, blood was oozing from her left ear — blood diluted by the clear fluid that surrounded the spinal cord and brain. The fluid leak meant that beneath the bandage, behind the woman's ear, her skull was fractured. Abby would have a sense of just how bad the fracture was when she felt back there. But first she shined her ophthalmoscope light into both eyes. The pupils were large and absolutely unreactive. She then ran the pointed end of her reflex hammer up the soles of Peggy's feet. On both the right and the left, the great toe reacted to the stroke by pointing upward rather than curling downward. The findings — both in the eyes and feet — were grave.

Around the room three nurses and the

pediatrician waited expectantly for her orders. Abby knew that at that moment none of them appreciated the situation the way she did. Peggy Wheaton, though breathing and maintaining a blood pressure, was quite possibly brain-dead.

Dreading what she was going to feel, she cut the gauze bandage away and, from both sides, carefully slid her fingers behind the woman's skull. The damage was massive — a broad, deeply depressed fracture beneath a large laceration. Abby withdrew her gloved hands slowly and glanced down at her bloodied fingertips. On several of them were strands of what she was certain was brain tissue. Breathing or not, blood pressure or not, it was already over. No medical miracle would save Peggy Wheaton.

"Get MedFlight up here," she said. "Give her Decadron, ten IV. Get set to intubate her. She needs a neurosurgeon."

Or, more likely, a priest.

"Please, let me in. Excuse me." A graying, extremely handsome man in his forties rushed to the bedside. His tanned face was pale. "I'm Gary Wheaton," he said.

"Abby Dolan."

Abby stripped off her rubber gloves and pulled the sheet up to Peggy Wheaton's shoulders.

"Dr. Dolan, I've heard many good things about you. I'm glad you're on duty today. How is she doing?"

Abby glanced down at the woman, searching for the right words, the right tone, but knowing that what she had to say could never be done right.

"She's not doing well, Mr. Wheaton." Abby looked around the room and realized that the staff, too, were hanging on her words. "She has a fractured skull, and my initial exam suggests that there may be extensive damage beneath the fracture."

"Oh, my God. Is she . . . I mean, she's going to make it, isn't she?"

Abby shrugged.

"I've sent for MedFlight. She needs a neurosurgical evaluation."

Just then the nurse in charge of Willie Cardoza hurried in.

"Dr. Dolan, his pressure's fifty."

"Is that the man who did this to my wife?" Gary Wheaton demanded to know.

"Dr. Torrance," Abby said, pointedly ignoring the husband's question, "please keep an eye on things here. I'll be back as soon as I can. Once they're set to intubate her, go ahead if her breathing deteriorates."

"I, um, I think I'd best call you if that happens," the pediatrician said.

"Fine. Mr. Wheaton, you can wait in the family room if you want."

"I'm staying right here. Dr. Dolan, I don't want you leaving my wife."

"I know," she said, moving to the door. *Nobody does.*

Before reentering Cardoza's room, Abby glanced about the ER. The orthopedist was in, examining Rebecca Mason's fractured leg. But Abby knew he was less equipped to perform an emergency abdominal exploration than she was.

Cardoza was slipping away.

Desperately, Abby tried to remain calm, to sort through the possibilities. If he was bleeding that badly into his belly, there was probably nothing she could do. The answer was to start from the beginning — the ABCs. His airway was fine, as was his monitor pattern. But while examining his chest, she hit pay dirt. The tube she had inserted was kinked, and Cardoza's original problem had recurred. She straightened the tube without much difficulty and tacked it down. Once again Cardoza's pressure came up and his color improved.

"Please get some blood up now," she ordered. "Un-cross-matched if they have his blood type. O negative if they don't. I'll take responsibility."

She was in the middle of inserting the gastric lavage tube when Mary Wilder called from the door.

"Peggy's having difficulty breathing. She's stopped completely twice. Dr. Torrance is trying to get a tube in, but she's having trouble."

"Tell her to stop trying to intubate and just use a bag and mask. I'll be there in a minute."

"But —"

"Please!"

215

Abby completed the insertion of the abdominal tube and watched as the saline she put in, then drained out of the cavity, came back bloody.

"Hang two units as soon as possible," she ordered.

She was racing back into the trauma room when both George Oleander and Martin Bartholomew entered the ER. They followed her into the room. Abby was not the least surprised that both were on a first-name basis with Gary Wheaton.

"Thank God you're here," Wheaton said to the two men. "This woman left my wife to go in there with the man who hit her. Now Peggy's not breathing."

"I just can't ventilate her by mask with that collar on," Susan Torrance explained.

Then take it off! Abby wanted to scream. *Breathing first. Everything else next!*

"Abby, what's going on here?" Oleander demanded.

Abby didn't bother responding. She loosened Peggy Wheaton's collar and gave her several good, ventilating breaths through the bag and mask. The woman's heart rate, which had dropped dangerously, sped up. Still, Abby knew, it was an exercise in futility. She prepared to insert a breathing tube through Peggy's nose and into her lungs. But at that instant Dr. Mehta, the anesthesiologist, arrived.

"Abby, let Dr. Mehta take over," Oleander ordered with far too much bluster. "San-don, Mrs. Wheaton needs a nasotracheal tube. Would you insert it, please?"

"Right away, George."

Abby backed away. She was expert at putting in breathing tubes. But this was not the time for debate or ego. The anesthesiologist inserted the tube with ease.

"MedFlight's been sent for, Dr. Oleander," Abby said with exaggerated evenness. "The problem's in her left occipital region. You should glove and check it out yourself, as I did. Dr. Bartholomew, I need you for the man in major medical. He's got a positive abdominal lavage. We're getting blood running, but I'm certain you're going to have to explore him soon."

"Is he the one who did this?" Bartholomew asked.

Abby tried ignoring the question.

"He had a tension pneumothorax," she said, "but a chest tube seems to have stabilized that. We're having trouble keeping his pressure up, though."

"I asked if he's the man."

"Yes."

"I'll be in there when I'm sure of the situation with Mrs. Wheaton. Not before."

Abby didn't respond for fear of what she might say.

"I'm truly sorry about your wife," she muttered to Gary Wheaton as she left the room.

Willie Cardoza had responded well to the repositioning of the chest tube and to an

217

infusion of blood. He was now fully awake, though dazed.

"Willie," Abby said, "I'm Dr. Dolan. You're doing better, but you've got some problems in your belly. Maybe a tear in your spleen. Do you understand me?"

Cardoza nodded. He tried to look at her, but flinched.

"There's something in my right eye," he rasped.

Abby noted tiny shards of glass remaining throughout the man's brows and in his hair. Carefully, she lifted his lid, but the discomfort made it impossible for him to keep the eye open. She inserted a drop of anesthetic, and seconds later his eyes opened. Abby slipped on a pair of magnifying glasses.

"There's a tiny piece of glass stuck in your cornea, Mr. Cardoza. Just stare at a spot on the ceiling and I'll get it out. Whatever spot you choose, stay right on it. Don't move."

Despite his distress, Cardoza was the perfect patient. Abby took a fine needle, slipped it under the edge of the embedded glass, and popped it free. The cornea, a clear dome over the front of the eye, looked okay. But to be certain it hadn't been damaged in a way she couldn't see, Abby put in a drop of fluorescent dye. Any cuts in the cornea would fill with the dye and would light up brightly under a black light.

She ordered the overheads cut. The cornea looked fine, but a golden ring glowed around the base. She had never seen anything quite like it. Some sort of irritant, she thought — a roughened area that was picking up the dye. Then she noticed that under the black light, the other eye had a glowing ring of equal brightness in exactly the same place. And that eye had gotten no dye at all.

She was trying to connect with something to explain the fascinating finding when, from the doorway, a throat was cleared. Abby looked up. Framed by the light behind him was George Oleander.

"Peggy Wheaton's dead," he said. "Why in the hell did you leave her like that?"

Chapter Seventeen

T ed Bogarsky, Abby's ER backup, arrived soon after Peggy Wheaton died. Together the two doctors worked their way through the huge backlog of patients that had developed during the hours following the nightmare at the country club. Still, it was after six in the evening before the waiting room was empty.

Willie Cardoza had made it into and out of the operating room and was now stable in the ICU under round-the-clock police guard. Martin Bartholomew reluctantly performed the surgery on him and, as Abby had suspected, found a tear in Cardoza's spleen. Aside from that and the chest trauma, he had no other critical injuries. Barring an unforeseen complication, there was no reason he wouldn't make it, unless, of course, the unmitigated hatred seething through the hospital and the town led someone to proclaim himself Cardoza's executioner.

Abby did her best to focus one by one on each patient she saw, but it was hardly easy. The staff was extremely distant and uncooperative. Finally she gave up asking for assistance and got her own suture set-ups and discharge sheets. Shortly after she had left Peggy Wheaton in the care of Drs. Oleander, Bartholomew, and Mehta, the woman had lost her blood pressure and her heart rate had dropped into the teens. Massive doses of medication held her for a short time, but the MedFlight chopper had not even arrived when she suffered an irreversible cardiac standstill.

Abby had little doubt that the coroner would document the lethal nature of Wheaton's head injury. But she also had little doubt that the finding would not matter to many people in Patience.

She had just finished suturing a child's knee when Ted Bogarsky came over. He was a jovial family man and a steady ER doc. He lived some distance from the hospital and had always seemed removed from the politics and personalities of the place. If, like the others, he condemned Abby for deserting an all-American mother of three to care for the lowlife who destroyed her, Bogarsky hid it well.

"Why don't you go on home?" he said now. "I'm on tonight, anyhow. Besides, we just found out our ten-year-old's going to need braces, so I can use the overtime."

"Ted, you're already getting the overtime. I don't think I should leave early. I'm just not sure what it would say to people if I did."

"I understand. It's been a hell of a day. For what it's worth, I think you handled everything brilliantly — as well as anyone possibly could have. If I'd been in your place, I know I'd have come completely unglued."

"Nonsense, but thank you. I need to know that at least someone understands what went on here."

"Everyone will with time. People are just a little raw right now."

"I hope so. Ted, let me ask you something. Have you ever seen or heard of any condition that causes a ring around the base of the cornea, bilateral, that can't be seen normally, but glows under a strong UV light?"

"Like the rings in copper poisoning? What are they called?"

"Kayser-Fleischer rings. They don't fluoresce. But, yes, that's the idea. Same exact place in the eye."

Bogarsky shook his head.

"Why do you ask?"

"Just something I read. I can't remember the details, though. Look, why don't I stick around for a while longer? If it stays slow, maybe I will leave a little early."

"Fine."

"I'll be in the on-call room for a few minutes. I just want to wash up."

Abby wanted to explain that she had seen the curious rings in the eyes of Willie Cardoza. But there was nothing to be gained by doing that until she understood more. As far as she could remember, none of the articles she had read on cadmium toxicity spoke of eye findings. But there was something in one of them — something that seemed to be just eluding her. The articles were in her briefcase in the on-call room, although she hadn't had time to read any of them today before the ER had gone crazy.

She set them on the desk, wondering if someone was sitting at a monitoring console someplace watching her. Skimming the articles quickly, she stopped at one entitled "Medical Findings in Nickel-Cadmium Battery Workers." Thirty-eight workers were studied. Thirty-four of them had headache; twenty-six had weakness, fatigue, and lassitude; sixteen had dizziness; one died from a syndrome like Lou Gehrig's disease; and CT scans on six of the workers revealed brain atrophy.

She set the article aside. It was impressive for the number of central-nervous toxic effects of the metal. But it wasn't the information that was nagging at her. Ten minutes later she was about to give up and rejoin Bogarsky when she found it. It was an article in a chemistry journal.

Cadmium in the liver and in the kidney, the abstract read, *can be measured in the lab by the technique of X-ray fluorescence.*

The science was simply too technical for her to understand. But at least the hint was there. Under certain circumstances cadmium in tissues *did* glow. She would have to try to get the original article and then maybe ask a biochemist to explain it.

She massaged her aching neck and shoulders. Tension, strain, and nearly ten hours of nonstop work had taken a toll on her body. It felt as if she had gone ten rounds with a heavyweight. *Enough,* she decided. She had had enough of this day. If it wasn't busy out there, she *would* leave. She opened the door and nearly collided with Joe Henderson, the president of the hospital. Henderson was a well-built, balding outdoorsman who had lacquered trophy fish on his office wall along with an NRA poster extolling the constitutional right to bear arms. No matter how grim or intense the subject he was discussing, Henderson always seemed to be grinning. Not today, though.

"Abby," he said, "they told me I'd find you here. Got a minute to speak with me and a couple of others?"

"Well, I don't know how things are going out there."

"They're fine. I just checked with Ted Bogarsky."

"Then I guess I've got a minute."

"Terrible thing that happened to Peggy Wheaton. Just terrible," he said as he led her to the small conference room just off the ER.

Len McCabe, the elder statesman of her ER group, was there along with George Oleander and a third man, who introduced himself as Terry Cox. Cox looked like a person whose passions included good food, fine wine, and money.

"I work for the hospital," he said. "I'm an attorney. But I'm also an old friend of Gary and Peggy Wheaton."

An attorney. What a surprise.

"Should I be getting a lawyer of my own?" Abby asked, far too weary to be civil.

"Abby," McCabe said, "there's no need to get angry. We'd just like to know what went on out there today."

"With a lawyer present?"

"A concerned friend," Cox corrected. "And a hospital representative. Needless to say, Gary and his family are distraught. I thought I could help explain things to them."

Abby calmed herself with a deep breath.

"Okay," she said. "What happened out there was that for almost twenty minutes our disaster-alert system failed to bring in another physician except for one pediatrician. I examined Mrs. Wheaton and determined that she would not benefit from my time and effort as much as Mr. Cardoza would. I felt that his life was on the line, while hers was already lost."

Cox grimaced.

"You mean," he said, "that after less than a minute with Peggy Wheaton — a young woman with a pulse and blood pressure, breathing on her own — you could tell that she wasn't worth trying to save, while the man who murdered her was?"

"Mr. Cox, this isn't a courtroom," Abby

225

said, "and I don't like the sense that you're cross-examining me." She paused while the lawyer mumbled an apology. "I'm horribly saddened by Mrs. Wheaton's death," she went on. "But I'm trained to evaluate patients quickly and to make decisions. That's what ER doctors do every moment they're on duty. Most of those decisions are quite minor and routine, some are life-and-death. The decision to concentrate on Mr. Cardoza was an extremely painful and difficult one for me to make, but it was the right one. I felt so at the time. I feel it even more strongly now."

At that moment, inexplicably, she flashed on Willie Cardoza on his back on the Colstar Park grass, holding Angela Cristoforo tightly, yet tenderly, as he kept her from hurting herself any more.

She would have done the same for me, he had said to Abby. *We company grunts have to stick together.*

"Would you have done things differently if you had had more time?" Cox was asking.

Abby didn't answer him. Instead, she turned to Oleander.

"George, did you examine Mrs. Wheaton's skull? Did you see the extent of the damage?"

The medical chief flushed.

"I . . . no. No, I didn't," he admitted. "There was too much happening too fast. Abby, please understand, we're not accusing you of doing anything wrong. I've been trying to

226

explain to you some of the differences between a city like San Francisco and a place like Patience. By now everyone in town has heard some version of what went on here today. We just want to make sure that when we tell the hospital's side of it, we're all on the same page."

"And are we?"

"What?"

"On the same page."

Abby had no intention of making excuses for anything she had done. For years she had feared being faced with a day like this. Now it had happened. And whether this impromptu men's club wanted to accept it or not, she had performed damn well. Whether they were pleased about it or not, a man's life had been saved. And whether they truly believed it or not, Peggy Wheaton was doomed before she had ever entered the ER.

"I . . . yes, I suppose we are," Oleander said. "Joe, Terry, Len?"

The men exchanged glances. None of them looked pleased, although none of them looked as if he had anything further to say. Abby thought she could read their eyes, though, and the set of their jaws. *Our community has its way of dealing with people who turn their backs on us, Dr. Dolan. You've had a number of chances to demonstrate you really want to fit in here. Don't count on being around much longer.*

She shook hands with each of the men

227

and asked Cox to extend her condolences to Gary Wheaton. Then she gathered her things from the on-call room, signed out to Ted Bogarsky, and left the hospital, surprised that it was still light out. As she headed across the ER parking lot toward the doctors' parking lot, she didn't notice a thin young woman who stepped from the lengthening shadows and followed her.

Abby was nearing the far end of the lot when the woman called to her. Abby turned as she approached. The stranger looked to be in her thirties. Her hair was dark and tied back in a ponytail that reached her midback. Her narrow face was plain, although her dark eyes were large and childlike. She wore jeans and a tie-dyed blouse.

"Dr. Dolan," she said, stammering nervously, "I'm sorry to run after you like this. I tried speaking to you inside, but there were always too many people around."

"What can I do for you?"

"My name is Colette Simmons. Willie Cardoza is my boyfriend. We've been together for almost five years now."

"Why didn't you come up to me earlier?"

"I waitress at a restaurant twenty miles away. I didn't even know about the accident until I got home a little while ago. My girlfriend is a nurse on the second floor. She called me and told me what happened. She said you saved Willie's life."

"I'm glad he made it."

"Dr. Dolan, I'm so upset. Willie would

never hurt anyone unless they hurt him first. The policeman told me he's been arrested for murder. They're going to take him to a prison hospital as soon as they can. But I think he was real sick before this ever happened."

"Would you like to sit down and talk?"

"Please."

Abby motioned her to the low, secluded bench where Lew had first told her about the Alliance.

"What do you mean, Willie was sick?"

"Doctor, Willie 'n' me have been together for almost five years. We live in a trailer east of town. We don't bother folks and they don't bother us. But Willie has always tried to do what little things he could for people who were old or sick — fix their fence, pick up their groceries, things like that. He even helped that girl at the company picnic who was cutting herself. I don't know if you heard about that."

"Actually, I was there, Colette. I saw what he did."

"Then you know he's a good man."

"What's been happening to him?"

"For about four months he's been acting real strange. He's been, I don't know, moody. Everything gets on his nerves. And that's just not like him."

Abby felt the tension building inside her with every word of the woman's story.

"Please, go on," she said.

"Well, on top of everything else, he's been

having these terrible headaches. He gets this bad taste in his mouth, then he gets a headache. We think it has something to do with a fall he took off a ladder last March. He smashed his head on a rock and was knocked out for a few seconds. The cut took twenty-five stitches. After that he began to have trouble."

"Sounds like a concussion. Did he have a CT scan? You know what that is?"

"Yes, I know. He had one several months ago. The doctor at the Colstar clinic said it didn't show anything."

"What did they say was wrong with him?"

"Migraine headaches. They gave him some medicine, but he kept getting worse and worse. Finally, a couple of days ago, he had a fight with his boss about missing so much work, and Willie punched him. Dr. Dolan, that's not like Willie Cardoza. None of this is."

"I understand," Abby said. "Do you have any idea what happened today?"

Colette shook her head.

"I left for work before he got up. He was bad yesterday, I can tell you that much. Real bad. Ranting and raving, and full of hate. *Rich* people. That's all he kept talkin' about, how much *rich* people were ruining his life. My friend told me the police were talking about how much everyone hates *him* now for what he did. I'm so frightened for him. Is there anything you can do to help him?"

"I don't know, Colette."

Abby started to say something about Josh but thought better of it. Colette Simmons might be a loose cannon in this situation. Instead, she wrote down her phone number.

"Here," Abby said. "If you need to call me anytime, day or night, just do it. I'll either be at this number or at the hospital."

"Please try to help him."

"I'll do what I can."

"Dr. Dolan, is there any chance that it wasn't Willie who did this?"

"No," Abby said sadly. "That's about the only thing I'm certain of right now."

"Thank you."

The woman shook her hand gratefully and then hurried back into the hospital. Driven by a surge of nervous energy, Abby stayed on the bench, trying to figure out what her next move should be. Cardoza and Josh — both Colstar employees, both with bizarre headaches and deteriorating behavior, both with violent, paranoid outbursts. Were there others? Did some of those on the Alliance's list fit the pattern? And what about the strange eye findings — did Josh have them? It was time to put some data together. And soon, maybe later tonight, it would be time to share what she had learned with Lew.

She collected her things. A shower at home, then maybe some Italian food at the Tower of Pizza. After that, she would return to the hospital to check on Willie Cardoza, reexamine his eyes, and review the information in his hospital record. Finally, she would take the list of names Barbara Torres had given her and get to work in the record room. A picture was emerging. Now it was time to color it in.

Ahead of her, above the trees, eight-foot-high illuminated letters watched over the valley.

Colstar International, Patience, CA. Employee Safety Is Our Highest Priority.

Abby laughed bitterly at the memory of the sign as she headed for her car. She was actually unlocking the driver's-side door when she noticed the broken glass covering most of her backseat. A small boulder rested in the center. Above the seat the rear window — what remained of it — was shattered.

Dismayed, Abby looked about. No one.

She checked her tires. The window seemed to be the only casualty — this time.

"Idiots," she muttered.

She took her briefcase down from where she had set it on the roof and relocked the Mazda. There was nothing she wanted less right now than to report the incident to hospital security or the police. But, almost certainly, her insurance carrier would not cover the replacement unless she did. And the last thing she needed at the moment was to pile up any unnecessary expenses. Soon, possibly very soon, she might be out of a job.

Chapter Eighteen

The intensive care unit on the second floor of PRH was, like almost everything else in the hospital, state of the art. It handled cardiac and major trauma cases as well as post-ops who were too shaky to go directly to a med-surg floor from the recovery room. Abby went up to the unit frequently to check on patients she had admitted there. Never had she seen it as busy as on this night. There were ten glass-enclosed cubicles arranged around the central nursing/monitoring station. The beds in all of them were filled.

Abby's first stop was the nurses' station, where she reviewed Willie Cardoza's chart. Although some 50 percent of PRH's records were still kept in manila binders, the hospital's record keeping was in the process of being upgraded to a system nicknamed KarMen — the Karsten-Mendenhall voice-activated data-encodement system. Compared to it, the record keeping at St. John's was chisel-and-stone tablet. KarMen, a recent product of a Silicon Valley company, was built upon the instantaneous computer transcription of dictated notes. The dictation was then immediately printed out for inpatient use and also stored electronically for future reference. The hard copy and records yet to be switched to KarMen were kept in a fireproof vault as backup. KarMen was so sophisticated that physicians and nurses with foreign accents or speech impediments could "register" them by reading a series of prescribed words and phrases into the dictation phone. The system adjusted itself so that their variations in speech would not affect the transcription. Record retrieval was carefully guarded through a series of passwords unique to each physician and nurse, and not to be shared under any circumstances.

Abby reviewed the operative notes from Martin Bartholomew and had to admit that the bombastic surgeon had done a professional job. Cardoza had remained stable throughout his surgery, with no significant blood loss once the circulation to his spleen was tied off.

Bartholomew's admission note cited an arthroscopic knee operation three years before, and a four-day hospitalization for pneumonia four years before that. There was no mention of the head injury that Colette Simmons believed was responsible for Cardoza's deteriorating condition. Abby wanted to check with KarMen for those records, but the nurses'-station terminals were all in use. She made a mental note to check Cardoza's record after she had finished examining him, then headed for his cubicle. Wedged in her clinic-coat pocket was the combination black light and magnifier she had borrowed from the ER. And folded alongside it was a copy of the report she had filed with hospital security.

After discovering the shattered window in her car, Abby had reluctantly sought out the guard on duty, a huge, porcine-faced man who chewed nonstop on a toothpick while he took down her complaint. His blatant lack of outrage at the damage to her car made it clear that he had been exposed to some version of the Cardoza-Wheaton story.

"We'll look into it, Doc," he said, scuffing at a few shards of glass on the tarmac by her car. "Looks like whoever did it had some muscles, though. That rock must weigh twenty pounds at least."

Abby left, having little difficulty imagining the guard himself heaving the boulder through the rear window of her Mazda.

It was on her way up to the ICU that she had stopped by the ER for the ophthalmologic ultraviolet light. Before pursuing the strange eye findings on Willie Cardoza, she had wanted to verify them. Entering and leaving the ENT room, she passed several nurses and aides. Not one of them spoke to her except Bud Perlow, who seemed genuinely concerned for what she was going through. Rarely in her medical career had she clashed with physicians or nurses. In fact, during tough times she had drawn strength from the respect they had for her skill, her attitude, and even her worrywart approach to solving problems. Now she had performed almost flawlessly in the most challenging situation. And, as a result, she had placed her job and even her career in jeopardy. Welcome to Patience, CA.

The police officer seated on a folding chair just outside Willie Cardoza's cubicle, looked ridiculously out of place in the bustling unit. If he knew who she was, he hid it well. He glanced at the plastic ID on her clinic coat but could not possibly have read her name as she walked straight past him and into the room.

Willie, eyes closed, was breathing comfortably on his own. Overhead, the monitoring equipment continuously traced out his EKG, blood pressure, central-venous pressure, pulmonary-artery pressure, and blood-oxygen concentration. State of the art. The lights were dim. The whirring, hissing, and gurgling of Willie's oxygen-delivery system and chest-tube suction apparatus droned white noise in concert with the sounds from the other nine rooms. But within the cacophony Abby also heard the alarm on one of Cardoza's IV infusion pumps beeping that the line was obstructed. The nurses were occupied with other patients and might not have heard it. But she wondered if the policeman was unaware of the significance of the sound, or was simply ignoring it.

She followed the IV tubing from the plas-

236

tic bottle through the pump and down to Willie's hand. No kinks. Next she gently straightened his arm out at the elbow. The alarm stopped almost immediately, and the red warning light went out. At the base of the plastic bottle she could see the droplets begin to flow once again. Instead of confronting the nurses with the information that the IV was easily occluded by Cardoza bending his elbow, she wrote it on a note and taped it to the infusion unit. It would be interesting to see if anyone bothered to splint his arm to keep it from bending.

"Everything okay?"

Willie was peering up at her through half-open eyes. He had on an oxygen mask, and there was a tube in his nose that kept his stomach from overfilling with acid. His lips were dry and cracked. There were faint bruises on his forehead. His voice had the raspiness of a patient who had been on artificial ventilation through a breathing tube. Abby moved to the side of the bed where the dim fluorescent light could best shine on her face.

"So far, so good," she said. "How're you doing?"

"Who are you?"

"My name's Dr. Abby Dolan. I'm the emergency doctor who took care of you when you first came in."

"Did I really kill someone like they say?"

"Don't you remember what happened?"

"I remember I was angry and . . . and sick.

237

And my head wouldn't stop hurting."

"That's all you remember?"

"Did I really kill someone?"

Abby could feel his confusion and anguish. She took his hand in hers.

"You hit some people with your car, Mr. Cardoza. Three women. I'm very sorry, but one of them *did* die."

Cardoza's eyes closed.

"Oh, God," he moaned softly.

There were many questions Abby wanted to ask him about the headaches and the months that preceded the violence at the country club. But there would be time later on or in the morning. She plugged the black light into one of the wall sockets over the bed.

"Mr. Cardoza," she said, "I know you're tired, and I know I just gave you some awful news. But if you can help me, I'd like to examine your eyes with this special light. I took a piece of glass out of your eye earlier today, and I'd like to check and see if everything's okay."

For several seconds Cardoza remained as he was, eyes closed. Then, slowly, he opened them. As he did, a tear broke free from the corner of his right eye and glided down along the edge of the oxygen mask.

"Thank you," Abby whispered. "I want to help you, Willie. I really do."

She shined the light in Cardoza's eyes. The glowing golden ring was there in each eye — thin as a pencil lead, but definite.

She examined Cardoza's eyes for half a minute and then allowed them to close. Except in textbooks she had never seen the golden-brown Kayser-Fleischer rings that were diagnostic of copper toxicity. But from what she remembered, the thickness and location were almost identical to these. And didn't poisoning with silver and gold do something to the cornea as well? An hour or two in the library would fill the gaps in her memory. The rings didn't mean anything yet in terms of signifying an underlying problem, but she strongly sensed they were going to. Later tonight or tomorrow she would discuss the bizarre finding with Lew. In the meantime, as long as her nervous energy was keeping her awake and keen, she would see what the record room had to offer.

She pulled up the sheet and adjusted the pillow beneath Willie's head.

"Hang in there," she said.

The record room at PRH, as in many hospitals, was located in the basement. Abby walked down from the ICU, aware of the toll that the stressful day was beginning to take on her mind and body. But there were too many unanswered questions for her to stop now. And, besides, she had little desire to hurry home for yet another night in an empty house.

The record-room door was locked, although light shone through the opaque glass panel. Abby knocked once, then again.

"Just a minute," a woman called out.

Through the glass Abby saw her approaching. The door opened, and before Abby could place the woman, she identified herself.

"Dr. Dolan, hi — I'm Donna Tracy, Bill's daughter. Come in."

"How's your dad?"

"He's home and doing very well, thanks to you. You know that the test for Cushing's disease did come back positive."

"I did know that, yes."

"He's gone to see a specialist at University Hospital in San Francisco. Dr. Fitzgerald. Do you know him?"

"He's the best around."

"That's great to hear."

Bill Tracy, Willie Cardoza — two lives she had been directly responsible for saving. But for one she was criticized for embarrassing another physician, and for the other she was an instant pariah just for succeeding. Tough gig, this place.

"I heard about that woman who got killed today."

"It was pretty bad."

"I don't know how you do it."

"Sometimes I don't know either."

"How can I help you?"

"I'm doing a little research about allergic reactions seen in the ER. Since I'm still a little wound up from all that's happened today, I thought I'd begin to put together some of the data. I don't know how many of the cases I want to review are on Kar-Men, and how many are still in regular files."

Donna Tracy bit at her lower lip.

"Dr. Dolan, I'm not sure you can do that," she said.

"Why? I have a password to get into the retrieval side of KarMen. I just need to know where to find things. I won't be in your way, I promise."

"I may have to clear this with my boss."

Abby glanced at the clock.

"It won't take me long. Maybe an hour or two at the most. I really am glad your dad's doing so well."

"Thank you. Oh, well, I suppose while I'm trying to get in touch with Joanne Ricci, you can get started. I'm sure she'll say it's okay. I do need to check, though."

"Thank you, Donna."

"Do you have the names and hospital numbers? . . . Good. Just give them to me, and I'll check off which ones are in the new system and which ones are still in files. The ER and the OR are the only parts of the hospital completely on KarMen, but they have two people working every day to load in the rest of the medical records. We still have everything on hard copy, and I suspect we will for a long time to come. But KarMen is much easier to use and certainly takes up a lot less space."

"Let's do it. One thing?"

"Yes?"

"Do you have a street map of Patience and the rest of the valley?"

"No, but I imagine security does. Harvey's around someplace. Do you want me to call and check with him?"

"No, no, that's all right."

Harvey. Abby handed over the first half of the Alliance's list, then took the other half and settled in at the nearest dictation carrel.

Patient name, age, sex, address, marital status, date, time, presenting complaint, discharge diagnosis, private physician, treating physician, blood work, X rays. Meticulously, Abby set up her database. As ER residents, she and each of the others in her program had been required to spend three months writing a literature-review article or conducting a retrospective record review. Abby's research, involving the correlation of internal damage with the entry location of gunshot wounds that had no exit holes, had actually been published. At the time, she and the others had groused about the impracticality of forcing action-oriented ER trainees to develop techniques of setting up databases and to relearn the various statistical tests for data analysis. Now she was grateful.

By the time Abby had completed setting up the data grid she would be filling in, Donna Tracy returned with half of her list, along with a stack of records.

"Some of these people have never been inpatients here," Donna said. "The ones on the list marked *K* are in KarMen. You can access them right there with your pass-word. Most are ER records of people who have never been admitted."

It was well after nine by the time Abby began reviewing the charts. The process was more difficult than she had anticipated for several reasons, the first of which was that she was absolutely exhausted. Her concentration was compromised, and she was reduced to logging in the data on each patient without trying to reach any conclu-sions. Another problem was the lack of a clearly defined hypothesis — the postulate that she intended to prove or disprove through her research. Instead, she was taking the scattershot approach of amass-ing as much information as possible in hopes that some similarities or, better still, a pattern, would emerge.

By ten she had completed the review on eight cases. Half were Colstar employees, three of whom had George Oleander as their primary doctor. One from the non-Col-star group had also been a patient of Ole-ander. None of the eight had a final diagnosis that was confirmed by a positive laboratory test, although all of them had been put through impressively detailed workups.

Abby checked the time. Something about

what she was seeing was bothering her, but she was too tired to put her finger on what it might be. Instead, she pulled out one last record. If she didn't quit for the night very soon, she was sure to start missing things. It was then that she noticed that she still had the ultraviolet light in her pocket. The way things were going, Harvey would be waiting outside the hospital to arrest her for grand larceny. The black light drew her thoughts back to the unfinished business of reviewing the record of Willie Cardoza's head injury.

She entered the KarMen retrieval system and typed in JOSHWY, the first of her two passwords. After responding to a series of questions about who she was and why she wanted the record, she logged in her other password, KILKENNY, the county in Ireland where her father had been born. Willie's KarMen record quickly appeared on the screen. It showed precisely what Bartholomew had noted in his workup: an outpatient knee operation and a four-day stay for pneumococcal pneumonia. No head injury.

"Donna," she called out, "sorry to bother you, but do you happen to have the actual chart for Willie Cardoza?"

"The patient who's in the unit?"

"Yes."

"It may have gone up, but I'll check." She disappeared into the record vault for only a minute. "I can't find it. It must be —"

The door to the record room slammed

244

open, and a middle-aged woman strode in, followed closely by Harvey, the guard. She clearly had come directly from some sort of dress-up affair and was wearing an evening pants suit and a great deal of makeup and jewelry.

"Mrs. Ricci!" Donna exclaimed, clearly startled and concerned by the woman's arrival.

"Donna, instead of leaving a message on my machine, you should have had me paged. This situation is an emergency that requires my immediate attention."

Harvey's pig face looked down at Abby. He shook his massive head reprovingly.

"I . . . I'm sorry," Donna stammered. "I didn't think —"

"This was not the time for thinking," Ricci snapped. "It was the time for knowing our policy."

By now Abby had regained her composure. Ignoring the guard, she stood to confront the woman.

"Excuse me, but what is this all about?" she asked.

Joanne Ricci met her gaze with the ease of someone used to being in charge.

"Donna left a message that you were here. Obviously, she saw nothing wrong with allowing you to examine the charts of our patients, but I do. And so does the medical records committee of *your* medical staff. It was just fortunate that I called into my answering machine from the dinner party I was attending."

"All I was doing was checking for patients who might have been having allergic reactions," Abby said.

"Frankly, Dr. Dolan, I have no interest in what you were looking for, only in the rule you" — she shot a withering look at Donna — "*and* you, were breaking. Now, if you'd please set those records on the counter, I'd like you to leave."

Abby wasn't certain, but it seemed to her that the woman's bravado was forced and unnatural, and her response, including bringing along Harvey, was well out of proportion to the offense. Was she as angry and dismayed as she seemed, or was she frightened of something?

"Mrs. Ricci," Abby said, "I still don't understand. Exactly what rule is it that I'm violating?"

"There is an expressed hospital policy against any sort of chart review without written permission from the medical-records committee. It's in the hospital bylaws, which you were supposed to have read when you accepted a position on the staff."

Abby had never heard of a hospital law prohibiting physicians from conducting a chart review without someone's written permission. But, clearly, the records librarian was in no mood for a discussion.

"Well, could you at least tell me who the chairman of the records committee is?"

"Dr. Martin Bartholomew has been in charge for years."

Inwardly, Abby groaned. *Another confrontation with Bartholomew.* Just what she needed. Well, the showdown wasn't going to happen tonight. For the moment she had seen about as much of Patience Regional Hospital as she cared to.

"Sorry," she said to Donna Tracy, who looked pale and shaken.

She picked up her briefcase and turned toward the door. Harvey, arms folded, puffed himself up like a eunuch at a harem-tent doorway, barring her return into the room. Suddenly, Abby turned back.

"Mrs. Ricci," she said, "I just want you to know that Donna did not want me looking at any charts. She tried to explain the rules, and I just pooh-poohed them."

"Well, she should have been more forceful."

"That's not so easy when you're young and working in a hospital, and a physician orders you to do something."

"That may be so. But it remains to be seen whether or not it is an acceptable excuse. I don't know what it is with you ER doctors."

"What do you mean?"

"I've been here for twelve years. The policy regarding chart reviews has been in place all that time, and you're only the second doctor to violate it. But the other one was an emergency doctor, too."

"Who?" Abby asked, trying to seem casual about the question while doing her best to match the woman's glare.

"It was Dr. Brooks," Joanne Ricci said. "David Brooks. I don't know what, if anything, the records committee decided to do to him, but they insisted that I fire the girl who let him stay down here."

Chapter Nineteen

Abby drove the Mazda home and then spent half an hour vacuuming out the glass. She felt tired, bewildered, and angry. It was as if she had done nothing more than buy a ticket to a play and suddenly found herself the protagonist . . . and the villain.

Leaving Patience was occupying more and more of her thoughts. In the morning, she decided, she would call her old boss at St. John's. If he had a position for her, well . . . she would be very tempted to take it. Cadmium poisoning, mental breakdown, or whatever — Josh's strange, threatening note had been very unsettling. She had done her best to get him diagnosed and treated. But from what she could tell, he was more irrational and uncooperative than ever. Where did her responsibility to him end?

Thanks to his last visit, there was no beer in the refrigerator. She settled instead for some iced tea and what remained of a box of vanilla fingers. She took a framed photograph of her and Josh from the counter and set it on the table. They had been hiking up Mt. Tamalpais in Marin County, ten miles northwest of San Francisco. Josh had wedged his Nikon on a tree branch and taken the snapshot using the automatic timer. The resulting inadvertent tilt of the frame had turned a pleasant shot into art. Abby closed her eyes and relived the warmth and even the scents of that perfect autumn day. But the emotions — the incredible feelings of connection, of closeness — were harder to capture.

On an impulse she brought out the regional phone book. Josh had rented from people named Sawicki, Quinn had said. There couldn't be too many of those in the book. Perhaps there had been some developments with the neurologist, she thought. Perhaps Josh was just too embarrassed by his recent behavior to call — or too pigheaded.

She was about to look up the name when her pager went off. The number that appeared on the liquid display was one she didn't recognize. *There are no coincidences*, she thought. She dialed, expecting to hear Josh. But it was Lew Alvarez who answered on the first ring.

"Abby, I'm really glad I caught up with you. Where are you calling from — the hospital?"

"Home. I guess you heard about today."

"I knew there was a multiple-injury accident of some sort when they tried to get me to come in. But when I called later in the day, they said everything was under control. I heard that Gary Wheaton's wife got

250

killed. I feel awful for you about that. I'm just calling to find out exactly what happened and if you're okay."

"What happened depends on who you talk to. And I'm okay, but I've certainly been better."

"Tell me about it."

Abby glanced through the empty dining room into the empty living room. As tired as she was, spending the rest of the evening alone had no appeal. It wasn't sex she was after, but somehow the timing of Lew's call, just when she was about to give in and try to reconnect with Josh, *had* to mean something.

"Are you busy right now?" she suddenly heard herself ask.

"Not really. My shift at the state hospital was only twelve hours, and not a bad twelve hours at that. I was going to do some reading and then call it a night."

"Well, would you like to get together? I have a great deal to tell you about."

Lew's hesitation, although brief, made her uncomfortable. He *had* to be involved with someone. That must be it. And the woman was probably sitting right there.

"The night is very clear," he said, "and the view from the meadow up here is spectacular. If you'd like to come up, I'd be very happy to see you."

Abby set the Tamalpais photo on the table, facedown.

"Is twenty minutes too soon?"

251

"I'm not a bit surprised by all this," Lew said, after Abby had reviewed the events in the ER and her subsequent meeting with Oleander, Henderson, McCabe, and Terry Cox, the attorney. "I doubt anyone who matters in Patience even knew this Willie Cardoza existed before today. And if they did, I doubt they thought much of him. Even before I began making enemies around here by siding with Dave Brooks, I was treated like an outsider. At the time they hired me, they were in pretty desperate need of good help in the ER — desperate enough to overlook my being Hispanic. But I was certainly never invited to belong to the country club."

Abby thought about the country-club feelers she had already received from both Oleander and Lyle Quinn.

"I think you should be proud of that," she said.

They were on a weathered wooden-slatted swing, placed atop a knoll in the meadow beyond Lew's house. The night was intensely clear and just chilly enough to warrant the frayed quilt he had carried up. In less than an hour Abby had counted half a dozen shooting stars. But although Lew was certainly warm toward her, as understanding and supportive as she could wish, he had not responded at all to the romantic setting. He sat well to his side of the swing, absorbed in her story, but hardly lost in her eyes.

"How was Cardoza when you left?" he asked.

"Well, let's see. He'd been charged with murder and was under police guard, plus being cared for by a staff that would have been much happier if he had died. Other than that, I would say he was doing okay."

"There's a prison hospital at Las Rosas. He'll probably be moved there soon — maybe even tomorrow."

"Not *that* soon."

"Don't be surprised if it happens. The hospital there is not that bad. They even have an ICU and a couple of ORs. And the last thing Patience wants is a crazed killer lolling around its hospital's ICU."

"Well, then, there's another big part of the story I think you should know about."

Abby began with the bizarre ocular findings on Willie, followed by the meeting with Colette Simmons in the hospital parking lot.

"So you think these rings in this man's eyes might be a manifestation of cadmium poisoning?" Lew asked, clearly intrigued.

"It's possible."

"Needless to say, I've read a great deal on the subject. Why haven't I ever run into anything like this?"

"I'm not sure anything's been published describing it. The two thoughts I had were, first, that the rings need a black light to be seen, and maybe no one with cadmium poisoning has ever been examined that way before."

"Possibly."

"And, second, maybe the amount of cadmium exposure in Willie's case is exceedingly high. Most of what I've read describes the effects of a low-dose, cumulative exposure over a long period of time. Perhaps the ocular rings come from a one-time, or short-term, high-dose exposure."

"A single spill. An accident of some sort."

"Air or water."

"Abby, we've got to test him, and soon."

"I'd already decided he should have blood sent for a cadmium level at some point, but until you told me about the prison hospital, I didn't think there was any rush."

"There is."

Abby wanted to share everything with him, to tell him about her odd experience with Joanne Ricci in the record room and the visit from Lyle Quinn and subsequent tour of Colstar with Kelly Franklin. But could she do that without firmly committing herself to the Alliance? She was in a very shaky position at PRH. Openly joining the Alliance would almost certainly put her on the unemployment line.

She wasn't certain anymore how she felt about helping Josh get to the bottom of his problem. But losing her job at the hospital would effectively relieve her of the chance to decide, as well as the opportunity to determine whether her efforts on Willie Cardoza had saved the life of a man who should not be held responsible for what he had done. Joining the Alliance now, she reasoned, would cause her more problems than it would solve. Besides, the truth was, the only objective finding they had was the rings in Willie's eyes. Everything else was still speculation.

"Lew, I just don't know about ordering any tests on Willie," she said. "I got into trouble with George this morning for ordering cadmium levels on three of his patients."

"You did that?"

"I . . . I thought there were good indications."

She could tell he was thrilled with the news.

"I knew you were impressed by what you learned at the meeting. I could tell. The tests were done at the hospital?"

"Yes."

"Then I assume they were negative."

"Lew, I need to think about this. Willie is Martin Bartholomew's patient. He and George are like this." She crossed two fingers. "If George finds out I had anything to do with sending off more blood tests for cadmium, I'm finished."

"That's the point, Abby. We don't order any tests."

The excitement blazing in his dark eyes made him that much more appealing to her.

255

"I don't understand," she said.

"We draw the blood ourselves. Right now. You said at the meeting you had a friend who was a toxicologist at St. John's."

"Sandy Stuart. She's the best."

"We just get the blood to her for testing."

"And what if it's positive?"

"We use the result as a lever to pry some cooperation from OSHA and the EPA. They go to wherever Willie Cardoza is and draw the blood themselves for retesting, and just like that, we've got a foothold."

"And what if it's negative?"

"Then I back off, and you don't hear another word from the Alliance. But it's not going to be negative. I know it in my bones. Oh, Abby, we've worked so damn hard for this breakthrough. We need your help right now. We need it so much."

Before Abby even realized what she was doing, she had reached across to him. He took her hands, then gently drew her toward him. His kiss was tentative at first, asking.

I don't know, Lew, her mind cried out. *I don't know what in the hell I'm doing. . . . But, please, don't stop.*

She cupped his face in her hands and brought his lips against hers. His arms tightened around her. His lips parted as the uncertainty in his kiss vanished.

"I've wanted to hold you and kiss you like this since the day we met," he said. "I just . . . didn't know your situation. I didn't want to do anything wrong."

She tucked her legs beneath her and rested her head against his chest. Across the valley a shooting star held on for longer than any of the others.

"The only thing you could do wrong at this moment," she whispered, "is to let go of me."

They arrived at the hospital separately and parked in different lots. He would enter first and go to the ICU through the ER, stopping only to pick up the ophthalmologic black light. His excuse for being in the ICU would be to visit a coronary patient he had admitted the day before. She would enter through the ER five minutes later and immediately cut over to the laboratory. There she would pick up two large blood-collection tubes with anticoagulant and a large syringe.

Abby drove to the hospital listening to Van Morrison and thinking about what it had been like to be kissed and touched for the first time in over two years by a man other than Josh Wyler. Josh's kisses were always an urgent prelude to making love. Lew seemed satisfied just to be close to her — to have her respond to him. His touch was searching and sensual, but also tender and even protective. Had he moved toward making love with her, she probably would have declined. But she sensed that no matter how much he wanted her, he would not say anything until she had made it clear the time was right. For the moment, at least, she felt schoolgirl giddy, on the threshold of learning what this man was all about.

"More stuff for Old Man Ives?"

The twenty-year-old lab tech startled Abby as she was slipping a thirty-cc syringe and three collection tubes into her clinic-coat pocket.

"Oh, hi, Grace. That's right. His leg is improving every day. I appreciate everyone looking the other way when I make my raids. Ives appreciates it, too. How're *you* doing?"

"Okay. I heard about what happened in the ER today, Dr. Dolan. The tech who was on with you said you were absolutely amazing."

"He did?"

"He said he's never seen any ER doctor do all the things you did today, and do them so fast."

"Tell him thanks for saying those things. And thank you for telling me. That's really nice stuff to hear."

If she only knew.

Abby hurried up the stairs to the ICU. The moment she entered the unit, she knew Lew was there and that he had done his part. There was a great deal of commotion in the cubicle farthest from Willie Cardoza. The patient Lew had admitted the previous day was an eighty-year-old man who was extremely hard of hearing and prone to be combative when he was disturbed. He had a long history of recurring chest pain, but no evidence this time of any heart damage. Lew planned to examine the man enough to get him a bit riled, and then to express concern to the nurses that he might be slipping into heart failure. Rather than disturb the covering physician, he would order an EKG, stat blood work, a portable chest X ray, and a portable ultrasound, as well as an immediate weight to see if the man was retaining fluid. Now the old gent was letting the nursing staff know how he felt about the barrage of late-night tests.

Abby smiled warmly at the police officer, who did not seem to care, or even notice, that she was making a return trip to Cardoza's room. She paused by the bedside and studied the monitor screen while she looked through the glass wall at the dozing guard. There was no one else around. She moved quickly to the other side of the bed, her back to the guard so that her movements were shielded. Willie's monitor tracings were strong and steady. He was most definitely a save.

Abby's target now was the arterial line she had placed in the radial artery at the underside of Willie's right wrist. She had inserted a three-way stopcock valve in the line. One arm of the valve connected with the IV catheter and another with the monitor screen through an electrical transducer.

The third made it possible to draw blood with no further needle sticks. She slipped the large syringe from her clinic coat and attached it to the empty arm of the valve. The movement roused Willie, who looked up at her sleepily.

"Hey, Doc," he said, his voice still a raspy whisper.

"I'm just drawing a little blood, Willie."

"Go right ahead." He peered up at her. "Say, weren't you at that picnic at Colstar Park? Didn't I see you there?"

"Yes. I saw you there, too," she replied as she worked. "That was a very brave and kind thing you did for that woman."

Abby switched the flow of the three-way from vessel-to-transducer to vessel-to-syringe. A gentle pull, and the syringe instantly filled with bright-scarlet arterial blood. She then switched the valve back to its original setting.

"It was nothing," Willie said. "Angela has a lot of problems."

So do you, Abby thought.

Working as rapidly as she could, she attached a large needle onto the syringe and stuck it through the rubber stopper of the collection tubes. The vacuum in the tubes quickly drew the blood from the syringe. She had drawn up enough to fill two tubes completely and half of the third. Next she carefully capped the needle on the syringe, then slipped it and the three tubes back into her clinic coat.

"I see you've reconnected with our friend Willie."

The words, spoken loudly from behind her, stopped her heart. She whirled. Her knees, now Jell-O, nearly buckled.

"Mr. Quinn. Making rounds?"

She barely got the words out. *How long had he been there? What had he seen? What did he think she was doing?* Her mind was racing. She brushed her hand against her clinic-coat pocket. The tubes of freshly drawn blood were concealed, but the top of the syringe was protruding an inch or so. Quinn's bland smile was chilling.

"I was about to ask you the same question," he said. "I thought you went off duty a few hours ago."

"I . . . I was in the library. As you probably know, Mr. Cardoza and I spent a good bit of time together earlier today. I just wanted to see how he was before I went home."

Quinn knew. She could see it in his face. He knew what she had been doing, and he was just trying to come up with the most effective response. In all likelihood she was cooked — finished at PRH. She felt as if her face were the color of the blood in her pocket.

"Ah, yes, today," Quinn said. "I heard you performed quite admirably."

"Admirably enough to be reviled by everyone from the medical chief to the janitor." Abby turned to Willie, took his hand, and bent over him. "Willie, you take care, now.

261

I'll see you tomorrow."

"You take care of that blood, Doc," he replied.

She straightened up quickly and spun toward Quinn, uncertain whether Willie had whispered or shouted the words. But the Colstar security chief was standing with his back to her now, talking with the guard. She adjusted her clinic coat and its contents as best she could and left the room.

"So," she said to Quinn, "what brings *you* here?"

"Willie's Colstar. And what concerns Colstar concerns me."

Abby felt she could have recited the words in unison with him.

"He's doing well."

"I'd like to say I'm glad to hear that."

His flint eyes were the coldest Abby had ever confronted.

"Yes . . . well," she said, "he *is* under arrest. I'm sure he'll be punished for what he did."

"Peggy Wheaton was a very special person and a very good friend of mine."

Again Abby almost filled in the words. She was once more being criticized for saving Cardoza. But typical of Quinn, the chastisement was oblique. There was still a remote chance he hadn't seen her draw Willie's blood, but she doubted it. He was more likely just allowing her to make clear what she intended to do with it. Either way, all she wanted now was to leave. The commotion at the far end of the unit was calming down now. She caught Lew's eye for the briefest moment and cut her gaze quickly toward Quinn.

Stay away. Don't try to examine Willie's eyes.

Lew said something to one of the nurses and left by walking around the nurses' station. But Abby knew Quinn was far too observant to have missed that he was there.

"Well," she said, "I guess I'll be going."

"Neither you nor Dr. Alvarez is on duty, yet both of you are here. Is that a coincidence?"

Abby glanced over at where Lew had been while she concocted a response.

"We both had admitted patients to the unit. So here we are."

It was a lame explanation, but if Quinn had seen her drawing Cardoza's blood, it really didn't matter.

"Yes," Quinn said. "Here you are." He checked to ensure they were out of earshot of the policeman. "So I haven't heard from you since your tour of Colstar. My offer is still on the table, but I can't promise it will be there much longer. As you said, there are a number of people who are quite upset over some of the decisions you made today."

"I'm sorry about that. I did what I strongly believed was right."

"I'm sure you did. . . . Well, it's Sunday night. Suppose we decide that if I haven't heard from you by, say, Tuesday at noon,

I may conclude that you have no desire to serve as one of our consultants."

"I'm thinking it over."

"I hope you're also considering carefully what Dr. Oleander told you about independently sending off blood for cadmium testing."

He seemed to be looking directly at her clinic-coat pocket.

"I'm considering that, too."

"Do that." There was clear menace in his voice now. "And, by the way, would you happen to know why Mr. Wyler has been absent from work for the past few days? People have tried calling him at the house he's rented, but the phone's out of order."

"I haven't heard from Josh for a week," she lied. "If I do, I'll tell him you're looking for him. Good night, Mr. Quinn."

She started to walk away.

"Dr. Dolan," he called after her.

She turned back to face him.

"Yes?"

"Dr. Dolan, I just want to be certain you know how thin the thread is that's holding you up at this hospital. Please don't give us cause to cut it."

Chapter Twenty

The Patience Auto Glass people must be at the remote end of the town's grapevine, Abby thought. She was ecstatic when, just an hour after her call, the purple-and-yellow truck pulled up her drive. She had expected that services of all kinds would be harder and harder for her to come by as versions of the Wheaton/Cardoza story spread across the valley.

It was a gray, drizzly morning, hardly the weather she wanted for the spectacular drive through the mountains to Sacramento, then down to San Francisco. But she would take it. The tubes containing Willie Cardoza's blood were carefully wrapped in cloth and bubble plastic, and packed in the sort of cooler used to transport human hearts. Sandy Stuart was expecting her by early afternoon. The cadmium assay would take a day or so to complete, although in an absolute emergency it could be done faster. Abby had assured her friend that there was no reason for such measures. Now, as the glass man worked on in the light rain, she stood by the back door, fidgeting and mentally reviewing the route she would take. Planning a drive from Patience to anyplace was never simple.

"You just can't get here from there," was the way Josh had started his directions the first time she was preparing to drive up from the city to see him. "You can go north then east, or west then north then east, or just meander diagonally up the valley."

Today, she decided, she would start by taking the narrow state highway west, away from town. The serpentine two-lane road was one of her favorites, rising and falling through dense primeval forest. The air there, even on a day such as this, would be sweet with evergreen and natural mulch, and so oxygen rich that just standing still and breathing would be a rush. After twenty or so miles she would cut south on another two-lane state road, winding through the foothills of the Sierras to I-80. From there, it was an eight-lane shot through Sacramento to the bay.

The glass man was nearly through the job when Lew called.

"I'm at work at the state hospital," he said. "I thought you might be gone by now."

"Any minute."

"Any problem getting the auto-glass people to come?"

"None. I guess the owner's one of the few people in Patience who isn't a dear friend of Gary and Peggy Wheaton."

"As if you didn't feel lousy enough about her death, you have to live with hearing that over and over."

"Exactly. . . . Lew, I had a terrific time

266

with you last night."

"Thanks. So did I." His voice trailed off.

Though he didn't say the words, Abby knew how he felt. And she knew that she was close, very close, to feeling the same way. After leaving the hospital last night, as planned, Lew had waited for her on a little-traveled side street. She parked behind his Blazer and then slid onto the seat next to him. Her pulse was still hammering from her confrontation with Lyle Quinn in the ICU. Breathlessly, she recounted the scene.

"So, what do you think?" Lew asked when she had finished. "Did he see you take the blood or not?"

"I don't know. It seemed that he did. But he never really said anything. God, but I dislike that man."

"Are you going to be all right tonight?"

"I . . . I'll be fine."

"I have to be at the state hospital at seven in the morning, but if —"

"No, no. I'm fine. Really."

"Well, if you need me for *any* reason, just call me at Caledonia. On second thought, the switchboard there is totally incompetent. Better use my pager. You have the number, don't you?"

"I do. . . . Lew?"

"Yes?"

"I probably don't have to say this, but I just want to be sure you understand why I'm taking this chance. I want to get to the bottom of what's wrong with Willie, and I'm very worried about Josh. But I'm still no crusader."

"Abby, I know that. Probably more than you realize. I told you before and I still mean it: no one's going to pressure you about the Alliance, especially not me."

They kissed once, then again. He brushed her forehead with his lips, then her eyelids, her ear, and finally her lips once more. His mouth drew her in. His breath and the sound of his breathing were foreign to her, but incredibly comfortable. His hand touched her breast, lingering just long enough for her to know how badly he wanted her. She held him tightly and stroked the inside of his thigh.

"Soon," was all she had been able to say. . . .

Abby looked out the kitchen window. The glass man was packing his gear and assembling the insurance forms for her to sign.

"Listen, Lew, this is it," she said. "He's done, and I'm off to see the wizard."

"Just be careful, Abby. I don't trust Quinn any further than I can throw him. I was a little worried after you went home alone last night. In fact, I wasn't going to tell you this, but I drove past your place a few times during the night."

"What a waste."

"What?"

"Nothing. That was a very sweet thing for you to do, especially with an early shift staring you in the face."

"Just be careful," Lew said again. "And call me when you get home tomorrow."

Abby hung up and checked the house one final time. Then she signed the glass man's papers, tossed her overnight bag onto the backseat, placed the cooler with the blood samples on the floor, and headed off. The drizzle was just heavy enough for intermittent wipers, but the Mazda had a sure grip in almost any weather. She flipped through her case of tapes and whittled her choices down to Tracy Chapman and Mary-Chapin Carpenter. The grayness of the morning gave it to Tracy.

Traffic was virtually nonexistent. Abby opened the sunroof a crack and accelerated to fifty, the fastest the winding road would comfortably allow. She worked her head from side to side, front to back. Gradually, the tension in her neck and shoulders began to subside. Even though it was just an overnight trip, she felt a sense of freedom. It had been a hellish month and a half since she had last been home. *Home.* She wondered how long she would have to live in Patience before she stopped thinking of San Francisco that way. Forever might be a good guess.

A McDonald's tractor trailer roared by, no doubt headed for the glittering new addition to the chain at Five Corners. On either side of the road the forest deepened. Abby opened the sunroof another inch. Sweet, moist mountain air filled the car.

Everything is going to be all right, she told herself. Quite possibly, the answers for Willie Cardoza and Josh were as close as the cooler right behind her. And then, once that business was over, she could turn her attention to finding the answers for Abby Dolan.

She was reaching down to punch the repeat button for an encore of Chapman's "Fast Car," when the Mazda was hit from behind. Though the jolt itself was minor, the surprise was anything but. Abby shot upright, confused and frightened. Had she hit an animal or run over something? A second jolt, this time with a crunch of metal against metal, brought everything quickly into focus. She checked the rearview mirror and then risked a glance over her shoulder. A large battered red pickup with a black steel frame in front was no more than a few feet behind her. It had oversize tires that raised its cab a foot or two above the Mazda.

Abby's hands whitened on the wheel, and, instinctively, she jammed down the accelerator. The rain-slicked roadway flashed beneath her wheels, rising and falling like an amusement-park ride, twisting from right to left with no predictable pattern. The truck sped up once more. Abby glanced in the mirror just as it hit her again. The jolt was harder than the others, though she still had no trouble maintaining control.

The unbroken double yellow line was

snaking under the driver's side whenever she chanced looking behind her. She was constantly whipping the wheel to the right to correct. Suddenly, just as she was drifting again, a massive tractor trailer shot up from a deep swale, barreling past just a foot or so from her. The roar was deafening. The vacuum it created nearly tore the Mazda from the road. Abby screamed out loud as she wrenched the wheel to the right. The pickup, which had backed off a bit, began to close in once more. Was she unlucky enough to have happened into the path of a madman? Or was she specifically the target? Through her rearview mirror she caught a glimpse of the driver. At first it appeared as if a demon of some sort were behind the wheel of the pickup. Then it registered. The driver was wearing a ski mask. This was no chance encounter. It had to be Quinn or someone who worked for him.

Determined to avoid being hit again, Abby accelerated. She was nearing seventy. It was only a matter of time before she failed to handle a curve or simply skidded into the trees. Her hands and arms were shaking on the wheel. Her mind, though, was responding reflexively, in the way it had been programmed to react over twelve years of medical crises. Her thoughts were becoming clearer, more focused. The movement around her, as it had done so many times in the ER, was actually beginning to slow down.

The truck crept up on her again, closer and closer still. There was no way she could chance going any faster. Any substantial bump was bound to send her spinning out of control. But the nudge this time was much less than that — a tap, perhaps a reminder that she was at the madman's mercy. Her speedometer hit seventy. The truck pulled out to the left, intending, it seemed, to force her off the road to the right. Just as quickly it swung back as a convertible flashed past, its horn blaring.

The road turned sharply to the right, then dipped. For a moment the pickup dropped out of sight. Abby wondered why Quinn, or whoever it was, hadn't just bashed her from behind until she lost control. One explanation, a lame one, was that he wanted to frighten her without actually killing her. More likely, though, he was toying with her. *Toying.* Vintage Quinn.

With the driver allowing some daylight between them, Abby hoped he was simply giving up on her. But she knew that possibility was unlikely. She had to take action. There were no gas stations, houses, or restaurants along this stretch that she could remember, and there was no sense in trying to attract the attention of someone speeding the other way. Her choices were either to stop and run, or to find some way off the road.

The roller coaster was going uphill in

stages now — a rise, a small dip, another rise. The Mazda actually left the road at the top, slamming down hard enough to grind the chassis into the pavement. Abby's teeth snapped together, biting the inside of her cheek. She tasted her own blood and imagined it all ending right there with a ruptured gas tank and a fireball explosion. But after the vicious bounce the Mazda sped on.

Suddenly, as Abby crested another hill, a car emerged from the woods beyond the right-hand soft shoulder not that far ahead. It hesitated for a fraction of a second, then sped across both lanes and vanished into the trees to the left. A crossroad of some sort! It had to be. She glanced in the rearview. The pickup was still some distance back but seemed to be gaining again. She might be able to make the turnoff before it crested the hill. No time to process. No time to reason. *Just act.*

Holding her speed, Abby pulled off the road, skimming along the gravel shoulder just a few feet from the trees. She waited as long as she dared, then slammed on the brakes and swung the wheel sharply to the right. The antilock system stammered like a machine gun as the car skidded into what was nearly a perfect right-angle turn. Almost before she realized she had done it, she was jouncing mercilessly down a narrow dirt two-track logging road. She tried glancing behind her, but the turns were too treacherous. All she could do was barrel ahead and hope for the best. She was going forty now, but given the circumstances, that speed was nearly suicidal. She had to slow down. As she rounded a sharp curve, the dirt road forked. For no reason other than her right-handedness, she swung the wheel that way. The parallel tracks dropped quite steeply and looked for a moment as if they were going to end altogether. Branches whipped wildly at the windshield and scratched along the doors. The car lurched on, scraping rock as it bumped through a dry streambed, then shot upward on the other side.

How long had it been since she'd left the highway — a minute? Five? Maybe thirty seconds. Reluctant to slow down, Abby continued to lean on the accelerator as hard as she dared. Her arms were aching horribly. Her hands felt welded to the wheel. Spewing dust and gravel, the Mazda bottomed out again and again. She tore up an embankment and once more became airborne. This time, though, the car slammed down on pavement. It was another road, even narrower than the two-laner she had been on, but fairly well maintained. She jerked the wheel hard to the left and skidded to a stop, shaking as if she had been dunked in icy water. The road was utterly deserted. With some effort she flicked off Tracy Chapman and opened the door. The silence was consuming. She turned her ear toward the dirt road she had left, straining to hear the truck's engine. Nothing. Still wary, she forced herself to stand on rubbery legs and opened the cooler, which was upside down, wedged between the rear and front seat. The tubes were intact.

"Thank God for bubble wrap," she whispered.

She breathed the oxygen-rich air. Gradually, her pulse rate slowed toward normal. Her trembling ceased. But her thoughts continued to race. Lyle Quinn, or someone sent by him, had just tried to kill her.

Or had they?

The truck, with its mammoth tires, was certainly capable of stopping, turning around, and catching her in the woods. Perhaps her pursuer had missed seeing her turn off the highway. Perhaps something mechanical had gone wrong with the truck. One thing was clear. Quinn knew of her cargo. He had to know. She patted the Mazda's roof, then slid back behind the wheel. Perhaps the Colstar security chief had just meant to send a message that would frighten her back to the city for good. If that was the case, he had misjudged her. The harder he pushed, the more committed she would become to seeing things through. It had always been that way for her, and it would be that way this time as well.

Abby turned the key. The engine hummed to life as if nothing had happened. The light rain had stopped, and the smallest opening had appeared in the clouds. She took one final deep breath to purge the last of the shakes and drove toward what seemed to be east. The trip to San Francisco was going to take a little longer than she had intended. But, dammit, she was going to make it there . . . *and back.*

Lyle Quinn had just seen to it.

Chapter Twenty-One

It was late afternoon when Abby arrived at Sandra Stuart's office in the pathology building at St. John's. The toxicologist whose lab was going to assay Willie Cardoza's blood for cadmium left a message that she was delivering a lecture and would meet Abby in the hospital library at five-thirty. Meanwhile, the librarian would have a bibliography and articles waiting for her to begin reviewing.

After emerging from the narrow logging road, it had taken Abby nearly half an hour to locate a gas station and get pointed toward San Francisco. She had given some thought to reporting the attack to the state police but quickly discarded the notion. What could possibly come of it? They'd never find the truck, and she certainly didn't need the police to explain what had happened to her, and why.

She was ensconced behind a fortress of bound journals when Sandy arrived at the library. To many the toxicologist seemed taciturn and introspective, but Abby had always found her to be droll, compassionate, and a terrific listener. And before a class she transformed into an animated, invariably fascinating teacher. A meticulous academician, Sandy was a few years older than Abby and was the mother of two young boys. Her husband, who was a pathologist at another hospital, had always seemed to Abby to be married more to his work than to his wife. But she had never once heard her friend complain about the man.

"Sorry I'm late," Sandy said. "This was my exotic-poisons lecture, and I can always count on an endless stream of questions at the end regarding everyone from Socrates to Napoleon to Howard Hughes."

"I just appreciate your being here for me."

"Nonsense. It's great to see you. After we finish here, Fred's going to watch the kids so we can go out for dinner and catch up. Ristorante Milano okay?"

"Only perfect. As I recall, you were the one who first brought me there. Now I obsess about the place every time I'm forced to patronize the Leaning Tower of Pizza in Patience."

"No wonder. Well, let's do our best here. Then tomorrow I'll get the lab geared up for your assay. I'll be teaching most of the day, so it will be late afternoon, or more likely sometime the day after tomorrow, before I have results for you."

"Listen, I'm relieved you can do this at all."

"I'll confess we don't get much call for cadmium assays these days, but I'm sure we can handle it. You said Josh might be involved in some way?"

Abby described the frightening changes in Josh that spanned nearly six months and seemed to be accelerating. Sandy listened intently, occasionally making a note on whatever paper was handy, studying it for a moment, then sliding it aside. When Abby had finished, Sandy sighed and reached across to pat her on the arm.

"I'm really sorry, Abby," she said. "I was so happy when you and Josh found one another."

"So was I."

"But I will admit that I always thought he kept his emotions somewhat pent up, especially when he was having such trouble finding work and constantly maintaining such an upbeat front. Still, I just can't imagine his behaving the way you describe unless he's sick from something, either a toxin or maybe a tumor of some sort."

Abby sighed. "I wish I could get him tested for cadmium, but there's no chance that's going to happen, not with the way things are now."

"Well, I don't consider myself exceptionally well versed on the nuances of cadmium toxicity, but I hope that by the time we finish plowing through that bibliography you sent me and the additional articles I've located, we both will be."

They stayed in the hospital library for three more hours, poring over journals and textbooks, searching especially for some reference to fluorescent ophthalmic rings and psychotic violence in cadmium-toxic patients. There were a number of allusions to acute mental illness, especially in workers who had ingested or inhaled massive amounts of the metal. And there was one particularly intriguing — and terrifying — article from Poland, reporting on a baker who had been a pillar of his community and had suddenly, viciously, stabbed his wife and two children to death. The baker's health had rapidly deteriorated, and one of the many blood tests performed on him disclosed high levels of cadmium. The source turned out to be a cadmium-contaminated gold dental implant. Removal of the prosthesis, and subsequent chelation therapy, resulted in negative blood levels and complete reversal of his symptoms.

A cure, Abby thought. *But, unfortunately, just a little late for his wife and children.*

There were no references to the specific eye findings Abby had discovered in Willie Cardoza, but as she suspected, it appeared that no researcher had ever had reason to examine such patients with a black light.

Finally Sandy closed the last of the latest pile of journals, set her glasses down, and rubbed at her eyes.

"Well, Abby, I don't know about you, but for the last ten minutes every other word I've read looks like either Ristorante or Milano."

"I'm ready."

"Well, I promise you some results on your Mr. Cardoza by the day after tomorrow at the latest. My lab will gear up and run the blood, and we'll also send it off to a commercial lab for confirmation of whatever we find."

"That would be great."

"But, tell me, what will you do if the findings are negative?"

The question took Abby by surprise. Swept along by Lew's enthusiasm, she had never really considered the possibility.

She thought for a moment, then said, "If the test is negative, I think I'll be coming home. Hopefully, some hospital around here will have an opening for me in their ER. If not, maybe I'll end up as a Doc-in-the-Box at some mall. Worse things could happen."

"I can't think of too much worse than having *you* drop out of emergency medicine."

What will you do if the findings are negative?

Sandy Stuart's question turned over and over in Abby's mind as she drove back to Patience. The more she thought about it, the more convinced she became that Willie Cardoza was toxic. After spending the night at Sandy's she had put in another two hours in the library before heading north. She steered clear of the mountain roads and took the interstates as far as she could.

The route wasn't nearly as scenic, but memories of her harrowing trip down would have made it hard to relax and keep her eyes off the rearview mirror.

The one issue still nagging at her was the simple fact that she was still alive. If Quinn was responsible for David Brooks's death, why hadn't he just followed through with another "accident"? Perhaps he and Colstar had secrets that he feared weren't buried deeply enough. Two accidental deaths among the emergency staff at the hospital were bound to prompt an investigation, especially with the Alliance around to call the question.

Abby drove into Patience from the west, along the same state road she had taken out of town the previous morning. The rain was gone, but a heavy blanket of clouds still covered the valley. In twenty-four hours she would have the answer from Sandy Stuart. For Willie's sake she hoped the test would be positive. Nothing would bring Peggy Wheaton back to life. But convicting a man of murder who was chemically insane would add no dignity or meaning to her death. That dignity would be achieved only by punishing those who had created her killer with their toxin.

On an impulse Abby cut off at Five Corners and headed north. Lew's farm was just a couple of miles away, and rather than drive all the way home just to call him, she could do it from a pay phone. She could

282

hear the relief in his voice.

"So, what's the verdict?" he asked excitedly. "Cardoza's blood has got to be positive, yes?"

"It's not done yet, Lew. Sandy's lab is just getting geared up. The blood'll be run late today or tomorrow. She wasn't sure which."

"But she's going to call as soon as she has some numbers?"

"The moment. . . . Lew, some things have happened on this trip that I want to talk to you about."

"Such as?"

"Such as someone in a big red pickup truck nearly running me off the road yesterday. I think Lyle Quinn or one of his Colstar goons may have been trying to kill me."

"But you're all right?"

"Barely."

"Thank God. After what happened to David, we shouldn't be surprised by anything that monster does. I was fearful from the moment you told me Quinn might have seen you draw Cardoza's blood. You're really okay, though?"

"Yes, yes, I'm fine. Lew, if you're free right now, I'd rather tell you about all this in person. I'm just past Five Corners."

"In that case the cows can wait."

"Want me to bring lunch? There're some golden arches right across the street."

"I might not be able to do better, but I'd like to try. Let's see. . . . Do you have any problem with shrimp or artichoke hearts?"

"I suppose the Big Mac I was planning on can wait," Abby said.

"I like to cook," Lew said as he set their lunch on the maple kitchen table.

"You also like to understate. This looks wonderful."

Abby had already finished a detailed account of her close call on the highway, and her evening with Sandy Stuart. Now, over strawberry soup, a shrimp-and-artichoke salad, and sourdough bread, she told him for the first time about the visit from Lyle Quinn following the Alliance meeting, and about her tour of Colstar with Kelly Franklin.

"They know we're getting close, Abby. That's why they're trying to woo you away. The more minds and hands we have working on this thing, the more likely it is we're going to figure out what they've done, and what they're doing now to cover it up. These people are vermin."

"I agree with you on Lyle Quinn, but I have to say that I liked Kelly Franklin."

"She's Quinn's stooge in this. Mark my words."

"Maybe. But if she's covering something up, I'm here to tell you she's a heck of an actress."

"They're all fakes. They've hurt people, lots of people, and they'll go to any lengths to avoid the blame. Colstar is an Ezra Black company, and everyone knows that man is a scorpion. The bottom line for anything he owns *is* the bottom line."

"Maybe," Abby said again.

"There will be no doubt in your mind when we get the results from your friend at St. John's, especially if we can make some headway with our analysis of the rest of the NIWWs."

He laughed at the initials, which he had embraced as if they were an actual medical diagnosis.

"Speaking of NIWWs, Lew, I'm beginning to wonder if Josh could be following Willie Cardoza's pattern. I'm very concerned about him, and I don't know who else to turn to. I hope you don't feel awkward talking about it."

Lew filled their cups with dark, aromatic coffee and settled back down in the chair across from her.

"Abby, I'd be a fool *and* a liar if I said I wanted things to work out between the two of you. But I certainly don't want anything bad to happen to him. What's going on?"

"I mentioned to you that some of Josh's symptoms resembled what Colette Simmons told me Willie was like."

"Yes. I was impressed with the similarities."

"Then there was the article I told you about. The one from Poland about the guy who stabbed his wife and kids to death."

"Cadmium contamination in the gold dental implant."

"Exactly. Well, Josh has been getting more and more irrational and more and more physically violent. He actually moved out because he was afraid he might hurt me. Now he seems to have disappeared. Quinn said he was missing from work and that no one had been able to reach him at home. Last night I tried calling him myself at the place he's living. The phone didn't even ring. I'm very worried, and I really don't know what to do."

Lew thought for a moment, then handed her the phone and the Patience Valley directory.

"Here. Try him where he's staying again."

"Thank you, Lew." Abby looked up the number and spoke as she dialed. "Orchard Road. Do you know where that is?"

"I do. It's not too far from that McDonald's you called me from."

"No ring at all," she said. She looked up Colstar's main number and called it. "Kelly Franklin's office, please."

"Into the lair of the enemy," Lew whispered.

"Kelly, it's Abby Dolan."

"Abby, it's nice to hear from you. What's happened with Josh?"

"Actually, that's what I was calling *you* about. Have you heard from him?"

"He hasn't been at work for several days. No one seems to know why. Today there was some talk about his being replaced if he doesn't show up or call in by tomorrow. He has several partially completed projects."

"Lord."

"Is there anything I can do to help you find him?"

"Just call me if he shows up or you hear anything. You have my number, don't you?"

"Yes. Abby, I heard what happened at the hospital the other day. It must have been awful for you, having to make a choice like that."

"It was, Kelly. Thank you for appreciating that. I haven't forgotten that I owe you a call and dinner when all of this business calms down."

"Don't worry about it. Just find Josh."

Abby set the receiver down, certain that Kelly Franklin's concern for Josh and for her was genuine. Lew was too invested in getting to the bottom of the Colstar syndrome to think otherwise. But this time he was wrong.

"Lew, I need to drive out to Orchard Road," she said suddenly. "Could you tell me exactly where it is?"

"I can do better than that," he replied, slipping into a tan windbreaker. "Let's go."

They left The Meadows and headed back toward Five Corners.

"Lew, tell me something," Abby said. "Assuming Willie's blood is positive for cadmium, what do we do then? Whom do we go to? The police? Joe Henderson at the hospital? State authorities? Federal?"

"How about all of the above?"

"Seriously."

"Well, let's start by remembering that, for all intents, Colstar owns the town, including, and maybe especially, the hospital. That eliminates Henderson, the locals, and even the state police. A good lawyer might get Willie off if we can prove he's been poisoned, but our goal is to shut the plant down right now, and to keep it closed until it comes clean and makes retribution. As far as I'm concerned, that leaves us back at OSHA and the EPA. Either of them could intervene if we could show conclusive proof that Colstar has acted irresponsibly, or has information on an environmental exposure — air or water — that they've held back."

"But you told me that both OSHA and the EPA have already sent teams in to investigate."

"Exactly. And there's not much chance they'd come back again, either, unless we present them with positive blood work and some sort of incontrovertible pattern pointing to the big concrete house on Colstar cliff. That's why we need more in-depth record study like what you were doing the other night. Age, sex, water supply, street location, driving route to work, medications, recreational habits — I don't know what it is, but I firmly believe the explanation is to be found somewhere in those records, or maybe in a combination of the records and a questionnaire to the NIWWs. We've just got to accumulate more data."

"It's just not possible, Lew. Joanne Ricci's got a lock on the system. I can't retrieve records anymore without going through the record-room person on duty. That woman is hard."

"Dave Brooks and I used to call her the Dragon Lady. Did you know she fired that poor girl who helped you out the other night?"

"Donna Tracy?"

"Yes. I called Len McCabe in the ER this morning to check on changing some shifts. He warned me against conducting any more unauthorized chart reviews and told me about the Tracy girl. The hospital is starting to resemble a stalag."

"I can't believe Donna lost her job because of me. That's horrible. She has little kids. After we check on Josh, I'm going to call her."

"Maybe she can come up with some way for you to crack back into the system."

"Lew, I would never ask her to do that."

"Why not? What does she have to lose — her job? I'm telling you, Abby, this is war. And until you came, we didn't have a hell of a lot of ammunition."

For the first time since she had begun to know Lew Alvarez as a person, Abby felt a spark of irritation at the man.

"I'm not here to join anyone's army, Lew,"

she said. "I keep telling you that. I just want to help the patient I'm being blamed for saving, and the man who, until just a month or so ago, was the most important person in my life."

"What about all those NIWWs? I suppose you don't give a damn about them."

"Okay, okay. I care about them, too. Lew, just don't push me. When people push me, all I ever seem to end up doing is pushing back. And I don't want that to happen between us."

"Understood. I'm sorry. I'll try to keep my feelings to myself."

Orchard Road was part of a middle-class housing development with no trees older than five years or so, and remarkably featureless rows of houses. The Sawicki place, number seventeen, was a modest ranch, white with maroon shutters, set on a typically small lot. The lawn was brown beyond reclamation, and the low shrubbery abutting the house was badly in need of attention. It saddened Abby to think of Josh living in such a place, even temporarily. She flashed on how excited he'd been, reporting that the house he'd found for them to rent was on a secluded dead-end street, backed up to the pine forest, and full of character.

The driveway, leading to a carport with a corrugated aluminum roof, was empty. They parked in the drive and rang the front doorbell. Nothing. Abby stepped behind the shrubs and peeked in the living-room window. What she could see of the room was a shambles, with newspapers and crumpled computer printouts everywhere. In addition, there were half-empty cartons of take-out food, beer bottles and soda cans, and an array of opened chip and pretzel bags.

"Let's go around back," she said in a half whisper.

She followed Lew around to the backyard with a sinking feeling in her chest. The side door, under the carport, was locked. The backyard, like the one in front, was barren and brown. A few weeds and low-lying vines had begun to encroach. Abby kicked at an empty tin can, one of several lying about. The shades were drawn on all the windows. She tried peering beneath but could see little. Then she tried the steel storm hatch leading to the basement. The heavy door swung open. Down a short flight of stairs, she found the basement door open as well.

"Lew, quick, down here," she called out.

"I'm not so sure this is a good idea," he replied, pulling the hatch closed behind him, then ducking to fit under the low door frame.

The basement was cluttered with tools and yard implements, plus a typical array of boxes and old furniture. They walked upstairs and cautiously entered the first floor near the kitchen. That room, like all the others, was untended and littered with trash. The sheets were torn off the beds. Josh's clothes were strewn about. The phones were unplugged or else torn from the wall. Abby moved apprehensively from room to room, peering behind the sofa and beds, dreading that at any moment she would see Josh's body. The smell from rancid food permeated the house.

Josh's computer and printer were set up on a Formica table at one corner of the living room. The floor around it was strewn with balled sheets of paper. Abby smoothed one out. It was a rambling, disjointed letter to the governor, decrying those industrial barons throughout the state who had forced their former employees into home-lessness and depravity. A second page, similar in tone and composition, was a fragment of a letter addressed to the Presi-dent. Abby was reaching for a third sheet when Lew called to her from the bathroom.

"Abby, come on in here."

She dropped the paper and hurried down the hallway, fearing the worst.

But there was no body. Instead, there was a message, crudely printed in reddish brown on the mirror.

VENGEANCE IS MINE
I WILL REPAY

"That's from the Bible," Lew said. "I can't say precisely where."

Abby moved forward and peered closely at the letters.

"Lew," she said, "this is dried blood."

292

Chapter Twenty-Two

The Patience Police Department was housed downtown in an elegant new building of cedar, redwood, and glass. The array of communication dishes and antennae on the roof suggested that, like the regional hospital, the station was state of the art. And to Abby that suggested Colstar.

She had driven alone to the station from Lew's farm to report Josh's disappearance and the frightening findings at the Sawicki place. The sergeant taking her report was a thick-necked moose of a man whose name tag identified him as Sullivan. His manner stopped just short of open contempt.

"I'd like to be of assistance to you, Miss Dolan, I really would," Sullivan said in an unabashedly patronizing tone. "But, frankly, I don't know what we can do about this situation."

Abby began to simmer.

"The first thing you can do is call me *Dr.* Dolan. And the next is to let me speak to your captain."

Sullivan reddened.

"Captain Gould is out, *Doctor* Dolan. He won't be back until later this afternoon. But I know he'd tell you the same thing. If the Sawickis file vandalism charges against this Wyler character, then we can get a warrant and put out a bulletin on him. But, otherwise, as far as we know at this point, the only crime that's been committed is unlawful entry — by you."

Just pray that you never get injured while I'm on duty, Abby wanted to say. But she knew such a threat would only cause her more trouble. Besides, there was no way she would ever treat Sergeant Sullivan differently from any other patient . . . except, perhaps, to order a rectal temp.

Smiling inwardly at the notion, she signed the report and headed home. She was anxious to call Josh's parents and a few of his friends to alert them to what was happening. The trick would be to do so without alarming them too much. But, then again, why shouldn't they be alarmed? She certainly was.

Before she began making *those* calls, however, there was one that was even more important to her — Donna Tracy. The young record-room attendant had become a victim of Abby's search for answers. An apology wouldn't replace the woman's job, but for today it would have to do.

Donna was furious at her boss, Joanne Ricci, but not at all angry with Abby.

"First of all, you saved Dad's life," she said. "You'd have to do something pretty horrible to offset that. But, second, as far as I was concerned, all we were trying to do was get some information on patients who were ill. That's what I don't under-stand. I don't think you deserved to be spoken to the way Joanne did the other night, and I told her so. *That's* why she fired me. Not for helping you, but for saying she was wrong, and for telling her that if you asked to check over some records again, I'd help you again."

Suddenly Abby found herself debating whether or not to request just that. Lew or no Lew, there was still part of her that wanted to keep some distance between her-self and the Alliance. But there was a much larger part that wanted to learn the truth. And Donna Tracy *had* opened the door.

"Donna, I want you to feel free to say no to what I'm about to propose," she said.

"Hey, that's easy. I'm a 'no' kind of person to begin with."

"Here's what's going on."

Carefully, completely, Abby reviewed the sorts of cases that had led her to believe that toxic exposure might be at work in Patience.

"You need to get back into KarMen," Donna said when she had finished.

"That's the request you can refuse."

"Do you have a computer with a modem?"

Abby considered whether she could re-turn to Orchard Road and either take Josh's computer or use it where it was. But she wasn't even certain that the phone lines were working, and with the police now aware of the situation, she would not feel at ease hanging around the house. Bringing the computer to her place was a possibility, but she was worried about infuriating Josh should he return home, and fearful that her well-documented lack of mechanical aptitude would make it nearly impossible to set up the system at home.

"Is there anyplace you can think of where I could find one?" she asked.

"Of course. The bookstore at the community college has about a dozen of them for rent in back. Meet me there at, say, seven. That way we'll be certain Joanne has gone home. I should be able to get you into the system. From there you're on your own."

"That's as much as I could have ever hoped for, Donna. I'm very grateful, but remember —"

"I know, I know. I don't have to help. But, Dr. Dolan, remember what my dad looked like lying there on that table in the ER with almost no heartbeat at all on his monitor?"

"Of course I do. I'll never forget that."

"Well, he just left with my mom for Hawaii."

It was nearing ten in the evening — one more hour before the Patience Community College Bookstore closed for the night. Abby was one of four still using the computers in the back room. She had yet to uncover any clear connections among the patients she had reviewed, but she *was* amassing information. She sensed that, sooner or later, a pattern would emerge.

Donna Tracy had tapped into the KarMen record-keeping system with no trouble whatsoever. When Abby asked her whose password she had used, all Donna would say was, "I have friends."

After Abby assured herself that she could find her way around the system, she insisted Donna return home. There were a dozen or so years separating them, but Abby enjoyed the younger woman's sarcastic humor and quickly felt comfortable around her. She had no wish to cause Donna more trouble.

"I can't tell you how much I appreciate what you've done tonight," Abby said, "and also how sad I am about your losing your job."

"There are more important things. The message to me was that I was working in the wrong place to begin with. I need to go back for some more schooling."

"Almost never a bad idea," Abby said. "Are you going to be all right?" she asked, uncertain how to approach the subject of money.

Donna made a theatrical show of looking at the data sheets and the screen.

"I don't know," she said. "You tell me."

She patted Abby fondly on the shoulder and left.

Now, almost three hours later, Abby summoned up the twentieth record to be examined, a forty-five-year-old father of three, named Henry Post. Post worked for the city as a groundskeeper/maintenance man in Colstar Park.

Name . . . Age . . . Birth Date . . . Address . . .

Abby logged each fact onto her data sheets. Then she referred to the map of the valley she had constructed and divided arbitrarily into a grid of twenty-five equal segments. She located the man's residence and work address with dots of colored pencil — segment eight for the house and twenty-two for the park. There seemed to be a slight clustering of dots in the southwestern part of the valley — the area farthest from the plant itself. But the grouping was not at all striking.

Status: Outpatient. Physician: G. Oleander. Admitting diagnosis: Chronic cough. Discharge diagnosis: Chronic bronchitis. Physical findings: none. Laboratory findings: CBC normal, Chest X ray normal, MRI unremarkable . . .

Abby dutifully recorded every available piece of information on the man. As she worked, she again became aware that something about the data was bothering her — something even beyond the fact that a predominance of the patients had George Oleander as their primary physician. The workups were, in most cases, simply *too* thorough. There were too many patients getting CT scans and way, way too many having MRIs, a sophisticated scan that was the diagnostic court of last resort — incredibly accurate, but very expensive. The patient was inserted into a total-body cylinder and had to lie motionless for nearly an hour while a three-dimensional picture of the body was generated — an unnerving experience for many people. But there was also an excessive number of blood counts, chemistry profiles, and standard X rays. In an age of medical-cost containment, peer review, and managed care, such overuse of the laboratory was almost unheard-of.

The finding did nothing to explain the NIWWs, but it did seem too close to universal to be considered coincidence, a fluke. An insurance scam of some sort — fee splitting with the radiologist or laboratory director — seemed possible. But it was hard to believe that a prosperous and patrician man like George Oleander would risk his reputation and career for that level of larceny.

Struggling to ignore the tightness in her back from three hours of work without a break, Abby finished with Henry Post and moved on to the next NIWW, a thirty-three-year-old teacher named Mildred Moore.

. . . *Admitting diagnosis: chronic skin abscesses. Discharge diagnosis: same. Physician: G. Oleander . . .*

The pile of data was growing. And with each additional fact Abby sensed there was something already there that she was overlooking — a pattern in those hundreds of pieces of information she had missed. But what?

She rubbed at her eyes, then stood and stretched. One more hour. She could do it. Tomorrow she wasn't on in the ER until the evening. That would leave her time to check on Ives's leg, and then to return to the bookstore computers for another go-round inside KarMen. And somewhere during that time, Sandy Stuart would be calling.

Abby twisted her neck until it cracked loudly, a habit that felt wonderful but used to irritate Josh beyond words. One of the remaining students looked up, startled. Abby grinned sheepishly and mouthed an apology. When she sat down at the computer again, the screen was blank. She dialed the access number for KarMen again. Nothing. There was trouble. She felt certain of it.

Quickly, she gathered her notes and hurried to the desk.

"I just lost my line," she said. "Are there any problems?"

"None that I know of."

"How much do I owe you?"

"Four hours — sixteen dollars."

Abby dropped a twenty on the counter and left without waiting for change.

About a hundred yards down the road a cruiser sped past her, lights flashing, headed toward the bookstore. She pulled over and watched through her rearview mirror until it turned into the parking lot.

"Sorry, Donna," she murmured.

Then she swung back onto the road and hurried home. There were plenty of places where her data sheets would be reasonably safe. She wondered if the same could be said for Abby Dolan.

Chapter Twenty-Three

Abby was suturing a child in the ER when she heard the screams from outside, followed moments later by the horrible screech of tires and brakes. She cut the fine nylon thread and had just set her instruments down when Josh's Wrangler exploded through the doors of the ambulance bay into the center of the ER, showering the floor with glass and debris and striking the nurse, Mary Wilder, head-on. Her body flew through the air and hit the wall at eye level with a sickening thud. In an instant there was chaos, with patients and staff screaming, running, and diving for cover.

The Jeep hurtled forward through the central examining area, slamming into a gurney in bay six with an elderly woman lying on it. The stretcher compressed like an accordion. The woman's body flew twenty feet across the room, limp as a rag doll. Then the Jeep struck the wall. The hood folded backward, shattering the windshield. Flames instantly leaped out from the engine.

Abby raced forward into the billowing black smoke. Through the cobwebbed windshield she could see Josh struggling with the door. His head and face were bloodied. She shouted his name, once, then again, but her cries were lost in the shrieks of others. She raced forward, stumbling over the body of Mary Wilder. The nurse's head was twisted at a repulsive angle. Blood trickled down from the corner of her mouth. She stared up at Abby with the vacant look of death.

Abby scrambled to her feet just as Josh stumbled from the Jeep. He was an apparition — the devil. His teeth were bared in a snarling rictus of hate. Blood was cascading over his face. But even through the crimson she could see his eyes, glowing like hot coals.

"Josh!" she screamed as he raised a pistol and aimed it point-blank at a nurse. "Josh, no!"

He heard her voice and lowered the gun a fraction. Then slowly, deliberately, he swung it around and pointed it at her face. She tried to call to him, to beg him, but there was no sound. All around her the scene blurred. Movement slowed. The panicked cries of others became muted. The swirling smoke hung motionless. And, finally, there was only the yawning maw of the revolver muzzle, and above it, Josh's eyes, flashing out searing laser streaks of gold. Suddenly, from somewhere far in the distance, a telephone began ringing. Abby struggled to locate the sound. The gun barrel expanded, then disappeared. The hideous eyes sparked, then dimmed, then vanished altogether. The smoke and the screams faded. Now there was only the ringing.

Shaken, disoriented, and struggling for air, Abby rolled over and slapped her hand down on the receiver. She rarely remembered dreams of any kind and had never experienced one with such horrible vividness. Her mouth was gravel and sand. The T-shirt she had been sleeping in was unpleasantly damp.

"Hello?" she croaked.

"Abby Dolan?"

Abby cleared her throat and worked herself up on one elbow. The images from her nightmare refused to be banished.

"Yes."

"Abby, I'm sorry if I woke you. It's Joe Henderson."

In an instant she was sitting up and forcing herself to concentrate. The hospital president had never called her at home before. It had to be trouble. She glanced at the alarm clock — almost nine-thirty, the latest she had slept in months.

"Just give me a second to get sorted out, Joe. I was up late last night."

"I know."

Uh-oh.

Abby took a sip of water from a half-filled glass on her night table, then dipped her fingers in it and rubbed them across her eyes. The Josh nightmare was just too goddamn real. Now, it seemed, reality was about to become a nightmare.

"Go ahead," she said.

"Abby, I wonder if you might be able to stop down at my office so that we might talk."

"About what?"

If Joe Henderson was going to take her off the ER staff, she had no intention of making things easy for him. There was a prolonged silence while he searched for the best response.

"Abby, it seems you've generated quite a bit of controversy these past couple of weeks. I think it's time I presented things to you the way they've been presented to me. That way you have a chance to respond to them."

Henderson always had some sort of twang or drawl to his speech. Now he seemed to have both. Abby found herself wondering if either was real.

"Is this going to be another committee?" she asked.

"Pardon?"

Abby ignored the voice in her head that was begging her to stay cool and simply agree to meet with the man.

"The last time you asked to have a word with me, the day of the accident, I ended up feeling as if I had mistakenly wandered into a fraternity induction ceremony."

"I'm afraid I still don't understand."

"Joe, just try to imagine yourself being

called into a room to explain your job performance to four women."

Certain that Henderson expected her to bow out without a struggle, she pictured him now, trying to maintain his never-faltering, political grin.

"It will be just you and me, Abby. You have my word."

"What time?"

"One?"

She glanced at the clock again. There would be plenty of time to hike up to Ives's camp.

"I'll be there," she said.

Abby trudged up the trail to Sam Ives's place with an uncharacteristic heaviness in her chest. In her career as an ER doc she had been party to incalculable tragedies. But until she'd come to Patience, her life outside the hospital had been more tranquil than most. Now, it seemed, she was being attacked from all sides. Oleander, Quinn, Josh, and now Joe Henderson. She had never shied away from making tough choices. It was one part of her job that *had* spilled over into her personal life. But she hated the straitjacket feeling of having others make decisions for her. And in just an hour or so, she assumed, Henderson was going to do just that.

Before driving to Ives's mountain she had stopped by the hospital and stocked up on more than the usual number of dressings.

In the event she was fired or suspended, it would become considerably more difficult, if not impossible, to obtain the bandages, instruments, and especially the drugs she had been using. The antibiotic was too expensive for the hospital pharmacy to give away, but in response to Abby's urging, the head pharmacist had worked out a deal with one of the drug houses. The cost to Abby was quite manageable.

She was also worried about the treatments — the regular debridement of infected tissue — that was allowing Ives's wound to heal from the base. She hoped that Lew might take over if she was forced out of town. Of course, if the Colstar forces went for a complete purge, Lew might find himself right behind her on the unemployment line. The truth was, though, she had never gotten even the hint from him or anyone else that his job was in jeopardy. Oleander knew of his anti-Colstar activities, as did Quinn. But somehow Lew had mastered the ability to stay out of the limelight, and out of the way of those who could cause him trouble. Perhaps sometime soon he could give her lessons — Invisibility 101.

Abby stopped at the edge of the clearing and was about to yell out her usual warning not to shoot when she spotted him. He was swinging in a homemade hammock, suspended between two trees about twelve feet off the ground. A paperback book was propped on his belly.

"Hey, Doc," he called out, "I thought you said you'd be up today, but I wasn't sure."

"Ives, how do you get up there?"

"Same way as I'm about to get down."

He grabbed a heavy cabled rope and flipped off the hammock without a bit of preparation. He descended under complete control, not even bothering to use his legs. It was only then, for the first time, that Abby realized how powerfully sinewy his arms were.

"Tell me something," she said. "The night you got beaten up, did you get any decent punches in at the guys who did it?"

"You know the answer to that."

"You don't hurt people."

"I don't even hurt *insects* if I can help it." He flipped the book onto his worktable. "Louis L'Amour," he said. "You ever read westerns?"

"I thought you were into the classics."

"Obviously you haven't ever read Louis L'Amour. Do yourself a favor some day. In fact, here. I've read this one a couple of times."

Abby knew better than to refuse even though she hadn't read a novel since the day she'd decided to apply for the PRH job. She thanked him and dropped the frayed paperback into her pack.

"Okay, let's have a look."

The dual attack of germ-specific antibiotics and the surgical removal of diseased tissue was working. Healthy pink skin was appearing around the edges of the wound. Abby wondered what would happen to Ives if she had to leave Patience entirely.

"So what's going on with you?" he asked as she cleaned away what little obvious infection remained.

"What do you mean?"

"Something's not right with you."

"How do you know?"

"Well, it's either the negative ionic aura that's emanating from you, or the terribly sad expression on your face."

"I didn't realize it was so obvious."

"Anything you want to talk about?"

"I've been summoned by the president of the hospital. We're meeting in about an hour. I think he's going to fire me."

"For what?"

"I don't know how he'll choose to word the royal decree, but the real reason is that I've been studying the records of patients at the hospital. I feel some of their problems may be due to a toxic exposure from Colstar."

"Last time you were here, you mentioned something about cadmium."

"Exactly. So far all the tests run at the hospital for cadmium have been negative. But just in case there's a problem with the lab here, I took some blood from one patient down to San Francisco for analysis at my old hospital."

"Excellent move."

"I've been trying to review the hospital records of patients I suspect might have been victims, but I'm in hot water for not getting permission from some stupid committee. I haven't identified a cause or pinned down the time of the exposure, but there's some sort of pattern linking these patients. I'm certain of it."

"Then you've got to keep looking."

"That's like telling a turtle who's been flipped on her back that she's got to keep walking."

"Well, my money, if I had any, would be betting you get some sort of warning. From what I've been able to tell, Colstar is a very confident company. I suspect you're a lot less of a concern for them than you think you are."

"How do you know so much about them?"

"Like I've told you, I keep an eye on the place. A couple of friends who visit me from time to time used to work there. We talk."

"Can you help me out in any way? I mean, do you think your friends know anything about a toxic spill or poor handling of cadmium?"

The hermit shook his head.

"Doubtful. I *can* tell you that over the last couple of days there's been a lot of activity around the place. As soon as you've wrapped that leg, I'll get my logbook and show you what I mean."

Abby finished her work and watched as Ives went to his hut for his sack. His limp was barely perceptible now, even though the wound was far from healed. She remembered how badly hobbled he had been just a few weeks ago and wondered how much pain he must have been having, to give in that much. Ives hadn't talked much about his past, but he did share that he had been a philosophy professor at one of the state schools and, before that, had served in Vietnam. He was uncomplicated and often childishly simplistic in his views of things. Yet he appreciated life on a daily basis more than anyone she had ever known. If — oh, hell, *when* — she left Patience, she would miss him.

Ives set his sack on his worktable and opened the logbook.

"There have been a number of big-shot-type cars cruising up Colstar Hill over the last four days. Two Jags, a Mercedes, a Porsche. I didn't recognize any of them. But the big company event was yesterday," he said. "A stretch limo with none other than Senator Mark Corman in it. You know him?"

"*Of* him."

"He was accompanied by a fellow in a suit — maybe his aide — and the guy I call the Man in Black. My friends tell me his name is Quinn. He must not like making decisions about what to wear each day, because I've never seen him dressed any other way."

"His name's *Lyle* Quinn. He's head of security. He may dress like a cartoon, but I believe he's a very dangerous man."

"Hmmm. Big-shot senator visits battery

factory. What do you suppose that means?"

"Well, for one thing, he's originally from Patience."

"That's right. I knew that."

"And for another, according to Josh, Colstar is always competing with other manufacturers for government contracts."

"I imagine that's it. Corman is probably adding to his store of pork barrels. Speaking of our friend Josh, any word from him?"

Abby shook her head. She had shared some of what she and Josh had been going through, but this wasn't the time to bring Ives up to speed on the latest sad developments.

"Listen," she said, "I'm sorry I can't stay, but I've got to go face the music at the hospital. Whatever happens, job or no job, I'll try to be back to see you in three days, right about this time."

"They won't fire you. Mark my words."

"We'll see." She started to leave, then returned and gave him a quick hug. "Take care."

"*You* take care," he said. "Between now and when I see you again, I'm going to be keeping an eye on my favorite factory and thinking about why a U.S. senator is so interested in batteries."

Chapter Twenty-Four

Joe Henderson was resplendent in a blue-and-white seersucker suit. His office was on the second floor of the hospital, and Abby noted that he had almost the same view as did George Oleander — across the meadow to the Colstar cliff. She had been interviewed by Henderson on her first visit to the hospital, and although he had made any number of inadvertent remarks that some would have considered sexist, she felt they had hit it off reasonably well. Seated in his pine-paneled office with its hunting trophies, Abby had had no trouble attributing the insensitivity to a man who simply wasn't aware that there was anything objectionable in telling her how unusual it was to see a woman physician as attractive as she was. It was no surprise, then, when he had followed up the inappropriate compliment by asking, "So how'd you end up becomin' a doctor, anyhow?"

Now she sat rigidly in a low-backed leather chair, waiting for the man to finish praising her skill as an emergency physician and get to the point of their meeting.

"It's not your overall knowledge or your ability in question here. I want you to know that," he was saying.

313

"Then what is it?"

"Well, frankly, some fairly influential members of the board of trustees and also some members of the medical staff believe they have good reason to question your maturity and your judgment."

Abby felt some weakening in her resolve *not* to lose her temper.

"Explain," she said.

Henderson ran his fingers through his thinning hair and fiddled with a desk game shaped like a putting green.

"Well, let's start with the fact that some of our doctors feel you've gone out of your way to make them look or feel inferior to you. As far as I know, none of them has suffered too badly because of your remarks. But this is a very tight community, and the thing we all treasure and protect the most is our reputation."

Abby was gripping the arms of her chair now.

"Please, go on," she said.

"Next there's this business of Peggy Wheaton. There are those who were there that day who feel you had no right to desert her in her moment of crisis in order to tend to . . . to the man who killed her in cold blood. Even if, as you say you believed, Peggy had no chance, folks still think that leavin' her the way you did showed poor judgment on your part."

He paused to give her a chance to comment, but she said nothing. Her jaws were

314

locked as tightly as her hands. Ives was wrong. Henderson was building to a carefully orchestrated crescendo, the grand finale of her termination.

"And, finally," he went on, "there's this business of your conducting an unauthorized review of hospital records. The rules of this hospital are spelled out quite clearly in our staff bylaws. Because our community *is* such a closely knit one, the hospital staff felt it was essential to protect patient confidentiality as much as possible. We also wanted to prevent any unauthorized audits that might pit one physician against another. The other night in the record room Mrs. Ricci expressly spelled out the rules to you. Yet we have reason to believe that last evening you again were calling up records, this time from a computer at the community college. Now, I will admit that we don't have absolute proof it was you. But the security built into our new record-keeping system identified that the intrusion was taking place and found the phone number of the bookstore. We got a detailed description from the girl who was working behind the counter."

"It *was* me," Abby said.

"Why? Why would you do such a thing when you knew it was forbidden by hospital law?"

Abby hesitated, uncertain of how much to share with the hospital president. Obviously, he had ties to Colstar. Everyone in

Patience did. But he also ran the institution that was caring for all these patients. It was certain that since Oleander and Quinn knew about the continuing existence of the Alliance, Henderson did, too. But maybe he didn't realize how extensive the toxicity problem seemed to be — and how explosive. Maybe it was time for her to start getting the word out. She tried to think of what damage Henderson could do if he was committed to helping Colstar cover up whatever it was they had done. True, he could fire her. But he was about to do that anyhow. She decided to chance imparting at least some of what she believed was going on.

"Joe, you said the hospital bylaws were established to protect patient confidentiality. Well, I violated those laws because I believe those same patients' lives may be at stake. And I believe Colstar may be at fault."

Henderson sat forward and pushed aside his putting green.

"Then why in the hell didn't you talk to someone?" he asked.

"Who? Dr. Oleander almost jumped down my throat for ordering cadmium levels on a couple of his patients."

"All negative, I've been told."

"See? That's a perfect example of how there are no secrets in this town at all. The things I believe Colstar might have done are crimes. People may even have died because of them. The company could be heavily

316

fined and even shut down. If there's been a deliberate cover-up, people could be sent to prison. So who am I supposed to talk to? Do you want me to ask permission from the record-room committee to investigate? Well, Martin Bartholomew is the head of that committee, and he's also the head of the employees' clinic at Colstar."

"I see."

"So I just decided that the welfare of my patients — *your* patients, too, incidentally, since they all have been inpatients or out-patients here — was worth breaking that bylaw for."

"Abby, how can you believe the company is responsible for exposing people to cadmium when there is absolutely no proof? No positive tests. Nothing!"

"I'm waiting for an independent lab in San Francisco to call with the results on some samples of blood I brought to them."

"You don't trust our lab?"

"Quite frankly, I don't trust anyone right now."

"What patient was it?"

Again Abby resisted any knee-jerk response. Was there any way she would be putting Cardoza at risk by revealing that it was his blood? Considering her encounter with the man in the ski mask and his pickup, it seemed clear that nothing she could say was going to be hot-off-the-press news.

"Willie Cardoza," she responded.

Henderson's attempt at looking surprised missed badly, she thought.

"You think he was poisoned with cadmium?" he asked.

"I do, actually. That would explain the violence, the insanity inherent in what he did. I've researched the subject quite thoroughly. Violent, psychotic behavior has been reported from cadmium, especially with high-dose exposure. Cardoza has some physical findings in his eyes, as well, that I think may quite possibly be due to some sort of heavy-metal poisoning. And cadmium is a heavy metal. It would certainly make me feel better to know that he wasn't responsible for what he did, although no matter how the tests turn out, I still defend my decision to work on him and not Peggy Wheaton. I did what every ER doctor is trained to do in a triage situation — treat those who have a chance of making it."

"Chance of making it *in your opinion.*"

"Dammit, Joe! All right, all right. If it would make you any happier, I'll say it. In *my* opinion. Now, let's just drop it."

"Did anyone else see these findings in Cardoza's eyes?"

"Not yet. But anyone who wants to can do it anytime."

"It won't be quite as easy as that. Cardoza was transferred to a prison hospital early this morning."

"Which one?"

"I'm afraid I'm not permitted to give that information to anyone."

Abby sighed.

"What a carnival."

Henderson clearly found her remark offensive.

"We don't think so, Doctor," he snapped. "This hospital and the Colstar corporation take the health of the people in this area very seriously. Two and a half years ago, when the community first raised health concerns about the company, investigators from the Environmental Protection Agency and the Occupational Safety and Health Administration were welcomed up on the hill and given free rein. The two teams were each here for almost a week. They found a few minor violations, which were dealt with immediately, but nothing that could have caused any health danger in the valley or to the plant workers. You were up there. You saw how they operate that plant."

Another nonsecret.

"How do you know I was up there?" she asked.

"Abby, what difference does it make? The problem is that you have gone out of your way to create conflict where none existed. It seems to us that your temperament, your way of doing things, is much more suited to . . . to a place that's not as . . . tightly woven as our valley. The letters of recommendation from your directors at St. John's were glowing. Superb. Perhaps you should consider returning to some sort of academic environment, where controversy is more a way of life."

"Joe, I don't think patients like Bill Tracy and Hazel Cookman and a number of others I've cared for would say that I foster controversy and conflict. I know I'm having trouble adjusting to some aspects of living in this community, but once I step through the doors of the emergency room, I feel totally at ease. Before I came here, I was dreading having to work with no backup in the hospital. Now I've discovered that I actually enjoy the challenge. I don't want to leave. At least not right now."

Henderson shook his head.

"I heard there are some nurses and doctors who aren't even speaking to you anymore."

"They're upset about Peggy Wheaton. That's understandable. Just about everyone is. But they'll come around. And those who don't, still have to take care of the patients."

"Abby, I'm sorry. It just isn't working."

She took a deep, calming breath.

"Joe, after you called this morning, I read over my contract. It spells out very clearly what I can be fired for. I don't believe that anything you've said this morning about me and my job performance qualifies."

"I don't want to fire you, Abby. I want you to consider resigning."

"And if I say no?"

Henderson drummed his fingers on the desktop, then removed a folder from his desk.

"I believe that one of those reasons spelled out in your contract has to do with demonstrating flawed judgment in critical situations. I have here the autopsy report on Peggy Wheaton."

He opened the report to a specific page, studied it for a very dramatic ten or fifteen seconds, and then slid it and another page across to her.

Abby looked at him quizzically.

"I was present for the autopsy," she said. "The whole thing. Start to finish. I don't understand what —"

"Just read those pages, Abby."

The first page in the technically written document was the description of the removal of the top of Peggy Wheaton's head, and the examination of the trauma to her skull and brain. The single-spaced, computer-printed paragraph covered most of the sheet. Abby read it in shocked disbelief. The injury described was far less serious than the massive fractures and brain damage that Abby had diagnosed in the ER and confirmed through her observation of the autopsy. In fact, as described, the trauma was minor enough to have easily *not* caused Peggy's death.

"This is a lie," she said. "Every word of it."

"I think you should read the next page as well."

The second sheet described the findings in Peggy's chest — a contusion to the heart with a traumatic hemopericardium — a constricting accumulation of blood between the heart muscle and covering membrane. If the finding was true, and Abby knew from having seen Peggy's perfectly normal heart that it wasn't, she would have been guilty of missing the very treatable cause of the woman's death.

"You're crazy if you think you can get away with this. I'll just insist that the tissues be reexamined."

"Feel free. I believe what tissue remains will conform completely with this report. The report is official, signed by the medical examiner, Dr. Barrett."

Abby groaned. Barrett was the chief of pathology at Patience Regional. He also ran the laboratory that had never found cadmium in anyone.

"I can't believe you all would sink to this."

"Abby, I assure you that no one wants this report to become public knowledge. It would reflect badly on the hospital, and terribly on you. In fact, I wouldn't be a bit surprised if Gary Wheaton and his attorney choose to pursue the matter in court. That would tie you up indefinitely."

"Am I that great a threat to Colstar, that you all would do this? What in the hell is going on here?"

"We would like you to give us two weeks' notice."

"If I refuse?"

"Then I'm afraid we'll just have to decide what's in the best interests of this hospital and this community."

At that moment Abby's pager went off, and at almost the same instant the loudspeaker outside Henderson's office sounded.

"Code ninety-nine, X ray. Code ninety-nine, X ray."

Abby glanced down at her page.

"It's the ER, and it's urgent," she said, pushing back from the desk. "They need help at the code."

"We can complete our conversation later," Henderson replied icily. "Perhaps we'd better see what's going on in radiology."

"Tell your secretary to call and say I'm on my way. And in case I forget to say it later, Joe, you're a son of a bitch."

The overhead page was continuing to broadcast the location of the code ninety-nine as Abby sprinted down the hall to the stairway. The radiology department was on the ground floor, not far from the ER. She tried to recall what doctor from her ER group was on the schedule for today. Whoever it was would certainly be there running the code. Just as she raced through the open doors to radiology, she remembered that the ER doc on duty was Jill Anderson.

And that, she knew, could mean trouble. Jill was skittish and insecure, and prone to bursts of temper. *Talk about impaired critical judgment!* Abby had wondered more than once what Jill was doing in a specialty that required nothing if not a cool head. She was a disaster waiting to happen every time she put on her clinic coat.

A technician stationed by the doors pointed down the brightly lit corridor.

"The MRI suite, Dr. Dolan!" she called out. "Please hurry!"

The magnetic resonance imaging suite consisted of a small waiting/reception area, a dressing room, and the room housing the massive MRI unit itself. The code ninety-nine was being conducted in there. Several people, including two nurses, were standing outside, craning to see through the thick glass walls.

"Just bump someone out and go right in," one of them said.

Over her years as a med student, resident, and then emergency specialist, Abby had been involved in hundreds of code ninety-nines. But the bizarre scene in the crowded MRI room was one she would never forget. Jill Anderson, tears streaming down her face, muttering to herself, was fumbling with the equipment to do a subclavian IV insertion in a woman who was kicking and flailing her arms about desperately. Every bit of the patient's skin that Abby could see was flaming red. Standing across from Jill, Dr. Del Marshall, a radiologist in his sixties, was trying to ventilate the patient with a black Ambu breathing bag. Even from the doorway Abby could tell he was doing an ineffective job of getting air into her lungs.

"What's up?" Abby asked as a nurse stepped back to give her room by the stretcher.

"Anaphylactic shock," Jill said. "She went into it while she was inside the MRI cylinder. Her jaws are clenched too tightly to get a tube in. She's hardly breathing."

Why in the hell didn't you wheel her out of this closet and back to the ER? Abby wanted to scream. The forty-five seconds or so that such a move would have taken would have been repaid a thousandfold with the space and equipment at their disposal in the ER. Now Abby couldn't tell if time was too precious for that.

She moved behind Del Marshall to get a better look at the patient, and at what the radiologist was doing. Above the black rubber face mask, she saw the patient's bright-red hair. Marshall backed away and let Abby handle the breathing bag. She lifted it from the woman's face. Lying there, her eyes wide with panic, fighting desperately and futilely to get air past the swollen tissues in her throat, was Claire Buchanan.

Chapter Twenty-Five

Claire Buchanan's face, puffed and crimson, was barely recognizable. She was thrashing about as if someone were smothering her with a pillow.

Jill Anderson looked only marginally better. Her mascara was beginning to smear beneath both eyes, and her normally pale complexion was bloodless.

"I've got to get this line in so we can paralyze her with some Anectine," she said. "Once her jaws are relaxed, maybe I can get a tube in."

Paralyze. Tube. From what Abby could tell, Claire Buchanan was still conscious. The use of such words in this situation was totally inappropriate. To make matters worse, the time that was being lost as Jill struggled to get an IV in could prove fatal. The lactic acid that was rapidly building up in Claire's bloodstream from her low oxygen levels could cause a cardiac arrest at any moment.

By the accepted rules of practice Jill was in charge of the code ninety-nine. But there was no way Abby could allow things to continue as they were. Besides, what did she have to lose? Henderson had more or less just fired her.

"Jill," she said with undisguised firmness, "let me help."

At that moment Jill looked like a frantic, treed animal who had just realized there was no place else to run.

"Take over," she said.

Thank God.

Abby was already experiencing the familiar slowing of movement and muffling of sound as her mind and body homed in on the critical elements of the situation at hand. In just a few seconds she understood the crisis and what she and the others had to do to reverse it.

"Jill, please get a tourniquet on that arm," she said. "Someone else keep a couple of fingers on her femoral pulse until we can get our portable monitor hooked up."

She next turned to the nurse, Mary Wilder. Before Peggy Wheaton's death they had been on a first-name basis — allies in the ER war. Since the triage episode the nurse hadn't spoken a kind word to her.

"Mrs. Wilder, please give Dr. Anderson point eight of epinephrine on a twenty-seven needle."

Wilder looked at her dispassionately.

"Yes, Doctor."

Despite the situation, and in spite of herself, Abby flashed on the nurse's horrible death in her nightmare. *If you only knew . . .*

"Jill, don't worry about a line," Abby said. "Just find some little vein and get the epi in. You can do it. I know you can. Put it in her femoral or external jugular if you have to. Just make sure it's IV."

She checked Claire's jaws, which were, in fact, rigidly closed. Trying to get a breathing tube through her mouth was out of the question. But there was another way — in fact, there were two. One of the techniques, nasotracheal intubation, she could possibly do right there. The other, an emergency tracheotomy, would require the surgical lighting, wall suction, and equipment of the ER. And that meant a risky dash.

"I need a six-oh nasotracheal tube," she said.

The nasotracheal breathing tube was made to be passed through the nose, down the back of the throat, and between the vocal cords. Because the NT tube was held tightly in place by the long nasal passage, it caused less tissue injury over long periods of assisted ventilation than the more wobbly endotracheal tube, inserted through the patient's mouth. But the nasal technique was slower to perform, technically more difficult, and damaging to the nose if not done correctly. Usually, when inserting the nasal tube, a lighted laryngoscope blade would be slipped into the patient's mouth to push the tongue aside and allow the physician to use a long-handled clamp to guide the NT tube downward through the vocal cords. This time, though, because of Claire's tightly clenched jaws, using the laryngoscope was out of the question. Abby would have to do the insertion blind, by feel — and hearing — alone. It was a technique she had practiced many times but had seldom used in an emergency situation, especially with a patient who was still awake and thrashing about.

She turned away from Claire Buchanan for a moment and added softly, "And somebody please get over to the ER and get us ready for a tracheotomy if I can't get this in."

She turned back to the stretcher and set about trying to calm Claire down. She also used the mask and bag to deliver high-flow oxygen along with what little air the woman was managing to get in on her own.

Their worst enemies right now were time and the cramped quarters in which Jill had opted to work. Abby identified the people who were not essential to the moment and asked them to wait outside. Del Marshall she motioned back to a corner, out of the way. The radiologist, who was hardly used to this kind of crisis, readily complied. He was tight-lipped and plaster pale. For a moment Abby worried he was going to pass out. As she watched him move aside and brace himself against the wall, her line of vision connected with Joe Henderson, who was watching and listening from just outside the doorway. For the briefest moment their eyes met and held. Then, with no other acknowledgment, she turned away.

Claire's face was horribly swollen now and a mottled crimson. Her lips were like sausages. Her eyelids and the surrounding tissues were so puffed that it was impossible to tell whether her eyes could even open. And to make matters worse, her struggles were weakening.

Come on, Jill, Abby urged silently. *Get that epi in. . . . Dammit, come on!*

The nurse working the crash cart handed over the nasotracheal tube.

"Did you check the balloon?" Abby asked.

Too often she had seen a breathing tube inserted flawlessly, only to discover that the circumferential balloon used to seal the space between the tube and the inner wall of the trachea was defective. The insertion would have to be repeated with another tube, but this time through vocal cords that were often traumatized and swollen from the initial attempt.

"No, Doctor," the nurse muttered. "Sorry."

"Do it, please," Abby demanded. "And it's got to be lubricated better."

Keep upsetting people like Jill and this nurse, and it will be a miracle if you're not lynched, she was thinking.

"I've got it, Abby!" Jill exclaimed suddenly. "Epi's in!"

"Way to go. I knew you could do it. Now, please get to work on that subclavian, and take your time. As soon as it's in, give her some IV steroids — make it forty of Solu-

Medrol — and also give her fifty of Benadryl."

Claire had stopped breathing altogether. In a few more seconds they would have to begin doing CPR. But without a way to get oxygen in, the pulmonary part of the CPR would not be possible. Abby couldn't remember the last time she had seen an anaphylactic-shock patient die in the emergency ward. The treatment was usually effective, and at St. John's there was just too much talent around, including skilled trauma surgeons who could perform a perfect tracheotomy in just a minute or two. But this time the severity of Claire's allergic reaction, plus Jill's indecisiveness and poor judgment, had put them in a deep hole.

Abby tried one last blast of oxygen from the breathing bag. Claire's neck was as rigid as her jaws. The resistance to proper air flow was intense. On the other side of the litter Jill was moving with agonizing slowness. There was no way Abby could wait for the IV to be established.

She tried to rid her mind of all extraneous thoughts. But some images of Claire Buchanan — snippets of their two encounters — refused to be dispatched.

". . . *Are you the nervous type?*"

"*I don't think so, except that I'm very claustrophobic. . . .*"

Abby glanced down the long, gleaming MRI cylinder. How in the hell could anyone with true claustrophobia make it in there for the forty-five minutes usually required to complete a study?

Hang in there, Claire. . . . Please, just a little bit longer. . . .

Abby felt the icy fingers of panic beginning to take hold.

". . . I was a damn good dancer, at least for Sioux City. . . ."

Don't leave us, Claire. . . . Don't leave us now. . . .

"Okay, everyone, let's get this tube down. Mrs. Wilder, put your hands on both sides of her rib cage. When I ask you to, give her some rhythmic compressions. That way at least I'll have a little bit of a target. I'm making one pass. If I don't get it, we're going to the ER for a trach. Are we sure there's no surgeon in the house?"

"The one on call has been paged, but he's coming in from his office."

It had been six or seven years since Abby had performed her last emergency tracheotomy. But if she failed to get the ventilation tube in, there was no other option. If she had to, she would race Claire Buchanan over to the ER, suck up her courage, and do it.

"Jill, hold off until I get this tube in, please. Everyone else, I need perfect silence so I can hear air moving through her cords. Ready, Mrs. Wilder?"

Instantly the room was totally quiet. Abby bent down, her lips next to Claire's ear.

"Claire, can you hear me?" No response.

No movement. "Claire, you're going to feel a plastic tube inside your nose. It's to help you breathe." Still no reaction.

There was no time left for explanations. And no need. Claire Buchanan, though her jaws were still rigidly locked, was on the brink. The two nurses who could backed out of the room to allow more work space. Abby took the lubricated tube in one hand and slid it into Claire's right nostril. The one-time Rockette barely moved. Next, Abby slipped her free hand beneath the woman's head and cradled it. The tube caught briefly on one of the nasal ridges, but a little rotating and some gentle pressure freed it and allowed Abby to advance it into the back of Claire's throat. Step one was done — the easy part.

Abby hunched over now, her ear just above the opening of the tube.

"All right, Mrs. Wilder," she said into the silence, "compress about once every three seconds."

Faintly, Abby heard the puff of air. She advanced the tube another half inch. This time she heard nothing. She guessed that she had gone behind the opening of the trachea into the beginning of the esophagus. She withdrew the tube an inch and rotated it slightly to angle the tip more forward.

"Dr. Dolan, I'm not feeling a femoral pulse anymore."

Abby checked Claire's carotid pulse. It

was still there, but very faint. Time was just about up.

"Hold off on the compressions, Mrs. Wilder," she said. "If we have to race to the ER, we're going to do it without any CPR until we get there. So everyone get ready."

She was down to it. One more try, ten more seconds, and she would have to make the time-consuming sprint to the ER and perform a tracheotomy under the worst circumstances.

"Quiet, everyone," she said again, although there was hardly any noise. "Okay, Mrs. Wilder, compressions, please."

Abby hunched over the tube opening once more.

The nurse squeezed down rhythmically, once, then again. Claire Buchanan's arms and legs were twitching spasmodically now, purposelessly. Suddenly Abby heard it again, the faint hiss of moving air. She advanced the tube down a quarter of an inch. The sound was louder. Suddenly she encountered resistance again. Was she against the epiglottis, deep in the throat? The bony ridge above the larynx? Or perhaps even the swollen vocal cords themselves?

Abby felt herself beginning to panic once more. This whole thing was a nightmare. An absolute disaster. Should she try forcing the tube down, hoping she was against the vocal cords, or give up and risk the mad dash to the ER for an emergency tracheotomy by a doctor who hadn't performed one in years? She waited for another wisp of air, and when she heard it, forced the tube down as hard as she dared. If she fractured or tore a crucial structure, with possibly fatal hemorrhage into Claire's lungs, she would bear the full responsibility.

There was momentary, total resistance. Then, with a soft popping sound, the tube advanced almost an inch. Abby knew she was in. The tip had pushed between the obstructing vocal cords and was now in the lower trachea, just above its split into the main bronchial tubes to Claire's right and left lungs. There might be some swelling in *those* tubes, but with epinephrine already on board, the blockage shouldn't be enough to keep them from ventilating her.

"Ambu bag, please," she said. "Quickly!"

Mary Wilder passed over the breathing bag. Abby attached it to the top of the tube and began ventilating as fast as she could. There was a tank of oxygen beneath the stretcher. Abby connected it to the breathing bag through a plastic tube.

"I think I feel a femoral pulse," the nurse called out.

"Excellent. Jill, you've got one more shot at that subclavian. Then, in or out, we make tracks for the ER. Take your time. I know you can do it. Just like the epi."

Jill Anderson, her tears no longer flowing, seemed as if she were about to back off entirely. Then, with a glance at Abby, she located her landmarks and slid the needle in beneath Claire's collarbone. The blood return was immediate. A perfect shot.

"Yes!" Jill exclaimed unabashedly. "Yes!"

One nurse applauded.

With a good intravenous route established, the steroids, some more epinephrine, and the antihistamine, Benadryl, could be given IV.

In less than a minute Claire began more purposeful movements of her limbs.

"Her pulse is much better now," the nurse exclaimed. "*Much* better."

"Great," Abby said. "Let's get her the hell out of this box and over to the ER. Mrs. Wilder, would you please lead the charge?"

The graying nurse looked over at Abby with unbridled relief.

"It's Mary," she said.

Chapter Twenty-Six

By the time Claire Buchanan was transferred from the ER to the ICU, her symptoms had begun to recede. She was groggy, but clearly awake. George Oleander, who had come in immediately to take over her care, expressed gratitude to Abby for her treatment success, but he had no explanation to offer for Claire's severe allergic reaction. He also made no defense of his insistence not to refer her for a dermatologic consult. Abby wanted to suggest sending off a cadmium-level stat, but given the controversy swirling around her, she decided the suggestion could wait.

Her actual shift in the ER wasn't scheduled to begin for a few more hours, and she was hardly in the mood to offer to take over early for Jill Anderson. Instead, she decided, she would go up to the unit to check on Claire, then maybe take a walk, and, finally, have dinner at the Peking Pagoda. With all she had been through today, the very least she could do for herself was a PuPu Platter.

Before heading up to the unit Abby went to a pay phone to check in with Sandy Stuart at St. John's. The toxicologist was at a conference for another two hours, and her secretary had no idea who would have been in charge of a cadmium assay. Abby left her beeper number and instructions for Sandy to call as soon as she had any information.

The unit was fairly quiet, due in part to Willie Cardoza's transfer. Abby immediately sensed a change in the attitude of the unit nurses toward her. Two of them made a point of coming over to congratulate her for "the save." One of them actually muttered something about "that Wheaton thing." Clearly, the pendulum of hospital opinion was swinging back in her favor. Abby wondered how far it would head in the other direction again if Henderson began leaking the lie that she had not only overestimated the severity of Peggy's head injuries, but that in her haste to tend to Peggy's murderer she had completely missed the constrictive hemopericardium that had probably cost the woman her life.

A wave of loneliness washed over her. She glanced at the time and wondered where Lew was. He had been working a fair amount at the state hospital lately because the main-coverage doctor had left without notice. She wondered what would happen to her embryonic relationship with him if she was forced to resign and move out of Patience. She believed something very special might be developing with Lew, but the two of them were hardly far enough along for her to stay in Patience just for him or for him to leave because of her. And, besides, the situation with Josh remained unresolved. Maybe it would be best if she simply ditched them all — Josh, Lew, the hospital, everything — and started over someplace. That notion was not very appealing, especially since leaving would vindicate the slimy methods of Joe Henderson, to say nothing of the heavy-handed approach of Mr. Ski Mask in his red pickup.

Love, marriage, kids, a reasonably inter-esting job, a nice place to live. Her goals in moving to Patience had always seemed per-fectly straightforward — never far-fetched or self-serving. And it had all started out so right, so innocent. *How in the hell had all this happened?*

Ironically, Claire Buchanan had been placed in the same cubicle Willie Cardoza had occupied. She still had the lifesaving NT tube in place, but Abby noted through the glass wall that the tube was now at-tached to moisturized oxygen, not to a ven-tilator. A very good sign. There was a beefy man in a turtleneck and sports coat seated next to her stroking her hand. Dennis Buchanan, the man who could sell iceboxes to Eskimos, the man who had rescued Claire from the Rockettes. Watching his gentle, concerned attentiveness brought a bitter-sweet fullness to Abby's throat. Once upon a time Josh had cared for her like that. And knowing that he did had made almost every problem in life bearable.

She shook off her melancholy as best she could and moved closer to the glass. Claire's lips were much less swollen already, and her eyes, though still puffy, were open. The terrible inflammation in her skin had also begun to ebb. With any luck she would have the tube removed before long. Abby saw no sense in trying to speak with her at this point, especially while her husband was there. But later tonight she would stop by again. Even if the tube was still in, Claire would probably be alert and strong enough to communicate in writing. And there were a number of questions Abby wanted answered, the most pressing being: What happened?

Abby started out of the unit. Then, bothered by the persistent gnawing feeling that she was missing something, she suddenly turned and went to the nurses' station. Claire's old hospital record was in a slot just below the loose-leaf-bound current record. The old record wasn't large. There were no inpatient stays before this one, except for the delivery of a healthy baby girl sixteen years before, and only five emergency-room visits: the two in which Abby had been her doctor, a sprained ankle, removal of a piece of glass from her foot, and an episode of upper-abdominal pain that was believed to be gastritis.

Gastritis. Claire had said something about that, something that Abby thought was unusual at the time. She flipped through the laboratory and X-ray reports. Blood counts had been done on the evening Claire had come into the ER with belly pain. Then, a day later, she'd had an MRI, which was normal. That was it. That was what had seemed so weird when Claire had first mentioned it.

An MRI, appropriate when a doctor suspected a condition not easily visualized by conventional X rays, seemed an odd and extravagantly expensive choice in view of Claire's symptoms. And for someone with claustrophobia, like Claire, it was bound to be an ordeal. In addition, the time required to run each study meant that there was often a long waiting period to get one done. Yet George Oleander had ordered an MRI without first going to an upper GI series, or even, from what Abby could tell, a trial course of treatment. Why?

And why had he ordered a second MRI today?

Abby left the unit and returned to the MRI suite. It occurred to her for the first time how unusual it was for a hospital the size of Patience Regional to have its own MRI machine at all. Granted, the facility served a fairly large geographic area. But as far as she knew, most hospitals this size referred patients to a free-standing MRI center that served several hospitals. And some facilities actually contracted with a mobile unit that was built inside a tractor trailer and hauled from hospital to hospital. Yet here was PRH with not only an MRI, but a very up-to-date CT scanner as well. And there was a great deal of crossover in the diagnostic capabilities of the two techniques.

The room housing the gleaming MRI unit showed no hint of the drama that had unfolded there just two hours before. The floor was polished and the machine was already in operation again. Del Marshall sat outside the room at a console, checking the remarkably precise images as the machine produced them. Inside, the sheet-covered feet of the patient could be seen just inside the cylinder.

"Hi," Abby said. "How're you doing?"

Marshall looked up at her and smiled warmly. He was a lean, fatherly man, with Ben Franklin glasses and razor-cut gray hair.

"I didn't have a coronary in there, if that's what you mean."

"You actually seemed to be handling yourself pretty well."

"That's kind of you to say, but I know better. It's one thing to take all those courses in CPR and advanced CPR. It's quite another to be confronted with a flesh-and-blood patient who's stopped breathing — especially when it happens in your MRI machine. I can understand my being a basket case, but I confess I was a little surprised Jill Anderson wasn't more up to the task. I don't know what would have become of that poor Buchanan woman if you hadn't been there."

"Thanks. Del, do you have any idea what happened in there?"

"No, no idea at all," he responded with knee-jerk quickness. "One moment she was perfectly peaceful, the next she was thrashing about violently, kicking the inside of the tube. We pulled her out, and she was already swelling up and turning beet-red."

"Well, I just stopped by the unit, and she seems to be making a nice recovery. I was wondering if you would happen to have Mrs. Buchanan's request sheet in there. I just want to get some data for my dictation."

Abby phrased the question carefully. She had no idea how connected the radiologist was to Henderson or to George Oleander. And the last thing she wanted was for either of them to know she was poking around for more information.

Marshall called up Claire's sheet on one of the screens. The specific line Abby was looking for was *Provisional Diagnosis*. According to it, Oleander had requested the study for *recurrent hives, possible occult malignancy.*

The diagnosis of possible occult malignancy was reasonable enough. Hives sometimes *were* the outward manifestation of serious internal disease. But this MRI, like Claire's previous one, seemed to have been ordered prematurely. Of course, there could have been any number of diagnostic studies done through Oleander's office of which

Abby would have been unaware. But she sensed that was not the case. Oleander had a strange predilection for ordering MRIs, as did the other physicians with NIWW patients. But there was something else about the MRIs — something that seemed to be floating just beyond her grasp.

There was just enough time before her ER shift to go home and review the data she had managed to gather so far — focusing this time on the MRIs. The PuPu Platter would have to wait for another day.

Abby thanked the radiologist and left the hospital trying to sort out what she was discovering, and what pieces were missing. Pending the results of the assay of Willie Cardoza's blood, she would try assuming for the moment that all of the NIWWs, including Cardoza, Claire Buchanan, and even Josh, were cadmium toxic to one degree or another. How could that possibly tie in with the inappropriate, excessively ordered MRIs?

Unlike standard X rays or even CT scans, which were a computerized integration of hundreds of individual X rays, magnetic resonance imaging involved placing the patient in a magnetic field and then bombarding that person with radio waves. The billions of hydrogen ions in the body, mostly located in water, would vibrate under the influence of the magnet in such a way that their density could be measured and then converted to incredibly detailed slices through the body. The slices were used to create three-dimensional pictures of any organ. The science behind an MRI was straight out of *Star Trek*, and for years many distinguished scholars had derided the believers. But scholars had laughed at Newton, too.

As far as Abby knew, no adverse effects of any real consequence had been attributed to magnetic resonance imaging. At a lecture on the technique sometime in the past year, she had learned that there was a slight but significant rise in body temperature in patients undergoing the test, possibly caused by the intense radio-wave bombardment. With time and a massive volume of cases it seemed possible something else would show up. But for the time being the temperature rise was it — except, of course, for the psychological trauma of lying in a metal tube for most of an hour, unable to move at all, surrounded by the echoing pings, hums, and clangs of the charging and discharging electromagnet.

The problem, as Abby saw it, was coming up with a workable explanation for how the MRIs fit in with the varied clinical presentations of the NIWWs. The understanding of the biochemistry of the brain was still in its infancy. Perhaps, she reasoned, the radio waves, the magnetic field, or even the claustrophobic effects of being slid into the narrow tube set off some sort of chemical discharge. And perhaps, in the presence of cadmium, that chemical discharge short-circuited the brain. *Perhaps. Perhaps. Perhaps.*

The truth was, the explanations she was conjuring up didn't make much sense. Some cases fit, some didn't. There simply wasn't any consistent pattern. Willie Cardoza had an MRI after his head injury. Josh had never been ill before coming to Patience, and had never had an MRI. Claire Buchanan seemed to be having trouble with her immune system — especially the immune chemicals in the skin. Other NIWW patients had nothing more than persistent fatigue, and still others, a chronic cough that was unresponsive to antibiotics.

By the time Abby arrived home, the best theory she had come up with was that she had stumbled by accident on a scam to raise revenues for the hospital or justify its MRI unit by ordering an excessive number of tests. What did the scam have to do with the NIWWs? Probably nothing.

Upon her hurried return home from the computer room at the community-college bookstore, Abby had searched for a spot to hide the loose-leaf notebook containing her data sheets. She thought there was a good chance that someone, probably Lyle Quinn, would try to find and destroy them. Finally she had settled on a hollowed-out area just behind the furnace in the basement. The spot would probably yield to a careful search, but the searcher would have to wade through a hell of a lot of junk first.

She carried the notebook upstairs to the dining-room table and brought out a blank sheet of paper. This time she would concentrate on just the MRIs. She jotted down the dates when the tests had been done, the doctor, the diagnosis, the results. Nothing. The only finding that looked like a pattern was that in most cases the study was negative. She rubbed at her eyes and paced around the house. Something was there. She felt certain of it. Maybe she needed more cases. But more likely she was approaching her work with a burden of preconceived notions. If she could only clear her mind of expectations . . .

She was still pacing when her beeper went off. The return number was not local, but still in the 916 area. Lew answered on the first ring. Abby had never heard him so excited.

"I'm at the state hospital in Caledonia," he said. "And one of the patients we have here right now is Angela Cristoforo. Do you know who that is?"

"Yes, the girl who cuts herself."

"Exactly. Well, this is the second time she's been here since that incident at the Colstar picnic. This time her mother found her burning herself with a curling iron. Apparently she had set her bed on fire as well."

Abby flashed on the scene at Colstar Park — Angela screaming at Lyle Quinn, with

Willie Cardoza approaching her, ever so carefully, from behind.

"*. . . Let me die! I deserve to die!*"

"Poor baby," she said.

"Poor baby, maybe," Lew said, "but she's also the break we've been waiting for. And you did it."

"I don't understand."

"Her eyes. I finished doing an intake exam on her, and then I started thinking about the rings you found in Willie Cardoza. Angela Cristoforo *has* them, Abby! The same ones you described. Invisible under regular light, glowing like fire under a black light. Both of them are poisoned, both of them are violently insane, and both of them worked for you-know-who. Have you heard anything from your friend in San Francisco?"

"Not yet. Soon, I think. In fact, I thought this page from you might be Sandy. Have you drawn blood on Angela?"

"I'm about to. Abby, we're going to *get* them. I knew we would. As soon as you mentioned those NIWWs of yours, I knew we'd get them. All we need now is a little more time — just a little more time to get everything organized and put our findings together."

A little more time may be all I have left around here.

"Lew, that's great news. You've worked very hard for this these past years. You deserve a breakthrough."

"You were the breakthrough, Abby. You did it. Will you page me as soon as you hear about Cardoza's blood?"

"Of course. Where are you now?"

"In the on-call room. But I have to see some patients. It's a full moon."

"Lord. That bodes ill for my shift in the ER tonight."

Abby decided against telling him anything about her meeting with Joe Henderson or the fabricated autopsy report. This was Lew's moment. There was no reason to spoil it.

"Abby, I can't wait to see you again. How about tomorrow? We can have lunch at my place."

"Sure. That would be fine."

"You don't sound that enthused."

"Oh, I am, Lew. I just have a lot on my mind. Remember, Colstar has been your fight for several years. I'm just trying to keep my head above water here."

"I understand. I'm sorry — I keep making the same dumb assumption about you and the Alliance over and over again."

"It's all right. I'm on your side. You know that."

"Are you headed into the hospital now?"

"Yes. There's a patient in the unit whose eyes *I* want to check."

"Just keep me posted."

Abby set the receiver down, replaced the notebook behind the furnace, and gathered her things for work. Lew was right. She had sounded lukewarm about having lunch with him. And he didn't deserve that. She was justifiably upset over what had happened with Henderson and *un*justifiably angry at Lew for not being around to help her come up with the appropriate response. Little Abby Dolan, feeling sorry for herself. That was it in a nutshell. Lew was off now seeing patients. But as soon as there was a chance later on, she would call and apologize. She was down to one ally she could really count on in Patience. Now she was trying to drive him off.

Dusk was already settling in when she drove back to the hospital. Even though there were still almost two weeks left in August, the air smelled like autumn. The summer that had once held so much promise was nearly over. *What next?* she wondered.

Lew's finding in Angela Cristoforo was sure to stir up the hornets. Abby hoped he had sense enough not to disclose his discovery prematurely. Tonight, when she called him to apologize for sounding like a brat, she would warn him. The bogus autopsy report on Peggy Wheaton demonstrated that the opposition was resourceful and not about to cave in on any point without a fight.

She stopped by the ER and once again slipped the ophthalmologic black light into her clinic-coat pocket. First Willie Cardoza, now Angela Cristoforo. Their symptoms were similar, they were both employed at Colstar, and both of them had telltale eye findings. Now it was time to see if one of the NIWWs was a member of that club.

Claire Buchanan was alone in her cubicle in the ICU. Abby was grateful to see that the NT tube had been pulled. Instead, Claire had only oxygen prongs. Mindful of having been surprised in the unit by Lyle Quinn, Abby was careful to stand facing the door.

"Hi," she said, "remember me?"

"Dr. Dolan from the ER."

Claire's vocal cords, swollen from the intubation and her allergic reaction, made her voice barely audible. Her lips and eyelids were puffy, but less so than even a little while ago. Her skin remained somewhat mottled, but now with varying shades of pale and pink. The allergic reaction she had endured was one of the most virulent Abby had ever seen. But thank God she was going to make it.

"How're you feeling?" Abby asked.

The one-time Rockette smiled weakly.

"Been better."

"If you feel too tired to talk to me, I can come back."

"It's okay. I remember your trying to help me in that MRI room. Thank you."

Claire still had to pause for breath every few words. Their conversation would have to be brief.

"It was a close call," Abby said. "I'm glad

you made it. Can I get you anything? Some water?"

"That would be great."

Abby held the paper cup and straw for her.

"Claire, I don't want you to try to say too much right now, but do you think you could tell me what happened down there?"

The woman shrugged.

"I really don't know. I hated having the MRI test, so I took the tranquilizer pills Dr. Oleander gave me."

"Pills? More than one?"

"Three, I think. I don't really remember. Then, when I was ready to go into the tube, they gave me an eye cover — black cloth, like the one some people use to sleep with."

She stopped to take some breaths and another sip of water.

"Claire, we can talk about this later."

"No, it's okay. At first I . . . I thought I was doing pretty well. Then, suddenly, I felt like I was having trouble breathing. The air seemed heavy, like it was liquid or something. It even had a weird taste."

"A taste?"

"That's just the way it seemed. All of a sudden my itching got worse. Much worse. Then I couldn't breathe at all. It was horrible. I'll never go inside one of those things again, I promise you that."

"Well, try not to make promises like that. That test is coming up more and more in people's lives."

"Not mine."

"Claire, I'm just grateful you're getting better. I'll stop back to see you later. But before I go, I want to check your eyes with this light."

Abby glanced outside the cubicle. No one was close by. Quickly, she pulled the curtain and cut the lights. She was aware of her own heartbeat as she clicked on the black light, leaned over the bed, and looked through the built-in magnifier. Claire's eyes were perfectly normal. No rings. No abnormal glow of any kind. Abby rubbed her own eyes and looked again. Nothing.

"See anything I should know about?" Claire asked.

"They look perfect," Abby said, still straining to see some telltale color. "Absolutely perfect."

Finally she flipped on the lights and opened the curtains. The movement caught the attention of one of the nurses, who left the others and approached the cubicle.

"Claire, I'll be back to see you later," Abby said, adding loudly, "Just take it easy and do whatever the nurses tell you."

She smiled at the nurse and left without waiting for questions to be asked. But now, with the lack of findings in Claire's eyes, she had a bunch of questions of her own — and there was absolutely no one she knew of who could answer them. She was almost at the ER when her pager went off again, this time displaying a call from the 415 area — San Francisco. Abby hurried to an out-of-the-way pay phone, fumbling for her calling card as she ran. For a moment she wondered if it might be Josh. But Sandy Stuart answered after one ring.

"Sorry to take so long to get back to you, Abby," she said. "But we ran the sample twice with two different methods. Then I got caught in a meeting. I didn't even know the final results until just a few minutes ago."

After the negative eye findings on Claire, Abby sensed that she was not going to hear good news. And negative findings on Willie Cardoza's blood would mean they were back to square one. Assuming there was a square one.

"I'm ready," she said. "What'd you find?"

"You hit it right on the button, Abby. Your patient's loaded with cadmium. Any level of that stuff is toxic, but his was over ten micrograms per deciliter. People can get quite ill at levels of just one point five or two, so this guy has been exposed to the stuff big time. What kind of a town is that you're living in, anyhow?"

Chapter Twenty-Seven

How long have you had this ingrown toenail?" . . . "Three weeks? Sir, it's two-thirty in the morning. What made you come in now?" . . . "Of course, of course. You couldn't sleep. . . ."

The steady stream of patients with nonemergency complaints would have been demoralizing under the best of circumstances. But tonight, over the seemingly endless twelve-hour night shift, Abby was in constant danger of letting her impatience boil over.

She was also in constant danger of violating a critical ER maxim: never assume anything. Almost lost among the barrage of chronic sore throats, six-day-old ankle sprains ("The doctor told me I'd be feeling better in a week, but I know I won't feel any better tomorrow than I do tonight"), and cranky babies, was an elderly gentleman complaining of "indigestion." Distracted by the news from Sandy Stuart's lab, and numbed by the parade of mundane cases, Abby had examined the man too briefly and was about to give him some samples of antacids along with the usual come-back-if-you're-not-better instructions, when Providence made her slow down a beat and look at his face. There was something there — a sallowness to his complexion or a flicker of fear in his eyes — that caused her to back off on discharging him and instead order an electrocardiogram. The EKG showed a rather large heart attack in process. Within an hour of admission to the ICU the man suffered a cardiac arrest, which was quickly and effectively treated by the nurses.

By morning Abby knew she was hanging on by her fingernails, checking the clock every ten minutes or so, dreading the next patient, the next potential error. The news of Willie Cardoza's cadmium toxicity and Angela Cristoforo's eye pathology was certainly vindicating for her, and probably lifesaving for the two of them. But it was also terrifying in its implications for Josh. And unlike Willie and Angela, who were in hospitals and would soon be undergoing chelation therapy, Josh was out there someplace, on a mission of vengeance against God-only-knew-who. Willie had killed Peggy Wheaton. Angela had come close to killing herself. Could there be any doubt that Josh, too, was capable of homicidal rage?

So much of his behavior these past weeks made sense now. Yet how he and the others could have become so seriously cadmium toxic remained the darkest mystery. It had to have been a spill of some sort — a one-time release of the metal into water or air, with Josh, Willie, Angela, and probably others being at the epicenter of the accident.

While Abby was writing discharge instructions for the last patient she would see on her shift, she asked the night nurse to call the record room and ask whether Angela Cristoforo had ever had an MRI. Abby was certain that a request from Dr. Dolan to the record room for information of any kind would trigger a call to Joanne Ricci or even Joe Henderson. The nurse made the call, no questions asked. Fifteen minutes later, just as Abby was packing to leave, the woman returned with the report. No MRIs on Angela.

Instead of driving home, Abby headed for Five Corners at the other end of town. She felt desperate to find Josh. And the only place she could think of to start was the house on Orchard Road. Unless he had come back and cleaned up, there were angry letters and parts of letters still strewn about the floor, at least one of them addressed to the President. Then there was also Josh's computer. Somewhere among those files there had to be a clue.

But first there was the matter of breakfast. She hadn't had anything to eat since midnight but a few packets of saltines and a dish of institutional Jell-O, probably strawberry. Having missed out on dinner at the Peking Pagoda, it seemed only appropriate to reward herself for making it

357

through the night with an Egg McMuffin and a hash brown or two. She wasn't proud of her eating habits, but neither was she all that upset by them. Her parents were doing well in their midseventies, despite her mother's being a horrible and totally indifferent cook. It was ironic that of all her friends, the one who was the least appalled by her junk-food habit was Josh, who could probably count his lifetime consumption of Egg McMuffins on his thumbs.

She flashed on the cupcake wrappers and such that she had found in his Jeep, and on the Styrofoam carry-out containers strewn about the house on Orchard Road. If she ever needed proof positive that he was insane, there it was. Her feelings toward Josh as a mate for life might have been driven off for good, but she still cared about him too deeply to endure the thought of his hurting someone, or being hurt or sick himself. She simply had to find him.

She sat at a corner table in McDonald's, sipping coffee. All around her, people were preparing to start their day. It was life as usual in Patience, California, the community perfect.

Surely, there had to be someone besides her and the three Alliance members who knew that the town was sick. Surely, Lyle Quinn or Kelly Franklin, or more likely both, were aware that some sort of environmental spill had taken place, or was even ongoing. Surely, Joe Henderson was acting on the orders of someone to get Abby Dolan out of the hospital and out of Patience before she figured out what was going on.

She scanned the restaurant again, wondering how these people and the rest of the valley would react if they knew that Colstar had endangered their health and the health of their loved ones. The truth was, it wouldn't be easy to convince any of them. Evidence would have to be overwhelming — airtight. And even then Lew's story of the tire company in Texas proved how irrational people could be when their way of life was at stake.

Maybe the status quo was in most people's best interest anyway, regardless of what it was. Maybe the best thing she could do, once she had found Josh, was to get him the medical help he needed and then get out of town for good. She could leave the infighting to Lew, the Alliance, and anyone else he could recruit.

She left the restaurant just as a busload of laughing, chattering seventy- and eighty-year-olds emptied out in front. A sign on the bus said Vegas or Bust. One of the tourists, a sprightly gent with a Forty-niners cap, looked about at the shopping center and the hills beyond.

"Nice town," she heard him say. "Very nice."

There was no evidence on the outside of the house on Orchard Road that anyone had been there over the past two days. The storm hatch in the back was still unlocked. The basement and upstairs were in the same awful shape. And the terrifying dried-blood message remained on the bathroom mirror.

VENGEANCE IS MINE
I WILL REPAY

The smell from rotting food was more intense. Abby opened some windows, then found a trash bag in one of the kitchen drawers. First she discarded all of the carry-out containers and obvious garbage. Then she turned her attention to the balled sheets of correspondence scattered on the floor. One by one, she smoothed the letters out and read them. Forty-five minutes later she had a list of nineteen names and businesses, including the President, the governor, the CEO of IBM, and even a woman Josh identified as his third-grade teacher. According to an especially venomous letter, replete with invective that Abby had never heard Josh use, the teacher was guilty of stifling the creativity of her students and of trying to inflict her jaded view of life on impressionable children.

In every paragraph, every word, Abby could feel her former lover's pain, confusion, anguish. But none of the subjects seemed like an actual target for murder.

Vengeance is mine.

She threw the last of the papers into the trash bag and turned on Josh's PC. She had used the computer for correspondence and, on two occasions, to prepare lectures, so she knew her way around it easily enough. It was almost ten. Outside, rain had begun falling steadily from a slate sky. Abby rubbed at the gritty fatigue that was beginning to settle in her eyes. Her nervous energy was starting to fade. She thought about making some coffee but decided against it and called up the first of Josh's folders, this one labeled Correspondence A. There were similar folders alphabetically labeled through *H.*

To her absolute dismay the folder consisted of thirty-five letters, memos, and even some poems, almost all of them tirades of hatred and anger. Some were later drafts of letters she had already read. Abby skimmed each one and added names to her list where appropriate. Of necessity she had to go faster and faster. Her concentration was getting feebler by the minute. She finished *A* and went on to *B.* When she realized there were another twenty-five files in Correspondence B, she decided she could make it through *C,* then she would have to take a break. She could have some lunch with Lew and maybe doze off at his place. Afterward she would hit the caffeine and keep going. She had to keep going.

Correspondence B was more of the same — a letter to a restaurant that had once improperly prepared his medallions of veal; a letter to the owner of the house they were renting, complaining about the poor quality of the construction. Then, suddenly, she noticed a file with her name on it. The date the file had last been worked on was just five days ago. It consisted of a single paragraph.

Dear one —
I didn't ask for this. I don't understand why I have been chosen. But I know what I have to do. It is clear that I will not be allowed to have you, to love you, until I am free. That is why I am going mad. I have fought it and battled it, when all I ever had to do was give in. Give in and accept that I am being tested. Vengeance is the Lord's and vengeance is mine. I must earn your love and respect. I must repay what was done to me. I must avenge my shame. And now I am off to do just that. When I have met them face-to-face, and ended their lives just as they have ended mine, I will be ready to reclaim your love. Killing them will be a gift — a gift to you, a gift to us, a gift to the man I once was. Pray for me, Abby. Pray for us. Pray

the pain ends once and for all.
And mostly pray for them. Vengeance is mine. I shall repay.
Bricker . . . Golden . . . Gentry
. . . Forrester.
BrickerGoldenGentryForrester-
Brickergoldengentryforrester

Abby stared at the names. She knew them all. Steve Bricker was Josh's immediate supervisor at Seradyne and had once been his friend. Nancy Golden was a colleague in Josh's lab. When the personnel cuts were made, Josh had been convinced that Nancy was kept, even though her work was inferior to his, because of an extracurricular relationship she had with Pete Gentry, the head of the research-and-development section. Alan Forrester was the president of the company.

For the year after his termination from Seradyne, Josh had handled the whole business philosophically, with his typical wry humor. But now his insanity-fueled hatred, almost certainly a manifestation of cadmium toxicity, had marked these four Seradyne employees for death.

Abby had no idea where Josh was. But now, at least, she knew where he was headed. Suddenly her fatigue was gone. She printed out a copy of the letter, hurried from the house, and sped to Lew's farm, praying all the way that Josh had not yet acted on his plan.

The short drive seemed interminable. Lew's Blazer was parked by the split-rail fence. As she skidded to a stop on the dirt-and-gravel drive, Abby honked the horn to give him some warning she was there. There was no need. He was approaching the Mazda's door as she was opening it.

"I heard you spin into the driveway down at the bottom of the hill," he said. "I'm so attuned to the quiet up here, sometimes I can tell when one of the cows isn't breathing right. What's happening?"

Abby jumped out, kissed him lightly on the lips, and handed him the letter.

"I got this out of Josh's computer," she said, heading toward the house. "Those four people all worked with him at the lab in Fremont. I've got to call and warn them."

Fremont was located on the Oakland side of the bay, about two-thirds of the way to San Jose. Abby had no problem reaching the Seradyne operator.

"Steve Bricker, please," she said.

She held her breath, half expecting a pregnant pause as the operator debated whether and how to tell her that Steve Bricker was dead.

"This is Steve Bricker."

"Thank God," Abby whispered. "Steve, this is Dr. Abby Dolan. Do you remember me?"

"Josh Wyler's Abby?"

"That's right."

"Is he okay?"

"Well, actually, he's not."

Abby imagined the man, sitting in stunned disbelief, as she reviewed the evidence that Josh was psychotic from heavy-metal poisoning and was headed toward Seradyne, intent on exacting vengeance.

"Abby, I find this all a little hard to accept. Josh was always such an easygoing guy. I know he was upset about the cutbacks and reorganization here, but, hey, I thought the severance package he got was pretty fair."

Abby had met Steve Bricker only once and remembered him as being very much taken with himself. Now, after just a brief conversation, she knew why she hadn't much liked him. The man had all the sensitivity of a football.

"Josh didn't want a severance package, Steve. He wanted his job. Things haven't worked out too well up here, and right or wrong, he blames you."

"That's crazy."

"That's exactly the point, Steve. Josh needs help badly. If we can find him, there's a decent treatment to remove the cadmium from his system."

"Well, for his sake he'd better not try anything. I have a permit and a gun, and I damn well know how to use it."

Abby groaned. This was precisely what she didn't want to have happen — a macho man ready to defend his turf. Shoot first, ask questions later.

"Steve, I'll call the others. I don't want Josh to get hurt."

"As long as he doesn't try anything, he won't be. Alan Forrester's on vacation. Nancy Golden's right down the hall. So's Gentry. I can talk with them. I'll talk with security also. Maybe they'll put someone extra on. Not that we need it. Place is tight as a drum."

"Steve, whatever happens, please try not to let him get hurt. That's the least you can do."

Bricker refused to back down.

"If it looks like he's going to hurt me or any of the others, I can tell you this — he'll be the one to get hurt first. That's the way it is. You know, back when they were making the cuts, I actually tried to talk Forrester into keeping him. Now look what I get for it."

Abby sighed and set the receiver down. She could try to explain more about Josh's condition, but Steve Bricker would never understand. She would call the Fremont police and then, just in case, Josh's brother in LA. There was no sense in worrying his mother, who was already frantic from Abby's last call. After that there wasn't much she could think of to do.

"How'd it go?"

Lew sat down across the table from her, his eyes full of concern.

"Bricker's cleaning out his revolver. Looking forward to the gunfight at the O.K.

Corral," she said.

"Just what you needed."

Lew came around the table and massaged her shoulders and temples.

"Oh, that feels wonderful."

Abby allowed her eyes to close for just a minute. He buried his face in her hair and pressed his lips against her.

"We'll find him," he whispered.

"Thank you, Lew. I don't know what I'd do if you didn't understand about Josh. Were you able to reach the prison hospital?"

"I did. The stupid doctor at Las Rosas wouldn't confirm or deny that Willie Cardoza was a patient there. I told him what he needed to do, and I think he understood me, but I'm not sure. Maybe you could get in touch with Willie's girlfriend. She has to know for certain where he was sent."

"Good idea. What about Barbara Torres and the pharmacist — what's his name?"

"Gil Brant. I'll call them and set up a meeting to bring them up to speed. But, frankly, Abby, I think they're both cardboard warriors. It's one thing to attend meetings. It's quite another to put your position in town on the line by bucking the establishment. That's why Dave Brooks was so valuable. He was absolutely relentless — fearless. You've got a lot of his qualities."

"Nonsense. I'm thinking more and more

about just pulling up stakes and getting out."

"You can't do that, Abby! Not when we're so close to breaking this whole thing wide-open."

"We're not that close, and you know it. We have a positive blood test, and after the O.J. trial, you know how much that means. Plus we have eye findings that suggest some people are cadmium toxic. But we still have no idea how it could have happened. And I don't think Colstar is just going to roll over and hand us evidence of what they did. In fact, I've been thinking that we may be putting Angela Cristoforo and Willie Cardoza in danger just by getting the word out that they're cadmium toxic. Besides, Lew, no matter how hard I try, I still don't feel as if this is my town or my fight. I've been staying involved because of Willie and Josh. Now one of them's going to be taken care of, and hopefully the other one will be, too. Colstar influences everything and everyone around here."

"I know they're powerful, but —"

"Lew, they've manufactured evidence that I'm responsible for Peggy Wheaton's death. If I don't resign, they're going to make it public."

Lew listened in agonized silence as she filled him in on her meeting with Joe Henderson.

"Damn them," was all he could say. "Damn them to hell." He knelt beside her.

"I'm so sorry, Abby. I'm so sorry they've done this to you. But we still need you. I need you."

He drew her lips close to his. His arms tightened about her as his lips parted. His tongue and his gentle hands became more searching. Abby found herself wondering what it would be like to lie naked next to him, to feel him on top of her, inside her.

"Lew, please," she managed, pulling away. "I love having you touch me. I love being with you. But I'm just too distracted. Right now I've got to follow through with finding Josh."

"Sorry. You're right. It's not the time."

"Don't be sorry. When it happens between us, I want to be a hundred percent there."

She kissed him again, quickly, then picked up the phone.

"Who now?"

"The Fremont police, then maybe Josh's brother in LA. And then I thought I might call Kelly Franklin again."

"Don't you think that's risky? I mean, you said yourself that Colstar might try to eliminate the toxic patients."

"Colstar, maybe, but not Kelly. I just don't believe she has that in her."

"That's where you and I differ," Lew said. "She's a snake, just like the rest of them."

"You'll just have to call it my woman's intuition and bear with me."

As she had expected, Abby got little encouragement from the Fremont police or

369

from Josh's vapid, money-conscious sister-in-law. The conversation with Kelly Franklin didn't start out much better.

"How certain are you about this Cardoza's blood work?" Kelly asked.

"Very certain. The woman who ran the test is one of the foremost toxicologists in the country."

"I just don't believe it. I've been over every inch of this company and the way we handle toxic substances. Dozens of times. I just don't see any way this could have happened."

"The exposure may be widespread," Abby added. "I have over a hundred fifty patients on a printout who've had strange, ill-defined symptoms that are quite consistent with cadmium toxicity."

"Those are the ones you mentioned with the excess MRI tests?"

"Exactly."

"But I don't see the connection."

"Neither do I. At least not yet. But I'm fairly certain there is one. The cadmium levels are no coincidence, and neither are all the MRIs."

"What do you want me to do about it?"

"Kelly, I don't know. It looks like Colstar is making people sick — very sick in some cases. What are you *supposed* to do about it?"

"You know, this is crazy. You have one positive blood test in a man who once worked for us, and some sort of rings in the eyes of a lady who's probably on multiple powerful psychiatric medications, and you want me to close down the company! I'll look into things, Abby, but I need much more than what you've given me to take any action at all."

"Just do me one favor, then."

"What?"

"If you're not going to take any action, please don't share this discussion yet with Lyle Quinn. I don't trust him."

"Abby, I don't think I can promise that."

"Please? Just for a day. Twenty-four hours."

"I'll consider it. But no promises."

"Thank you."

"And Abby —"

"Yes."

"I really don't think Lyle is all that bad. If you look past the posing and the theatrics, he's not nearly as hard as he wants everyone to believe."

"If that's true, he's sure got me fooled," Abby said.

She set the receiver down.

"What did she say?" Lew asked.

"Just about what you'd expect. At least I've got her thinking. Lew, I'm going to take a rain check on lunch. I want to stop by the hospital and speak with the patient who had the bad reaction in the MRI tube. Then I want to shower off this all-nighter grunge and crash for a few hours."

She could see his disappointment.

"Listen, whatever you say. I'm better at dinner than lunch anyway. When you wake up, you're bound to be hungry."

"Dinner sounds great. I'll call you as soon as I get up. If you don't hear from me by five, feel free to call."

"Perfect. If our cause can't get you to stay around, maybe my salmon poached in brown ale can."

"Lew, come on."

"Just kidding. I know you'll do whatever you need to do."

Abby pulled him to his feet and kissed him on the mouth.

"I love that you understand that," she whispered.

Chapter Twenty-Eight

Abby had no desire to run into Joe Henderson at this point, but she did want to speak with Claire Buchanan again. And if Claire's allergic reaction continued to respond rapidly to treatment, she might be discharged as soon as tomorrow morning.

Abby rationalized to herself that she wanted to check on the woman's condition and wish her well. Together they had faced death and won a reprieve. But she knew that was only part of the story. Something about the MRI tests was still gnawing at her — something that might become clear by going over Claire's story one more time. And Abby knew that with her own decision to leave Patience all but made, there would probably not be another chance.

What she had told Lew was true. She had been willing to stay at the hospital and in the town until Willie Cardoza was properly diagnosed and treated. She owed the same to Josh. But now there was nothing for her to gain by staying, and much to lose. She had underestimated the resolve and resourcefulness of Colstar and, in particular, of Lyle Quinn. The struggle to expose the truth about Colstar might continue, but in the end, she suspected, the Alliance would lose. And if she chose to remain and fight beside them, she would almost certainly become a casualty. Joe Henderson held all the cards — evidence that her critical judgment was impaired, and a community that had already joined ranks against her. She was history at PRH. Nothing could change that now. But a malpractice suit holding her responsible for Peggy Wheaton's wrongful death could tie her up indefinitely and jeopardize her ability to find another ER job, maybe kill it altogether.

Clearly, the best thing she could do for Abby Dolan at this point was to admit that she was overmatched and get out. People were being harmed by Colstar. That was a given. But people all over the world were being harmed by corrupt corporations and governments. Those tragedies weren't her responsibility, and neither was this one. And, dammit, she had tried. She had stuck her neck out for Lew and the Alliance, and now the blade was about to fall.

The arguments for leaving were perfectly sensible. And yet she remained on the fence. She had been working at the hospital for less than two months, but she had become part of a number of patients' lives in ways she never had at St. John's. Feeling as if she had deserted them — deserted herself — would hurt as much as knowing that she had been beaten so badly when she was in the right.

Then there were her deepening feelings for Lew. Her choosing to stay in Patience and fight Henderson, Quinn, and Colstar might be the best thing for their embryonic relationship, or the worst. She had already sacrificed her academic appointment for one man. Was she ready to risk her entire career for another? If she abandoned the cause, though, would Lew ever forgive her?

And, finally, there was Josh. If their situations were reversed, he would make any sacrifice to save her, she was certain of that. She stood a much better chance of locating him if she wasn't spending long hours at the hospital.

No, she told herself. This time her head had to prevail over her emotions and her instincts. There was too much to lose by staying in Patience. She would bequeath her data sheets to Lew and be off for San Francisco as soon as possible. With any luck she would be somewhere not too far from Seradyne when Josh made his move.

Feeling relieved at having closed in on a decision, she entered the hospital through the ER, and called the operator to check on Claire Buchanan's status. The one-time Rockette was out of the ICU and in a single just down the hall from it. Abby found her in a recliner in the bright, airy room, gazing out the picture window at the Colstar cliff. Claire lit up at the sight of her.

"Boy, am I glad to see you again," she said, her hoarseness now much improved.

"The nurses told me you saved my bacon by getting that breathing tube in. I remember you were there, but to tell you the truth, I didn't know what was going on. That's why I didn't thank you before."

"There were a lot of people helping you. I'm just glad you're okay."

"I would be if I could get rid of this itching."

Claire pointed to some patches of the same skin lesions Abby had seen on her in the ER. They still looked like small blood-vessel inflammation.

"Claire, tell me something if you can. You've had two MRIs, right?"

"Yes."

"Any other X rays?"

"Not really. They did a chest X ray just a little while ago."

"But before that?"

"None."

"How about blood tests?"

"Dr. Oleander's done some, and you did some. I don't think I had any before my first MRI, though. That was when I was having that stomach pain."

Abby stared at the woman in disbelief.

"Are you sure?"

"I may be nothing much more than an old chorus girl, but I have a heck of a memory. He did some blood tests after the first MRI, but none before."

Now it was Abby who was gazing out the window, past the meadow and the barbed-wire-topped fence. The Colstar cliff and the massive plant atop it looked somber and foreboding in the gray midday light. She closed her eyes. The pattern that had seemed so elusive to her, so nebulous, was coming into focus. Claire Buchanan had provided the lens. Not only were the MRI studies at Patience Regional Hospital ordered and performed in excess, but many of them were done *before* the actual problem that brought the subjects into the hospital. It was almost as if the studies themselves were causing illness. The confirmation of her theory lay in the KarMen record-keeping system of the hospital. But she thought she had enough data of her own in the loose-leaf notebook packed in the wall behind her furnace.

"Claire, it's been a pleasure meeting you," she said, now suddenly impatient to get home. "I'm very glad you're doing so well."

"Thank you. Tell me, Dr. Dolan, do you think I'll ever get rid of this rash and itch?"

Abby took the woman's hand in hers.

"You know, Claire, they teach us from day one in medical school never to make any promises to patients. But I'll tell you what — I'm going to promise you that before long you'll have some answers as to what's wrong. And with any luck those answers will point the way to the right treatment."

Claire Buchanan stood and hugged her.

"You take care, now, Doctor," she said.

"And don't forget to leave yourself some time for fun."

Abby took the staircase to the basement and left the hospital through the service door. The notebook, and the conclusions buried within the data, were the legacy she would leave for Lew and the Alliance. A significant number of the NIWWs had had an MRI that preceded their major complaints. There was some sort of scam going on at PRH, she reasoned — some sort of kickback deal with the radiologists, the hospital, or both. But no one appreciated that many of the patients involved in the scam had been exposed to cadmium. And, together, the magnetic field and the intense ultrasound were somehow interacting with the cadmium to produce symptoms.

Abby mulled over the explanation as she drove home. It was weak, she acknowledged — as tenuous as wet tissue paper. It was a square peg she was trying to hammer into a round hole. But it *was* a theory with some data to back it up. And that was more than the Alliance had been able to accomplish in their three years of trying. There was no reason for her to feel she had failed.

She pulled into her driveway with no recollection of having gotten into the car or driven home. It was a familiar phenomenon Abby had long ago labeled autohypnosis — one of the most consistent signs of extreme exhaustion. For nearly twenty-nine hours now, from the moment the phone in her bedroom had rung with Joe Henderson's call, she had been awake and on the move. Studying the data in her notebook could wait, she decided. She could not function without a few hours of sleep.

She entered the house through the back door and went immediately to the answering machine, desperately hoping for some news of Josh. There were two messages. A woman from Patience Auto Glass had called to see if there had been any problem with their service. Then there was a no-message hang-up. Abby rewound the tape just a bit and listened again. Whoever it was had waited through her greeting message and a good ten seconds into the recording before hanging up. She turned up the volume and listened a third time. It was a stretch, but she swore she could hear breathing. *Josh!*

"Say something," she muttered. "Come on, say something."

She took off her slacks and blouse — the outfit she had worn for her ill-fated appointment with Henderson — and put on a light cotton nightshirt. Then she opened the front door to check on two days' worth of mail. The metal mailbox was screwed to the house, just beside the front door. She opened the top of the box and was about to reach in when the wooden doorjamb next to her face burst apart, showering her with splintered wood. An instant later, there was a soft crack from somewhere up the hill far to her right. Before she could even react, there was a metallic snap from the mailbox, and the side blew off. Abby cried out and instinctively ducked and backed away. Then she saw the bullet holes above her in the wood. She flattened out on the stoop and pulled the screen door open with her fingertips. As she did, another bullet tore through the screen and snapped a hole in the partially open front door. Except for the single faint crack, she hadn't even heard any of the shots.

Her body was on red alert now, her heart hammering against the inside of her chest, her lungs unwilling to accept air. She had completely misjudged Kelly Franklin. The woman had sold her out to Quinn as soon as she had hung up. Damage control was now being initiated.

I think he's not as hard as he wants everyone to believe. Isn't that what Franklin had said about her pal, Quinn? *Well, screw you, lady,* Abby thought. *Screw you.*

Desperately, she scrambled back into the house on her hands and knees and kicked the door closed with her feet. Then, gasping for breath, she snaked on her belly to the bedroom phone. Behind her the picture window in the living room shattered inward, showering the sofa and braided rug with glass. Cringing from the noise, she dived between the bed and the wall. She was reaching across the quilt to call 911 when the phone rang. She hesitated, then snatched up the receiver.

The voice, almost certainly a man's, was raspy and muffled.

"Get out!" it said. "Get out now!"

Bathed in an icy sweat, she put down the receiver, then snatched it up again and called the police. The officer who answered knew immediately who she was and where she lived.

"We'll send someone over soon, ma'am," he said as if she had just called to report a stray dog in the neighborhood.

Make it someone other than the man who just shot at me, she wanted to reply.

She set the receiver down, and then, over-whelmed by the adrenaline of fear and anger, she cried. Fifteen minutes later, when two police cars pulled up in front of the house, she had washed her face, put on a Stanford Med sweatshirt and a pair of jeans, and brewed a cup of tea. Through the shattered plate-glass window she saw Sergeant Sullivan emerge from the front cruiser, laughing and chatting with a man wearing jeans and an Oakland Raiders windbreaker. Without bothering to announce their arrival, they began inspecting the carnage around the front stoop. The other cruiser, Abby noted, had "Captain" painted just above the blue accent stripe on the right fender. The officer who stepped out — Captain Gould, Abby remembered Sullivan calling him — was in uniform, complete with cap. He looked to be six four or five and had on mirrored sunglasses and cowboy boots.

From bad to worse, was all Abby could think.

As Gould approached up the front walk, he noticed her watching and gave her a half salute. She nodded and motioned him in. He paused briefly to speak with the two men inspecting the bullet holes, then entered without knocking. Abby predicted with exact accuracy the first words out of his mouth.

"Dr. Dolan, I'm Captain Gould. I've heard a lot about you."

"Well, now you're hearing that someone tried to kill me."

Gould slipped off his sunglasses with Clint Eastwood deliberateness and dropped them into a case on his belt.

"Who?"

Abby debated what her answer should be, then finally shrugged and said, "I think it was Lyle Quinn."

The policeman laughed out loud.

"Pardon me, Captain," Abby said, "but I don't think this situation is particularly funny."

She knew that her temper, under marginal control in the best of circumstances, was already smoldering from profound fatigue and anger. The last thing she needed to do now was to blow up at the captain of the Patience police force.

"Pardon *me,* Doctor," he replied, "but there are two things I think you should know. First of all, Lyle Quinn and his wife are at

St. Margaret's Church right now helping my wife, among a dozen or so others, prepare for tonight's auction and dance."

Abby felt embarrassment burn in her cheeks, along with irritation at this latest example of Patience cronyism.

"What's the other thing?" she asked stonily.

"Well, excuse me if this seems insensitive, Dr. Dolan, but Sergeant Sullivan and Detective Jacques out there tell me that the shots that hit your house were most likely fired from a ledge on the side of that hill over there." He pointed toward the spot. "I make that three hundred yards, maybe a little more. Lyle was a decorated officer in the Rangers. With the sort of high-powered rifle and sniper scope available at any army/navy store, he could have put a hole in the O in Stanford if he had wanted to." He gestured at the lettering on her sweatshirt. "Same goes for most of the hunters in this community, which is to say most of the men. Believe me, Doctor, the fact that you're alive means that nobody was trying to kill you."

"Right after the shots were fired, a man called me. He muffled his voice with a handkerchief or something, but his message was clear enough."

"And it was?"

" 'Get out.' That's all he said. 'Get out now.' "

"See, I told you whoever was up on that

383

ledge was just trying to make a point."

"Get out, Captain," Abby said sweetly.

"What?"

"That was the message to me. Now it's *my* message to *you*. I was shot at, Captain, not picketed. I'm simply not in the mood for your smug sarcasm right now. So, please, leave me alone. I'm tired, I have a headache, I want to get some sleep, and it's clear that this farce of an investigation is going to lead nowhere."

Gould hesitated for a few seconds, then shrugged and said, "Suit yourself."

He took a step toward the door before turning back to her.

"Dr. Dolan, I don't approve of that caller's methods, but I believe you should pay attention to what he said. There's a lot about this town that you just don't understand. We depend on each other a great deal here. You stamp on someone's toe on the east side of the valley, and someone on the west side is sure to say, 'Ouch!' "

"Nicely put. Thanks for your advice. I'll watch where I step."

Gould glared at her and looked for a moment as if he was going to say something else. Then he simply marched down the walk to his cruiser and drove away. A few minutes later, without so much as a word to her, Sergeant Sullivan and the detective left as well.

Abby found a handyman listed in the local paper who was willing to bring a sheet of plywood right over and nail it across the window. When she had finished cleaning up the glass in the living room, she considered trying to doze off in a chair until the repairman arrived, but she was too wired from her ordeal and too furious at just about everyone who had anything to do with Patience, California.

First the red pickup, now this. *Get out! Get out now.* Lyle Quinn was delivering his message with all the subtlety of a wrecking ball.

Well, I've got news for you, Lyle, Abby thought. *I'm off the fence now — but not on the side you expected.*

She went to the basement, retrieved her notebook, and began plodding through the data once more. Unlike her previous efforts, though, this time she knew what question to ask: which came first, the illness or the test?

Abby wasn't surprised when the repairman took much longer to arrive than he had promised. Although there was no way the man could have any idea what she was doing, she was just paranoid enough to close her notebook and conceal it in a kitchen cabinet until he was finished. Her preliminary survey of the data was confirming what she suspected. Somehow the MRIs were *preceding* certain symptoms, not just diagnosing them.

It was after three. Almost thirty sleepless hours now. The handyman talked incessantly as he worked, sharing town gossip with no regard for whether Abby knew the person or not. She brushed off several questions about the nature of the damage to the front of the house, then finally explained it away as blandly as she could — some vandals on a spree.

Still, bullet holes were bullet holes, and she could only imagine what a juicy yarn he would be spinning for his next customer about the crazy lady from the big city. She was smiling at the notion that no story the man could conjure up would come close to matching the truth, when the phone began ringing.

Reflexively, Abby hurried to the bedroom nightstand. But then she could only stand there, staring down at the phone through one ring, two, three. One more ring and the answering machine would kick in. Thinking about the hang-up she was certain had been Josh, she forced herself to pick up the receiver.

"Hello?"

"Abby, this is Kelly Franklin." The woman spoke in a near whisper. "Are you alone?"

Abby felt her temperature rise a degree at the mention of the woman's name.

"I'm not," she said coolly. "There's a repairman fixing a shattered window in my living room. What do you want?"

"Please get rid of him, Abby. I have to know you're alone before we can talk. I need to change phones and call you back. Is ten minutes long enough?"

"What's this all about?"

"Please. It's very, very important."

"Where are you?"

"Right now I'm at the library. Please — trust me."

Abby sank onto the bed. *Why should I, lady?*

"Okay, Kelly," she said. "Ten minutes."

Chapter Twenty-Nine

It took some fast talking and a twenty-dollar tip, but at last the handyman got the message that Abby wanted him to take a break — now. He was halfway down the front walk when Kelly Franklin called again. This time Abby snatched up the phone.

"Your friend Quinn had someone deliver an ultimatum to me with a high-powered rifle, Kelly," she said. "You led me to believe you wouldn't tell him about our conversation for twenty-four hours. It was more like twenty-four minutes."

"I never said a word to him. I swear I didn't."

"Spare me. You said you thought he was all bark and no bite. Well, those bullets were the real thing. They wrecked the front of my house, and they scared the hell out of me. Our staunch protector, Captain Gould, pooh-poohed the whole deal. He thinks that whoever pulled the trigger was an expert marksman who was just trying to frighten me out of town. I didn't bother pointing out to the man that one hiccup, one little gnat in his expert marksman's eye, and any further attempts to frighten me out of town would have been unnecessary."

"Abby, please believe me. I never even saw Lyle after we spoke. Of course, he may have a tap on my phone — that doesn't seem beyond him. But I never said a word to him or anyone else. I was far too busy following up on some of the things you told me."

She was clearly upset at Abby's accusation, but Abby reminded herself of Lew's warning that the woman was a consummate actor. Still, according to Captain Gould, Lyle Quinn was at church all afternoon. If Kelly hadn't called him, she had to be right about the tap on her office phone. Abby felt some of the hard edge of her anger toward Kelly begin to soften.

"Where are you calling from now?" she asked.

"My car. I don't trust the office phone. And there are always people hanging around pay phones, waiting to make a call."

"All of a sudden you're starting to sound as paranoid as the rest of us."

"I'm beginning to feel that way. Abby, I was bothered by some things you said the first night we were together. Especially a question you asked about openings on the northeast face of the cliff. You didn't explain the question, but it seemed clear to me you wouldn't have brought the subject up unless you knew something."

"I saw an old slide of the cliff, and it looked as if there were openings then. So a friend of mine and I scanned the face with high-powered binoculars. There almost certainly *were* openings there at one time — three of them. But they've been sealed off or camouflaged somehow."

"I know."

"What?"

"I know there were three windows. One of *my* good friends works at the library. I told her I wanted a book on the Patience mine. She found one locked away in the archive room. It's waiting on reserve for you."

"I'll stop by there tomorrow."

"If it's possible, it might be better if you could go now. The library's closed tomorrow until one."

"I haven't been to sleep since yesterday morning," Abby said, rubbing at her eyes.

"Abby, I believe you now. Something has to be going on at Colstar. Something that I don't know anything about. And I'm frightened. I left a note for you in the book explaining some things I've found. I . . . I probably shouldn't have done that."

Resigned as much as curious, Abby stuffed her nightshirt under the pillow and dragged a brush through her hair.

"I'll be at the library in fifteen minutes," she said.

"Thank you. You'll understand more when you read my note to you. But, first, stop by the registry of deeds in the basement of town hall. Ask for volume fifty-eight, and look on page one-seventeen."

"Page one-seventeen, volume fifty-eight."

"The registry's open until four. The library closes at five."

"Anything else?"

"Yes. Forgive me for doubting you. Whatever it takes, I'm going to find out why people in this company have been keeping secrets from me."

"Just be careful."

"I will. Read the note I left for you and do what it says. I'll contact you through your pager later today or this evening. And, please, *don't* call me at the office."

She sounded agitated now, her words spilling out one on top of the last.

"Easy does it, Kelly. We'll get to the bottom of things."

"No!" she snapped. "They lied to me. I hate being lied to. I don't detest anything else as much."

Without waiting for a reply, she slammed the receiver down.

Abby gazed longingly at the bed. As a resident, she had once done four straight months of alternating thirty-six hours on, twelve hours off, and had held up reasonably well. In fact, during training there was a certain cachet that surrounded "doing a thirty-six." But now she knew there was nothing heroic about long stretches without sleep, and a lot that was not only stupid, but for a physician, downright dangerous.

The Patience town hall, located on the small village green not far from the police station, was the only granite building in town. Like most everything else in the valley, it was postcard perfect, with a manicured lawn and a tree-lined duck pond in back. The cornerstone put the construction of the building at 1922.

On the way into town Abby stopped at the convenience store for a sixteen-ounce cup of hi-test coffee and a sugar fix in the guise of a jelly doughnut. In fifteen or twenty minutes she would feel as if another thirty or forty sleepless hours were quite within her capabilities. The chemically induced bravado would last for an hour or two, but the crash that followed would be the biologic equivalent of Black Monday.

No one took any particular notice of her as she crossed the marble-floored foyer and followed the signs down to the registry of deeds. The wizened man dozing behind the counter could well have been there since the cornerstone was laid.

Abby cleared her throat, startling him to his feet.

"Excuse me, I need to review some records," Abby said. "Volume fifty-eight."

"Can't take the volumes out of that room."

"I know."

"We close in an hour."

"I know."

"You real estate?"

"Medicine."

"Oh."

The man had resumed his nap before

Abby passed by him into the dimly lit registry. The space smelled of mold, dust, and old paper. The volumes, hundreds of them bound in khaki, canvaslike fabric and embossed in gold, filled five or six long rows of shelves, as well as shelves lining the stone walls. She found volume fifty-eight with ease, but wondered how she would have found anything if she had had to depend on the man at the desk. What, she wondered, had brought Kelly Franklin here in the first place?

Page 117 was the first of a series of documents dealing with the Patience mine. It recorded the seizure of the property known as the Patience Gold Mine in 1919, by the village of Patience. The reason given was failure to pay taxes and other bills. The next document registered the purchase of the property from the village by the California Battery Company. The date was October 18, 1925.

The several succeeding pages described and depicted plans to build an alkaline-battery manufacturing plant on the site of the old mine. Abby scanned the architectural drawings and knew immediately why Kelly had started her there. Fifty feet in from the cliff was the main shaft of the Patience mine, descending over a hundred feet from the surface, and terminating beneath ground level at the bottom of the cliff. There was an artist's arrow pointing at the shaft with the notation "To be sealed off." Nothing else.

Wedged into the binding was a small slip of paper. *A,* it read, *I had no idea this shaft even existed. I don't believe it was ever sealed.* Signed, *K.*

Abby traced the main aspects of the drawing on typing paper and tiptoed past the now-sleeping clerk. The existence of the shaft was not that surprising. But keeping it secret from the environmental health and safety officer of the plant certainly was. The caffeine-and-sugar mix, which had kicked in some time ago, was now augmented by a jet of her own adrenaline. Her initial take on Kelly Franklin, dating back to the ball field in Colstar Park, had been on the mark, after all.

Lyle Quinn had pushed Abby over the edge with bullets and a battered red pickup. Abby had done the same to Kelly Franklin with a barrage of facts. And the Colstar house of cards was beginning to quiver.

The library was directly on the opposite side of the green from town hall, but Abby walked casually around the green rather than across, careful to stay as far away from the police station as possible. There was a pay phone on a pole by the front lawn — undoubtedly the one Kelly had used to call her. Abby fished out the number of Seradyne in Fremont and called Steve Bricker.

"Steve, it's Abby Dolan," she said. "Anything?"

He laughed.

"Peaceful as a manger," he said. "Abby, don't you think you're blowing this whole business out of proportion?"

"Actually, I don't. A woman here is dead. She was run down by a man who —"

"I know. I know. Who was poisoned with cadmium, just like Josh. You told me that."

"Objects of hatred seem to become magnified in these people's minds."

"And Josh hates the four of us because we cost him his job. Abby, it just isn't going to happen. We've got an extra security man inside the factory, the Fremont police are circling the block every fifteen or twenty minutes, and Pete Gentry and I are carrying guns just in case. Now, if I were you, I'd be calling hospitals. If Josh is as sick as you say he is, maybe he'll show up at one of them."

"That's a good idea. Maybe I'll do that."

"Say, listen, Abby. You said you were coming down here."

"As soon as I arrange for coverage at work."

"I always thought you were a real interesting woman. How about we meet someplace for a drink?"

"Good-bye, Steve."

Ass.

The book Kelly had left on reserve, *A Brief History of the Patience Mine*, was narrow and threadbare. It was held closed with a rubber band that kept Kelly's envelope in place, and possibly kept the binding from falling apart as well. "Property of the Patience Historical Society" was stamped on the inside of the cover.

Abby took the book to a carrel in the stacks and opened Kelly's note.

> A —
>
> *I have worked for Colstar for five years and have studied detailed blueprints of the plant for hours and hours. Until you suggested it, I had no idea there were any subterranean areas beneath the company. But there are.*
>
> *After you have finished with this book, please ask the librarian named Esther to direct you to the two issues of the Patience Valley Chronicle I alerted her to. Look at the obituary for Schumacher, and the story and obit for Black. Good luck.*
>
> K.

The Patience Gold Mine, first opened in 1850, produced a steady yield of ore for almost fifty years before going dry. Abby flipped through the pages of the small volume, which was written by one of the last owners of the mine, William H. Gardner. In addition to creating incredible profits for some, the mine seemed to have spawned intrigue, financial ruin, suicide, and even murder.

What goes around comes around, Abby thought as she flipped through the pages.

Colstar International, through the California Battery Company, seemed to have inherited some of the Patience Gold Mine genes.

There was a small piece of paper — Kelly's paper — protruding from between pages thirty-eight and thirty-nine. Those pages and the ones following showed sketches of the mine. Extending some ninety or a hundred feet from the main shaft through the outer wall of the cliff face were three ventilation shafts that correlated perfectly with the three windows on Lew's slide. The highest of the openings was twenty-five feet below the mesa surface, the next, twenty-five feet below that, and the lowest, another twenty-five feet down, which placed it twenty-five feet above the ground. On the other side of the main shaft were two enormous man-made caverns, which expanded each year as miners chipped away at the rock. One of them appeared to be at about forty feet down and the other just below ground level. The drawings were fairly crude, but there was one, captioned "Piercing an Imposing Wall of Rock," that showed the ventilation openings clearly.

Abby traced that one and then skimmed the rest of the book. It was past four-thirty, and the caffeine was beginning to wear off. She returned to the front desk and found Esther, a cherubic woman with a large button on her blouse proclaiming that Readers Are Leaders.

"Here's the *Chronicle* from the twelfth," she said. "The one from last February is on this microfiche. The machines are in the central hall, just through those doors."

"Thank you."

Abby tucked the paper under her arm and turned away.

"Kelly's a fine woman, isn't she?" Esther said.

It was a statement, not a question. Abby turned back and smiled at the librarian.

"The best," she said.

There was an open microfiche reader, so Abby decided to start there. The newspaper issue was from February 3 — six and a half months ago. The front-page headline heralded the upcoming election to fill a vacancy on the regional planning board. The sports page praised the Valley Regional High School basketball team for once again winning its league. So normal. However, one of the obituaries that day was anything but.

Gustav "Gus" Schumacher, 44 Was Foreman at Colstar

A memorial service attended by two hundred relatives and friends was held at the Congregational Church for Gustav W. "Gus" Schumacher, a Colstar employee for twenty years and a foreman in the packaging unit for ten. A friend to many in Patience and a devoted father, Mr. Schumacher died in Las Vegas on January 15 in a gun battle with police. Immediately prior to his death, Mr. Schumacher is alleged to have shot and killed three employees of the Golden Nugget Casino.

Family members relate that Mr. Schumacher had once incurred heavy losses in that casino but that he had not gambled in several years and, in fact, had been active in founding the Valley chapter of Gamblers Anonymous. They also report that Mr. Schumacher had not been feeling well and had recently been under a doctor's care.

Schumacher leaves his wife, Dorothy, two sons, Gregory and Lance, a daughter, Heidi, and two grandchildren.

Memorial donations may be made to the Valley Region Little League.

Stunned, Abby read then reread the obituary. A triple murderer, eventually gunned down by police, yet thought enough of in the community to have a well-attended memorial service. *Schumacher had not been feeling well and had recently been under a doctor's care.* She had no doubt that the symptoms he was experiencing would include blinding headaches and violent, unpredictable mood changes. A call to his widow was all that would be needed for confirmation.

The second death was as fascinating — and disconcerting — as Schumacher's. It was written up on the front page and in the obituary section of the August 12 *Chronicle*. Abby had read about it and even discussed it at work. But at the time there was no reason, other than the obvious, to be interested in it. Now there was.

Twenty-seven-year-old Ethan Black, son of the industrial baron, Ezra Black, had ended his own life with a leap from the twenty-third-story office of noted San Francisco psychiatrist, Graham DeShield. Ethan held a degree in accounting from Cal State Fullerton and had been employed as comptroller at Colstar for the last two and a half years. He was a pilot and had done some set design for the Valley Players. In addition to Ezra and Estelle Black of Feather Falls, California, he left a sister, Ellen St. Germaine, of Berne, Switzerland.

DeShield refused comment to the press except to issue a statement that said Ethan had been responding well to treatment of his severe depression, and that his death was a terrible shock.

Ezra Black, the billionaire industrialist, speaking from his Feather Falls ranch, expressed his profound grief at his son's death and also some frustration with the medical establishment for not having solved the mystery of depression. Ironically, one of Black's companies, Coulter Pharmaceuticals, manufactured the antidepressant

Xerane, one of the most widely prescribed drugs in the world.

Abby took notes on the article and the obituary. She knew of Dr. Graham DeShield and, in fact, had once attended a lecture he had given to a packed house at grand rounds. It had been several years, maybe five or six, but she remembered feeling that he had described some of his celebrity patients in enough detail so that they were identifiable by anyone who read the papers or watched TV.

The self-aggrandizing allusions had made his talk fascinating, but Abby remembered feeling grateful that for the brief period of her life when she had seen a therapist, it wasn't DeShield. She set aside her notes and studied the face of the young man who was heir to a billionaire's fortune.

It was the headaches, Ethan, wasn't it? she thought. *But how did you get exposed? You worked in the accounting office. How on earth did you get exposed?*

CARDOZA . . . CRISTOFORO . . . SCHU-MACHER . . . BLACK . . . JOSH . . .

Abby printed the names out block style, then added, . . . **HOW MANY OTHERS???**

She packed her things in her briefcase, then gathered two more pieces of information before leaving the library. The first was the telephone number of Gustav Schumacher's widow, and the second was the location of Feather Falls. The town, on the edge of Lake Oroville and the Plumas National Forest, was barely a dot on the state map. But Abby suspected that most of that dot belonged to Ezra Black. She recalled reading articles about his vast ranch and estate — a splendidly isolated, rustic palace with its own helipad and game preserve. Depending on the roads, Feather Falls looked like a one- to two-hour drive south. It wouldn't be the first time she had used her M.D. to get through operators to unlisted numbers. Whether Ezra would be there, and whether he would see her, were other matters altogether.

It sounded insane to be trying to approach the owner of Colstar about the cadmium crisis caused by his own company. But his son had died a horrible death. And possibly, just possibly, Ezra Black had no idea why.

Chapter Thirty

Dorothy Schumacher, Gus's widow, lived in a modest red-shingled ranch on the west end of the valley. It was just after eight in the morning when Abby pulled up in front. The previous evening she had succeeded in convincing an operator that there was a medical emergency that required her to speak with Ezra Black in Feather Falls. The tycoon had spoken with her, although he was clearly annoyed with her ploy.

"My daughter is in Europe, my wife is here with me, and my son is dead, Dr. Dolan," he said. "There is *no* medical emergency that could possibly be of interest to me. So state the business that is so important you had to abuse your privilege as a physician. If I sense you have done so to request money from me in any form, I shall hang up, and you can expect to hear from the state medical board first thing in the morning."

In spite of herself Abby felt intimidated talking to the man whose face she had seen on the cover of *Time*, and whose reputation as a maker and breaker of people was universal.

"I want to talk about your son."

"Go on."

"I would prefer to speak with you in person, Mr. Black."

"Why?"

"I have reason, good reason, to believe that Ethan might have been chemically toxic when he died."

"What sort of chemical?"

"Please, Mr. Black. This would be much easier for me to explain in person."

"Dr. Dolan, we have not met, but I am well aware of your role in the death of Gary Wheaton's wife. And what I know does not sit well with me. So kindly answer my question, or this conversation is over."

Abby felt flustered and frightened. Black was used to being The Man. And there was no way he was going to relinquish an iota of control to her. She had somehow expected that getting hold of him would be the hard part. Now she knew better. She tried to choose her words carefully, knowing that if she was too careful, Black would sense it at once and might close up shop on her. She wished she had done some research into Ethan Black's medical history, but there simply wasn't time. All she had were the few facts she had read in his obituary and a lot of hunches. She knew that he had been an employee of Colstar, that he had been depressed, and that he had killed himself in a horribly violent manner. The rest was pure conjecture.

"I believe the chemical he was exposed to is cadmium."

"From the plant?"

"Exactly."

"Ridiculous."

"I have high blood levels documented on one patient, and evidence that several more have been exposed. All of them worked for Colstar at one time or another, and all of the patients I know about have exhibited violent behavior toward themselves or others."

There was a prolonged silence. Abby knew that something she'd said had struck a nerve.

"I'll see you at noon tomorrow here at Feather Ridge," Black ordered. "Just drive straight through the town of Feather Falls and keep going about half a mile. The main street ends at our ranch. The gateman will be expecting you."

"Thank you, Mr. Black."

"Just be sure to bring enough hard evidence to interest me in what you are saying. Because as things stand, I don't trust you, and I certainly don't believe you."

But you believe something I said, Abby thought as she set down the receiver. The main questions were, What? and Why?

Desperate for sleep, with her body rapidly running down, Abby tried unsuccessfully to locate Willie Cardoza's girlfriend. Colette Simmons's phone had been disconnected. According to Lew, Angela Cristoforo, Abby's second choice, lived with her mother. Abby tried the number but got no answer. There

405

were some notes regarding headaches in Angela's Caledonia State Hospital record, but nothing that well documented, and nothing Abby could get her hands on before she had to leave for Feather Ridge. That left only the widow of Gus Schumacher. Her number had been listed under "Dorothy and Gustave" in the Patience Valley phone directory.

"Gus was such a good man," Dorothy Schumacher said. "I knew there was something that caused him to do what he did."

"I can't make any promises," Abby replied. "But I'd like to meet with you for a short while tomorrow morning if that would be all right."

Dorothy gave her directions and made her promise to leave room for coffee and home-made strudel.

Abby set the alarm for six, located Josh's tape recorder, and set it on the dining-room table. Then she pressed her face into the pillow, almost too exhausted to fall asleep. Thirty-eight hours straight. She felt as if she had aged a year.

Dorothy Schumacher, soft and prematurely silver-haired, looked as if she had been put on earth to wear an apron and spoil her grandchildren. She greeted Abby with inborn warmth, but Abby could tell that she was putting up a brave front. Dorothy brought her directly into the kitchen, which was busily decorated with souvenir plates, collector spoons, and wrought-iron trivets. Lew had said to allow two and a half hours to make the eighty-mile drive to Feather Falls. Abby knew from the moment Dorothy started bustling about, talking nonstop about her late husband, that she would have to work hard to maintain some control over *this* conversation if she was to reach Ezra Black's home by noon.

"If it's all right with you, Mrs. Schumacher, I'd like to record what you have to say."

"Please call me Dotty. Nobody calls me Mrs. Schumacher or even Dorothy. Dotty always just seemed to fit, ever since —"

"Dotty, is it okay to record some of this?"

"I have no problem with that. No problem at all. When we were married twenty-three years ago, we recorded our wedding ceremony. Imagine, twenty-three years. I listened to it just the other night and — do you take cream in your coffee?"

"A little milk, please. No sugar."

Abby switched on the tape, then flicked it off again as the bereft woman began talking wistfully about the last bowling league she and Gus had been in. It was going to take some artful interviewing to keep Ezra Black listening for more than a few seconds. She waited until Dotty paused for a breath and switched on the machine again.

"Dotty, I don't want to put any words in

your mouth," she said quickly, "and I'll try not to. But could you please tell me what Gus was like for the few weeks before he went to Las Vegas and . . . and got into trouble."

Once again Dotty started rambling, giving a day-by-day account of Gus's life before he left on his fateful trip to the Golden Nugget Casino. Abby had spent many hours in medical school learning how to avoid asking patients closed-ended, leading questions such as, "Does the pain go up into your jaw?" Rather, no matter how much longer and more cumbersome the history taking would end up being, the request that needed to be made over and over again was, "Tell me about your chest pain. . . . Tell me more. . . . Is there anything else you can think of?" She knew that, as with patients, being forced to ask directive questions would greatly devalue Dotty's story. And Ezra Black would know it, too. Still, without several hours and a skillful sound editor, there was nothing else she could do.

"Dotty, did Gus have any headaches?"

"Oh, yes, they were very bad. One day while he was working in the garden, he actually had to lie down right back there on —"

It had been the right idea, just the wrong performer. Abby could feel any hope of presenting Black with this tape slipping away. Once again she flicked off the recorder. A frontal assault was going to be the only way.

"Dotty, I don't have a lot of time, so I'm going to try to keep the questions and answers short."

"Would you like some more strudel? I use that low-cholesterol, low-salt butter."

"It's wonderful, but no, thank you." She clicked on the tape once again. "Dotty, did anything unusual happen along with Gus's headaches?"

The woman stopped wrapping strudel for Abby to take home, actually stopped talking, and thought in silence for a surprisingly long time.

"By 'unusual,' " she said at last, "do you mean like the flashing lights he complained of before the headaches actually started?"

Shielded by the table, Abby clenched her fist and pumped it excitedly. *Nice going, Kelly,* she was thinking.

"Yes, Dotty," she said. "That's exactly what I mean. Tell me about the flashing lights. . . ."

As Lew had predicted, Abby made the spectacular drive down to Feather Falls in just over two hours. She had wanted to take him along for company, moral support, and to present a unified front to Ezra Black, but he was on duty in the ER. He would be working an extended shift — from eight A.M. until almost midnight — because Jill An-

409

derson and her husband had a wedding to attend.

Abby cruised down the neatly kept main street and was out of town in just a few blocks. The narrow road curved upward through rolling range, high above Lake Oroville. Then, past a small painted sign that said simply Feather Ridge, it entered a rich, perfectly planted orchard — oranges, pecans, avocados, and even several cork trees. About two hundred feet farther was the guardhouse, and beside it, an ornately wrought ten- or twelve-foot-high gate that spanned the roadway. The letters "EB" were scrolled on both sides in bronze. Extending out from either side of the gate as far as Abby could see was a seven-foot-high iron-rail fence topped with several tightly strung strands of thin wire that she guessed were electrified. And beyond the gate, beyond the orchard, there was only grassland and a gently rising tree-lined road.

So this is where the other zero point zero, zero, zero, one percent lives, she thought. *Not bad. Not bad.*

"Dr. Dolan, we've been expecting you," the gateman said. "Would you mind opening your trunk and stepping out of your car?"

Maybe not so great after all, she decided as the gateman and another identically uniformed guard checked her with a metal detector and carefully searched the Mazda inside and out, including beneath the hood. To amass wealth of this magnitude, there

410

must be countless casualties — and enemies. One of the guards examined the tape recorder and passed it over to her.

"Would you play this for me, please?"

Abby did as she was asked. The guard apologized to her for the inconvenience, made a call from a cellular phone, and opened the gate electronically.

"You'll be met at the house, Doctor. Have a good day."

Abby drove slowly through the gate and up the road, feeling slightly like Dorothy approaching Emerald City. The road continued upward for almost half a mile, then crested above a broad, verdant valley. On the far side of the valley, sprawling across the side of a small mountain, was a magnificent rustic estate — rough-hewn logs, massive windows, decks and balconies, and seven chimneys. Abby paused for a time to take in the entire panorama. The view to the north encompassed the lake. To the south was the heavily forested area she assumed was the game preserve, and behind her was a vista that might have extended to Japan. It was daunting to think of the movers, shakers, and world leaders who had driven in over this road or flown in by chopper.

Pay no attention to that man behind the curtain.

Abby rolled down into the valley past a dozen grazing horses, and up to the house on Feather Ridge. A security man opened the door for her and asked her to leave the key. Apparently, Ezra Black disliked automobiles cluttering his front drive. She mounted the broad stairs to the veranda, thinking about the modest home of Gus and Dotty Schumacher. How strange that suddenly their lives and Ezra Black's were so intimately entwined. But she knew, even without the full story on Ethan Black, that they were. The problem was going to be convincing Ezra Black.

She was shown to his study by a cadaverous servant wearing a white dress shirt and black vest, but no coat. He was the first man she had met on the property who she decided was not wearing a gun.

"Welcome to Feather Ridge," he said. "Mr. Black will be down presently."

He offered her a drink, and she opted for a Diet Pepsi — something to hang on to. The room was about as she would have expected — huge rough-hewn beams, animal heads on the walls, plush oriental carpets on the floors, perfectly worn leather furniture. Black's desk — mahogany, Abby guessed — could have been marked off in yards. Unimaginable wealth. Yet none of it had been enough to keep Ethan from diving out a twenty-third-story window.

There were several framed pictures on the desk. Not feeling comfortable walking around to view them, she turned the nearest frame around and then picked it up. It was an eight-by-ten black-and-white of

Ezra Black arm in arm with Senator Mark Corman. Several seconds passed before Abby recognized the backdrop, purposely blurred to get sharp detail of the two subjects. They were standing in front of the main entrance to Colstar.

She replaced the photo and picked up another. This one, in color, was of Black and a man who she felt certain was Ethan. He was a bit taller and huskier than his father, but there was no missing the likeness. They were wearing waist-high waders and standing knee-deep in a mountain stream, each proudly displaying a large trout. Ethan looked about eighteen. Suddenly Ezra Black's loss was real to her — more than just a link in a chain of events.

"Sorry to keep you waiting, Dr. Dolan."

Abby whirled, immediately self-conscious that she was still holding the photo. Ezra Black stepped forward and extended his hand. Abby shook it, then somewhat sheepishly set the frame back where she had found it.

"Thank you for seeing me," she managed.

Black motioned her to one of a pair of hand-tooled beige leather couches and settled himself on the other. He was bigger than life in print and on television, but in person he was rather ordinary in stature. In fact, he was actually slight, without an ounce of excess fat. His pale-blue shirt perfectly matched his piercing eyes. She could almost see the energy crackling off him.

Abby had long ago learned the distasteful feeling of having a man undress her with his eyes. Ezra Black's steady gaze was something else entirely. She was not being disrobed, she was being scanned. X-ray vision to her soul. The sensation was not disturbing, not even intimidating. It was, in fact, impressive. She bet herself that he was seldom very far off the mark in his assessment of people.

"I assume you deduced that photograph is of my son and me," he said.

"I felt very sad seeing the two of you together and obviously enjoying one another so much. You have my sympathy for what happened."

His expression, the slight raise of an eyebrow, suggested that he was surprised by her empathy.

"Ethan and I had our differences," he said. "What father and son don't? He was never ambitious enough for me; I suppose I was never understanding enough for him. But on the whole, we were reasonably close. Do you know much about him or about the way he died?"

"No, sir. Only what I read in the papers."

Abby was careful not to bend the truth in any way. She was struck by the fact that Black had asked her nothing about herself, her background, or how she came to be practicing at Patience Regional Hospital.

414

Then it occurred to her that within minutes of hanging up after their phone conversation last night, he probably knew a great deal. Unfortunately, that would mean he had probably gotten the Joe Henderson or Lyle Quinn version.

"If all you know is what you've read in the papers, why would you conclude my son was toxic from cadmium?"

No wasted time. No small talk. Ezra Black's way was strictly put up or shut up. She opened her briefcase and passed over what documents she had accumulated as she discussed each one.

"This is a list of over one hundred fifty cases treated at Patience Regional Hospital over the last two years, none of which has had a positive test leading to a specific diagnosis. All of their symptoms are consistent with the many faces of cadmium toxicity."

Black glanced at the list for no more than a few seconds and set it aside.

"It says that a number of these people have had negative tests for cadmium. Have any of them had a positive blood test?"

"No, sir, but —"

"What else do you have?"

Abby felt the already chilly atmosphere grow colder.

"I have five other people who are not on that printout," she said, passing over a chart she had made. "As you can see, all of them worked at one time or another for

Colstar. One of them is your son. Two of the five have died violently. One of the others, Angela, is a self-mutilator. Josh Wyler is off on some crazy mission of vengeance right now. Willie Cardoza is the one who ran down Peggy Wheaton." Abby sensed she was speaking too rapidly, but she feared that if she slowed down, Black would cut her off for good. "As you can see, four of the five, not counting Ethan, whom I don't know about, had severe, distinctive headaches. This cassette is of an interview I did this morning with Dotty Schumacher, the widow of the third person on the list. I thought maybe something she said would resonate with what you know of your son's case."

Black popped the cassette into the player and listened stonily for ten minutes. It was impossible to read what he was thinking. He clicked off the machine and gestured to the chart once again.

"If I understand this correctly, the one positive-cadmium blood test you have here was on the man who murdered Gary's wife?"

"Yes. The test was run by a toxicologist at my old hospital in San Francisco. We have blood going out on Angela Cristoforo now."

"What about all these negative tests?"

Black was like a guided missile. Abby knew this was not the time to accuse his company of purposely switching samples or

416

falsifying data. But since that probably was, in fact, the truth, there was no decent alternative explanation. She hoped her response didn't sound as feeble to him as it did to her.

"The cases on that printout, with a few exceptions, did not have symptoms as severe as the five people on that chart. They might have tested negative because their exposure to the metal wasn't that great."

"And this box, Eye Findings, that you've checked positive on Cardoza and Cristoforo?"

"A yellow glow around the iris of their eyes when looked at with an ultraviolet light."

"And you think this . . . this glow is from cadmium?"

"I do."

"You have scientific proof of that?"

Abby hesitated just a second, then shook her head.

"No. No, I don't."

She could sense that she had still not piqued his interest, and now she had played every card in her hand. There was half a minute of silence while the billionaire processed what she had presented. His face was still an undecipherable mask.

"Do you belong to the Alliance?" he asked suddenly.

Abby felt her hopes sink. Ezra Black had read the evidence, but he remained unconvinced. Now she was going to have to defend her motives in bringing it to him.

"I've been to one meeting. I confess that I felt sympathetic toward their issues. But I haven't considered myself a member, and I had no intention of actively supporting their cause until certain people started trying to frighten me into leaving Patience."

"Frighten you?"

"Someone tried to run me off the road while I was taking Willie Cardoza's blood to St. John's in San Francisco. Then, yesterday, that *same* someone, I suspect, shot at me in front of my house. The police think they were trying to miss. I'm not so sure."

"So instead of frightening you into leaving town, they've driven you to stay and fight."

"I think people are in great danger from this chemical. At first I didn't feel it was my fight. Now I do."

For the first time since meeting Ezra Black, Abby had no trouble reading his expression — utter disdain.

"Dr. Dolan," he said, "as far as I can see, you couldn't be further off base. Those misguided zealots in the Alliance have taken advantage of you. They've been tilting at the Colstar windmill for almost three years, and they have nothing to show for it. They knew you were looking for some explanation for your boyfriend's insane behavior and some way to justify your decision to treat that animal, Cardoza. So they fed you just enough lies to help you put

418

two and two together and come up with five!"

"That's not so."

"Trust me, Doctor. It is. There is no cadmium exposure. Never was, and from my plant, never will be. My son Ethan was always weak. From the time he was a child he had a great deal of difficulty in developing self-esteem. The two years he spent at Colstar were the longest time he had ever held a job. But, in general, he was managing fairly well. Then one night he skidded off the road going home from work in a storm. He was driving a stupid little sports car with no protection. That was his problem — that and the damn high-society psychiatrist I was foolish enough to trust. Ethan sustained head injuries, including a laceration and a severe concussion. He couldn't even remember the accident. That's when his personality began to change and he began to go downhill. Ethan's problems dated from that accident. Not from any goddamn cadmium exposure."

"But —"

"My son was a numbers cruncher, for crying out loud! An accountant. How in the hell would he have gotten poisoned from an industrial exposure? Well? Answer me. How could he?"

"I don't know."

"That's because he never did. You put words in this Schumacher woman's mouth, and you know it. She hears you, and suddenly she's thinking about how much she can extort from Colstar." He stood and handed the tape recorder back to her. "Dr. Dolan, my company is in a very delicate position right now in a number of areas. I warn you not to cause any more trouble for us. My man will show you out."

He turned and started out of the room.

"Mr. Black, you're wrong," she said firmly. "And I think you know it. There was a sustained cadmium exposure — a big one, I'd guess from Cardoza's blood levels. And somehow the people on those lists were hit, including your son. Go speak to Mrs. Schumacher yourself if you think you're such a good judge of who's misguided and who's not."

"Good day, Doctor," Black said without looking at her.

"Okay, have it your way. One more question, then I'm gone. Did Ethan have an MRI?"

Black turned around and eyed her evenly — another penetrating scan.

"That test was done the night of his injury," he said finally. "It showed nothing, just like all the other tests. Do you have some reason for asking me that question?"

Abby stared down at the floor, then back up at the man.

"When I do, sir," she said, "you'll be the first to know."

Chapter Thirty-One

Although Abby had been in the Feather Ridge mansion for less than an hour, by the time she left, the bright, crisp day had turned overcast and humid. She was somewhere between the house and the main gate when the first of a series of squalls hit. The drive back from Feather Ridge, hampered by the wind-driven rain and impassable truck traffic, took a seemingly endless three hours. When hunger got the better of her, she stopped at a roadside diner for an omelette and home fries.

The visit with Ezra Black had hardly gone as Abby had anticipated. But why? Black had been interested enough in what she had to say to invite her out to his home. Yet he refused even to admit to the possibility that Colstar was responsible for a cadmium leak. She had actually planned to suggest exhuming Ethan's body as confirmation of her theories. Fat chance. If digging up the man's son was somewhere between third base and home, she was still in the dugout waiting her turn at bat.

She pulled out of the diner lot just as a huge semi roared past ahead of her. The narrow highway looked as if it was going to be solid yellow line for miles, so she slowed down until she was out of exhaust range and cruised. For a time she lost herself in Nanci Griffith's latest album. But there was just too much going on in her head to stay distracted for too long. Time was running out for Josh and anyone else who had been exposed. And with that folder sitting inside Joe Henderson's desk, time was running out for her, too.

The only explanation that kept making sense for Black's rude behavior was that he knew something about what had happened at Colstar. He knew there had been a cadmium spill of some sort. Perhaps he was aware of, or even responsible for, the subsequent cover-up. But until her call he had no idea his accountant son had been a victim. Even now he wasn't sure. So he had invited Abby to Feather Ridge to size her up as opposition, and to hear what she had to say.

It had been ridiculously naive of her to believe that he would simply embrace all her facts and theories on the spot. The man had not become a billionaire by taking anyone's word on blind faith. He had listened to her, and now he was checking out her story.

"What did you expect him to do?" she asked out loud.

But even if Black had no idea that Ethan's death was connected to his employment at Colstar, *something* she had said over the phone had registered. For the final thirty miles of the drive back to Patience, she played that telephone conversation over and over in her head. She hadn't said much, really — only that a large number of still-undiagnosed cases had passed through the Patience Regional Hospital ER with symptoms consistent with cadmium toxicity, and a group of at least five Colstar employees had exhibited bizarre, often violent, behavior that she believed was caused by massive exposure to the metal.

Violent behavior. Was that it? Was that the hook that had gotten Ezra Black's attention? As she rolled down the final hillside into Patience, Abby mulled over the possibility. Although Ethan's suicide was tragic, it was explainable by his depression. According to Ezra, the depression was believed to be a product of his son's head injury and profound, preexisting low self-esteem. But supposing there had been more going on. Supposing Ethan had behaved with the same illogical, unbridled violence as Josh, Willie, and Gus Schumacher. There would be no reason for Ezra to share that information with her — especially if he had gone out of his way to cover it up. But if he knew that Ethan's violent behavior was no longer a secret, there was at least a chance he would allow his company to accept responsibility for what it had done . . . or was still doing.

There was only one person Abby could think of who might be able to confirm that

Ethan Black had demonstrated excessive, irrational violence before his death — one person who could effectively tie him to the other four cases — Dr. Graham DeShield. It was clear that Black Ezra blamed the therapist, at least in part, for his son's death. Considering Black's reputation, it wouldn't be surprising if he had already done something to make his displeasure with the psychiatrist known. If so, it was possible that a soothing feminine voice and a little pandering to DeShield's ego might get him to bend the laws of patient confidentiality just a bit. From what Abby remembered of the man, it was a distinct possibility.

It was just four and still raining when she reached home and swung into the driveway. The large sheet of plywood across her picture window was as obtrusive as missing front teeth. Mindful of her nocturnal visit from Lyle Quinn, she remained in her car for a minute until she sensed no one was about. As had been her habit since Josh moved out, she had left several lights on in the house. Against the dreary late afternoon the glow from the windows was comforting. She entered the kitchen and immediately checked around the house. There was no sign anyone had been there. Everything seemed to be in place.

She called information in San Francisco and got DeShield's office number. Then she left notice with his service that her call was an emergency regarding his patient Ethan Black, and that the operator should try to reach the doctor rather than wait for him to call in. Assuming he got her message, it was hard to imagine he wouldn't respond.

It was only then that she noticed the red light flashing on her answering machine. One message. Her first thought was, *Josh*.

"Abby, I'm assuming you recognize my voice," the tape said. In just the first few words Abby could feel Kelly Franklin's tension. "I'm calling from my car. I've left an envelope for you with the woman who gave you something from me yesterday. Please try to get it before this evening. If we miss connections, I'll be in touch."

Abby listened to the message a second time. Kelly's paranoia seemed to be building by the hour. But given her own experiences, first with Lyle Quinn, then with Joe Henderson, Abby was not surprised. The woman Kelly was referring to had to be Esther at the library. There was still half an hour before it closed. But what to do about DeShield? Clearly, she had to drive into town. The only thing she could think of was to change the greeting on her answering machine.

"This is Dr. Abby Dolan," she said. "I've had an emergency and will be away from my office until five. Dr. D., please leave a number where I can reach you then. It is very important. Thank you."

The repetition of her new message was

still playing when she snatched up her windbreaker and hurried out to her car. She reached the library at exactly four-thirty, just as Esther was locking the front door.

"We closed at four today," the librarian explained as they huddled in the doorway against the continued steady rain. "Kelly came by at about two with an envelope for you. She said I was to destroy it if you didn't pick it up before we closed."

"Damn," Abby murmured.

"Fortunately," Esther went on, with a tiny smile, "I decided to do so after I got home."

She passed the white business-sized envelope over, and Abby thanked her.

"I know it's probably none of my business, Dr. Dolan," Esther said, "but is Kelly in some sort of trouble? This is all very cloak-and-dagger, and she's seemed very nervous these last couple of days. That's just not like her."

"She's under some stress at work," Abby ventured. "But I'd rather let her tell you about it."

"We're in a quilting group together. Every Thursday night. The Thimblefingers. We raffle the quilts off for charity. I sure hope she's okay."

The woman was stalling for more information. Surely her interest was just the concern of a friend, but suddenly Abby felt herself prickle with caution. There was no telling how tightly the Patience grapevine was coiled. She thanked Esther and hurried back to her car, wondering how people who were intrinsically mistrustful ever managed to function in the world. Then she drove to a deserted street a mile out of her way before she would chance opening Kelly's envelope.

Abby, forgive me for dragging you out here, but Lyle's been hanging around a lot more than usual, and I'm afraid to leave much of a message on your machine. I sense that he knows we've been in contact, but he hasn't said anything.

I think I've found the staircase that leads to the lower chambers of the mine. Second shift will be the best time to see. The truth is, my job allows me access to any part of this plant, so even if I get stopped, I should have a decent excuse.

There's a small, very secluded park just a few blocks from my house. Enclosed is a map of how to get there. Let's meet there at seven. I don't know what's going on here, but I am convinced something is. And I believe it's happening right under me. I'm angry, but I'm calmer than you might think. Wish me luck. See you at seven.

Abby read the letter until she had nearly memorized it, then tore it up and studied the hand-drawn map. Kelly had marked the park and her house. She included her home

427

address and phone number, as well as a note at the bottom that the key to her house was beneath a large planter by the back door, and the phone number of her ex-husband was taped to the kitchen phone. Paranoid, frightened, or more likely both, Abby decided.

She hid the map beneath the repair records, owner's manual, and bag of corn chips in her glove compartment, and headed home. It was almost five. She would give Graham DeShield until six, and then would stop by the ER to bring Lew up to speed on all that had transpired. After three years of chipping away, he deserved to know that Colstar's facade was beginning to crumble.

Kelly Franklin sat in her locked office, the blinds drawn. She had been hunched over blueprints and builder's notes for most of a day and now could feel the strain at the base of her neck. The drawings and blueprints were kept in an archive room, and she was one of the few who had a key. As environmental health and safety officer, she had to be expert on the heating and ventilation systems of the plant, as well as on the disposal route for all toxic materials.

There were records dating back to the 1920's when the first construction of the California Battery Company began, and literally hundreds of sets of drawings and blueprints, many of which were rolled, held with rubber bands, and carelessly piled in bins. The newer drawings, necessary for occupational health and safety, were quite carefully filed. Because so many years elapsed between the initial building and the massive reconstruction by Colstar, Kelly had never examined the original plant blue-prints or the several additions that were completed before Colstar took over. But now she had spent much of the past night and all day scanning those earlier draw-ings, often beneath a magnifying lens, and comparing them to more recent ones. What she was looking for was a staircase or passageway of some sort that she knew nothing about. There were dozens of stair-ways leading down to the basement level where the power plant and some of the manufacturing units were housed. But the basement, she had been told, was built on solid rock.

Now, thanks to Abby Dolan's persistence and her own research, she knew better. There were huge, man-made caverns, two of them beneath the plant at depths of forty and one hundred feet. And somewhere in the massive factory there was access to them. At about one that afternoon she had found something in a drawing done in 1946 — a staircase at the very back of what would one day become C Concourse. The area containing the stairway was eventually partitioned with eight-foot-high walls that were still four feet short of the ceiling. The dozen or so large rooms created by the partitioning were used for warehousing and storage. Kelly had patrolled the spaces on any number of occasions searching for safety violations or potential sources of trouble. She did not recall seeing a door or staircase in the spot depicted in this one drawing. It was possible the flight had been sealed off, but there was no such notation as there were for other stairways on other drawings. It was as if, sometime between 1946 and the next set of blueprints in 1968, the staircase had simply disappeared.

It seemed to her that other drawings containing the area around the staircase might actually be missing, but there was no way to tell for certain. The only way she would ever know would be to check out the area for herself.

She carefully put the blueprints back together and returned them to the archive room, keeping only the ones showing the warehouse area. Then she clipped a small, powerful flashlight onto her belt, locked her office, and slipped behind the wheel of her golf cart. If she couldn't find the staircase, it was back to the drawing board. But Kelly was betting it was still there.

For whatever reason, no one at Colstar had ever told her about the caverns left over from the Patience Mine — caverns that could have been the source of natural-gas leaks, collapse during earthquakes, or even collapse from the weight of the plant itself.

As she rolled up A Concourse toward the reception area, careful to maintain a normal speed, she wondered who in the company might know. As far as she could tell, none of the officers had been there for more than ten years — none except Lyle. Was it possible that no one knew about the caverns or about the three ventilation shafts that had been sealed off? Not likely. As environmental health and safety officer, she reported directly to the president, a keen businessman named Roger Sealy. Together they had walked through every inch of the plant. If he knew there *were* subterranean spaces, she had to give him credit for being one hell of an actor. The same would go for Lyle Quinn.

Kelly felt her heart beating in her chest as she approached the mouth of C Concourse. She had never been foolhardy in any sense of the word, although she did have an adventurous streak that revealed itself in her love for scuba diving and rafting. Now she felt a bit frightened, but also keyed up and not a little angry. She had left a perfectly decent job with the Forestry Service to move to Patience and Colstar. What in the hell had she been doing here all these years? Had she really been just a shill — the frontman for a lie? Had her repeated, earnest denials of the allegations of the Alliance been just what Quinn or some of his cronies had brought her there to do? Soon she would have the answers.

Her plan was to drive along on a routine inspection tour, then to leave her golf cart inside one of the storage rooms at the end of C Concourse and make her way on foot to the rear of the area. Second shift was now well under way. Foot traffic was almost nil. Dan Gibson, a foreman Kelly knew well, passed by in a golf cart and waved cheerfully. Kelly hoped she looked more relaxed than she was feeling. There was no one around when she reached the first of the doorways to the warehouse area. They were all wide enough to fit a forklift and wooden pallet, and more than wide enough for the golf cart. She turned left through the second one, then immediately right into a room used to store cleaning supplies. She could hear men's voices coming over the top of the walls, but there was no one in sight. The blueprints with the partition walls drawn in did not include the staircase, so she was constantly forced to go from 1945 to 1968 to 1985 and back as she made her way through the maze of rooms toward the very rear of the factory.

"Can I help you?"

Kelly whirled, badly startled.

A young man in coveralls confronted her from about ten feet away. She had never seen him before. She took a moment to catch her breath and forced a smile. The man did not seem to recognize her, which was somewhat strange. There was a two-hour health-and-safety talk she gave to each shift every four months dealing with various topics including toxin containment, evacuation procedures, and even first aid. And although she had no way of knowing all the twenty-four hundred or so Colstar employees, they almost all had reason to know her. She moved close enough to see the man's ID badge and to give him a look at hers. *Jeff Kidd, Warehouseman.*

"I'm Kelly Franklin, environmental health and safety," she said, steadying herself with one hand against a wall until the rubberiness in her knees firmed up. "Just doing a routine walk-through of this section."

No glimmer of recognition from Kidd. But he did read her badge and nodded.

"I'm sorry," he said. "I've only been here a couple of months, and I've never seen you before."

Kelly tried unsuccessfully to remember when she had last given her talk to the second shift.

"No problem," she replied. "I'll be giving a talk to your shift real soon. You'll get to know me then. I'm going to be wandering around here for the next half hour or so. I don't need anything, so you might as well go on about your business."

The man met her gaze levelly — perhaps more self-assuredly than she might have expected from a relatively new warehouseman confronting a company VP.

"If you need anything or you get lost, Ms.

Franklin, just holler. I'll probably hear you over these walls."

"I'll do that."

Kelly moved slowly toward the next area, inspecting the overhead ventilation ducts. She sensed that Jeff Kidd was still watching her. And, in fact, only when she risked a glance in his direction did he finally turn and head off. Unsettled by the encounter, she came close to going back to her office. Instead, she wandered slowly from room to room, feigning an inspection. Except for Jeff Kidd, no one seemed to be around, although from somewhere she could hear a forklift whine. She checked the blueprints again. Just one more doorway to get through. Again, she glanced about. No one. She rolled up the blueprints and stepped into the last room. It was large — perhaps forty feet square — broken up by a network of floor-to-ceiling shelves containing boxes of nonflammable chemicals, packaging supplies, and paint.

Listening carefully for footsteps, Kelly worked her way to the west wall. According to the drawings, the staircase should have been almost at the midpoint. Right where she expected the door to be, there was a forklift, facing the wall, piled high with empty pallets. The ignition key was in place. Kelly had to peer between the adjacent shelves to see beyond the pallets, but the door was there — metal, unlabeled, not unlike hundreds of other doors throughout the plant, except that every one of those other doors had been opened by her at one time or another. If it was locked, she ought to have the key. She backed away to where she could view the entire room and separated the appropriate master from the other keys on her ring. Then she turned on the forklift and backed it away from the wall just far enough for her to squeeze in past the pallets. If anybody needed to come through that door, they would have to call someone in the warehouse to move the pallets. Was that someone Jeff Kidd?

The master key turned easily, and she pulled the door open an inch. Beyond it she could see only darkness. There was no way to get the pallets back in place. If anyone checked, they would know someone had gone down the stairs. The part of her that was urging a retreat until she could return with someone — perhaps Abby — who could stand guard, was outflanked by the part that was desperate to know what lay beyond the door. With a final check of the room, Kelly slipped inside, stepped onto the first of a flight of stairs, and closed the door behind her.

The darkness and the silence were total. The air was musty and damp. Kelly leaned against the wall, which seemed to be a mix of solid stone and cement. She felt air hungry. Her pulse refused to slow. It was the same panicky sensation she had experienced one hundred feet down on her first deep dive. Finally, a few slow, deep breaths helped her regain control. She clicked on her flashlight and panned down the concrete steps. There were thirty or more of them, steep and straight, ending at another door. Almost certainly they went beyond the basement floor of the factory.

Kelly walked halfway down the narrow flight, then shone her light back up at the door. There was still a chance to retreat — to try another time with more preparation and some help. She hesitated for a few anxious seconds, then headed down to the lower door.

The lower door was unlocked. She opened it a crack. Beyond it, as with the other, was only stygian darkness. But there was also a waft of cool, damp air. She opened the door a foot, slipped inside, and let it close silently behind her. Even in the dark she knew she was in a vast, open space — the uppermost cavern of the Patience Mine.

Cautiously, she panned her beam about. The space was rectangular, about 50 feet wide by 150 long, and only 7 feet or so from floor to ceiling. The walls were irregular rock as far as she could see. Ancient timber pilings, the size and shape of railroad ties, gave some added strength to the ceiling. Engineers must have determined that the rock could hold the massive weight of the factory, forty feet above. There were lightbulbs connected by metal tubing spaced out all along the ceiling, but nothing else that she could see.

Immediately Kelly began searching for the stairway to the deeper level. It took just a few minutes to find it — an open doorway, about twenty yards in the direction of the cliff face. The staircase, narrow and circular, seemed to be hewn into the rock. It was much longer than the upper flight and reminded her one moment of the stairways in medieval castles, and the next of a childhood trip she had taken up and down the stairs of the Statue of Liberty. But this stairway was pitch-black. Reluctant to switch on the flashlight, she kept one hand on the damp rock wall and cautiously worked her way down.

The air coming up from below seemed cool now, and clean. There was a hum that she at first thought was the response of her ears to the dense silence. Now, she realized, it was a machinery noise. Once again her pulse began to accelerate, this time as much from the excitement of imminent discovery as from any sense of danger. The machinery drone grew louder, and she knew she was reaching the lower cavern. According to the drawings in the Patience Mine book, she was nearly one hundred feet beneath the factory — level with the floor of Patience Valley, or even a bit below that.

As she rounded a bend in the spiraling stairs, she spotted light, spreading out from under a door. Six more steps and she was there. Suddenly she sensed movement behind her. She started to whirl, but a man's powerful hand clamped roughly over her mouth and pulled her tightly against his broad body. There was a sensation of cold metal pressing against her neck, followed almost immediately by a soft pop and a sharp sting at the spot. In seconds the world began to dissolve into a swirling haze. Her panic exploded, then vanished, as her vision blurred. Inexorably, her eyes closed. The single word she heard before unconsciousness swept over her was growled by a voice she knew well.

"Stupid," was all it said.

Chapter Thirty-Two

Yellow rings. Josh had examined his face in the bathroom mirror a dozen times over the last day alone. Granted, he looked like hell. But if there was anything wrong with his eyes, he'd damn well have seen it.

His fury growing with every step, he stalked out of the Ghost Ranch Saloon and across the busy road without checking for cars. Horns blasted at him, but he didn't notice.

The sparkling lights had begun again.

Josh raced back to the motel. There was still time, he was thinking. Time to do what God had been telling him to do. Time to end the pain once and for all. The shimmering diamonds of multicolored light snapped against the inside of his eyes like hailstones. He fumbled with the lock, then threw the door open and snatched the rucksack out from beneath the bed.

"Not this time," he said out loud.

This time there would be no headaches. There would be no begging God to take him. This time there would be only vengeance.

"Bricker . . . Golden . . . Gentry . . . Forrester . . ."

He recited the names in a litany as he

once again checked the two weapons.

Ever so slightly the flickering lights began to dim. It was a sign. The path he had chosen was the right one. He grabbed the rucksack and ran from the room. It was three or four blocks to the main entrance of the company. Five minutes, if that.

Josh started out the front door of the Fremont Motel, then stopped short as a police cruiser glided slowly past. He moved back into the entryway and waited. Minutes later a second cruiser drove by in the other direction, just as slowly and deliberately as the first. They were trying to look routine, but he knew they were searching for someone — almost certainly for him. How could they know? The only possible answer was Abby. She had been worried about him all along. Now she had broken into the house on Orchard, scanned through his computer, and found the letter he had written to her but never sent. Why hadn't he just erased the damn thing? Now Bricker and the rest would be on alert, and the police must have the description and plate number of his Wrangler.

He pressed himself deeper into the shadows. Abby had been wrong to try to stop him. As always, she probably meant well. But once again they were pushing against one another. He wondered how in the hell they had gotten so messed up. When did he make her the villain in his life? When did she stop giving him the unconditional love that she had always claimed meant everything to her?

He found himself wondering, too, about her relationship with Dr. Lew Alvarez. Frightened of the consequences of his nearly striking her, he had followed her to Alvarez's farm one night. Then he parked by the road, walked up the long, unpaved driveway, and spied on the two of them, sitting with two other people in Alvarez's den. After a time he had returned to his car and waited until Abby drove out and headed home. Alvarez was movie-star handsome and had impressed her with his work in the ER. Were they lovers? He felt his jaws clench. Was that why she was trying to get him caught here in Fremont?

Once Bricker and his cronies were taken care of, he would have to confront her and demand some answers to those questions. She wouldn't lie. Lying just wasn't in her. Her fidelity would be rewarded with the life they had always dreamed about. Desertion? . . .

He glanced down at the rucksack and feared that he would be spotted if he tried to lug it to Seradyne. One semiautomatic under his windbreaker — that's all he would be able to get away with. But, then again, that was all he would need. Reentering the motel, he exited through the rear to the lot where the Jeep was parked. The early evening was quite dark, and a fine rain had begun falling. He tossed the rucksack onto the floor and took a screwdriver from the tool kit. In seconds he had changed license plates with a van from Colorado. His headache was steady, but much less severe than he would have expected at this point.

He tucked the MAK-90 beneath his arm, zipped his windbreaker up, and headed away from the main drag. There were back streets and an alley he could take to get to the Seradyne building. Security there was always fairly tight — probably more so now. But he had no intention of entering the building. The parking garage made much more sense. He might get only Bricker, but that would be a hell of a start.

A cruiser passed by on the street ahead. He sensed they might have noticed him. He cut down a narrow alley. When he hit the street again, he was just a block from the garage. The Seradyne executives all had assigned parking slots there. One more year, maybe less, and he would have had one himself. His attitude and performance had gotten consistently superior ratings. But in the end superior ratings didn't matter. What mattered was that Nancy Golden was sleeping with Pete Gentry. *Some corporate restructuring.*

Bricker's Infiniti would be in his designated spot. A sexmobile, he had once called the car. With Bricker everything came down to sex. It would be relatively easy to make it up the back stairs and wait behind a nearby car. If the Infiniti was gone, he would search out Pete Gentry's Land Rover.

The lights were still flickering inside Josh's eyes as he approached the Seradyne garage from the rear. He dashed along a concrete wall and flattened himself behind a row of seven-foot-high shrubs. He stayed there for a time, breathless from the short sprint. Not too long ago he had run a half marathon with ease. It appeared his body was rotting as rapidly as his soul.

Please be patient with me, Abby, he thought. *Please understand that I have to do this.*

But there was no way she would understand, not until she saw him finally free of the headaches and the confusion. Not until she saw him as a whole man again. He waited until his breathing was normal and the street was deserted, then rolled over the concrete wall and dropped onto the first level. Bricker's parking space was on the second. Staying low, he worked his way between cars and the three-foot wall until he reached the second level. At the sight of Bricker's white Infiniti, his jackhammering pulse increased even more. Mortar shells burst behind his eyes.

He chose a spot just in front of the Grand Cherokee parked next to Bricker and was just about to sprint across to it when a sports car screeched around the corner and sped past him to the next level. Had he taken one more step, he would

443

have been as dead as Steve Bricker was about to be.

Careful to listen for oncoming traffic this time, he hunched very low and sprinted across to the spot between the grill of the Grand Cherokee and the wall. Again, he was gasping for breath. It felt as if his heart was just going to stop.

He checked to be sure he was concealed from the stairway door and the elevator, although he expected that Bricker would use the stairs. Then he brought the MAK-90 out and set it on his lap. He had practiced firing the gun in several different dumps. He wouldn't win any marksmanship prizes, but he wouldn't need to. All he had to do was aim at the right height, pull the trigger, and spray.

It was almost five. He would give Bricker until five-twenty, and then go looking for Pete Gentry's car, just in case. His headache was continuing unabated, though it was still manageable. If he had a major explosion like the two he had endured already today, he was cooked. Bricker would be able to walk right up and step on him, and he would be powerless to do a damn thing. But so far, so good.

Then, with no awareness that he had even opened his wallet, he realized that he was holding the laminated photo of Abby he kept there. God, he had loved her. She had given him everything — given up a life she was totally content with so that they could be together. What had he given her in return? Pain and confusion. Anger and anguish. What in the hell had happened to him? Was this insanity? Was this what it was like to be crazy? . . .

Footsteps echoed through the concrete cavern. His hand tensed on the semiautomatic. A couple, chatting and laughing, emerged from the stairwell and headed toward him. Kate Alston from the reception desk and a guy from the design office. Did they know, too? He glanced down at the MAK-90. If they saw him like this, what difference did it make whether they knew why he was there or not? If they spotted him, he would do what he had to do. He tightened his finger on the trigger and pressed himself against the bumper of the Grand Cherokee. They were about thirty feet away. Now twenty. If either of them owned this car or the one next to it, it was all over for them.

Josh held his breath. What in the hell was he going to do if they saw him? Just gun them down? Bricker was his target, not these people. Kate Alston, probably only twenty-three or -four, had always been great to him.

Help me, Abby. For God's sake tell me what to do.

Suddenly the footsteps stopped. A car door opened, then closed. Josh risked a look. Both of them had gotten into a white coupe — a Camaro or Firebird. The engine rumbled to life, and the car eased out of the spot two spaces down and across from Bricker's.

Abby, I didn't want to kill them. I just wanted things to be like they were for us. Bricker and the others did this to us. They've got to pay. Isn't that right? . . . Isn't it?

He slipped Abby's picture into the pocket of his windbreaker. The headache seemed to be getting worse again, and he was beginning to feel queasy.

Come on, dammit. . . . Come on. . . .

The stairway door opened again. Again there were voices — two men. He recognized one of them immediately. Bricker! He worked himself into a low crouch and tightened his grip on the MAK-90. Then he peered cautiously through the windows of Bricker's Infiniti. The other man was Pete Gentry! It was more than he could have hoped for — a true sign.

Almost over, Abby, he thought. *The end for them. A new beginning for us.*

He ducked down and tried to gauge their distance from him by the sound of their shoes on the pavement. *Twenty feet. Maybe fifteen. And . . . now!*

He stood up, took three quick steps to the rear of the Infiniti, and confronted the two startled men from a distance of no more than fifteen feet. Point blank.

"Josh, no!" Bricker cried out.

Pete Gentry dropped to his knees, head

down, but Bricker was fumbling inside his coat. A gun!

"Abby, forgive me!" Josh bellowed.

He brought the MAK-90 to his shoulder and fired.

Chapter Thirty-Three

The call came in at six, just as Abby was leaving for the hospital to see Lew. "Dr. Dolan, please."

Even though it had been years since she had attended Graham DeShield's presentation at St. John's, she recognized the society psychiatrist's voice — affected and nasal — immediately.

"This is Dr. Abby Dolan."

"DeShield here. Dr. Graham DeShield."

She remembered the therapist as tall and slim with wire-rimmed glasses and a receding hairline. Now she pictured him sitting in the paneled study of an opulent hillside home somewhere in Marin County.

"Thank you for calling me back so promptly, Dr. DeShield."

"My service said it was an emergency regarding Ethan Black, although how someone who's deceased could constitute an emergency is beyond me."

"Believe me, it is an emergency. Dr. DeShield, you have no reason to remember me, but I was on the staff at St. John's for a number of years before I moved here to Patience a few months ago. We met briefly some years back, after you gave very impressive grand rounds at our hospital."

"Yes, yes, I remember that particular lecture well. 'Narcissism and the Stars,' I called it. I very much enjoy teaching."

"It was an excellent presentation. One of the best on the subject I've ever heard."

"Are you a psychiatrist?"

"Ah, no, actually. I'm an emergency specialist."

"I see."

It was clear to Abby that he didn't, but she doubted Graham DeShield ever admitted to not understanding anything.

"Dr. DeShield, earlier today I had a meeting with Ezra Black."

"Ah, yes, my good friend Ezra."

"He told me how angry he is with you about his son's suicide. He's desperate to blame someone for it — anyone except himself."

"My feeling exactly. He's already begun to spread rumors about me."

"I would bet your reputation can withstand most of the dirt he could dish out."

"It's very kind of you to say so. What hospital were you at?"

Abby smiled. DeShield's hearing was clearly limited to facts that involved him.

"St. John's. I was there for ten years. I met with Mr. Black today to try to convince him that Colstar International, the company his son was working at, one of the companies *he* owns, was actually responsible for Ethan's death."

Abby could sense the heightened interest

449

at the other end of the line.

"Continue," DeShield said.

"There have been a number of cases here — four, not counting Ethan Black — of Colstar employees who have exhibited psychotic, violent behavior. A small group of us here in Patience is dedicated to getting at the truth about them. We believe that all four cases were toxic from a massive cadmium exposure, and that a large number of patients with lesser illnesses had proportionately less exposure. All four have been involved in violent incidents or have shown violent tendencies. One has now been charged with murder. He is the only one whose blood we have been able to test so far, but it showed an extremely high level of cadmium. We've sent off a level on one of the others, but it's not back. We wanted Ezra Black to close his plant down until he and the people there could determine what happened and assure everyone that the problem has been corrected."

"And?"

"At first Mr. Black seemed receptive to listening to me. Then he did a sudden about-face and as much as threw me out of his place."

"Sounds like Ezra."

"It's been very frustrating. No matter what evidence we produce, Colstar and the people Colstar controls have a response."

"The positive blood tests, too?"

"I'm sure they're going to demand that an

independent lab run the bloods again. Something like that. By the time their data and ours are evaluated and reevaluated, more people will have come to harm. We need Ezra Black on our side, or we don't have much chance of convincing anybody who matters that this is a dire emergency."

"Why call me? In case you didn't get it today, I'm the last person Black would listen to."

"That's his mistake." Abby wondered whether she was laying it on too thick, even for DeShield. "As to how you can help — I think the one thing I said that initially interested Black was about the four other employees becoming violent. Then, when it was clear I knew almost nothing about Ethan other than what I read in the papers, he suddenly became totally uninterested in me, cold as block ice. I left Feather Ridge with the feeling that if I had known that Ethan had been violent — if I had known precisely what he did under the influence of cadmium poisoning — Ezra Black would at least have heard me out. I was even going to suggest that he have his son's body exhumed and tested, but I never got that far."

"In other words, you want me to violate patient-physician confidentiality involving the son of one of the wealthiest, most powerful men in the world."

"I know from the sort of man, the sort of *physician,* you are, that speaking to someone about a patient would not be at all easy for you. It wouldn't be easy for me either if I were in your position. But we believe lives are very much at stake. And the truth is, we really have no one else to turn to."

"If Black learned that I did such a thing, his lawyers would hound me until . . . until I jumped out of my office window myself."

That the therapist didn't flatly say no was all that mattered. He was holding out to hear what Graham DeShield had to gain. And Abby had that argument ready and waiting.

"You have my word that I would never tell Mr. Black we spoke. And, in addition, it would seem that if we can prove it was the cadmium in Ethan's brain that caused him to kill himself, that would certainly absolve you of the responsibility Ezra Black is trying to stick you with."

During the extended silence that followed, Abby picked up a pen and readied it over a notepad.

Come on, Graham. Come on. . . .

"We haven't met since that conference, Abby, but somehow I feel I can trust you."

"You can, Dr. DeShield," she said, adding in a voice that was as close as she could get to seductive, "and, perhaps soon, we *could* meet again in person."

"It's Graham. And I think I should like that very much. The truth is, Abby, Ethan Black almost bludgeoned a man to death with a baseball bat. A farmer. It was in a

452

parking lot after a fight in a bar. Ezra saw to it that every witness said the farmer started it. Then he made certain the victim got cared for at the Stoneleigh Head Injury Center. You know that place?"

"Of course. The best."

"I believe the man will be there indefinitely. His injuries were that severe."

"What about Ethan's headaches?"

Black Ezra had said nothing about headaches, but Abby no longer doubted his son had them.

"They started following his accident," DeShield said. "Horrible, debilitating headaches that I felt were postconcussive. Were they caused by the cadmium, too?"

"I believe so. Tell me, were there any preceding sensory warnings? Strange tastes? Lights?"

"Funny you should mention that. Actually, he did complain of a smell. He said it was like . . . like rotten eggs."

Bingo!

"Dr. DeShield — *Graham* — did Ethan harm anyone else besides the farmer?"

"A number of people, actually, although the farmer got it the worst of all. Ethan seemed to have a smoldering anger against almost everyone, and periodically he would just blow. He beat up a prostitute last month. Broke her arm."

Abby was writing furiously.

"Daddy took care of her, too?"

"Of course."

"Graham, you won't regret having done this."

"I hope not, Abby. Just remember your promise to keep my name out of it, and be sure to give me a call to let me know what happens. Having Ezra Black bad-mouthing me from pillar to post is not going to be good for business."

"One last thing."

"Yes?"

"Do you by any chance have the phone number at Feather Ridge?"

"As a matter of fact, I do. Why?"

"I don't think Ezra Black is likely to say yes to another operator with an emergency call from me."

Despite a steady rain, the early evening was mild and quite bright. Driving to the hospital, Abby even caught a brief glimpse of the sun. There was still forty minutes before her meeting with Kelly. She couldn't wait to see Lew and share the two major developments of the day — her visit to Feather Ridge and Kelly's discovery of a secret staircase somewhere in Colstar.

She felt buoyed by her success with Graham DeShield. The real trick would be to honor her promise to keep his name out of the conversation when she called Ezra Black. She had decided to hold off on that call until she had learned what Kelly had found. Even if it turned out to be nothing — and she strongly doubted that would be the case — there was still the information she now had about Ethan. Black would have to be devoid of a conscience not to take action against the company that had contributed to his son's death — even if that company was his own.

As she pulled up the hospital drive, Abby mulled over the explanation she had given DeShield and Black for what had happened to Ethan and the four others, as well as to the 150 or so NIWWs. She strongly sensed — no, no, she *knew* — something was wrong with her reasoning. At first glance her logic held together reasonably well: a little cadmium exposure, especially when stimulated by an MRI, caused a variety of symptoms, depending on the patient; a heavy exposure, with or without the MRI, caused headaches, violent behavior, and eventual death. The theory certainly did what theories were supposed to do: integrated the facts. But each time she verbalized it — first to Lew, then to Black, and finally to DeShield — she felt uneasy.

There was an ambulance parked at the receiving platform, but Abby's highly developed sixth sense told her that things inside were reasonably calm. In fact, there was very little going on. In bay one, two nurses were checking in the elderly man from the ambulance. The only other action was in bay four, where Lew was listening to a young boy's chest. He noticed Abby the moment she came through the door and motioned toward the on-call room. She nodded that she would see him there and made her way inconspicuously along the outside corridor. During the few minutes she was alone in the room, she dialed her answering machine to check for a message from Kelly, or perhaps even Josh. Nothing.

She glanced about, wondering if, as Lew had warned, the room was bugged. Given the bogus autopsy report Joe Henderson had produced, a little electronic eavesdropping would hardly be a surprise. There was no reason she should have had any pangs about having to leave a hospital controlled by a corporation like Colstar and run by men like Henderson and George Oleander, but she did. She was angered beyond words at being squeezed out by lies and treachery. She was furious about having to leave a job that had taught her so much about herself and her capabilities. And she was upset about being forced to make decisions about her relationship with Lew Alvarez before she was ready.

"Damn you, Henderson," she muttered, "damn you."

At that moment the door opened and Lew stepped in. The instant the door clicked shut, her arms were around him, her lips pressed against his. He tensed with surprise. Then, with a soft sound of pleasure, he brought his hands up, buried them in her hair, and brought her mouth even more tightly against his. Even after she gently broke off their kiss, she held him against her.

"I feel like I just won the lottery," he whispered.

"Maybe you did."

He sat down and guided her onto his lap. She buried her face in the curve of his neck and savored the taste of his skin and the feel of his hardness against her thigh.

"Careful," he whispered. "Big Brother may be watching."

"Let 'em."

"Well said."

"Lew, I can't stay long."

He moved her away and kissed her lightly on the mouth.

"Why did I know you were going to say that? Is everything all right with you?"

"Better than all right, except that I haven't heard anything from Josh."

"I've been saying prayers for him."

"Thanks," she whispered. "Lew, do you think it's safe to talk in here?"

He shrugged *no idea* and motioned her to the bathroom, where he turned on the sink and the shower.

"I still think we ought to keep our voices down."

"Okay. Lew, I think something's breaking at Colstar. Kelly Franklin's found a staircase that she thinks might lead to the underground caverns I told you about."

"You really trust her?"

"I do. I never thought she was hiding anything. Now she's angry as hell that they've kept the underground spaces and ventilation windows beneath Colstar secret from her. We both feel there's got to be a damn good reason why they did. I'm meeting her at a park near her house in twenty minutes to hear what she found."

"And your visit to Ezra?"

"Went poorly, but there's still hope. He wanted nothing to do with me, but I think it's because he doesn't want anyone to know his kid beat a man senseless with a baseball bat and broke a prostitute's arm. And those are just samples of his cadmium-induced violence. Once Ezra knows there's nothing left to hide, maybe he'll relent and at least order some sort of investigation."

"Unless he already knows what Colstar is doing."

"It's possible. I just can't get a decent read on the man."

"I'll tell you one thing: if that company is responsible for those shootings in Las Vegas and the Wheaton woman's death, once the lawyers begin to gnaw at them, there's no way they're going to be able to stay in business. I'll be anxious to hear what Kelly finds."

"Soon."

Abby turned off the shower and sink and returned to the study for her jacket.

"You know," she said, "the one thing that

keeps bothering me is all those MRIs I told you about."

"You don't think it's just some sort of agreement between the family docs and the radiology department to run up as many MRI charges as possible? It is a hell of an expensive test."

"If that were the case, we'd be saying that it was a coincidence that something like ninety percent or more of the NIWWs have had one. I'm not much good at biostatistics, so I didn't even know if there was a formula that could be applied to all the data I gathered. But if there is, I bet it says all those MRIs done on our cases are statistically significant."

"You may be right, but I certainly can't come up with an explanation that makes sense."

"The MRI machine's an electromagnet, and cadmium's a heavy metal. It wouldn't be much of a stretch to imagine the two interacting in some way."

"I guess."

Abby slipped on her windbreaker.

"Gotta go."

"I'll be off by midnight. Maybe a little earlier," he said hopefully.

"Hey, listen, I'll be back here as soon as I learn what Kelly's discovered."

"Abby, for God's sake, be careful. Be very, very careful."

Abby held his face in her hands and kissed him lightly.

"In case you hadn't noticed," she said, "I'm not exactly the biggest risk taker in the world."

The park Kelly had designated as their meeting spot was a rarity for public places in Patience — a space that was poorly maintained. It was a postage-stamp-sized play area at the end of a rather long drive. There were homes visible from the small gravel parking lot, but none that was close. The grass, much of which had yielded to weeds, was badly in need of cutting. And the swings, slide, and wooden seesaw were begging for repair. The playground was certainly private enough, but viewed in the rainy, late-evening gloom, it was also somewhat forbidding. To Abby it was something of a metaphor for the whole town.

She arrived at the parking area several minutes early, cut her lights and windshield wipers, and slid in one of the three Beethoven-symphony tapes in her case. She listened to them frequently but had never concentrated on the music enough to be able to distinguish one symphony from another. There was a third of a Heath Bar resting in the compartment by the gear shift. The rest of the bar was all she had eaten since her trip back from Feather Ridge. Minimal exercise, lousy eating habits, even worse sleeping habits, unstable emotional life — what a wonderful example she was for the patients of the world. Someday, she told herself. Someday it would all settle down. She polished off the remaining Heath morsel and glanced in the direction of the drive. No one. It was just seven. The steady, fine rain continued, warm and cleansing. Abby glanced about once again and instinctively locked her doors. The windows began to fog. Beethoven filled the Mazda — his Eighth, she guessed, although for no particular reason. Her thoughts floated free for a time, then came to rest, once again, on the most irregular of the shapes she had been trying to force into the Colstar puzzle: the MRIs.

Nearly every one of the NIWW patients had had the test done. In many, if not all of them, the date of the MRI actually *preceded* the onset of the symptoms that placed the patients in the NIWW group. Her theory was that these patients had already been exposed to cadmium, and that somehow the combination of the heavy-metal poisoning and magnetic resonance imaging triggered the rashes, fatigue, susceptibility to infection, headaches, and other complaints.

Combination. That was the key, the most disturbing word. First the cadmium exposure, then the MRI. That combination was the concept she was having trouble with — the square peg that kept refusing to be jammed into the round hole. Her explanation required a pairing of events in 150 or so patients — what amounted to 150 coincidences. It simply didn't wash.

She glanced at her watch. Seven-ten.

Come on, Kelly. Where the hell are you?

The windows of the Mazda were fogged too much to see outside. She opened the front ones an inch, started the motor, and turned on the defogger. Then she ejected Beethoven and listened to the deep silence, broken only by the brush of rain on the hood and roof.

Something had gone wrong.

Five more minutes, she decided. No, ten. She'd give her until seven-twenty, and then go looking — first at Kelly's house, then at Colstar.

Dammit, where are you?

A car's headlights at the end of the drive flickered off the trees, and for the briefest second Abby felt a flood of relief. Then the lights swung away and continued down the road.

She tried to make the minutes pass by focusing, once again, on the possible significance of all the MRIs. *Never postulate two diagnoses to explain a patient's symptoms when one will suffice.* The maxim was at the very heart of sound medical case synthesis, right next to the venerable adage warning young doctors, fascinated with the obscure, that when they hear hoofbeats on the plains of Arizona, they would do well *not* to look for zebras. Never two diagnoses when one will do. Abby wrote *Cd* in the condensation on the left side of her window and *MRI* on the right. Then she fingered a circle around each one. Cadmium exposure alone might explain each and every symptom in the NIWWs. But it would not explain the MRIs. Never two when one will do.

There was only one other option she could think of — that the NIWWs were not cadmium toxic but were somehow actually getting sick from the MRI test itself. Did that make any sense at all? Not from anything she had ever learned about the procedure. And what about the high levels in Willie Cardoza?

Perhaps the machine was defective in some way. But how would that explain the hundreds of MRI cases who weren't among the NIWWs? Her mind was tying itself in knots.

The ten minutes were up. She turned on the high beams and swung back so they shone down the drive. Nothing. Kelly's map was on the seat beside her. Abby checked it to get her bearings and drove to the house, just three blocks away. The rain continued — steady, gentle. The house was a prim stucco ranch with a neat shrub-lined lawn and an attached garage. Several lights were on inside. Abby snapped her windbreaker, then felt around the rear floor until she located her Giants baseball cap and pulled it on. She walked up the flag-stone path to the kitchen door and peered in the window. Nothing seemed out of place. To her right was half a small barrel, planted with a yucca, some geraniums, and ferns.

Abby lifted the planter on edge with both hands, braced it against her leg, and was about to reach underneath for the key when she heard the dull rumble of an automobile engine. She lowered the planter back down and listened. The street was deserted. Suddenly, she knew. Her heart in her throat, she raced around to the garage and pulled up the door. A dense haze of automobile exhaust billowed out. Abby stepped back and turned to get a lungful of fresh air, then pulled her shirt up over her nose and mouth and charged into the lethal fog. Kelly was lying motionless across the front seat of a small white convertible.

Abby snatched open the door, shut off the key, pulled her out by the waist, and dragged her out of the garage into the rain by her wrists. She didn't stop pulling until they were halfway down the drive. Then she sank down on one knee, gasping. Her breath was visible in the cool, rainy air. Kelly had a reasonable pulse although there were several skipped beats, but her breathing was exceedingly shallow. Abby slapped her face once, then again, and called her name. There was no reaction. She gave her several effective mouth-to-mouth breaths and repeated the attempts to rouse her. Then she checked her pupils, fearing the worst — fixed and dilated. Instead, she was able to make out that they were pinpoint small — the pupils of a narcotics overdose.

"Help!" she screamed as loud as she could. "Someone help!"

Her voice was swallowed by the dense night.

The house across the street had lights on, and Abby could actually see someone inside. She bent over one more time and gave Kelly three deep breaths. Next she stripped off her own windbreaker and bunched it beneath Kelly's neck to keep her airway straight.

"Hang in there, Kelly," she said.

Then she whirled and sprinted down the rain-slicked drive.

Chapter Thirty-Four

By the time the rescue squad arrived, Abby and the man across the street had lifted Kelly, carried her into his house, and placed her on the living-room rug. She remained unconscious. Her pupils were pinpoint and her respiratory rate still depressed. Neither of those were classic signs of carbon-monoxide poisoning. Almost certainly Kelly had been drugged before being placed in her garage.

Tears mixed with the rainwater on Abby's face as she did what little she could to help Kelly get air into her lungs. The rescue squad was just five minutes away. Carbon-monoxide poisoning — even a mild exposure — was one of the most challenging crises in emergency medicine. The monoxide literally forced oxygen off the hemoglobin molecules that normally carried it to the tissues of the body. The effect of the poisoning was extremely difficult to reverse, and the newly formed carboxyhemoglobin prevented vital structures, especially the brain and heart, from getting enough oxygen. In addition, the monoxide caused a dangerous buildup of acids in the blood, and a drop in blood pH, making the heart dangerously prone to life-threatening arrhythmias.

There were half a dozen neighbors standing around the living room. None of them had seen anything unusual around Kelly's house. In fact, none of them had even seen her come home. There was going to be no way to fix the length of exposure. Abby knew they all expected her to do something heroic. But without oxygen and some way to deliver it in high concentrations, there wasn't much she could do except continually monitor Kelly's pulse and be prepared to institute CPR at the first sign of a loss of blood pressure. She did have the presence of mind to send one of the men over to Kelly's car and house to look for pills.

"Open the car door carefully and don't touch anything except with a cloth," she warned.

"You mean you don't think this was an attempted suicide?" he asked.

"I don't know," she lied. "But let's not assume anything."

Abby wiped the rain from her cheeks with the back of her hand. Thank God it was Lew waiting there in the ER and not McCabe or Jill Anderson. Together they would do what they could do. She looked down at Kelly, who was laboring to breathe once again, and adjusted the jacket beneath her neck. The woman was a few years older than Abby, but without her tortoise-shell glasses it was easy to appreciate her youthful skin and fine, somehow innocent, little-girl's face.

You shouldn't have done it, Kelly, Abby was thinking. *You shouldn't have gone down there alone.*

Abby forced herself to stay focused. She was angry, shocked, and frightened, but determined not to be distracted by any emotion. This was the time to do things precisely right.

The immediate goal would be to get a breathing tube in and get Kelly onto a cardiac monitor. Next would be to deliver 100 percent oxygen and treat any cardiac irregularities. Once in the ER, they would measure the amount of circulating carboxy-hemoglobin, as well as Kelly's blood pH. The low pH could be corrected, but the dissociation of oxygen from hemoglobin was another story. The oxygen concentration of room air was about 20 percent. In a hospital setting they could deliver pure oxygen — 100 percent. Unfortunately, even pure oxygen was often not enough to break apart the carboxyhemoglobin in time to prevent serious brain damage. There was, however, a way to deliver *more* than 100 percent, and that was by giving 100 percent oxygen under increased atmospheric pressure. Hypersaturation, it was called. The technique would require transporting Kelly to a hyperbaric decompression chamber. Somebody at the hospital would know where the nearest ones were. There she would undergo a series of what amounted to deep dives into a sea of pure oxygen. The carboxyhemoglobin would yield to the technique much more quickly than it would to oxygen delivered at sea-level pressures, or worse, at the atmospheric pressure in Patience, which was located several hundred feet *above* sea level.

The key was remembering that carbon-monoxide poisoning was insidious. Patients could look fine, and even test fine in some respects. But until the oxygen-hemoglobin balance was restored to normal, irreversible brain-cell damage would continue to progress. Hundreds of fire fighters and victims of fires had had life as they knew it preserved by tenacious ER docs who got them into chambers despite no clinical evidence that they were in danger. They were breathing, their heart was generating a blood pressure, and they were awake and alert. Why push?

Abby knew why. She reached down and cradled Kelly's head in her hand. The woman remained motionless. From somewhere in the distance she heard the first siren.

"Okay," she said to the neighbors. "If you could all move away to give us room to work, that would be a help."

The man whom she had sent back to Kelly's car and house rushed in, carefully holding a pill bottle with a washcloth.

"I couldn't find anything in the house except Tylenol. But this was on the floor of the car," he said, breathless.

There were two pills in the rust-colored clear-plastic vial. Two pills and no label. Abby had no doubt the carefully placed tablets would coincide perfectly with whatever was depressing Kelly's respirations and constricting her pupils. And, of course, no one in the crack, unbiased Patience police department would question why a woman bent on suicide would bother to swallow the entire contents of a bottle of pills . . . except two.

The siren grew louder, and at least one more could now be heard. In seconds the strobes of the ambulance flashed through the windows. Abby remained kneeling beside Kelly until the three-person rescue squad rushed in. One of the paramedics was Tom Webb, whose feelings she had hurt during the resuscitation of the insurance man, Bill Tracy. She had gone out of her way that day to apologize for anything she might have done or said in the heat of battle. And since that time even after the Peggy Wheaton debacle, there seemed to be a decent relationship between the two of them. Now, seeing him was a boost.

"We need to intubate her, Tom," she said. "I have no idea how long she was in that garage. Maybe we should get her right on a monitor, too. The monoxide and the acidosis can wreak havoc on her cardiac rhythm. Also, she looks like a possible narcotics overdose. We're going to need an IV and oh-point-four of Narcan to reverse that. Have someone remember to repeat the dose in two minutes if she's no better, even if I forget to ask for it."

The young man just nodded and relayed her orders to the other two. Despite the minor clash over the technique used in pumping Bill Tracy's heart, the squad was damn good. In less than a minute one of them — a slight woman old enough to be Tom's mother — had a good IV line in place and the narcotic antagonist injected. A second paramedic worked on hooking up the portable monitor/defibrillator.

Tom Webb set out the equipment for tracheal intubation. All the paramedics were trained in performing the procedure, and every one Abby had ever known took great pride in being able to do it in the field. But after anesthesiologists, who intubated almost every surgical patient in the operating room, ER doctors were generally the next-most skilled. Abby had always had confidence in her ability to intubate anyone in any situation.

"Here you are, Doctor," Webb said, handing her the laryngoscope and a tube.

Abby looked over at the young man. Kelly was still breathing on her own, which made the situation a bit less critical. Several weeks ago she had inadvertently embarrassed Tom in front of a number of his co-workers. She was The Professor then, still operating on university mean time. Now she really was becoming someone else.

471

And one of many lessons she was learning at PRH was how important reputations were in a closed community, and how fragile.

"Go for it, Tom," she said. "I'll assist. She's still moving air, so we have time to get her up onto the stretcher if it would be easier for you."

She hoped he would know that she was telling him not to try to intubate Kelly while stretching himself out on the rug. If he attempted to do it that way and missed, she would have to step in and take over. If he missed while Kelly was up on the stretcher, she would have to decide whether or not Kelly's condition allowed him a second pass.

"Help me get her on the stretcher," Tom ordered.

With Abby holding Kelly's neck steady at just the right angle, the paramedic knelt at the head of the stretcher and got his body in perfect position. Then he slid the lighted, curved laryngoscope blade along Kelly's tongue and applied just enough upward pressure to lift her epiglottis away from the opening of her trachea. Abby could tell from his position and technique that he had given himself an excellent view of Kelly's vocal cords. She placed the breathing tube in his hand.

"Steady on," she whispered. "You're doing great."

The paramedic slipped the tube smoothly

into place between the cords. The woman who had inserted the IV had a breathing bag in hand with portable oxygen already attached.

"Nice shot, Tom," she said. Then she looked over at Abby and mouthed the word, *Thanks.*

By the time they wheeled Kelly out of the house and hoisted her into the ambulance, her pupils seemed a bit less constricted and her color was a tad better. But she still had not regained consciousness.

Abby knew that was a bad sign.

The moment Kelly's stretcher was pulled from the ambulance and into the ER, the dam that had been holding back Abby's emotions burst. Nearly consumed by fury, she paced behind the nurses' station. Lew stood nearby, keeping a constant eye on the ER. It was considerably busier than it had been just two hours ago.

"She found something," Abby said. "She found something in those caverns beneath Colstar, and that bastard Quinn tried to kill her."

Across from the nurses' station, in major medical, almost lost among the wires and the tubes, Kelly Franklin's profile was just visible. She had not moved voluntarily for the forty-five minutes since their arrival in the ER. Above Kelly a monitor scanned out a heartbeat that had been in nightmarish irregularity. To make matters much worse, they were having a hell of a time finding an accessible decompression chamber where the staff was willing to handle a patient as unstable and unresponsive as Kelly. And because of the low cloud ceiling and poor visibility, it was uncertain whether or not MedFlight would even be able to fly.

Abby felt tense, frantic, and absolutely helpless to alter the scenario that was unfolding around them. If she hadn't been so aggressive about condemning Colstar to Kelly . . . if she had tracked Kelly down and insisted that she not take any chances . . . if she had simply left town . . . if . . . if . . . if . . .

"Is there any chance she actually could have done this to herself?" Lew asked.

Abby whirled like a startled cat and nearly leaped at him.

"You sound like that policeman who just took a statement from me. Lew, she was supposed to meet me at seven. She was anxious, yes, but she was angry and excited, not depressed. She did not do this to herself. Something's going on in that place."

He quickly squeezed her hand.

"Sorry. I was just asking."

The physician whom Lew had called in to take over Kelly's care was a brilliant young cardiologist named Harvey Shulman. It had been a titanic struggle to tame Kelly's irregular heart rhythms, but Shulman seemed to be prevailing. Now he emerged from her room and approached them, studying some lab slips. His thick black brows were knit almost together. Abby sensed trouble.

"Her pH is up from six-point-nine to seven-three," he said. "That's the good news. The bad news is we just got her carboxyhemoglobin level back. It's thirty-five percent."

Abby and Lew exchanged concerned glances. They had both been programmed with the same carboxyhemoglobin numbers. Guru living on an isolated Tibetan mountain, 0 percent. Average person exposed to secondhand cigarette smoke, 1 to 2. Heavy smoker, 9. Threshold for admission and serious consideration for hyperbaric treatment, 18. Potentially lethal, 30 percent and up.

"She needs a chamber," Lew said.

"Any luck with that?"

Shulman's question was directed at Abby, who had been working with the charge nurse to find something. Now Abby found herself too choked up to speak. Instead, she shook her head. Lew patted her gently on the back.

"Abby, you're doing everything you can," he said.

Shulman passed over the lab reports, all of which looked reasonable except for the 35 percent.

"Her depressed consciousness is almost as disturbing as those numbers," he said. "I've got her on steroids to reduce any brain swelling. If we can't line up a chamber and transportation in another ten or fifteen minutes, the nurses want her transferred out of the ER and up to the unit. We can't keep them tied up like this."

"No!" Abby said, far too vehemently. "Let us try again. We'll find something."

From behind his glasses Shulman's dark eyes appraised her.

"Abby, I don't think MedFlight will fly on a night like this. The last thing we want is to push them into flying and have something happen. Besides, Kelly needs a chamber in a well-staffed hospital setting. Her cardiac situation is still too unstable for anything less."

Helpless to argue, Abby could only turn and head for the charge nurse's office to make more calls. Ten minutes later she returned, shaking her head. Her eyes were red from fatigue, strain, and tears. She motioned Lew into the glass-enclosed dictation cubicle, where they could speak in private while he kept an eye on the ER.

"The best MedFlight can do is remain on standby until morning," she said. "Sooner, if the weather breaks. The people at Eden Medical Center in Castro Valley say they might be able to handle her in their chamber by five or six tomorrow morning if we can transfer her safely. Patience can't spare an ambulance and crew for an eight-to-ten-hour round trip. I just can't believe this."

"They're coming down from the unit to get

her in just a few minutes."

"Lew, she's not going to make it."

"You don't know that."

"With that thirty-five-percent level, if she lives, we all might wish she hadn't."

"We've been able to reach her ex-husband. He's driving up from San Francisco with her daughters."

"Damn! I'd like to get my hands around Lyle Quinn's throat. Right now."

"Just don't let anyone provoke you, Abby. We're playing on their field with their ball and their referee. The only way we're going to win is if we play that much smarter and more determined than they do."

"I understand."

Hidden from anyone's view, Lew reached over and took her hand.

"Win or lose, I'm glad you're with me," he said.

"Don't talk like that, Lew. We're going to bring them down. I'm not going to have her end up like this for nothing."

"Maybe when the results of Angela Cristoforo's blood tests come back, we'll be able to attract someone's attention. Meanwhile, I don't know what else we can do."

"There is one thing. While I was waiting out in that park for Kelly, I tried to go over everything we've learned so far. One piece just wouldn't fit."

"Namely?"

"The MRIs."

"What do you mean?"

"Lew, most of the cases on the Alliance's list had an MRI *before* their symptoms developed. The reasons for ordering the tests in the first place were pretty damn thin in a lot of instances. From what you know, is there any way the MRI *itself* could be causing people to get sick?"

"I thought you were postulating some sort of interaction between the cadmium in the patient's system and the MRI."

"I was. But that requires a coincidence — first the exposure, then the test. The truth is, except for Willie Cardoza, we have no definitive lab proof of anyone being cadmium toxic."

"Colstar rigged the testing. You know that."

"I know they're capable of it, that's for sure."

"And what about the rings in Angela's eyes? And the other cases of violent behavior?"

"I don't know, Lew. But I do know I want to take a look at that MRI machine. And if I don't find anything, I'd like one of my radiologist friends from St. John's to come up here and check it out."

"When are you going to try to look at it?"

"As soon as I see that Kelly is settled in upstairs."

"I think you're barking up the wrong tree."

"Maybe. But ever since I started accumulating data on our cases, something's been bugging me. I think this is what."

"I'll be here."

"Do you have a good penlight I can borrow?"

"I do."

Lew unclipped it from his pocket and passed it over.

"Courtesy of Coulter Pharmaceuticals," he said, reading the printing embossed on the side.

Abby laughed sardonically.

"Believe it or not, that's one of Ezra Black's companies. Listen, as soon as I'm ready to go to the MRI unit, I'll need you to occupy the X-ray tech for twenty minutes or so."

"No problem. Hector Ortega's on tonight. He was born and raised in the Napa Valley, and he's sick of people thinking he should know Spanish. He loves it when I take a few minutes to speak it with him."

"Excellent." Abby motioned out the glass to where the nurses and a transportation worker were loading Kelly onto a gurney for transfer to the unit. "I'm going to go up with them and then I'll call. She shouldn't have gone down there by herself, Lew. I shouldn't have let her."

He turned her by her shoulders to face him. His dark eyes were deadly serious.

"Abby, we told you at the Alliance meeting that this was a war against corporate killers. We meant it. David Brooks was a casualty. So were Peggy Wheaton and Ezra

Black's kid, and those people in the casino in Las Vegas. And possibly even Josh. And now, maybe, so is Kelly. I'm sorry it's happened this way. But at least you and I are still here to fight back."

Abby wiped at the tears that had suddenly materialized at the corners of her eyes.

"You're right," she said. "I have to stay focused on that. One more thing just occurred to me."

"Yes?"

"If, as I think, Kelly discovered something beneath Colstar, she may be in danger even now. Shouldn't someone be guarding her?"

"I hadn't thought of that. Listen, I'm sure that once she understands what's at stake, Barbara Torres from the Alliance will do some special duty. She's the associate head of the VNA. I'll call her right now. After Jill Anderson relieves me tonight, I can make some excuse for relieving Barbara. We'll try to have someone watching her continuously."

"Great. I'll do a shift, too, although I hope that by morning Kelly will be out of here."

"Just give me a call when you want me to start Hector's Spanish lesson. And in the meantime, *buena suerte*."

"Quinn shouldn't have done this," Abby said, balling up a blank progress note sheet and snapping it into the trash. "And I promise you he's going to regret it."

Chapter Thirty-Five

U nwilling to leave, Abby stood beside Kelly Franklin's bed in the ICU. Kelly's condition remained essentially unchanged in that she was unresponsive even to painful stimuli. But a slightly more hopeful sign was her pupils, which were not excessively dilated and were slightly reactive to light. Her cardiac status had largely stabilized, although high doses of antiarrhythmic medications were still needed, and her blood pH was up to 7.42 — normal. The cardiologist's opinion was essentially the same as Abby's — persistent central-nervous and cardiac-oxygen deprivation due to carbon monoxide clogging the hemoglobin-carrying sites. The most likely explanation for her depressed consciousness was increased pressure within her skull caused by swelling of her brain. The high doses of intravenous steroids seemed to be helping to reduce the swelling some, but how much permanent brain damage she had already sustained was impossible to know.

Abby found herself praying that there hadn't been time for Kelly to experience much terror before the narcotics knocked her out. In the report she had given to the police a short while ago, she had strongly suggested that Kelly's blood would reveal a drug overdose. But she hadn't shared her belief that this was attempted murder. And she certainly hadn't mentioned anything about Colstar or Quinn. By doing so all she would have accomplished was to place herself in danger at a time when she needed, above all, to be mobile.

Quinn was going to pay for this, she vowed. She had never felt strongly enough about any cause to believe she was ready to die for it. But if Quinn and Colstar were responsible for this tragedy, as well as for Josh and the others, she would do whatever she had to — take whatever chances were necessary — in order to bring them down, along with anyone else who was involved. She checked the time. Just nine. It seemed a lifetime ago that she was sitting by the dilapidated park, waiting.

She looked about helplessly. She could stick around to be sure no one came in bent on finishing the job that was started somewhere in or beneath Colstar. But, otherwise, there wasn't much she could do — except take a close look at the MRI machine. She paced to the nurses' station and back, then pulled the blinds apart and checked the weather. The rain and the blackness seemed as before. There was no way Kelly was going to get to a decompression chamber before morning.

She went to the phone beside the central

monitoring station to call Lew, hoping he had been able to reach Barbara Torres. If she had agreed to come in, Abby would wait until she arrived before going to inspect the MRI unit, provided that the ER was still slow enough for Lew to divert the night X-ray tech.

At that moment, as if in answer to a prayer, Barbara Torres marched into the unit. She was wearing her blue VNA uniform and carrying a clipboard and stethoscope. Her expression and nod to Abby said that she knew everything and was ready to insert her not inconsiderable bulk and determination between Kelly and any threat. She walked right past Abby to the charge nurse and greeted the woman warmly.

"Kelly Franklin's an old friend," Abby heard her say. "It would mean a great deal to me to special her."

"No problem, Barb," the unit nurse replied. "We never turn down good help. I'll clear it with the supervisor and be in to give you the lowdown in ten or fifteen minutes. Meanwhile, just keep an eye on her vitals and urine output, and do a neuro check every fifteen minutes."

Barbara met Abby by the door to Kelly's cubicle.

"I came in as soon as Lew called," she whispered. "It doesn't look good in there."

"It isn't."

"Well, my husband's got a virus, so I may or may not stay the night depending on how he is and how Lew feels after his shift is done."

"I can special her, but I'm on the schedule for tomorrow at eight A.M.," Abby said. "A sixteen-hour shift, no less."

Abby had started her day with the visit to Dotty Schumacher and her strudel. She'd been sleep deprived when she'd gone to bed late the previous evening, and not much less sleep deprived when she awoke. Now, with all that had happened today, she was operating on raw, nervous energy. There was no way to guess how much fuel remained in her tank. But it was a safe bet that without five or six hours of decent sleep, she would never make it through her shift tomorrow without crashing.

"Don't you worry," Torres said. "Lew or I will handle things here. I stopped by the ER. He said for you to call as soon as you're ready to go down to the MRI unit. What's that all about?"

"Maybe nothing. I'll tell you as soon as I get back. Meanwhile, don't let anyone near her who doesn't have an ID tag."

"I used to do some per diem, and before that I was a med/surg nurse on two. I know a lot of the staff here."

"Any doubts about anyone, just bring them over to be eyeballed by one of the unit nurses."

"Done."

Barbara Torres moved into Kelly's room and set to work. Abby called Lew in the ER.

Spanish class for Hector Ortega would commence in three minutes.

The air seemed heavy, like it was liquid or something. It even had a weird taste. . . .

Claire Buchanan's words played over and over in Abby's head as she made her way cautiously down the back stairs to the radiology unit. The lights in the main corridor were dim, and the place seemed totally deserted. Several years ago she had bought herself a running watch as part of a pledge to jog more. The pledge lasted only a few weeks, if that, but the twenty-three-dollar watch was like Old Man River. Now, as she entered the blackened MRI unit, she put the watch in countdown mode, set it for twenty minutes, and began.

She first entered the control room, which was connected by a door to MRI radiologist Del Marshall's office. The area, housing the huge, complex electronic console and monitoring screens, was the purview of the imaging technologist. Beyond it, in a room the size of a large closet, was the integrating computer itself. The control area was separated by a heavy glass wall from the room housing the MRI machine.

The entire unit, including Marshall's office, was totally dark. Abby flipped on the lights in the main room and pulled the print curtains closed on the control-room side of the glass, cutting down on much of the glare. Then she stepped inside the pitch-black radiologist's office and closed the door. There was no light filtering in from the control room. As a last precaution she pulled a wastebasket over and left it by the door from the office to the main hall. The noise of the door bumping it might give her a few seconds of advance warning. Of course, doing anything beneficial with those seconds would be something else again.

She closed Marshall's office door behind her and passed through the control area to the actual MRI unit. The watch read 18:43.

As a resident Abby had taken a tour of the MRI unit serviced by the St. John's radiologists. Now she wished she had paid more attention. The machine was massive — a seven-foot-long tube, less than two feet in diameter, set inside the housing of the electromagnet, which was a huge gleaming cube, seven feet on a side. Extending from the cylinder was the track and movable platform on which the patient was placed to glide electronically into the machine.

Abby examined the track quickly, then peered into the tube. The opening was wide enough to admit an average-sized person. She suspected that anyone above 250 or so would have a problem even fitting inside, let alone fitting inside and remaining sane for three-quarters of an hour with shoulders pressed against the sides and nose just inches from the top. Claire Buchanan wasn't large, but she *was* claustrophobic.

Abby's estimation of the woman's determination went up several notches. Claire had wanted so much to be well again that she was willing to enter the lair of her dragon.

"What went wrong, Claire? What went wrong?"

Abby sang the words softly, tunelessly as she crawled around the base of the machine, looking for something, anything, out of place. At the rear of the unit the track extended several feet so that patients could be positioned with their torso and head outside and their lower body inside. In that way the pelvis and legs were easily scanned. Below the opening were the hydraulics that helped move the sled along the track. Nothing among the cables seemed unusual. Abby cursed herself for having absolutely no idea what she was looking for.

Suddenly, from beyond the control room, she heard the soft sound of the office door striking the waste can. She was as far away from the door to the waiting room and hallway as she could possibly be. There was no chance she could make it. She huddled behind the scanner and peered over the track, through the long cylinder. The door from the office to the control room opened, backlighting the curtains she had drawn. Seconds later they were pulled apart. From her position it was impossible to see who was there. She glanced at her watch. Fifteen minutes left. Unless Lew had failed miserably, it wasn't the X-ray technician.

She held her breath as the door from the control room slowly opened. She could see who the intruder was only if he or she passed directly beyond the cylinder opening. Abby sensed the footsteps moving around toward where she was crouched. Silently, she pulled herself facedown onto the track and then into the narrow cylinder. The footsteps continued around to where she would surely have been seen had she stayed crouched next to the hydraulics. Then they turned and headed back toward the front of the room. Abby pushed herself backward again until only her upper half was in the cylinder. She extended her neck, lifting her head so that she could see in front of her.

Suddenly, a man's broad back appeared to the left of the track. He was wearing white. Abby's mind was swirling. Was this a radiologist? If so, what was he there for? An emergency MRI? The man stepped away. He was wearing bright white coveralls, not a clinic coat. He began singing a woeful rendition of the "Folsom Prison Blues" as he dusted the floor. Abby barely took a breath as the janitor sang and dusted around her. She watched the time flash down on her watch. Eleven minutes. Ten. The singing stopped. Moments later the lights went out. The doors opened and closed. Soon the silence and the darkness were total.

Abby waited an extra thirty seconds, then

managed to roll over so that she was facing upward. How on earth had claustrophobic Claire allowed herself to be scanned even once, let alone a second time?

The air seemed heavy, like it was liquid or something. . . .

She took Lew's penlight from her breast pocket and ran the beam over the white enamel inside the tube. Inch by inch, she worked her way out of the cylinder in the direction she had entered, keeping her body extended by keeping her feet on the track. She was about eighteen inches from the opening when she saw them — a single row of minuscule pores in the enamel, extending in an arc directly over where a typical patient's nose or mouth would be. She held the light inches away from the openings — a row of, perhaps, thirty holes that were little more than pinpricks. Were they standard in an MRI? If so, what would they be for?

Abby's pulse was racing as she pulled herself out of the cylinder and turned on the overheads. There were eight minutes left by her watch. She took a step back and ran her gaze around the margin of the opening. At the twelve o'clock position there was a small fan that was used, she assumed, to keep air circulating over the patient during the test. At three o'clock there was a clear Plexiglas disc attached to the housing by a rivet and hinge in such a way that it could be swung over the opening

489

and fixed in place, effectively sealing the cylinder at that end. Abby went around and checked the other end. There was no similar piece there. Was that a standard part of the equipment?

Six minutes.

Abby hurried to the phone on the wall by the door and called Lew.

"Is the X-ray tech still there?" she asked.

"He's busy conjugating the verb *ir*. 'To go.'"

"Well, *menos prisa, por favor*."

"Go slow. Where did you learn — ?"

"Lew, I've found something, but I need more time."

"Tell me."

"Can you see Hector right now? We can't let him come back here yet."

"He's right over there at the nurses' station, wondering how so many people in the world who are not as smart as he is can speak Spanish so well. But a guy's just been brought in with a fractured hand from punching a tree instead of his girlfriend. Hector knows him and knows he's got work to do."

"Fifteen minutes. Can you give me that much?"

"What have you found?"

"Lew, there are tiny holes inside the cylinder just above where the patient's nose and mouth would be. Do you know if they're supposed to be there?"

"No idea."

"There's more. There's a Plexiglas plate that can be swung over the opening at that end, sealing it off and creating an enclosed space."

"But what for?"

"I don't know. Listen, Lew, I need to look some more, and I want to call the radiology resident on duty at St. John's. Can you give me fifteen minutes?"

"I can try. Maybe I'll have him conjugate *hacer el amor*."

" 'To make love.' From what I know of Hector, that might do it. I'm at extension three-three-eight-four. Call if you lose him. I'm going to check with St. John's, then I'm going to try to figure out what comes out of those little holes."

"Just be careful and keep me informed. Kelly underestimated those people."

"So did I."

Abby hung up, reset her watch for a thirteen-minute countdown, and used the switchboard operator to call St. John's. It took just a one-minute conversation for her to confirm what she intuitively suspected: there are no holes inside the standard MRI, and no technical reason ever to close off one end of the cylinder.

. . . It even had a weird taste. . . .

She returned to the massive housing and first examined the cables and tubes making up the hydraulic system for the sled, then the base of the machine. Nothing.

Nine minutes.

491

Feeling just a bit panicky from the press of time, she stepped back again, searching for something, anything, that looked out of place. It was fully half a minute before she realized she had not inspected the top of the unit. She pulled over a wooden straight-backed chair and stood on it. The missing piece was there — a small bundle of clear plastic tubes, each slightly smaller than IV tubing, rising from the floor next to the hydraulics, and running around the outside of the housing to a spot just above the ventilation fan. From there the bundle dropped into the machine through a black-rubber gasket.

Seven minutes.

Abby traced the bundle of tubes back down to the floor at the base of the unit, where they disappeared into a white enamel shield. Using the penlight, she tried peering down behind the shield. As far as she could tell, the tubes seemed to come right out of the tiled floor. Lying prone on the floor and using the penlight for an up-close examination, she studied the foot-square beige tiles, and the gray grout between them.

Six minutes.

Five.

Just as she was about to give up, she saw it — a thin space, less than a millimeter, through the grout bordering a two-foot square of tile. It was virtually invisible except at almost microscopic range and had to be a trapdoor of some sort. At that moment the wall phone began ringing. Abby sprang up and dashed to it.

"Hector's just gotten a call," Lew said. "One of the floors is sending someone down for an emergency belly film. He's meeting them in two minutes."

"Damn!"

"I really can't keep him here without having it look terribly suspicious."

"Lew, I've found it! The MRI machine is rigged to function as some sort of inhalation chamber. That was why Claire experienced what she did. The gas, whatever it is, comes up through the floor in six small tubes and enters the cylinder at the top, right by those little ports I told you about. If that Plexiglas panel is in place, it would be possible to deliver a very closely controlled dose."

"An inhalation chamber. God, as if that thing didn't feel enough like being pushed into a tomb."

"There's more. I traced the tubes down, and they seem to go straight into the floor. Lew, I think there's a trapdoor in the tile right near where they go in. I want to find a way to open it."

"What about Hector?"

"If all he's doing is a standard set of abdominal films, there's no reason why he should come in here. I'm going to chance it."

"I don't know if that's wise."

"I'll be back in the ER in ten minutes."

"Just —"

"I know. I know. It seems that 'be careful' is all you've been saying to me lately."

"I'm crazy about you. How's that?"

"That's much better," she said. "I'll see you in ten."

She went out and closed the curtain in the control room. Next she returned and checked the walls in the main room for any switch that might unlock the panel in the floor. Then she stopped, calmed herself, and struggled to overcome her limited mechanical aptitude. She began by reasoning the situation out piece by piece, the way she did in the ER when her first rapid-fire treatment of a crisis failed to work. Whatever was going on in the MRI scanner, it was unlikely that more than a very few people were in on it. Dozens of explanations could be given to any technician or physician who questioned the tubes or the Plexiglas. And the patients, many of whom wore coverings on their eyes to help them relax, were unlikely even to notice the pores in the cylinder, or to think them abnormal. A switch on the wall would be too prone to being thrown by mistake. Instead, she concluded, it had to be a lever, most likely concealed beneath the electromagnet housing itself. Something mechanical, not electric.

Abby got down on her hands and knees once again, feeling up underneath the cylinder where the track came out. It took several careful minutes, but finally her hand closed on a smooth curved handle hidden high up behind the housing, well away from any place it could be accidentally pulled. It was metal of some sort, although if so, it certainly had to be nonferromagnetic. She composed herself with a deep breath, curled her fingers around the handle, and pulled. With a soft pop the latch released. The four-tile segment of floor opened half an inch at one side. Abby's pulse was hammering again as she crawled over, lifted the hatch, and peered inside. Below her was a ladder, set in concrete, dropping six feet or so to the start of a concrete tunnel. The narrow plastic tubes, extending through the tunnel wall, appeared to run along the length of ceiling. The floor of the tunnel was slatted wood, like the floor of a sauna.

It took a few seconds for Abby to re-create the orientation of the hospital and the radiology suite and to get her bearings. But when she did, she became certain of what she already suspected — the tunnel was headed straight toward the Colstar cliff. From outside the unit, voices became audible. People were closer than she would have expected given the room where Hector would have been working. She hurried across and killed the overhead lights. Then she returned to the trapdoor, using the penlight. Suddenly there was a scraping, as if someone's shoe had brushed against the hallway door.

Quickly, she dropped onto the ladder and lowered herself into the tunnel. Then she checked that she could open the hatch from underneath before pulling it down over her.

She crouched at the base of the ladder and waited. A minute passed. Two. There was no sound from above. The tunnel was almost exactly her height — perhaps an inch or so more. The air was stagnant and dusty, the darkness total. Abby shined the penlight into the blackness. It illuminated a few feet, no more. Again she listened for sounds from above. Again there was nothing.

She had come too far, learned too much, to turn back now. Moving inches at a time, hunching her shoulders, and keeping the weak light trained on the floorboards, she took her first tentative steps toward what she knew was the man-made cavern within the Colstar cliff.

Chapter Thirty-Six

The concrete tunnel sloped downward and seemed to make a gradual bend to the right. As she moved through it, Abby tried to estimate where she might be relative to what she remembered of the terrain and the layout of PRH. Under the service parking lot behind the hospital. . . . Under the long gravel-and-dirt lot, staked out with flag sticks for some future addition. . . . Under the high chain-link fence topped with barbed wire. . . . Under the broad meadow of boulders, jagged rock, and wildflowers that led to the Colstar cliff. . . . And, finally, somewhere near or under the cliff itself.

Progress was slow. There was a row of bare incandescent lightbulbs, set about ten feet apart along the center of the ceiling, but none of them was lit. Abby cursed herself for not thinking to look for a switch somewhere around the ladder, although it was doubtful she would have felt safe turning it on. Running parallel to the row of lights was the bundle of six narrow plastic tubes, each color-coded by bands of tape spaced along its length: yellow, red, blue, green, pink, and black.

The small penlight succeeded a little in

piercing the dark, but the blackness was consuming when Abby turned it off. Gradually, the damp, musty taste to the air began to subside. Her estimate put her well beyond the base of the Colstar cliff now, but there was absolutely no way to know her position with any certainty. From somewhere up ahead, she could feel a faint breeze and hear the low hum of air-conditioning. Then, as she continued the gentle curve to the right, she saw a faint light. Her heart was pounding in her throat as she moved forward. Twice she had to stop and brace herself against the wall just to allow her pulse to slow down. With each step the light grew larger and brighter, until finally she could make out the outlines of a doorway. Her best guess was that she had traveled a quarter of a mile from the hospital. Maybe more.

Except for the faint hum of the air-conditioning unit, the silence was absolute. Abby turned off the penlight and inched her way along the wall. Her fight and flight reflexes were turned up to the maximum, but she knew that nothing was going to override her anger and her overwhelming curiosity. The light flowing through the doorway was fluorescent. As she moved to the end of the passageway, she realized that it was coming from around the side of a whitewashed concrete wall twenty feet away. She stepped around the doorway and was standing within a dimly lit space that rose into the rock as far as she could see. At the center of the space was an elevator, enclosed in a concrete shaft. A metal staircase wound around it like a serpent. At the base of the stairs, riveted to the stone wall, was a professionally painted sign:

<u>WARNING</u>
IN THE EVENT OF FIRE
OR GAS LEAK DO NOT
USE ELEVATOR. BE CERTAIN
SPRINKLER SYSTEM IS ON.
IF NOT, THROW LEVER BEFORE
LEAVING. TAKE STAIRWAY
TO 1ST OR 2ND LEVEL
EMERGENCY EXIT.

Beside the sign, encased in glass, were the fire alarm and the manual lever controlling the emergency sprinkler system. In a rack on the floor were half a dozen hand-held state-of-the-art fire extinguishers. And hanging on the wall were three rubberized exposure suits and an equal number of gas masks.

Abby flattened herself against the wall and listened for any hint that others were around. All was quiet. From her hours of reviewing Kelly's research in the registry of deeds office and the library, she knew exactly where she was — at the bottom of the main shaft of the Patience Mine. Unless she was badly off base, the emergency exits referred to on the sign were two of the three old ventilation shafts that were so carefully camouflaged on the rock face.

Grateful that she was wearing sneakers, Abby stepped cautiously onto the first metal step, waited there a few seconds, then quietly made her way upward. Lighting along the rock wall beside the staircase was minimal — widely spaced low-wattage incandescent bulbs covered by opaque plastic clip-on shades. She could look over the black iron-pipe railing and see straight down alongside the concrete elevator shaft. The first ventilation tunnel was twenty-five feet up the rock wall, exactly where she anticipated. However, the opening was sealed with a locked accordion-type metal gate. Just beyond the gate were tools, bags of concrete, and hand-held drilling equipment indicating that the shaft was undergoing some sort of repair.

USE 2ND EMERGENCY EXIT, the sign wired to the gate read. Abby tiptoed up to the next landing and was now looking a dizzying fifty feet straight down along the shaft. To her right was the emergency-escape passageway, beginning with an opening in the rock similar to the one at the end of the tunnel from the hospital. To her left was a concrete landing and a short flight of stairs going up. She tried the stairs first. At the top of the flight was the pitch-black space Abby knew from *A Brief History of the Patience Mine.* Although the soft glow from the stairway didn't allow her to see beyond ten or twelve feet, she strongly sensed that the entire cavernous area, called "The Upper Dig" in the monograph, was empty. According to the book, she was now about forty feet below the plant and sixty feet or so above "The Lower Dig."

Abby returned to the emergency-exit tunnel. It was totally unlit, about a foot lower than her height, and no more than two and a half feet from side to side. Once again she paused to listen to the deep silence. She had no sense that anyone was nearby, but her fight/flight mechanism remained on red alert. Cautiously, she made her way down the tunnel, clicking on the penlight every few steps. Ninety or a hundred feet, the diagrams in the mine book indicated. It took quite some time to reach the end of the passageway, because she was forced to move uncomfortably hunched over. She wondered if Kelly had made it this far. The thought of the woman, the image of what she looked like now, added a few more degrees to Abby's anger. Her boiling point wasn't too far off. The door, which she knew blended so well into the rock face on the other side, was plywood. It was painted black on this side, and fixed to holes in the rock walls by six sliding bolts, three on a side. DOOR IS ALARMED, the sign affixed to it read. USE ONLY FOR ABSOLUTE EMERGENCY.

Abby shined the penlight carefully around the margin of the door. Then she turned around with no little difficulty and retraced her steps to the staircase in the main shaft. She had started down, and was ten feet or so from the lowest level, when the elevator gears engaged with a clank that echoed off the rock and startled her into several missed heartbeats. The vestibule at the foot of the staircase was dimly lit and deserted. Uncertain whether the car was moving down or up, she raced to the bottom of the stairs and hid in the shadows of the hospital tunnel. In moments the grinding of the descending car stopped and the door swung open. A slight man with Coke-bottle glasses emerged. He was wearing a lab coat and studying a clipboard. Abby crouched farther back into the shadows, but still, had the man turned to look, he would have been staring right at her. Instead, totally engrossed in whatever was on the clipboard, he passed no more than six feet from her and headed toward the source of the fluorescent light.

Although a retreat back to the hospital seemed like a prudent course, Abby knew that she had come too far not to follow him. She crossed the vestibule, flattened herself against the concrete wall, and inched along it until she could peer around the corner. The space in front of her was vast and gleaming beneath a drop ceiling and brilliant fluorescent lighting. It was separated from the rock by a three-foot tarmac path and an encircling thick glass wall that reached the ceiling. Within the enclosed space were a number of rooms, partitioned by other walls of glass. The man with the lab coat was about twenty feet away, working at a computer in a well-equipped office with four desks. No one else was around. On one wall of the office was a large cork board with an assortment of newspaper and magazine articles pinned up, as well as a number of documents. On the opposite glass wall, hanging from a metal strip, was an American flag.

Still in a crouch, she inched her way along the outside glass wall. Looking through the transparent walls at the various rooms, she could see that one section — a square perhaps twenty feet on a side — was sealed across the ceiling with painted plaster. In addition, it was equipped with four sets of closed ports along with thick gloves that were attached on the inner side to manipulate robot arms. Seated at one of the ports, working on the contents of a small brass vat, was another scientist — a large black man, also wearing a knee-length lab coat. Abby moved back into the shadows, though, as before, she would have been seen easily had the man's attention not been fixed on the mechanical arms.

To her left, in a small area marked with the black-on-yellow universal symbol for dangerous materials, were two dozen or more gas tanks of varying sizes painted in colors identical to markings on the six tubes entering the MRI scanner. They were secured in metal racks and labeled with stenciled lettering. From where she was, it was impossible to read any of the names. But moving much closer — moving at all, for that matter — would greatly increase her risk of being spotted by the man at the computer, who was facing almost in her direction.

Her choices seemed limited: stay partially secluded and risk the arrival of more people and almost certain discovery, or chance moving nearer to the storage area to learn what she could about the contents of the tanks and get back to the hospital. She flattened out on the gray tile floor and moved in a crawl toward the glass outer wall. She was shielded in part by some equipment and was at an angle where the man at the computer would have to turn thirty or forty degrees to spot her. Within ten feet she had moved directly behind the scientist working the robotics. The tanks were no more than fifteen feet away now, the stenciling almost legible. She crawled a few feet closer before risking another look. The word stenciled in black on the red tube made her blood freeze: SARIN.

Following the disaster in the Tokyo subway system, when a radical religious cult had exposed hundreds to the gas, Abby had attended an ER-department briefing on sarin and other chemical weapons. Ironically, the presentation had been made by her friend, toxicologist Sandra Stuart. Sandra was assisted by a physician/researcher from the U.S. Army Chemical School at Fort Something-or-other in Alabama, who spiced up his portion of the talk with a number of terrifying slides dating back to World War I.

Sarin was in the organophosphate class of chemicals and, as such, had a modestly effective antidote. But the molecule-for-molecule potency of the neuroparalytic agent was so intense that even a small exposure would often cause death by suffocation before any treatment could be administered. Suddenly Abby remembered the patient of George Oleander's whose blood had lit up for small amounts of organophosphate. Exposure to fertilizer, Oleander had said. A yearly event for the careless farmer. Nothing to worry about. *Bullshit, George!*

Abby peered through the legs of a table and between two workbenches in time to see the man with the thick glasses push back from his computer and head toward the robotics room. For one paralyzing moment he was directly facing her. She forced herself down and tried to make her body melt into the floor. Then, after half a minute, she risked a peek, half expecting to see him standing right there on the other side of the glass wall staring down at her. Instead, his back was to her as he spoke with the other scientist. The larger man had pulled his arms out of the protective gloves and was laughing. He had a jovial face and wonderfully animated hands when he spoke. Abby wondered how he felt, knowing that he was working every day with a substance so lethal that the contents of a single tank, properly released, could probably wipe out a large city.

After a conversation that lasted only a few minutes, the myopic researcher patted the other man on the shoulder and headed for the elevator. Moments later Abby heard the gears engage. She had dodged a good-sized bullet. And for the moment, at least, it was just Abby and one very absorbed scientist. Immediately, her game plan changed. She was still going to identify the contents of the gas cylinders. But before she retreated through the tunnel to the hospital, she was now intent on getting into the office and seeing exactly what items were tacked on the cork board.

On her hands and knees she moved a few feet closer to the gas-storage room. The stenciling on the yellow tanks became discernible first — TRICHOTHECENE. The chemical — an irritant better known as TTC — was another of the weapons described at the St. John's toxicology lecture. Along with mustard gas, which she then noticed was in the blue cylinders, TTC was one of the most debilitating of the so-called blistering agents.

The pink tanks held something called

mycotoxin, and the black ones were labeled VX in white. Neither name rang any bells. The last set of cylinders, green labeled in white, contained phosgene oxime, which the expert from Alabama said had been in worldwide use for well over seventy-five years, most recently by the Soviets against the Afghans and by the Iraqis against the Kurds. Now, it appeared, the U.S. government against Claire Buchanan and others at Patience Regional Hospital could be added to the list.

Had Claire almost died from an accidental overdose, or was it an allergic reaction? If Del Marshall knew this experimentation, or whatever it was, was going on in his department — and it was certainly hard to imagine he didn't — no wonder he looked so pale as Claire was being resuscitated.

Abby had been inside the lab now for twenty minutes. It was time to get out and get back to Lew with what she had found. There were still a number of missing pieces, among them the connection between this subterranean operation and the cadmium exposures in Josh, Willie Cardoza, and the rest. But at this point she had seen enough of what was going on so that the Alliance could try to enlist the intervention of someone with political influence and a conscience — provided, of course, there was such a person.

Once more in the shadows, she worked her way back toward the tunnel. A short run and she would be safely there. Instead, she stopped opposite the door to the glass-enclosed office, essentially out of sight of the robotics man. But once she was inside the office, she would be fair game again.

She dropped back down to her hands and knees. Then she moved to the doorway of the office. Through the far glass wall she could see what was almost certainly the gas-delivery area — a chamber containing tanks of all six colors, plus two other large gas cylinders, one white and one orange. Abby bet herself that one of those tanks contained some sort of cadmium fumes. She remembered Kelly's description of the maximum allowable circulating cadmium — two aspirins pulverized and blown into the air in the Astrodome. Impressive. In vapor form the heavy metal would be right up there in toxicity with some of these other gases.

The more Abby thought about the possibility, the more sense it made. Another puzzle piece might well have fallen into place. A slipup with the cadmium fumes had resulted in the exposure of a number of Colstar employees, including Josh. Then she remembered that there would have to have been more than one slipup, since Gus Schumacher would have been exposed before Josh had even arrived in Patience. Postulating two accidental exposures didn't feel that comfortable as a theory, though it did explain the facts.

There was one thing Abby had no doubt about whatsoever. The array of cylinders in the dosing room were connected to a complex system of tubing, gauges, and digital displays. And at the receiving end of the tubes were the NIWWs.

From the office doorway she could clearly see the headlines on the articles tacked to the cork board.

MANY DEAD, HUNDREDS ILL IN TOKYO SUBWAY GAS ATTACK

KURDS CHARGE HUSSEIN WITH USING YELLOW RAIN CHEMICAL — Hundreds Claimed Dead, Thousands Sick

SARIN, DEADLY SARIN — WHO WILL BE NEXT?

VETERANS GROUPS RALLY TO PROTEST INACTION ON GULF WAR SYNDROME — "We Were Gassed," Vets Proclaim

There were at least two dozen articles dealing with confirmed or suspected chemical attacks on military and civilian targets around the world. Crouching low, Abby took a cautious step into the office. She was about to cross to the desk when she caught movement far to her left. The hulking scientist had left the robotics room and was

heading through the maze of glass doorways toward the office. She was frozen,
unable to decide whether to flee or try to
conceal herself in the office. The hesitation
cost her the option of running. Praying that
she hadn't yet been spotted, she dived into
the well beneath one of the desks, drew her
knees to her chin, and pulled the chair back
in place. It had been pure hubris not to
leave when she had the chance. Stupid and
reckless. And now she was going to pay —
possibly with her life. The scientist entered
the office humming and walked directly to
the desk. Abby breathed slowly through her
nose, trying desperately not to make a
movement or a sound. He stood behind the
chair and rummaged through some papers
that were two inches above her head. If he
pushed the chair under the desk now, it
would hit against her almost immediately.

Still humming, the man moved back from
the desk. Abby watched his scuffed shoes,
the cuffs of his trousers, and the lower edge
of his lab coat as he walked out through
the doorway where she had just been
standing. Then he turned left toward the
elevator. She wondered if he was planning
to leave the area completely unattended.
But with her heart rate still in the 150
range and her clothes damp from tension,
she knew that even if he did, she was
finished there. Then, from just around the
corner, she heard a door open and close.
The toilet, she thought, remembering now

that she had seen the door near the elevator with the man and woman symbols on it.

Breathless, she scrambled out from under the desk and sprinted down the corridor and into the tunnel. Almost home. After fifty feet or so she paused and allowed herself a grim smile. She had finished what Kelly had started. Now it was Lew's turn — his and the others in the Alliance. She started back along the pitch-black passageway, praying that Kelly had begun to regain consciousness.

Familiar with the terrain, she moved much more quickly than she had before. She slowed only when she sensed she was reaching the ladder and hatchway beneath the MRI scanner. All that mattered now was making it to Lew without being spotted. Quinn and his Colstar cronies would know that they had been penetrated once, by a woman who was now unconscious. But they would have no idea their secrecy had been pierced a second time. It would be business as usual as long as Kelly was in a coma.

When Abby reached the ladder at the end of the tunnel, she used her penlight for the first time. Everything was as it had been. It was well after ten now. There was no reason to expect anyone to be around the scanner or, in fact, the MRI unit. Still, she slid the latch back very carefully and pushed the hatch open an inch. The scanner room was as dark as the tunnel. She

511

stepped up a rung and guided the hatch back silently until it touched the floor. Then she quietly stepped up another rung, bringing her waist to the level of the floor. At that instant the overhead fluorescent lights winked on.

Abby blinked until her dilated pupils adjusted to the brightness. Standing a few feet away, legs apart, arms folded across his chest, was Lyle Quinn. Behind him were George Oleander, Joe Henderson, Martin Bartholomew, radiologist Del Marshall, and Police Captain Gould.

"Welcome back, Abby," Quinn said. "We've been waiting for you."

Chapter Thirty-Seven

Abby stared in stunned silence as Lyle Quinn took a step forward and extended his hand. His black sports coat fell away just enough to reveal a shoulder holster and gun.

"Here, let me help you out of there," he said.

"Don't touch me!"

Abby shrieked the warning.

Quinn retreated.

"Have it your way."

For a few uncomfortable seconds there was total silence. From her spot on the ladder Abby surveyed the group. Only Del Marshall, perhaps unable to get past her lifesaving performance in his department, looked uncomfortable at her situation. He shifted from one foot to the other and stared off at one wall. Finally George Oleander stepped forward. Quinn, his body tensed, his eyes fixed on her like lasers, took a single step to the side.

"Abby, nine or so years ago the town of Patience — the *whole valley* — was dying," Oleander began in his most paternal voice. "Directly or indirectly, almost everyone's livelihood depended — and still does — on Colstar. And Colstar was going under.

Senator Corman did his best to send what military contracts he could our way, and for a time the company looked as if it was going to make it. As you know, Ezra Black lives not too far from here. So even though he owns companies around the world, he feels a special connection to Colstar and Patience Valley. He did his best to hang on while Corman did what he could in Washington."

Oleander looked around for approval of his story. Martin Bartholomew and Del Marshall nodded that he was doing well. Captain Gould and Joe Henderson remained statuelike, their arms folded across their chests. Quinn, his silver hair fairly glowing beneath the bright fluorescents, made no acknowledgment at all. He appeared ready for action. His hands hung loose at his sides, but his fingers were in minute, constant movement. His linebacker's shoulders were square to her, his feet apart. He looked like a panther, getting set to spring.

The medical chief cleared his throat, shifted uneasily, then knelt so that he was speaking directly at Abby. His tone now was somewhere between pleading and patronizing.

"For a while, with some government contracts coming in, it looked like things might turn around for us. Then, about eight years ago, some terrorists in South America blew up the huge Colstar plant that mined and refined most of the raw materials used in our manufacturing operation here on the mesa. Five Colstar employees were killed in the blast. After the explosion no one down there would help the corporation rebuild. It looked like that was the death knell for all of us up here. That's when Senator Corman stepped forward with a proposition."

"An offer you couldn't refuse," Abby said, keeping Oleander and the others in check with her eyes, while her mind evaluated and discarded one possible move after another.

Run . . . scream . . . give in . . . fight . . . grovel . . . try to win the weak ones over . . .

"I suppose you could say that," Oleander responded. "The truth is, we didn't *want* to refuse. Every other day, in some country or another, a new chemical weapon was popping up. Our scientists were working with animals to develop antidotes to them. But as often as not, the *treatments* that seemed to work all right on some pig or sheep or monkey ended up making our troops sicker than the *chemicals*. The Gulf War syndrome is a perfect example. Half the symptoms in our troops were from chemicals Hussein was exposing them to. The rest were the result of the so-called protecting drugs *we* were feeding them."

The NIWWs, Abby realized. The Alliance had been in the right church by suspecting that an exposure of some sort was what unified the patients on their list. But they

515

were mostly in the wrong pew. Cadmium was only part of the nasty picture. The NIWWs' varied symptoms were certainly consistent with those reported from heavy-metal exposure, but they were positively identical to the myriad complaints issued by returning Gulf War veterans.

"So Corman wanted a human laboratory," Abby said. "A controlled environment where microscopic amounts of gases could be pitted against microscopic amounts of antidotes."

"Something like that. At one time the government worked with prisoners. But that just isn't allowed anymore. Besides, they needed an even more rigidly controlled situation."

"Like a hospital," Abby said.

"Initially we used our CT scanner. Then, when MRIs became available, we were able to get one when no other hospital our size in the country could. Some people have been . . . inconvenienced. I won't deny that. But in addition to our scanner, what we got in exchange for agreeing to cooperate with our country's needs was a rebirth of the entire valley — the businesses, the schools, the parks, and especially this hospital."

And a hefty payday for each of you.

Perhaps sensing from Abby's expression that she had not been moved by Oleander's explanation, Joe Henderson stepped forward. The medical chief got to his feet wearily and moved to one side.

"Abby, I'm sorry about that autopsy thing," the husky hospital president began, grinning his superficial Henderson grin, and not bothering to kneel. "But you were like a pit bull about this thing. You had your teeth into our leg, and you wouldn't let up. We decided it was best for all concerned if you just left Patience. Maybe we should have sat down with you and explained."

"Maybe you should have," Abby said hollowly, knowing there was no way that option had ever been considered before the red pickup, fake autopsy report, and high-powered rifle were rolled out.

The corner of Henderson's mouth twitched. His plastic smile vanished for a second. Then, just as quickly, it returned.

"Well, we're doing that now, aren't we?" he said in his bogus drawl.

His manner and expression indicated that he was about finished reasoning with her.

Abby looked up at Lyle Quinn and saw the emptiness in his eyes. He was a soldier, but a soldier devoid of conscience. Welcome to My Lai, Lieutenant Calley. She knew there had to be a reason why she wasn't already dead — and it had nothing to do with Quinn's compassion.

"How did you know where I was just now?" she asked.

The chorus deferred to Quinn.

"You set off a silent alarm," he said. "A photoelectric beam at the other end of this tunnel. Unfortunately, it functioned improperly. The lights went on all over the cliff outside, but there was no alert to me or the security man on duty — or I should say, *not* on duty. By the time we picked you up on our monitors, you were crawling around in the office. I assumed you were headed back to the hospital and decided it would be best if we met you here."

"Why?"

"I don't understand."

"Why did you let me get all the way back here? Why didn't you drug me, stick me in a car in a garage, and turn on the engine, like you did to Kelly Franklin?"

As she made the statement, Abby was focused on the chorus standing to Quinn's right. Bartholomew, Oleander, and Del Marshall looked surprised. Gould and Henderson knew.

"I don't know what you're talking about," Quinn said vehemently. "I'm sorry about Kelly. I like her very much. But I certainly had nothing to do with her suicide attempt. Abby, we need your cooperation. We need to know *who* else in this hospital — this town — knows *what* about Colstar. We need to know how you knew your way into our facility. And mostly we need to know whether you will join us in keeping this program, and with it this whole valley, alive."

"I . . . I need some time to think about it."

"About what?" Quinn said, an unmistakable note of impatience in his voice.

He stared down at her, and Abby could tell — the Colstar security chief had decided that he had seen and heard enough.

"There are several others who know where I am and what I'm doing," she tried.

Quinn's icy eyes studied her for just a few more seconds.

"This is bullshit," he snapped suddenly. "We tried it your way, George. Now we'll do it mine. Out of here, all of you. Except Gould."

It seemed as if the four hospital men were glad to be let off the hook. They left quickly. Abby knew that their mute departure was her death sentence.

Quinn's eyes now were menacing. Standing behind him, the tall police chief wore an unnerving half smile. Unconsciously, he wet his lips with his tongue. Whatever was about to happen to her he was going to enjoy.

"Abby, suppose we three go on back to my office in the plant," Quinn said, stepping toward her. "We'll have a talk."

Abby flashed on Kelly's inert body, stretched across the front seat of her car. The men standing above her were remorseless. Whether with drugs or torture or both, Quinn would find a way to get his answers. Then Abby Dolan would simply vanish. And in all likelihood Lew Alvarez would end up missing or dead, as well.

Quinn had done it to David Brooks and Kelly. There was no reason to suspect she had anything better in store.

The prospect of Quinn merely touching her was terrifying. The thought of being completely helpless before him refused to register at all. She felt as frightened as she could ever remember, and as defenseless. Still, there was no way she was going to allow herself to be taken without a fight. It was possible that screaming might have some effect — possible, but highly doubtful. Instead, she slid one foot back from the rung on which she was standing, and as Quinn moved toward her, she pushed back with the other and dropped into the tunnel. Above her, Quinn quickly issued an order to Gould, then headed down after her. But Abby, hunched over, arms spread to maintain herself between the rock walls, was already running awkwardly along the wood-slatted floor, through the consuming darkness.

"Abby, don't do this," Quinn called out, his voice flooding the tunnel. "It's not necessary. And it won't help."

At that instant the row of ceiling bulbs flashed on, stretching out ahead of her like some obscene carnival attraction. Momentarily blinded, Abby lurched ahead, losing her balance and stumbling heavily against the wall. She cried out, as much from the surprise as from the jolt to her shoulder.

Now she could hear Quinn's leather soles,

snapping down on the wooden slats like pistol shots. He was moving quickly. The darkness and the low ceiling height had been to her advantage. Now they had essentially been neutralized. Desperately, she reached up her fist and snapped the next lightbulb off with a sideways blow. If the glass cut her hand, it wasn't bad enough to matter. Head down, she sprinted ahead, hammering the fleshy side of her fist against bulb after bulb, spraying herself and the area around her with glass, but also restoring the blackness. Behind her the footfalls slowed.

"Abby, give it up!" Quinn cried.

He tried to sound confident, but Abby sensed he was frustrated. The notion brought her a burst of energy and more resolve. As long as there was no one coming at her from the other end of the tunnel, she had a chance. And if there was someone moving toward her, he had better be ready. She had a decent mental picture of the entire Patience mine and, before, had made it up as far as the Upper Dig. Somehow the elevator or the circular staircase connected with the main plant. They had to. And there was bound to be at least one more staircase somewhere — probably off the cavernous Upper Dig itself. If she could only make it to *that* stairway, she had a chance.

Running with lights ahead of her, Abby knew she had to be moving faster than Quinn. She sensed herself making the final, protracted curve to the right and wished the tunnel were longer. But at least no one had intercepted her. She wondered if Quinn had ordered Gould to call over to the lab, and the cop had failed to reach anyone. Whatever had happened, the end of the tunnel was in sight and unobstructed. She had gotten a major lucky break. The next one she would have to manufacture for herself.

It would be obvious to Quinn that she had gone up the circular staircase. With walls of glass throughout the lab, there was simply no place else she could go. For that reason alone she frantically tried to think of an option. The bathroom came immediately to mind. If she could get in there and Quinn ran up the stairs, she could head back through the tunnel to the hospital. But if he spotted her going in, or thought to look there, it was over.

She wondered if she could outrun him up the stairs by enough of a margin to give her a shot at finding the stairway in the upper chamber — if, in fact, there even was one. She had fifteen years or so on him, but he looked to be in great shape, and she knew she wasn't. From a dead-even start she probably couldn't outrun him at all. That depressing notion was dominating her thoughts as she reached the end of the tunnel. The elevator and staircase were right in front of her. The bathroom was about twenty feet away. But she could hear

Quinn coming hard. Within a few seconds he would be there. Then she noticed the emergency fire alarm and manual sprinkler lever, and below them, the row of fire extinguishers. With no time left to reason things through, she grabbed the small hammer suspended on a chain, smashed the glass, and activated both the alarm and the sprinkler systems. Instantly there was a powerful whooping from sirens throughout the lab. Seconds later dozens of overhead nozzles erupted in the equivalent of a typhoon rainstorm.

Abby snatched up one of the fire extinguishers, pulled the safety pin, and stepped back from the tunnel just as Quinn charged through. He was only a few feet away when he turned toward her, already sodden from the downpour. No longer composed and confident, he was actually snarling. She aimed the broad nozzle at the center of his face and fired. Instantly, his head vanished within a burst of chemical foam. He cried out and sank to one knee as he pawed at his eyes. But the sprinklers, moments ago her ally, were already rapidly washing away the foam.

Frightened of getting any nearer to the man, and panicked at losing her advantage so quickly, Abby hoisted the heavy extinguisher to her chin and hurled it across at him with an awkward chest pass. It struck him on the front of his shoulder and the side of his face, bowling him over backward onto the rapidly flooding tile. But Abby could tell he was not badly injured. She whirled and raced up the stairs, three at a time.

The lower stairs were dangerously slippery. Abby's foot skidded out from under her. She slammed her shin into the steel edge of the stair above. Electric pain shot up her leg, and for the briefest moment she thought it was broken. She cried out and stumbled, barely managing to keep from falling. But she knew she had been badly gashed. She glanced back. Quinn was on his feet, still pawing at his eyes, but obviously regaining his vision. There were no sprinklers past the ceiling of the Lower Dig, so the stairs were dry. And although Abby's lungs were beginning to burn, adrenaline enabled her to continue taking two or three steps at a time. Then, just as she passed the locked accordion gate at the first emergency tunnel, she heard the clanging of heavy footsteps from the stairway high above her.

It wasn't even worth slowing to look back. She knew Quinn was coming. The vise was closing. The only hope she had — a wafer-thin chance, at that — was to make it to the vast Upper Dig and pray she could find a staircase up to the plant.

No, she realized suddenly. No, that wasn't her only hope. There was another option — not much better, but possible. The landing at the upper escape tunnel was just a short distance above her. If she could make it there without running into the man who was charging down from above, there would be some confusion between him and Quinn about whether she had gone left to the short flight of stairs leading to the Upper Dig, or right, into the old ventilation shaft. That hesitation might give her time to reach the emergency exit and throw the six bolts holding the door. Once outside, she would just have to improvise. But she had been doing that since she had entered the MRI unit in the first place. From that point there had to be grips built into the rock to get down to the meadow or up to the mesa.

The man clanging down from above couldn't have been any farther away than a single loop of the staircase when Abby hunched down and plunged to her right, into the tunnel that the Gardner monograph on the Patience Mine had captioned "Piercing an Imposing Wall of Rock." The ceiling of the passageway, a foot or so lower than the tunnel to the hospital, was worth maybe another ten or fifteen seconds to her. But even for her the run along the hundred-foot channel was awkward and difficult. What little light penetrated from the main shaft disappeared within a few feet. The darkness was stifling. Again and again she lurched heavily against the rock walls. Her shirt, soaked through from the sprinklers, shredded at the point of her left shoulder, along with the skin underneath it. The pain barely registered.

The burning in her lungs was a wildfire now. The heavy, stale air refused to allow her a decent breath. The hundred feet seemed like a mile. Suddenly she hit the door — a stunning blow off the side of her forehead. She fell backward, dazed. Then, frantically battling dizziness, pain, and a wave of nausea, she scrambled to her knees and pulled Lew's penlight from the pocket of her sodden jeans. Remarkably, the promotional gift from Ezra Black's pharmaceutical company was still working. She pulled one bolt back, then another and another. Her knuckles scraped against the rock. From behind her in the tunnel she could hear the continued wailing of the emergency sirens. But now she could hear footsteps as well. Then, as she threw the fourth and fifth bolts, Lyle Quinn's voice filled the darkness.

"Give it up, Abby! There's an arrest warrant being put together right now saying that you tried to kill Kelly! Working with us is your only hope! Only we can save you now."

Desperately, Abby clawed at the last bolt.

"Abby, stay right there! You'll never get down the rock alive!"

The bolt wouldn't budge. There were no hinges, so the door had to be removable. But inward or out? Quinn's footsteps were drawing closer. Abby dropped to her back, drew both knees to her chin, and shot her legs out with all the force she could manage. The door broke free, splintering at the bolt, and flew out into the cool night. Instantly the tunnel was flooded with fresh air . . . and light.

Abby peered out. She was far above the valley and the town. From beyond the meadow below, at the base of the fence, widely spaced spotlights were illuminating much of the cliff. Steady rain — now wind-blown — was continuing to fall, making the dark rock glisten. In the distance, near the center of town, she could see the blue strobes of two police cruisers heading toward the plant. If Quinn was telling the truth — and on this she had no reason to doubt him — the drivers of those cruisers had been dispatched with a warrant for the arrest of one Abby Dolan. If Joe Henderson could come up with a bogus but totally legal autopsy report, and George Oleander could arrange to have toxic chemicals instilled into his trusting patients, a mere fraudulent arrest warrant had to be child's play for the men of Patience.

As far as she could see, there were no man-made handholds on the rock. But to her relieved surprise, although the cliff was frighteningly steep, it wasn't perfectly sheer. There was more slope than she had appreciated from Lew's slides or even from looking up the rock. Not much slope, but some. Given optimum conditions on a dry day, if she was in no particular hurry and never looked down, it was likely she could have found enough purchase and footholds to make the descent. But no situation could have been further from optimum than the one she was in now.

She would have done almost anything to keep from stepping out onto the rock face. But measured against her fear of being killed on the jagged boulders at the base of the cliff was the unthinkable prospect of becoming Lyle Quinn's captive.

Without hesitating she set her feet on a ledge no more than six inches wide, dug her fingers into a shallow crevice, and pulled herself out onto the slippery rock.

Chapter Thirty-Eight

Willing herself not to look down, Abby clung to the wet rock with her fingertips, moving steadily sideways as swirling gusts threatened, again and again, to tear her away into the blackness. The cliff curved gently to her right. The farther she could move around the bend, the more difficult it would be for Quinn to shoot at her if, in fact, that was his intention. It was hard to imagine that Quinn, or whoever conceived of the laboratory escape routes, had ever tried getting down from here. But, then again, the exit they were probably expecting to use was the one at twenty-five feet.

Abby focused desperately on the rock to her right. Each time it seemed there was no place for her to go, a crack in the rock and foothold would become apparent, and she could move on. She uttered a soft little-girl's cry with each breath, trying her best to ignore burning pains in her shin and shoulder. A piece of lightbulb glass, embedded in the side of her palm, now felt like a deep needle jab every time she tightened her grip. Still, she moved laterally, trying to put some distance between her and the ventilation shaft opening before Quinn reached it.

She was almost midway between the top of the mesa and the ground. The slope of the rock was such that while climbing down was a possibility, there was absolutely no way to go up. From far above, the glow from the giant neon COLSTAR sign reflected obscenely off the rain, staining the pitch-black sky crimson.

Finally Abby worked herself to a position that was secure enough for her to pause and look about. She was some fifty feet from the opening in the rock. The spot she had found was in the shadow between two beams knifing upward from the powerful lights below. Quinn was still nowhere to be seen. Wind-whipped rain continued to make even standing motionless treacherous. Abby clung to her hold and scanned the boulders and meadow below. The chain-link fence, topped by barbed wire, was unscalable. To the north it was built up into the cliff itself. No chance there. But the south end looked possible. The fence ended against a high wall of almost sheer rock. There was clearly no way over it from the outside. But the fence had been built to keep intruders *out*. The rock on this side looked to be sloped. If she could get to the fence, it might be possible to climb back up the cliff there and slide or tumble down the other side. The prospect of trying that route was only slightly less terrifying than the notion of giving up. In the distance the blue strobes of the police cruisers were moving closer.

Having decided on a course of action, Abby took a single step to her right. Still distracted by Quinn's failure to appear at the opening, she missed her footing and slipped. Before she could even react, her feet were out from under her. Clawing frantically at the wet rock, she slid downward, scraping her belly, chest, and arms. Ten feet, twenty. Suddenly her feet bounced off a large, jagged spire of rock, slowing her fall enough for her to twist her body and grab hold of the spire as she slid past. Her full weight snapped down, nearly tearing her hands away. Her arms were stretched out painfully straight. Her legs dangled like a doll's. She locked her fingers around the spire and peered down over her shoulder. Below her stretched thirty feet or more of rain-slicked rock, ending at the boulders. The glass shard in her right hand was a stiletto now, sending continuous electric shocks up her arm. Her shoulder and chest throbbed unbearably. Still, she managed to hold her grip as she searched frantically with her feet for purchase.

At the moment when she felt she could hold on no longer, the toe of her right sneaker landed on a tiny prominence and held. Gingerly, she pushed upward, taking some of the strain off her hands. Six or eight inches above her right foot, her left connected with a more substantial ledge — twelve inches wide at least and sloped downward into the cliff. She planted her full weight on that ledge, released her hands one at a time, and slowly worked them into cracks in the cliff face.

She clung there, gasping in air until gradually her breathing eased. Tears mixed with the rainwater cascading over her face — tears of relief and anger and pain. The bruises over the front of her body were throbbing mercilessly — worse than what she remembered from the broken arm she had suffered in a high-school soccer game. But she was much closer to the ground now. The rock below her seemed craggier and may have even had a bit more slope. She could almost completely visualize her path of descent. If she could stay focused and careful, she could make it down. But where in the hell was Quinn?

Suddenly, through the darkness and the downpour, from far to her left, he hollered out to her.

"That was a close one, Abby! Good thing you eat your Wheaties!"

He had unlocked the accordion gate and gone through the lower escape tunnel. Now he was out on the rock, about thirty yards to her left. A spotlight was directly on him. He had discarded his black sports jacket, but his turtleneck and trousers blended in totally with the cliff face. The light shimmered eerily off his face, hands, and especially his hair.

Abby glanced down at the fence. If she could get to the south corner, there was the very definite possibility of climbing back up the rock and vaulting over. As quickly as she dared, she began moving diagonally downward.

"I could shoot you, Abby! Right here, right now! Wanna see?"

There was a firecracker snap, and a bullet pinged off the rock three feet from her face. A second shot sprayed her with chips. She cringed and reflexively slowed, then, helpless and wondering what it felt like to be shot, she continued lowering herself toward the meadow.

"You're better off up there than down below!" Quinn called out.

He was moving toward her now, and fairly rapidly. He paused long enough to fire twice more, the first time just above her head, and the second time ricocheting off the rock and actually tearing across the back of her calf. The sharp sting was nearly lost among a dozen other, much deeper, pains.

So now you've been shot, she thought. The sight of the bastard moving confidently toward her brought as much anger as terror. Abby tried to shut him out of her mind and concentrate on each placement of her feet and hands. But she knew she wasn't going to come close to making it. Once she reached the bottom of the cliff, she would be scrambling over huge boulders for fifty yards before she reached the corner of the fence. Then she would have an almost impossible fifteen-foot climb up the rock and a drop down the other side at least that far. She was moving on adrenaline, but the heavy humidity, plus her gashed leg, multiple bruises, and mediocre conditioning, were all working against her.

"Abby, you'd better listen to me! The guards aren't going to like you invading their turf!"

Abby was no more than ten feet from the ground and just a few feet from the top of the largest boulder. For the moment she was out of Quinn's line of sight. She squinted up through the rain. The Colstar cliff looked like a windowless skyscraper. Above it the garish neon sign, hidden by the jutting edge of the mesa, bloodied the night. Her best bet, she decided, was to go around the boulders, not over them. If Quinn's guards showed up, then that would be that. But Quinn wouldn't have warned her to stop if he was confident they were going to reach her.

When she was six feet above the ground, Abby dropped, landing in some muddy dirt between a boulder and the cliff. She huddled there for a few seconds, catching her breath and listening for Quinn or his guards.

"Abby — !"

Quinn's voice still seemed some distance away. Abby felt renewed hope that if she could skirt the huge rocks, stay low, and steer clear of his line of sight, she might actually make it to the end of the fence.

"Allee, allee in free! . . . Come out, come out, wherever you are. . . . Our guards are going to be very annoyed —"

Abby stayed in a crouch and moved quickly around the boulder. There was almost no way that Quinn could spot her unless he came off the cliff and stepped away from it into the meadow, toward the fence. If he did that, and he spotted her, it would be a race. There was still no sign of Quinn's guards.

Abby hurried across six feet of wild grass to a series of smaller rocks. She had a sense of where Quinn was. And if she was right, there was absolutely no way he could see her. Advantage Dolan. She was no more than thirty or forty feet from the end of the fence now. It was possible she'd get there and find the rock wall on this side too steep to climb. But since that horrible moment in the scanner room, each time she needed a break or a miracle, she had gotten one.

"Hey, Doc, last chance," Quinn called out coyly. "I've got the whistle in my hand. One blast and the guards are loose in the meadow. The good news is that two toots and they'll stop whatever it is they're doing to you. At least I think they will. . . ."

Abby moved around another rock. The meadow was narrowing as the fence drew nearer to the cliff.

"Okay, Abby. Have it your way. Go ahead, guys. Soup's on!"

There was no whistle blast, but in an

instant Abby understood why. The long fenced-in field was patrolled not by guards, but by guard *dogs*. She looked up the meadow to the north and saw them — two ebony torpedoes, streaking across the undulating terrain, closing on her with terrifying speed. Instinctively, she took several steps backward into the open meadow. Then, suddenly, just as she was about to turn and run, Quinn appeared on the top of a large boulder. He was still twenty-five yards from her — far enough away so that she might actually have made it to the corner of the fence, but close enough now to have a decent shot at her whenever he wanted to. Instead, he stood atop the rock, hands at his sides, legs spread. The vision of haughtiness.

"Heeeere's Johnny," he shouted.

Trying to outrun the dogs, Abby knew, was futile. But there were really no other options. She whirled but almost immediately slipped on the muddy ground, stumbled, and fell. She could see the dogs flashing past the boulder where Quinn was standing. They were huge Dobermans — black-and-gold phantoms, streaking through the bright wash from the spotlights, one slightly ahead of the other. She could hear their snarling now.

Oh, my God . . .

The first dog hit the top of the small rise in front of her at full stride and leaped, its body stretched outward like a sprint swimmer leaving the mark. Abby screamed and instinctively lifted her forearm up to shield her face. Suddenly the hurtling shadow changed direction in midair and landed heavily on the ground beside her face. The second Doberman had come over the rise and begun its charge. This time, just as it left the ground, moving upward toward her face, there was a whiplike snapping sound from off to her left. The animal pitched toward the cliff and fell to the ground with a heavy thud, a long hunting arrow through its neck. Only then did Abby notice the arrow shaft protruding from the thorax of the first Doberman.

"Ives!"

As she shouted the word, a gunshot rang out from where Quinn was perched. She felt a sharp bite through the skin at her right hip and knew that again she had been hit. The shot was still echoing across the meadow, and the pain in her hip was still burning when she heard the snapping bow-string from her left once more. Quinn cried out, fired wildly, and then toppled off the rock.

"Quick, Abby! Over here!"

Ives was on his knees by the fence, rapidly snapping through the links with enormous wire shears. As Abby hurried to him, she could see Quinn writhing on the sodden ground, Ives's long arrow through his knee. Only then did she appreciate that the her-mit had made his three incredible shots through a small opening he had cut in the chain-link fence. Ives pulled a corner of the fence up enough for Abby to scramble through on her belly. Then, albeit briefly, he allowed her to throw her arms around his neck.

"You look like you met up with an angry mob," he said.

"I'm okay, thanks to you." She glanced back at the meadow. "Ives, I'm sorry about the dogs," she said. "I know how hard that must have been for you."

The hermit squeezed her hand.

"We'd better get going. Two police cruisers just headed up the Colstar drive." He gestured to the field and added, "I don't think they're going to have much trouble figuring out who did this."

"Damn you, Ives!" Quinn was bellowing now. "I'm going to get you for this, you son of a bitch . . . !"

"Do you think the arrow broke his leg?" Abby asked as they scrambled along the fence toward Ives's mountain.

"I don't know. If it did, it means I'm in need of much practice. I wasn't aiming for bone."

Chapter Thirty-Nine

With Sam Ives leading the way, they hurried north along a corridor of shadow just outside the fence. Although Abby was battered and exhausted, she had little trouble keeping up. Ives's leg was healing well, but the muscles that had been destroyed by chronic infection were gone for good. As a result he ran with a stiff, syncopated gait that Abby sensed was causing him some pain.

She glanced over at the hospital as they passed and realized that somewhere just a few feet below them was the tunnel from the MRI unit to the Colstar lab. She wondered about Kelly Franklin — whether Barbara Torres was still standing guard, whether Lew planned to take over when his relief showed up at the ER. Abby had said she'd be back in ten or fifteen minutes, and that had been a lifetime ago. He must be frantic, wondering what had happened to her.

She peered up into the rain. The ceiling was still too low for a MedFlight landing and transfer. If Kelly hadn't regained consciousness, morning was going to be too late for her. Hell, the truth was, it was probably too late for her already.

To her right she could see the two open emergency exits gaping like wounds on the rock face of the Colstar cliff. In a few minutes or a few hours the holes would be sealed and the Colstar spin doctors would be meeting. The story they would concoct was sure to do nothing to slow her plummeting reputation. She glanced back just as one of the police cruisers, blue strobe flashing, siren wailing, sped down the Colstar drive. It was disgusting, but totally typical of the man, that before Quinn climbed into the tunnel to pursue her, he would have issued orders to Gould to get a warrant for her arrest. Human experimentation, falsified autopsy report, murder, attempted murder, fabricated arrest warrant. The Colstar Golden Rule: we have the gold, so we make the rules.

Well, you haven't got me yet, she thought angrily. And later on, when she connected with Lew, one would be two. Then there would be more — Torres and Gil Brant, and surely others when the word got out. The dike was leaking — one hole after another. And soon Colstar was going to run out of fingers.

By the time they passed the north corner of the fence, Abby was gasping for breath again. She stumbled crossing the narrow footbridge over the Oxbow River and tripped on the gentle slope leading up to the foothills.

"Ives, I've got to stop," she begged.

Ives glanced nervously back at the valley.

"Do whatever you have to do," he replied. "You've been through a lot. Are the police after you, too?"

"I think so."

"Do you have anyplace to go?"

"No place that's safe. My best bet is Dr. Alvarez's farm. I could hide out there until he gets home."

"I call him Dr. Lew. I did some work for him."

"I know."

"Good man. Where's your car?"

"At the hospital. But I could never go there. Ives, I'm in real trouble."

"I guess you could say we both are. Are you ready to move?"

"I can handle a fast walk," she said.

"Fine."

"Where are we going?"

"My place, for starters. The back way — the way I got down. There's some climbing involved. Think you can make it?"

Abby looked back at the Colstar cliff.

"I can make it."

Ives slipped his longbow onto his back, and they headed upward at a brisk pace, Ives in front, Abby a few steps behind.

"Ives," she said as they neared some very steep terrain, "the police know where you live, don't they?"

"I imagine they do. We won't be able to stay for very long. But there's some clean, dry clothes for you — your clothes, as a matter of fact, at least the clothes you brought me. Then I'll head up to where some friends of mine have a place. None of them is too fond of the police. Besides, I doubt anyone could follow me up where I'll be going. You can head over to Dr. Lew's."

"His place is a few miles from here. How'll I get there?"

"Unless you suddenly sprout wings, you'll walk. Come on, let's go. You can explain how you ended up popping out of the Colstar cliff when we get to my place."

"And you can explain how you managed to show up like you did."

"Deal."

The back way to Ives's camp was an ingenious series of heavy ropes strung from tree limbs and roots at strategic intervals. The ropes, along with some carefully carved toeholds in the rock, enabled him to make a near-vertical ascent without too much difficulty, although Abby needed some help. The hike up to the camp by the usual way took thirty to forty-five minutes. By this route they made it up in not much more than ten. Having seen the hermit drop down the rope from his hammock, Abby bet that the descent to the meadow took him five minutes, if that.

Once they'd reached Ives's compound, he hurried into his hut and came out with a small knapsack, a dozen more perfectly hewn arrows, an old sweat suit and black rain slicker of Josh's. It was strange to see

Ives anxious or rushed.

"Go ahead in there and change," he said. "I'll be sitting right here, so you can tell me what's going on."

Abby did as he asked. The inside of his hut was always surprisingly neat. Tonight it was lit warmly with a Coleman lantern. She glanced over at the cinder-block-and-boards bookcase, filled to overflowing with well-worn paperbacks. It made her deeply sad to think about Ives having to leave his place on her account. But at the moment there was nothing she could do about it. She stripped her sodden clothes off with some difficulty. The gash over her shin, and the many other abrasions, welts, and cuts, were ugly but tolerable. The bullets that had torn through the skin of her calf and hip had done no serious damage.

She took some of the dressings she had brought for Ives and bandaged the most troublesome wounds on her leg, hip, and shoulder.

"Ives, there's a laboratory inside the base of the cliff," she said as she worked. "Colstar's getting hefty government contracts for their batteries. In exchange they're testing chemical weapons and the antidotes for them on patients in the hospital. I found their lab, but then Quinn found me."

"Well, you set off the alarms inside the plant, and all the spotlights went on across the fence line," Ives replied. "I had never seen that before, so I got out my field

543

glasses. Then, while I was watching the cliff, out you popped. Right out of one of those openings you once called to my attention. I had a sense you might need some help, so I took the back way down."

"I'm very grateful you did," Abby said.

"You're a good person. You do good things for folks like me. From time to time we get the chance to do something back."

"Ives, absolutely everyone with any power in this town is involved in this thing, and they're all after me. Quinn, the chief of police, the president of the hospital, the chief of medicine, even that boor who sewed up your face — they made a pact with the devil in the form of Senator Corman. In exchange for turning the town over as a lab, and running the experiments, they get full employment for the region, beautiful parks, great schools."

"Faustville."

"Exactly."

Abby emerged from the hut wearing Josh's frayed sweat suit, rubber rain jacket, and even an old green-and-gold Oakland A's baseball cap that he had given up on for one reason or another. Wearing his clothes was something she had always enjoyed. And although she had stopped the day he left, it felt strange, but not uncomfortable, to be doing it again.

"We ought to get cracking," Ives said. "You can come with me if you want."

"I can't put you in even more jeopardy.

My only real hope is to connect with Lew."

"The trail I'll show you runs along the hillside through the woods. Use the flashlight I'll give you sparingly, and I doubt you'll be seen from down below."

He took a powerful four-battery flashlight from his knapsack and handed it to her.

"Ives, I can't take this. You're going to need it as much as I will."

Sam Ives looked at her. From above his thick beard, his eyes sparkled.

"As I recall, you and I have already had a conversation about the circumstances in which I can and cannot see. Don't make me show off."

Abby tested the flashlight and nodded her acceptance of it. Then, after Ives shut off the lantern in his hut, he allowed his gaze to make one final sweep of the camp before they set off toward the west.

The forest was fully saturated, the branches dripping so steadily, Abby could not tell how much rain was still falling. They hiked downward for a time until she could easily make out the town, perhaps two hundred feet below them and to their left. Some distance from Ives's camp they connected with a partially overgrown trail.

"Get used to the way this path looks," he said. "It's like this all the way along the rim of the valley. Keep your eyes sharp and you should be able to stay on it all the way. If you get lost, just keep Patience on your left, don't go up and don't go down, and you should make it okay."

Suddenly he raised his hand and put one finger over his lips. Then he pointed down the hill. Through the dense woods Abby could see a car approaching down a straight road that appeared to end right below where they were standing. Then she recognized the street as the one she took to visit Ives's camp.

"Police," he whispered, well before she could make out the unlit lights on the roof.

"That didn't take long."

"They'll be going the other direction up to my place, but we'd better keep moving."

For the next fifteen minutes they hiked in silence with Abby leading the way. Only once, for just a minute or so, did she stray from the trail. She recovered smoothly, backtracked, and found the trail once more. Apparently, Ives decided he had seen enough.

"Okay, this is it," he said. "From here you go straight and I go up. You know the town well enough to tell approximately where you are. You've got about three miles to go. When you get near Dr. Lew's place, you can go up into the hills and come down in the field beyond the house, or drop down to the road and take your chances going up his drive."

"I think I'll probably do the hill. Ives, if the police or any of Quinn's people catch me, I don't think I'll be allowed to live. There's no way they can let me get out of

Patience. I've seen too much. Before we split up, I want to tell you what I know.

"The lab beneath the Colstar cliff pumps small amounts of toxic gas through tubes that run along a tunnel into the MRI scanner in the hospital. There's a trapdoor in the floor by the MRI machine. The lever to open it is beneath the machine in the back. If an antidote to the gases is being tested, the patients get it from their doctors. The people *I know* are involved are Quinn, Joe Henderson, the hospital president, Dr. Bartholomew, Dr. George Oleander, Dr. Del Marshall, and Captain Gould of the Patience police. There are almost certainly others. Can you remember most of those names?"

"My brain is extremely uncluttered these days. There's plenty of room for a few names or facts."

"Sorry I even asked. Dr. Sandra Stuart is a friend of mine at St. John's Hospital in San Francisco. If you get the chance, call her and tell her what you know."

"I still have some colleagues at the university who would be interested in your findings and might have some influence."

"Excellent. Ives, please be careful."

"And you, Dr. Abby."

"When I get out of this, I'm coming back to find you and finish working on that leg. I'll also make sure everyone who'll listen knows why you put that arrow through Quinn."

She embraced him, and he awkwardly responded in kind. Then he headed up the steep slope to their right. Abby stood there watching him. After a few yards the hermit stopped and turned back to her.

"You're a credit to your profession," he said.

He resumed his climb into the blackness, and within half a minute he was gone.

Abby remained there in the dark, listening to the noisy silence of the forest, feeling acutely alone and painfully melancholy. *At least you have someplace to go,* she reminded herself. She glanced down at the town in time to see a police strobe flashing in the distance. They would be out in force by now, and every road out of the valley would be blocked.

She risked a few seconds illuminating the trail. Finally she broke through her inertia and continued west. With each step her mood improved and her resolve deepened. She hadn't come this far — hadn't been *brought* this far — to lose. Lew was scheduled to stay on at the hospital after his shift to take over from Barbara Torres. But perhaps Barbara's husband was having a turn for the better and she had decided to stay the night. It would be wonderful to reach Lew's place and find him waiting there.

The hike, in sodden sneakers through the sodden forest, seemed endless. Dry clothes and the slicker definitely helped, but within half an hour Abby was soaked from the waist down, chilled to the bone, and shivering whenever she stopped. The trail was, as Ives had promised, not that difficult to follow. Each time she worried that she might be drifting, there was a break in the foliage and a vista of the town. Occasionally, in one part of the valley or another, she could see the distinctive flashing blue of a cruiser. She imagined the frantic goings-on at the station and on the roads and wondered whether Lyle Quinn had been taken to the ER for treatment of his leg wound. She laughed out loud at the irony of Lew being on duty when Quinn was rolled in.

After more than an hour of walking Abby knew she was close. She could see the neon of Five Corners in the distance and gauged that the driveway up to Lew's place was almost directly below her. She was battling exhaustion now, aching in places she didn't even remember injuring, and working with each breath to get the moisture-laden night air into her lungs. And to make matters worse, as Ives had warned her, the trail took a turn to her right and began a fairly steep upward incline. This was where she could bushwhack down to the road and try walking up the driveway, or go up, around, and down, approaching the house from across the fields in the back.

She pictured what she remembered of the topography of the farm from her visits there. To the southwest there were two broad, flat planted fields, one of corn and one of wheat or hay. Bordering them on the south and east were deeply undulating meadows, and beyond the meadows, to the east and north, were the hills — steep, rocky, and sparsely forested.

The rain had lessened to a heavy mist, but there was some wind, and the temperature had fallen below the comfort zone. Abby drove herself up the slope with mental images of crackling fires, warm, dry clothes, and steaming cocoa. She had no idea what Lew would come up with to get her out of the valley, but she felt certain he would find a way. San Francisco would be best. St. John's was a safe house for her. And once she had made it there, once she had told her story, she would no longer be the liability for Quinn and his people that she was now. Of course, there was the very strong possibility that no one with any clout would believe her account or dare to go up against Mark Corman and Ezra Black. But she couldn't afford to start thinking that way.

The lights of town were no longer visible from where she was, so there was no easy way to judge her position. If she started down too soon, she would waste a great deal of time and energy and end up dangerously visible on the road — on the long driveway leading up to the farm. She leveled off, now essentially bushwhacking through low brush and wild, thorny brambles that raked her legs through the sweatpants.

Finally, she decided, it was time. She cut to her left and battled her way downhill, slipping on rocks and stumbling over tree roots hidden beneath the dense ground cover.

Now, the lights of the town were visible again in the distance. She had judged her position perfectly — another hopeful sign. A dozen more steps and the last of the forest was behind her. She was on the top of a broad, smooth ledge. To her left, a few hundred yards away, were the house, barn, and outbuildings of the farm. There was a light on outside the back door of the house, but otherwise it appeared dark. Barbara hadn't stayed at the hospital, after all.

Abby slid down the ledge in a sitting position, then made her way across the meadow. In addition to the back-door light, there was a spotlight high up on the side of the barn illuminating the empty parking area and the top of the driveway. The silence was pervasive. She glanced about warily, gave brief thought to breaking a window to get into the house, and then decided that the barn would be a satisfactory place for her to hide out until Lew's return.

At that instant she heard an automobile approaching up the drive. She flattened herself against the barn by the side door, reached back, and assured herself that the door was open. Silently, she prayed to see Lew's Blazer pop over the top of the drive.

What she saw instead was a black-and-white police cruiser, rolling slowly with its lights cut. Quickly, she ducked into the barn. It was dark inside, but thanks to the back-door light filtering in through numerous cracks, not totally so. Although two of the four horse stalls were covered with straw, the large old structure was the home to equipment and baled hay, not animals.

From outside she heard hushed voices but could not make out what they were saying. There was a wooden ladder leading up to a hayloft, but she rejected that option, sensing that they might look up there first. Instead, she hurried to the last stall, where a truck or car was covered by a large vinyl tarp.

She was huddled on the ground between the tarp and the wall when the huge front door of the barn creaked open. A powerful flashlight beam shot from one wall to another, to the loft, and back. As Abby predicted, the ladder to the loft was the policeman's first choice. She heard him walking overhead, at one point directly above her, scuffing at the hay. She wondered whether or not he had his gun drawn. After a few minutes he came back down and began moving her way. Abby dropped to her belly, pulled the tarp over her, and squirmed well under the vehicle, which was some sort of old truck. The chassis smelled of dried mud and oil. The footsteps shuffled closer. By holding her breath she could hear the man breathing. She sensed him standing not six feet away and buried her forehead in her hands, expecting any moment to have the tarp whisked aside and to be skewered by his flashlight beam.

Please no . . . please no . . . please . . .

Suddenly the footsteps retreated. Abby remained motionless, exhaling slowly, silently, then filling her lungs the same way. The barn was totally quiet now. Outside, there was a brief hushed exchange. Then the cruiser rumbled to life and pulled away. For five minutes, ten, Abby remained in her hiding place. Finally she decided it was safe. She squirmed out from under the old truck, standing with the creaking, aching difficulty of the Tin Man. Another bullet dodged.

As she rose, the vinyl tarp snagged on the bill of her A's cap, and pulled upward. Abby turned to free it, and froze. Her hand shaking, she drew her flashlight from the waistband of her sweatpants and shined it on the truck. Her pulse began to race as a tidal wave of uncertainty and confusion washed over her. The truck under which she had been hiding was a battered red pickup with oversize tires.

No longer worried about whether one of the officers might have stayed on, she threw a flap of the tarp over the top of the cab. The black steel plow frame that had slammed into the rear of her Mazda was still there, bolted over the grill.

The door to the cab was locked. Abby shined her flash inside. On the floor by the passenger seat was a black ski mask and a box of bullets. And on a rack in front of the rear window was a high-powered rifle with a telescopic sight.

There was a cellular phone on a stand bolted between the two seats.

Get out! the muffled male voice had demanded just a minute or so after she had nearly been shot. *Get out now.*

Chapter Forty

Abby pulled the vinyl tarp back into place and leaned against the barnside, her mind unwilling or unable to wrap itself around the significance of what she had just discovered. It was Lew, not Quinn, who had come at her with the pickup — Lew, not Quinn, who had fired at her outside her house, then called her with a menacing message. *But why?* Why would he want to frighten her into leaving Patience?

She had sensed that day on the road that the ski-masked assailant in the battered pickup had passed up the opportunity to force her off the road and into the trees. And Gould was right that the sniper who had shot at her could have killed her had that been his intention. But why would Lew want to frighten her? She hadn't been hurt either time, but she might have been. Why was he willing to take that chance just to scare her out of town?

Why . . . ?

Bewildered, she wandered out the side door of the barn into the drizzly night. The lights of Patience winked through the rain like a Christmas display. So charming. So innocent. Faustville. Beyond the lights was the ebony hole in the night sky that she knew was the Colstar cliff. And glowing above the rock were the seven letters that had so changed her life.

Why . . . ?

Lew was totally dedicated to proving that Colstar was making people sick. That much was indisputable. And Abby had done much to forward his cause. It simply made no sense for him to try to drive her away. Abby forced herself to reject the obvious conclusion that Lew was out to intimidate her into leaving Patience. And the moment she did so, she knew the truth.

It had never been his intention to frighten her — at least not for long. He had made it a point to get to know her — to understand what might make her recoil, and what was more likely to make her arch her back and take a stand. He had done his homework well — no, not well, *masterfully*. His goal was to *anger* her — to make her so furious with Lyle Quinn and Colstar that she would do anything to help bring them down. Initially, her commitment to the Alliance had been lukewarm. She wasn't a fighter or a crusader, she had told them. She was apolitical — put together to deal with the pain and suffering of others on an intimate, one-to-one basis.

Yet since that Alliance meeting, thanks in no small measure to Lew's attacks on her, she had ended up leading the battle against Colstar while he had remained in the shadows. All along he had been the one supplying the information. She had been the one acting on it. She was the catalyst. It was she who had used her academic connection to get the definitive blood analysis for cadmium, she who had won Kelly Franklin over, she who had discovered the Colstar lab, and she who had almost died as a consequence. Lew remained as removed from the spotlight as he had been the day they had met.

Why . . . ?

Heedless of the rain, Abby paced to the end of the gravel parking area and back. A memory kept flashing like neon in her head — a snippet of a conversation with Lew.

I would suggest part of Garrett Owen's evaluation of your friend should be a serum-cadmium level. . . .

He had said that about Josh the night of the Alliance meeting. He had seemed so confident. And although he was completely right about Josh, he was absolutely off base about all the other NIWWs. It wasn't cadmium at the root of most of their symptoms. It was the gases and, at times, the antidotes. Lew blamed Colstar's control of the PRH laboratory for all the negative cadmium tests. He was certain of it. But now Abby knew that the tests for cadmium were negative in all those patients because the heavy metal simply wasn't there. How could Lew have been so insistent, so certain it was going to be present in Josh? Unless . . .

He's the one who sewed up my thigh when
I tore it on that nail, remember? . . .

The words were Josh's, speaking about
Lew, about the one time the two of them
had met. Willie Cardoza had fallen off a
ladder and gashed his scalp. Ethan Black's
father and his shrink dated his violence
problem from an auto accident in which he
suffered a head injury and a laceration. All
along it had seemed as if the three of them,
plus Angela Cristoforo and more recently,
Gus Schumacher, had been a group apart
from the rest of the NIWWs — sicker than
the others, with probable or proved evidence of cadmium toxicity, and with no
history of having gotten an MRI before their
symptoms began. And each of them was a
Colstar employee. Lew had definitely sutured Josh. Could he have sewn the others
as well? If so, what had he done at the time
he was treating them?

Abby glanced at her watch. Assuming
Kelly wasn't going to be MedFlighted out
until five or six in the morning, she had
several safe hours to find out if Lew's house
held the answers. Without hesitating she
raced to the kitchen door and snapped her
elbow through the glass. Then, tensed and
ready to flee, she reached in and slowly
opened the door. No alarm went off. If there
was one that sounded at the police station,
she was cooked. But she doubted there
was. She wanted to call the hospital and
speak with Lew in the ER or ICU just to be

certain he would be there for a while. But if, as he feared, his calls were monitored, she would be delivering herself into Quinn's hands.

Not at all certain of what she was looking for, she started in the basement, a damp, confined space, cluttered with tools, boxes, and gardening implements. After just a few minutes of rummaging around, she gave up. If Lew's secrets were hidden down there, she was never going to find them.

She went back up to the first floor and pulled open the drawers and cabinets in the kitchen, sensing this wasn't the spot either. Next, she bypassed the dining room and headed to the den — the room where the Alliance meeting had been held. In the hallway she stopped, drawn, as she had been the first time she saw them, to the dozen or more framed photographs of a country . . . and a woman. Paraguay, Lew had said. Paraguay and his late wife. During the many hours Abby had spent with him, he had not spoken at all of her or, for that matter, of his native land. But Abby remembered clearly his deep sadness when responding to her question about the photos that first night. *Paraguay . . .*

Something about the country began reverberating in her mind. She studied the bronze-skinned, dark-eyed beauty. There was an alluring gentleness to her and a striking intelligence in her eyes.

The woman in the picture is . . . was . . .

my wife. She's dead.

That was all Lew said that night. In fact, that was all he had ever said.

She's dead. . . .

Abby opened a few cupboards in the paneled den. She was nervous about using a lamp or the overhead light, for fear that the police would be making a return trip. Using her flashlight, she skimmed over shelves of books, many of them older or more modern classics in Spanish, and a great number of them books on ecology and the environment.

Paraguay . . .

What was it about that country? She pulled out one of the books in Spanish, a novel by the Nobel laureate, Gabriel García Marquez, the author of one of her favorite books, *One Hundred Years of Solitude.* The volume in Lew's collection was one she had meant to read but had never gotten around to. *El amor en los tiempos del cólera. Love in the Time of Cholera.* There was an elegant bookplate pasted on the first page — a pair of dragons coiled about an open book. *Ex Libris Dr. Luis María Galatín,* the ornate printing read.

Luis . . .

Abby slid the book back in place. Dr. Luis Maria Galatín was Lew. She felt certain of it. She checked the time and decided to give up on the den and try the upstairs. She would give herself another twenty minutes or so. If she hadn't found anything by then, her plan was to get to a pay phone and try calling Ezra Black. But unless she could find something more, she would be telling Black only part of the story — and not the part that had much to do with his son.

She tiptoed up the narrow farmhouse staircase as if there were someone home and found herself on a short corridor with two braided rugs on the floor. There were four closed walnut-stained doors off the hallway. The first one she chose to open, just to the right of the stairs, was Lew's bedroom — walnut four-poster bed, dresser, TV, free-standing bookcase, closet.

Possible, she thought. Especially the closet.

She decided to check the other rooms and then return to the bedroom. The second door she opened was to Lew's bathroom, and the third to a neatly kept guest room with two single beds. The fourth door, at the end of the hallway to the left, was locked. Instantly, Abby was dizzied by a massive adrenaline rush. This room was what she had been searching for. Behind it were the answers she had been missing. She tested the door with her shoulder, then with a sharp, thrusting kick from the sole of her sneaker. No chance. Finally she remembered seeing a crowbar hooked over a nail on the basement wall. She hurried down there and returned with the tool and a hammer.

Even with the crowbar, the solid oak door

yielded reluctantly. And by the time it finally crunched free, wood fragments from it and the jamb were scattered on the floor. Abby snapped on her flash. Then silently, slowly, she eased open the door. She was standing in a room cluttered with stacks of newspapers, scrapbooks, boxes of correspondence and other papers, books about Paraguay, and old Paraguayan picture calendars. The two windows of the room were boarded over and covered with large tourist-office posters of Paraguay. On the floor by the wall opposite where Abby was standing, was a posterboard-mounted, two-foot-high color photo of Lew's late wife. In the photo — a head and shoulders shot against a verdant background — she was even more stunning than she was in the pictures downstairs — almost mystically alluring. The notion of the woman's life being cut short brought a sharp pang.

Even though the room faced the back of the house, Abby checked to ensure that the plywood on which the window posters were mounted would, indeed, keep any light from being seen outside. Then she flicked on the overhead. Except for the windows and a large, ornate crucifix, the walls of the room were bare. Most of the yellowing newspapers were from Asunción and San Juan Bautista. In one corner of the room, leaning against the wall, were two full newspaper pages, each one framed in dark wood and kept under glass. The pages were both page one from the Asunción paper, *Diario Hoy* — almost nine years ago and three months apart.

Abby's Spanish was adequate enough to translate most of the two-headline articles. She sat down, braced herself against a wall, and propped the heavy frame containing the older page on her lap. The main article described a lethal mudslide that had destroyed a neighborhood on the outskirts of the town of San Ignacio, twenty kilometers from the city of San Juan Bautista, killing at least eighty people. Included in the article was an angry quote from a physician whose clinic was destroyed and whose wife lost her life in the disaster. The physician's name was Luis María Galatín.

. . . *"This horrible tragedy should never have happened," Galatín said. "And it is clear who bears the responsibility for it. For years the Colstar Mining Company has been raping the mountainside with no regard for the ground cover or forests. For years authorities have turned their backs as they opened their wallets."*

It was only then Abby remembered what George Oleander had said about an incident in South America. Terrorists had blown up a huge Colstar refinery, killing a number of Colstar employees. The attack was almost the coup de grâce for the company, and eventually led to the deal with Senator Corman and the military.

Ironic, she thought. The death of Colstar

563

in Paraguay had essentially led to the creation of the underground laboratory and to the survival and renaissance of Patience, California.

The second, more recent, *Diario Hoy* page only confirmed what Abby already knew. A band of terrorists had blown up the Colstar refinery, killing three security guards and two night-shift workers, and injuring dozens of others, some seriously. A nationwide manhunt was under way for the man believed to be the leader of the terrorists, Dr. Luis María Galatín, and a reward was being offered by Colstar International for information leading to his capture. The picture of Galatín, without a mustache and a decade younger, was Lew, yet it wasn't. Somewhere along the line, a cosmetic surgical genius had altered his nose and jaw and narrowed the corners of his eyes, creating a striking ruggedness in a face that had once been quite boyish — borderline pretty.

Abby studied the photo for several minutes as one missing piece after another clicked into place. Having been through the licensing and credentialing process herself, she knew it wouldn't have been that hard for a man with Galatín's intelligence and resourcefulness to become Dr. Lew Alvarez — especially having been educated and trained in California. But she also knew that no alias was impenetrable. The last thing Luis Galatín would ever want to do was to call much attention to himself.

Which was why he had needed her.

Lewis Alvarez got on the medical staff at Patience Regional Hospital. But he must have quickly realized that he couldn't simply march up the hill and blow up this plant as well. Too big, too inaccessible, too closely guarded. Alvarez knew that he couldn't physically destroy the Colstar factory as he had done in San Juan Bautista, so he set about to find a weakness he could exploit — a soft underbelly. And Mark Corman, Lyle Quinn, and all the rest who had sold out the people of the valley provided Lew with just that in the form of dozens of NIWWs.

You just misinterpreted the data, Lew, Abby thought. With all those tons of cadmium being trucked into the place, who wouldn't have? Cadmium toxicity seemed so logical that there was no reason to search for an alternative explanation. Once he recognized that a pattern was there, all that stood between Lew and a paralyzing, possibly fatal, series of suits and shutdowns, was the proof.

She set the framed pages back in their place and rummaged through a small box of correspondence — perhaps thirty pieces from all over the world, most of them in Spanish. One most definitely wasn't. It was a handwritten letter, undated, on the stationery of David Brooks, M.D.

Lew —

I am writing this letter in hopes that you will read it, reread it, and do what is right. When you first invited me over and presented your series of unusual cases, along with your theory of a cadmium spill or persistent leak from Colstar, I was most intrigued. Indeed, I have worked on behalf of environmental causes all my life. I agreed to join you and the others in the Alliance because I believed there were serious health issues involved. I still do. There are far too many unusual cases to be coincidental.

But as much as I respect you, I cannot ally myself with a man who I know has willfully taken human lives, regardless of the justification of the act. While I was at the recent ER meetings in New York City, I decided to spend some time doing research on the company that we had both decided was an enemy of the environment and of the people. . . .

Brooks's letter went on to describe his almost accidental deduction of Alvarez's identity and the crime for which he was an international fugitive. From what Abby had been told by many, her predecessor was as gentle and kind as he was principled. Abby set the letter back in the box. There was no mention of the underground lab, no hint that Brooks had discovered anything that might cost him his life — anything, that is, except Lew Alvarez's real identity.

Abby felt sick. Alvarez had used David Brooks just as he was using her now. And when Brooks became a direct threat, Luis María Galatín simply eliminated him. There was no way she could expect a kinder fate.

Abby knew that there was no one in Patience whom she could trust. Being caught by the police was a death sentence. Even escaping to San Francisco would probably do her no good. Lyle Quinn was as ruthless as Alvarez. His treatment of Kelly Franklin made that quite clear. In addition, he possessed almost limitless resources. The moment Abby surfaced with her unsubstantiated story, something was certain to happen to her — a suicide or fatal accident. Or perhaps she would simply vanish. It was doubtful Quinn would even have to bother permanently sealing off the trapdoor in the MRI room floor or the tunnel. A little time off, a little expert PR work, and they would probably be back in business.

No, trying to run wasn't the answer. Her best bet continued to be Ezra Black. She was in the process of proving that his son's "suicide" death was, for all intents, murder. That was really her only tangible bargaining chip. Even though Black certainly knew about the Colstar testing program, and somewhere along the line had probably even authorized it, there had to be limits. Black impressed her as a tough businessman, but not a monster. He had a conscience. Every fiber of Abby's intuition told her so.

The Colstar program hadn't directly resulted in the deaths of Peggy Wheaton, Gus Schumacher and his victims, and Black's son. But it had spawned the man who *was* responsible. Surely, Ezra Black would be able to see that. But before she called him, there was one final piece that remained unaccounted for.

Abby found it in a shoe box held shut with a rubber band, and containing several vials of a grayish-white powder from a chemical supply house in the Midwest. "Cadmium sulfide," the labels read. Beneath the vials was the list — dates, names, and amounts of those whom Alvarez had infused with intravenous cadmium under the guise of dosing them with prophylactic antibiotics. There were nine subjects in all, including the five Abby already knew about. The doses Alvarez had chosen varied somewhat, but Josh, Willie Cardoza, Angela Cristoforo, Ethan Black, and Gustav Schumacher had received by far the largest amounts.

Intravenous cadmium. Toxicity by inhalation, or ingestion, or even through the skin had been extensively studied and reported. But she was certain that nowhere would there be any data on intravenous injection. Lew Alvarez had injected those ER patients with absolutely no knowledge of the consequences. And the truth was, he didn't care. As long as Abby Dolan pushed the right buttons, Colstar would be exposed for poisoning its employees and others in the valley. And that was what mattered.

Abby hurried to the kitchen and found a box of kitchen-sized white plastic garbage bags. She put one bag inside another for strength, then returned to the upstairs room and placed the cadmium, the letters, and some of the newspaper articles inside. What she had ought to be enough to interest Black. If she sensed he couldn't be trusted to hear her out and make some sort of deal, she would try her luck in San Francisco — provided, of course, that she could find some way out of the valley.

Thanks to Graham DeShield, she had Ezra Black's number at Feather Ridge. Now, all she needed was a phone that wasn't tapped and a car. Then, suddenly, she thought about Alvarez's truck. She always kept a spare set of keys to the Mazda in a kitchen drawer. If there were keys for the truck somewhere in the house, she had both the transportation and the phone.

After a brief search of the den and a more extensive search of the kitchen, she gave up. Then it occurred to her that although she couldn't *start* the truck, she could certainly bludgeon her way inside it. And inside it were two things she needed very much at this point — the cellular phone and the rifle that had been fired at her.

She raced upstairs and grabbed the hammer she had used to break into the locked room. Then she put her rain slicker on black side out, cautiously left the house, and jogged painfully toward the barn. She had just reached the side door when she sensed someone nearby.

"Freeze! Right there! Drop the hammer!" the hoarse, almost inhuman voice barked out.

Abby did as she was told and turned slowly. Bracing himself against the corner of the barn, the muzzle of his gun pointed shakily at the center of her chest, was Josh.

Chapter Forty-One

Through the fine rain, illuminated from the side by the back-door light, Josh was an apparition. Abby recoiled a step from the man with whom she had shared her life and her bed for two years. This was not the fire-eyed demon of her nightmare — far from it. Josh's face was drawn and ashen, his eyes little more than black hollows in his skull. His speech was strained and halting. The gun he was pointing at her — some kind of military weapon — seemed too heavy for him. The barrel would shake, then drift. Then he would regain control and fix it once again at the center of her chest.

"Josh, I . . . I've been really worried about you."

"I can take care of myself."

He was no more than ten feet away. Abby strained to get a sense of his anger — of the danger she was in.

"Why are you pointing that at me?" she said finally. "Did you come here to kill me?"

"Yes . . . no . . . I mean, I don't know."

She spoke slowly, evenly, wary of saying anything that might set him off.

"Did you find Bricker and the others?"

"Yes."

"And did you . . . ?"

She held her breath.

"Kill them? I should have. . . . They were right there. . . . Bricker and Gentry. . . . Both of them . . . I should have blown them to hell."

Abby felt a flood of relief.

"But you didn't?"

"No. I . . . I shot up the ceiling of the garage and some cars, and then took off. . . . Abby, why didn't you just let me *do* it? . . . Bricker deserved to die. . . . He stole my life."

Abby took a tentative step toward him. Seeing him this way, she felt a consuming sorrow — and an unbridled fury at Lew Alvarez.

"You did the right thing, Josh."

Once again the muzzle of the gun sagged toward the ground. This time Josh made no effort to pull it back up. Abby turned her flashlight on, handed it to him, and motioned to the barn door.

"Come in where it's dry so we can talk," she said. "I've been worried sick about you."

He hesitated, then followed her inside. His clothes — sneakers, jeans, and a dark sweatshirt — were soaked through. Abby could appreciate now that he had the frightened, bewildered, wild-eyed look she had seen any number of times in patients who were dying. He stood five feet away from her, braced against the wall, holding the gun now with both hands. It was almost impossible to connect him with the loose, graceful man she had watched holding his own in playground basketball games with youths half his age.

"You should have let me kill them," he said again.

"I'm glad you didn't. How did you find me here?"

He squinted at her, then released the gun with one hand and rubbed at his eyes. Abby sensed she could have simply reached out and taken the weapon from him. Instead, she stood her ground and waited.

"I drove past the house. . . . The police are there. . . . Two cruisers. They're looking for me."

"Maybe so, but they're also looking for *me*. And if they catch me, they may kill me. How did you know about *this* place? Have you been here before?"

"Once. . . . Where's Alvarez?"

"Josh, why don't you sit down before you fall down?"

"Shut up! . . . Where's Alvarez?"

"At the hospital."

"Everything would have been all right . . . if you had just let me kill Bricker."

"Killing someone wouldn't have made anything all right. Josh, you're sick. You've been poisoned — with cadmium. You need help. You need treatment."

"Are you two lovers?"

"Josh —"

"Are you?"

"No."

"You are! I can tell."

"Will you please put that gun down? Josh, we've got to get you to a hospital."

Josh rubbed at his eyes again and stumbled back a step. This time, when Abby gently implored him to sit down, he did so. The semiautomatic was awkwardly heavy for her. She set it aside, then knelt beside him and supported him with her arm around his shoulders. She could smell alcohol on his breath and clothes.

"Are the headaches bad?" she asked.

Josh buried his face in his hands, then pressed in at his temples.

"I can't take them anymore. . . . If I had killed Bricker and Gentry, they . . . would be gone. . . . Why did you stop me?"

"I didn't want you to kill, that's why. Josh, where's the Jeep?"

"In the woods . . . a mile from here. . . . It's out of gas."

Abby cursed under her breath. There was probably a filled gasoline can somewhere around the barn or in one of the sheds. But no doubt the Jeep was a police target as well. Whether they ended up trying for San Francisco or Feather Ridge, their best bet was clearly the truck. But with no key, that meant dealing with Alvarez.

Perhaps that's the way it should be, she thought.

She looked down at Josh and wondered how much he could be counted on. With surprise and Alvarez's rifle or Josh's gun on her side, it was just possible she wouldn't need him.

She found a coil of clothesline hanging on the wall and some duct tape on a shelf. She set them both beside the truck. Then she stripped off the tarp, smashed in the driver's-side window with the hammer, and used the ski mask to sweep the fragments of glass onto the hay-strewn floor. Across from her, Josh was now slumped against the wall, asleep or unconscious.

Abby hefted the high-powered rifle, then pulled open the magazine, loaded it with three rounds, and used the bolt to thrust one bullet into the firing chamber. As a kid, she had done a little riflery in summer camp — strictly twenty-twos. But since then, the only time she had ever pulled the trigger of a gun was in amusement parks. She opened the barn door and peered through the telescopic sight at the rooster weather vane mounted on the roof of the house. The metal head of the bird, a dark shadow against the lighter sky, filled the scope. The *O* in Stanford — that's what Gould had said the sniper could have hit had he wanted to. Now she understood. She took a step through the door to shield Josh from the noise. Then she braced herself, set the crosshairs on where it seemed the rooster's eye might be, and fired. The recoil was like a heavyweight punch to her shoulder, but she was balanced for it. Almost on top of the sharp report from the rifle, there was a muted clang. The vane spun like a pinwheel.

Piece of cake.

Abby stepped back inside the barn. Josh stared at her briefly with exhausted eyes, then slumped back against the wall. Abby set a new shell in the chamber and laid the rifle down by the rope. Then she fished out her wallet from the pocket of her slicker, found the slip with Ezra Black's number on it, and called. She wondered if, at this hour, Black would answer his own phone.

"Feather Ridge," a cultured voice said.

Abby pictured the skeletal houseman.

"This is Dr. Abby Dolan. I'd like to speak with Mr. Black."

"Is this an emergency?"

"It is."

"One moment, please."

In fact, it was almost a minute before Black came on the line. There was no hint in his voice that he had been sleeping. And Abby sensed from his first words that he was well aware she had penetrated the lab.

"So, Doctor, did you abuse your degree with the operator again, or do I have to get this number changed?"

"You can keep it."

"Might I ask how you came by it?"

"We have more important things to talk about, Mr. Black."

"Such as?"

"I'm in some trouble here in Patience."

"So I've been told. Attempted murder is a

very serious charge."

"Kelly Franklin and I were on the same side. We both wanted to get at the truth. There's no way I would have hurt her. It was Lyle Quinn who tried to kill her."

The momentary silence that followed was telltale. Black didn't know! Quinn might or might not have told him about Abby's finding the lab but had not been honest about Kelly.

"And just who tried to kill Mr. Quinn?" he asked.

This time the silent pause was Abby's.

"A man who was trying to save my life. What's Quinn's status?"

"His assistant told me that his knee has been shattered by an arrow from a high-powered bow. He's going to require surgery."

In spite of her situation and her sensibilities, Abby smiled at the news.

"He tried to kill Kelly Franklin. And I'm certain his men are out looking to kill me right now."

"Is that what you called to say?"

"No. I need you to call off Captain Gould and the rest of the people who are after me."

"If you're wanted by the police, Dr. Dolan, I would suggest the prudent thing to do would be to give yourself up."

"I don't feel safe doing that. Mr. Black, you impressed me as being tough, but not the sort of man who would allow his employees to go out and murder people."

"I'm not."

"In that case I don't think Lyle Quinn has told you everything. I'm calling now because I have a trade to offer."

"Go on."

"Sir, I spoke to you yesterday about my belief that your son was inadvertently poisoned with cadmium by some sort of accident at the plant."

"And I told you what I thought of your theory."

"And you were right. I know now that there was nothing inadvertent about it, and that it wasn't Colstar's fault. Ethan was *intentionally* poisoned. I have absolute proof of how, who, and why. Mr. Black, your son was no more responsible for assaulting that farmer with a baseball bat than he was for jumping out that window."

Abby could feel Black dissecting her revelation about the farmer. It didn't take him long.

"Dr. DeShield will feel the sting of abusing his relationship with me," he said. "And I *will* have this number changed."

"Mr. Black, we're talking about your son and his murderer."

"And exactly what is it you want from me in exchange for your information?"

"I want the dogs who are chasing me called off. I want something done about the laboratory in the old Patience mine. And I want justice for Lyle Quinn for whatever happens to Kelly Franklin."

This time the silence was prolonged.

"Have you anything else to say to me?" Black asked finally.

Abby felt her hopes sink. She had clearly read the man wrong.

"No," she said. "That's it."

"Well, first of all, if the police have a warrant out for your arrest, it would behoove you to turn yourself in before you get hurt. Second, I know nothing about any laboratory in a mine. And as far as Mr. Quinn goes, his situation is no different from your own. If he's charged with a crime, he will have to answer for it. In the meantime, as far as I know, he is not. I'm his employer, not his judge, jury, or executioner."

"Good-bye, Mr. Black."

"If what you're saying about my son is true, Doctor, I promise you that one way or the other I'll find out."

The thinly veiled threat was chilling, but Abby's frustration and anger quickly overrode any fear.

"Not before a lot of people find out about Mark Corman and that underground lab," she snapped. "Think over my offer. I might call you back later."

"Do what you wish, Dr. Dolan."

Abby slammed the phone down on the seat. Black's final words had left the door slightly ajar for her to call him again. But her friends in San Francisco were a far safer bet. Just then she heard the thumping rotors of a helicopter not far overhead. She raced past Josh and through the door. A good-sized helicopter, landing lights on, was swooping over the valley toward the hospital. *MedFlight!* Assuming they were coming to transport Kelly to a decompression chamber, Lew would be home before long.

Abby knelt beside Josh and assured herself that his carotid pulses were decent. Then she checked his pupils. They were nearly pinpoint. Almost certainly he had augmented whatever he had been drinking with narcotic painkillers.

"Josh," she whispered, shaking him gently. "Josh, wake up. I need to talk to you."

He stirred, then opened his eyes dreamily.

"Leave me alone," he muttered.

"Josh, listen. It was Dr. Alvarez who did this to you. He poisoned you with the cadmium. He did it when he sewed up your leg. Remember?"

Josh's sleepy eyes widened.

"Why?"

"He thought Colstar was trying to cover up a cadmium spill by faking lab results. He thought they were succeeding because none of the exposure cases was terribly sick. So he decided to create cases that would be seriously ill enough to indict the company and close it down."

And of course, she thought, but didn't bother to add, *he also created an ally in one*

580

Abby Dolan — a sap who would be certain the blood work was sent off to the right place and the battle against Colstar would escalate.

Josh struggled to his feet.

"Where is he now?"

"He'll be home soon. But we don't want to hurt him. The law will do that. With the proof I have, I promise you they will. Understand?"

For the first time Abby felt she saw a spark of life in Josh's eyes.

"What do you want me to do?" he asked.

Abby called the ER and was told that Dr. Alvarez was outside at the helipad, helping to load Kelly Franklin onto the MedFlight chopper for a trip to the hyperbaric chamber in Castro Valley. She insisted that her call was an emergency and waited until Alvarez came on the line.

"God, but I've been worried about you," he said in a near whisper. "The police have been here twice asking about you. I think they're still around. Where are you?"

"I'm at a phone booth at Five Corners."

"I'll pick you up there."

"No! I mean, I told a guy here that my car had broken down. He's waiting to take me to your place. Just meet me there. I'll wait by the barn."

"I'll be there in five minutes. If you wait inside the barn, be careful not to go walking around. There are rotting floorboards all over the place."

Abby glanced over at the pickup.

"Thanks for the warning," she said.

"Abby, the news on Kelly is good. She's lighter. Much lighter. I think the steroids are kicking in. MedFlight's just taking off with her. Apparently the decompression chamber is ready."

"What about Quinn?"

"Did that hermit Ives do that to his leg?"

"Do what?"

"He was shot with an arrow — the same sort of arrow Ives makes. His kneecap is shattered. I mean blown to bits. The arrow went right through it, then right through the joint. It may have severed the popliteal artery. Ortho's in with him now. So's the vascular team. They may not be able to save the leg."

"Ives did what he had to, to save my life. Lew, I've got to get going. I'll see you at the farm."

"I'm so glad you're all right, darling."

"I know you are, Lew. Hurry home and I'll tell you what I found."

Chapter Forty-Two

Five minutes. Abby felt wired — the same tense anticipation as she had felt so many times in the ER.

We are on our way to your facility with Priority One traffic. Repeat, Priority One traffic. Our ETA is five minutes. . . .

Organize the troops. Start thinking through treatment protocols. Check off a mental list of potential problems and responses. And above all, no matter how shaky you're feeling, get ready to be composed — prepare to be the eye of the storm.

Her mouth unpleasantly dry, Abby swung open the large front doors of the barn and positioned the rifle just a few feet inside, in the deep shadow between two rough-hewn supports. Then she returned to the truck, set the plastic garbage bag on the floor in the cab, and helped Josh up onto the cargo bay. He was definitely too weak, too ill, to rely upon, except perhaps for helping to tie up Alvarez once she had the rifle pointed squarely at him.

As a precaution, she tore off several two-foot lengths of duct tape and hung them on the door of the truck. Then she made a loop and slip knot at one end of the clothesline.

If she had to work alone, she would be ready.

"It's almost over, Josh," she said, handing him his gun. "A few more minutes, and we'll be headed to the city. We'll go straight to St. John's. Once they get you on treatment, you're going to feel much better."

Josh propped himself up against the metal side wall, steadied the gun with two hands, and aimed it at a spot in the darkness.

"Ka-pow!" he whispered.

"Please, honey. Please don't do anything except wait. I want to take him with us and hand him over to the police in San Francisco. So, please, just keep out of the way. . . . Promise? . . . Josh, I'm begging you."

"Promise," he muttered.

He rubbed at his eyes again and shook his head as if trying to dislodge claws that were piercing his brain.

Abby hopped down from the truck. With the front doors open, light from the outside illuminated most of the barn. She made certain the wooden wall of the stall kept the pickup from being spotted from the doorway.

"Stay still and stay quiet," she whispered.

She moved to the front of the barn, leaned against the siding, and waited. Five minutes went by. Then another five. Nothing. She left her post and hurried back to check on Josh. He was still sitting, but he was asleep, his head lolling to one shoulder. His hands were still wrapped around the grip of his gun. *Just as well,* she thought.

Abby checked her watch again. For the first time a knot of panic began to tighten in her chest. Something was wrong. She stepped outside the barn and peered down the driveway. Another five minutes passed. Alvarez had said five minutes. Now it was more than fifteen.

She had placed the rifle in the shadows for surprise. Now, suddenly, she felt as if she needed it for protection. She turned toward the back of the barn and gasped. Alvarez was standing behind her, not five feet away, grinning at her arrogantly.

"I know you too well, Abby," he said. "I've known you inside out since the day we met. That's why you've been so easy to control. You didn't sound quite like yourself when you called me from the so-called pay phone. And there was no traffic noise in the background. So just in case, I decided to come up an old logging road and walk across the fields to the door back there. I notice you broke the window in my kitchen door."

"Just to use the phone."

"How I wish I could believe that. I also noticed my old pickup over there is uncovered. Is that the phone you used? I assume tonight you stumbled on it by accident and recognized it from that day on the road. That's why you broke into the house."

Without taking a step Abby took a quick, vicious kick at Alvarez's groin. Before she connected, he snapped one hand down and caught her ankle. Then he twisted her foot until she fell heavily to the floor.

"You know," he said, "I was going to have that truck painted sometime before you asked to move in with me. Now I guess I don't have to bother."

"I would never have moved in with you."

"As I said, I know you like a book. Two or three weeks ago, before your friend Wyler even moved out on you, I circled tomorrow's date on my calendar. That was the day we were going to become lovers."

"Go to hell."

Abby forced her eyes to remain locked on his. The rifle was just a few feet away, but Alvarez hadn't spotted it. He hadn't discovered Josh yet, either. Perhaps if she could just head him toward the house and make some noise, she might be able to wake Josh up.

"You hurt a lot of people," she said. "A number of them are dead."

"You were in my house. I assume you saw pictures of my village. This is war. In war there are casualties. I want to know how you got from the hospital to Colstar, and what you found there that upset Lyle Quinn so."

"The police have been up here twice looking for me. They're due again any minute."

Alvarez snatched her wrist, yanked her to her feet, and twisted her arm high behind her back. Abby cried out in pain. Tears instantly filled her eyes.

"I asked you a question," he said, forcing her deeper into the barn.

"Let go of me!" she screamed.

Alvarez released some of the tension on her arm. They were moving closer and closer to the truck.

"Tell me!" he snapped.

"You were wrong all the time," she said loudly. "Wrong! It was never cadmium. They have a lab down there set up for testing sarin, phosgene, and a bunch of newer chemical weapons, and for trying out antidotes to them."

"They put the gas in through the MRI?"

"Yes! Now let me go!"

She shouted the words again. It was no use. Apparently Josh was comatose.

"Did you take things from Gabriella's room upstairs?" He twisted her arm even more viciously than before. "Did you?"

"In the truck," she sobbed.

Alvarez eased the force on her arm and dragged her several feet closer to the pickup. One or two more steps and there was no way he could avoid spotting Josh sprawled in the back. All Abby could think about now was the weapon in Josh's lap. Which would give her the better chance — trying to rouse him somehow, or trying to pull free and vault into the cargo bay her-self? She decided to do both.

"Josh!"

She screamed the word at the same instant she yanked her arm free and dived headfirst over the side wall of the pickup. The metal rim caught her at the waist, sending pain screaming from her pelvic bones. The cargo bay was empty. Alvarez whirled, caught her by the leg, and threw her back to the floor. She rolled away from him, over and over, until she was well outside the stall. Alvarez came after her quickly, but he was still several feet away when Josh stepped out of the dimness on the far side of the truck.

"Hold it!" he ordered.

There was little strength in Josh's voice. Alvarez stopped short and turned slowly, his hands open in front of him. Abby scrambled to her feet. She could see that Josh was able to stand only because his back was braced against the wall. He was struggling to keep his gun trained on Alvarez's chest.

His icy smile unwavering, Alvarez slid several paces to his left. He was now no more than ten feet from the side door — about the same distance he was from Josh and from Abby.

"Wyler, you don't look well," he said.

"Don't . . . move."

The words were barely audible.

Abby could see the pain and confusion in Josh's eyes, and she had no doubt that Alvarez could see it, too. If Alvarez dived for the door, he was almost certain to make it before Josh reacted. Instead, he stood his ground. His expression was bemused, his eyes were riveted on Josh.

"Josh, give me the gun," Abby said, taking a tentative step toward him.

There was no response.

"Josh?" she said again.

The barrel of the gun sank toward the floor. She realized that Josh was virtually unconscious on his feet. Alvarez tested the situation with a slight move toward the door. Then another. At that moment a dreadful gurgling rose from Josh's throat. His head snapped back and his body stiffened. Then he lurched to his left and fell, his back arched and his limbs pumping in a violent seizure. The weapon spun out of his hand and under the truck. Alvarez had a much better angle on the stall than did Abby. He dived headfirst toward the pickup and was scrambling over Josh when Abby whirled and sprinted for the spot against the front wall where she had propped the rifle.

She grabbed it just as Alvarez shoved Josh clear of the truck. He was on his belly, reaching for the gun, when she dropped to the floor about twenty feet away and leveled the rifle.

"Stop, Lew! Right there!"

She punctuated the command with a shot that splintered the floor beneath the truck, just a foot or so away from his face. Then she quickly bolted another round into the chamber. Slowly, he wriggled out backward from under the truck. She could see that he held the gun. Behind him, Josh had stopped seizing and was now lying motionless.

"Throw it away, Lew," she barked. "Now!"

He slithered around to face her. The gun was still in his hand, but turned almost under him so that it would be impossible to ready it and shoot before she fired. He tested her with a tiny movement.

"Okay, that's enough," she said.

He adjusted his arm another few inches.

"I said enough!" she snapped. "You say you know me so well. What does your wonderful insight say I'm going to do if you don't throw that gun away right now?"

He made a show of sizing her up.

"It says you won't fire," he said finally.

"Good. I'm glad that's how you feel. You haven't been wrong about me yet, so why don't you go ahead? *My* intuition tells me you're too much of an egomaniac to want to chance having the world endure without you forever. Let's see who's right."

Fifteen endless seconds passed. Then, finally, with a flick of his wrist, Dr. Luis María Galatín sent the weapon spinning across the coarse wooden floor.

"Stay on your belly," Abby barked, advancing to him, her rifle leveled at the base of his skull.

"How are you going to tie me up without setting that gun down?"

"Put your hands behind you, Lew. Now!"

"If I don't?"

"If you don't, I'm going to shoot you. Maybe in your leg, maybe in your groin. Do you believe that? . . . *Do you?*"

Slowly, Alvarez brought his hands behind his back. Abby dropped the loop of clothesline over his wrists and pulled the knot tight. Next, she wound the rope several times around his ankles, and then looped it around his neck. Only then, keeping constant tension on the rope, did she risk cradling the rifle as she reached for the duct tape.

It took more than twenty careful minutes, all of the clothesline, and most of the roll of duct tape before Abby felt certain she had bound Alvarez securely. He was on his belly, hands lashed behind him, ankles secured. It was only then that she felt able to tend to Josh.

He was in the condition Abby had observed hundreds of times after patients' seizures — conscious, but dazed, moaning softly with each breath. In the course of his fit, he had bitten his tongue and the inside of his lip. Now a trickle of blood had darkened the corner of his mouth. Abby gave passing thought to leaving him there and calling for an ambulance when — if — she got free of the valley. But she sensed she would never make it out of the area without his knowledge of the back roads through the hills.

She checked his pulses, which were strong, and his pupils, which were somewhat less pinpoint than they had been. The seizure was probably an effect of the cadmium, although it could have been alcohol. Either way, the narcotic painkillers may have kept it from being worse. The expertise to perform chelation therapy, and indeed, the chelating medication itself, was at St. John's, not here in Patience. But the drive to the city could prove disastrous for him. Even so, Abby knew they had to take the chance. She propped him up with an arm around his shoulder. His head lolled at first. But after a short time he began to regain some control.

"Josh, can you hear me?" A faint nod. "You had a seizure, probably from the poison in your body. We need to get out of here and down to St. John's. Do you understand?" Another nod.

Abby helped him to his feet. Then she belted him into the passenger seat of the truck. She found the key on a ring in Lew's pocket. Next she pulled on the clothesline, stretching his arms backward until he had to stand up. Then she ordered him to the back of the truck. He refused to move. Abby retrieved Josh's gun and held it against one of his thumbs.

"I have no patience for this," she said. "As far as I'm concerned, it's high time you were the one doing the suffering. Once I shoot this thumb off, I guarantee you, as only a doctor can, that it's not going to grow back. What does your precious sixth sense about me have to say about my willingness to do that?"

Without a word Lew hopped to the cargo bay and awkwardly rolled onto it. Abby searched the barn and found another length of rope. Then she wrapped him snugly and completely in the vinyl tarp and lashed him securely in place.

"Don't do this to me, Abby," he said. "I'll never survive in here like this. I'll suffocate."

"We'll see," Abby replied, securing the rear gate and taking her place behind the wheel. "We'll see."

The engine kicked over on the first try. With Lew's meticulous attention to the details of his life, she had never doubted that it would.

"Josh, I need to get out of the valley without going on any of the state roads. Can you do that?"

"Yes. . . . My head is . . . killing me."

He took the vial of pills from his pocket but was unable to open it. Abby helped him shake out two. He swallowed them without water.

"Which way?" she asked.

"South and west . . . toward the house."

The road to which Josh directed her was steep and rutted. By the time she was a mile into it, he was semiconscious again, with a rag doll's control of his body. Again and again jolts sent his head snapping against the window. As much as she could, she drove holding on to the neck of his sweatshirt. Once she stopped to check on the bundle in the cargo bay. Lew was furious, but uninjured.

There were no forks or turns off the dirt road, so there was no reason to try to rouse Josh. For forty-five minutes Abby drove through the rain-soaked forest. Suddenly, after a steep, mercilessly jouncing downhill stretch, she saw headlights flash past ahead. She slowed and crept forward, cutting the lights. Finally she reached the margin of the woods. Josh had done it. The highway was the two-lane state road through the mountains that she had taken to San Francisco, and then later to Feather Ridge.

"Josh, we made it!" she said excitedly.

He did not respond. His breathing was sonorous, unnatural.

"Josh?"

Abby shook him, but he did not respond. She turned his face toward her. The muscles in his face were twitching. Another seizure — this one more focal than the last.

"Damn," she said softly.

To the right, with luck, she still faced more than a four-hour drive to the city. To the left, half an hour back, was Patience — a viper-filled pit for her, without a single ally she could count on. She bit at her lower lip and looked again at Josh. Then she took a single deep breath, flipped on the headlights, and swung a right onto the road, headed south. Ten miles, twenty, fifty. Josh had long ago stopped seizing, but he remained in a coma. She was about five miles from the cutoff to the town of Feather Falls, and beyond that, Feather Ridge. Ezra Black had his own helicopter. With it Josh could be on the roof at St. John's in forty-five minutes or so. At the very least it was worth a call.

Abby was looking down at the floor for the cellular phone when the cab was lit up by a flashing blue-white strobe. Her heart froze. The cruiser was a few car lengths behind her, inching closer as the officer inside waited for her to pull over. The town was just ahead. Being stopped now might well mean being brought back to whatever unthinkable fate awaited her in Patience. It certainly meant delay and trouble for Josh. And with no arrest warrants out for Lew Alvarez, it was quite possible Galatin would be able to talk the police into setting him free and even into adding kidnapping to the charges against her. She was seven miles or so from Feather Ridge — no more.

"Hang on, baby," she said, though Josh was far beyond hearing her.

She rammed down on the accelerator and felt the truck surge forward with surprising power. Instantly, the siren from the cruiser pierced the night. Abby kept her foot tight to the floor. The cruiser tried to pull beside her, but the narrow road made it easy to keep it at bay. Luckily, at this hour there was little traffic. She flew over a small hill, bottoming out the chassis as she hit. Ahead, she could see Main Street. She was doing over eighty now. Wind was tearing through the open window, whipping her hair against her face and into her eyes. Josh was slumped over almost double, jostling violently from side to side. The cruiser pulled alongside her once more. Again she fought it off.

Then, up ahead, she spotted a second cruiser, parked across the middle of the road, strobes flashing. There was room for the truck to the right of it, but only if the pickup was tougher than a pedestrian bench and a stop sign. Eighty-five. Eighty-eight. Abby saw the officer standing by the cruiser realize that she wasn't slowing down, and dive off to the left. At the last moment she swung the pickup onto the sidewalk. Her head snapped forward as the steel plow frame took out the wooden bench. But the stop sign sheared off with just a minor jolt.

Seconds later she was beyond the town, flying up and down the roller-coaster hills toward Feather Ridge. Behind her the two cruisers were gaining. But now, she knew, they would not be driving with such a sense of urgency. She was trapped. Not a mile ahead was the massive gate to Feather Ridge. What they had *no* way of knowing, though, was that she had absolutely no intention of stopping.

Apparently, the police had been able to call ahead to the guardhouse. As Abby approached it, a dark sedan snapped its lights on, and a security man appeared at the roadside, gun in hand. Abby got her bearings, aimed for the center of the gate, gripped the wheel tightly, and ducked below the level of the dash. A bullet cracked through her window and thudded into the roof of the cab. Then a second shot must have hit the left front tire. It exploded with a bass-drum sound, tearing the wheel from her hands at precisely the moment the pickup slammed into the gate. Abby's forehead smacked against the steering wheel, dazing her and sending blood cascading down into her eyes. But the pickup barreled on through the gate, careening to the left into the orchard.

Abby kept her foot to the floor as she battled to regain control of the wheel. The truck flattened several young trees, then lurched to the right and back onto the pavement. The smell of burning rubber filled the cab. It took all her strength, pulling the wheel to the right, to keep the pickup on the road. Blood from her forehead had her nearly blind. The cruisers and the third car were pulling alongside again. But ahead of her now, sprawled across the side of the mountain, was the estate.

The battered truck careened down the last hill. Abby could see perhaps half a dozen guards running to take up positions in front of the house. With a final, unspoken prayer, she slammed on the brakes. There was a deafening screech as the pickup skidded sideways, spun completely around, tipped way up onto two wheels, then dropped back heavily onto four. The doors were snatched open. Rough hands pulled her and Josh out and threw them to the ground. Instantly, a dozen or more men, guns drawn, were around her. Half a dozen powerful flashlights shone on her face. One of the men kicked her onto her back with his boot, then roughly pulled her to a sitting position by the front of her sweatshirt.

Abby blinked, trying to focus on him, but could hardly see anything through the blood. Suddenly the guard let her go and stepped away. She wiped her eyes with her sleeve. Through the glare of the lights a man approached and handed her a handkerchief. She tied it around her head, putting pressure on the gash, which she now could appreciate was not that big. Then she peered up at him.

"You must have wanted very badly to see me," Ezra Black said.

Abby waved off help, stood by herself, and rushed around to where Josh lay. He was unconscious but crying out softly. His vital signs seemed strong, and there were no other indications that he had been injured in their ordeal.

She retrieved the plastic bag from the truck and motioned Black away from his men. Back at the pickup, she could see some of the guards untying the tarp. After the violent pounding Galatín must have taken during the harrowing chase, it was quite possible that there would be a corpse wrapped inside. But after a few seconds she heard him moaning.

"That man on the ground needs to get to St. John's in San Francisco," she said. "Could your helicopter take him?"

"What's the matter with him?"

"He's been poisoned with cadmium. Just like your son was. He'll die soon without help."

She reached into the plastic bag and brought out the box of cadmium and the article about the Colstar explosion. Black studied them. It was clear from his expression that the name Luis María Galatín was one he knew.

"Galatín is responsible for this?"

"He is."

"And where is he now?"

"There."

Abby motioned toward the truck, where Galatín was sitting, crying out about a pain in his arm.

"And is that all you want from me? A ride to San Francisco?"

"No. I want that lab beneath Colstar closed down for good."

Black eyed her for several seconds.

"Can I count on your total discretion if I guarantee that?"

"You have my word."

Abby unfolded the list of cadmium victims.

"This man, Josh Wyler, is the one on the ground. The next one, Willie Cardoza, is the one who ran down Peggy Wheaton. There's Ethan's name, right there. Galatín was working in the Patience Regional Hospital ER under the name Alvarez. These people all worked for Colstar. He gave the cadmium to all these people when he sewed up their cuts. He had no idea that given intravenously, the metal would become concentrated in a place in the brain where it would cause the sort of insanity that killed your son. He didn't care. He only wanted to get Colstar closed down."

"I see. . . . So, is this a trade?"

Abby glanced over at the truck.

"I want the best lawyers money can buy for Willie Cardoza and Josh. And I want something done about Quinn."

Black looked at her admiringly.

"You're tough," he said.

"I wasn't before this all happened."

"For what it's worth, I will promise you that Quinn is finished in Patience. I also have heard that they will not be able to save his leg."

"I'm not sorry. I want Kelly Franklin to get the very best medical care and rehabilitation. And if she doesn't make it, I'd like to contact you about having Colstar take care of her two daughters."

"Is that it?"

"Yes."

"You sure, now?"

Abby thought for a moment.

"I'm sure."

"Thank goodness. . . . Hey, Nick," he called out to one of the group of men. "Get ready to fly. This lady and her friend need to get to a hospital in San Francisco."

Abby motioned toward the truck with her head.

"What about him?"

"I don't recall that my sharing that information was part of our deal."

Abby hesitated, then said, "It wasn't."

"For what it's worth, I have no intention of killing Galatín, although at some point he may wish that I had. I have some good friends and business associates in the Paraguayan government. I know for a fact that they'll be most grateful for this . . . this scum's return home. Most grateful."

Abby held the billionaire's gaze for a time; then she nodded that their business was completed. She turned away and followed the men who were carrying Josh to the helipad. Minutes later they were airborne. Abby sat at one end of a plush, sofalike seat at the rear of the elegant aircraft. Josh was stretched out next to her, his head resting on her lap. He had regained consciousness only briefly, but long enough to

601

manage something of a smile.

The chopper banked a graceful arc over Ezra Black's estate and then headed southwest. Abby gazed out the window past the battered, exhausted reflection that looked vaguely like herself. She reached up and flicked off the cabin lights. Far to the north, almost lost in the pitch-black landscape and sky, she could just barely make out a smudge of red.

Epilogue

Three thousand miles away, just to the east of the Tennessee/North Carolina border, Lally Dorsett lay supine on the stretcher, watching the ceiling fluorescents flash past. Forty-five years she had lived in the town of Gilbert, nestled in the Blue Ridge Mountains, and she had not been sick a day. Now, because of a little dizziness, she was in the damn hospital. Hell, she thought, for most of those four and a half decades, Gilbert didn't even *have* a hospital. Now, suddenly, it seemed as if there were doctors coming out of the woodwork.

There was a time, not so long ago, when she would have simply written off her dizziness and waited it out. It would have gotten better, too. Problems like that always did. But now, because her children insisted, and because the hospital was there, here she was getting wheeled down for a test her doctor couldn't even explain to her. An MRI, he said. Well, this was the last time she was going to submit to any test without a fight. Her kids meant well, but they just didn't understand that there was a direct correlation between the number of doctors in a town and the number of sick people.

The stretcher was wheeled into the place Lally had been told to expect — a gleaming, bright room with something like a huge spaceship in the middle, a hollow tube running through its center. She refused the technician girl's offer of help and scooted herself from the stretcher to a sliding bed attached to the hole in the ship. At her doctor's recommendation, she consented to the earphones and black eye shield. Then she allowed herself to be pushed into the cylinder.

"Are you ready?" the girl asked through the earphones.

"Ready's I'll ever be."

Some George Strait began playing in the headset. Beneath the mask, Lally's eyes closed. The banging and clanging of the magnet that she had been told to expect was scarcely blocked at all by the music. From someplace behind and above her, a fan started blowing. The air in the tube began to smell sweet and just a bit heavy. Her doctor hadn't said anything at all about that. Lally wondered if she should say something to the girl.

Oh, hell, she decided, forcing her muscles to relax. *Let's just get it over with.*

About the Author

MICHAEL PALMER, M.D., is the author of *Silent Treatment, Natural Causes, Extreme Measures, Flashback, Side Effects*, and *The Sisterhood*. His books have been translated into twenty-two languages. He trained in internal medicine at Boston City and Massachusetts General hospitals, spent twenty years as a full-time practitioner of internal and emergency medicine, and is now involved in the treatment of alcoholism and chemical dependence. He lives in Massachusetts.